PLEASE STEP BACK
By Ben Greenman

MELVILLEHOUSE
BROOKLYN, NEW YORK

PLEASE STEP BACK

© 2009 Ben Greenman

Melville House Publishing
145 Plymouth Street
Brooklyn, NY 11201

www.mhpbooks.com

ISBN: 978-1-933633-70-1

First Melville House Printing: March 2009

Library of Congress Control Number: 2009901636

For Gail:

Thank you for letting me be myself, again and again

FADE IN

Robert
Boston 1954

"What is that shit?" Dre made Robert say it. Robert didn't want to. He tried to disguise his voice, make it low like Dre told him to, but he couldn't.

"Who that I hear talking?" Henry Petroski stayed in the car, head down on his chest, eyes closed.

Dre answered. "It don't matter who it is. Just tell us what that shit is. It's pussy music."

"It ain't no such thing. This here's Mantovani, playing the Blue Danube Waltz. And it's beautiful."

"Beautiful?" Dre snickered. "Your mama is beautiful, and I told her so myself last night."

"You want to come over here and say that, Andre?"

"Andre? There ain't no one here named that."

"Don't pretend you ain't there, Andre Sanders. I see you and your cousin Robert hiding there behind that car. I see your punk feet and your punk heads."

"I ain't scared of you, you big Polack cow," Dre said, winking at Robert. "You or Mountain Vinny."

"Okay." Henry sat up. His head bumped the ceiling of the car. "I'm about to come over there."

"No, man, wait. I'll send out Robert as a hostage." He pushed at Robert. "Go," he said, laughing.

"Hey, Roberto," Henry Petroski said when Robert came around the fence. "Long time no see."

"Yeah," said Robert.

"How old you now?"

"Eleven."

"Good, good. And how old," he said, raising his voice, "is that punk-ass cousin of yours?"

"*Mooo,*" said Dre from behind the fence. "Mooski." Robert giggled. He couldn't help it. Even Henry Petroski cracked a smile. Dre was always clowning, with his shiny eyes and his hair that went wild in all directions. He was a year older than Robert; Lucas, Dre's brother, was four years older than Dre, and he was always telling Robert that he shouldn't listen to Dre. "Every time that boy gets out of trouble," said Lucas, "he gets right back in." Dre was small, even smaller than Robert, but Lucas was already man-size.

The three of them were known around the neighborhood as the Three Musketeers, or had been until Lucas stopped running with them. What stopped him was a sweet young thing from the corner. Dre told Robert that she let Lucas go all the way with her. "Liar," said Robert, but Dre insisted. Robert tried to picture it but he wasn't sure what he was supposed to picture.

When they weren't the Three Musketeers, they were sometimes the Three Keys. They would go down to Dudley Street and sing, Lucas handling the low parts, Dre taking the high end, and Robert working the middle. "Close Your Eyes," "I Don't Stand a Ghost of a Chance," "Sh-Boom." They didn't dress to match but they had moves, lean-ins and head-bobs and snaps. Occasionally guys from walk-tough gangs like the Red Devils would come by to taunt them, but all Lucas had to do was draw himself up to his full height and the attackers backed off. Sometimes after they sang Lucas would have them in and show them how a song went on the bass guitar. He had one that his daddy, who was a musician, had left behind. Robert's daddy, who had owned a hardware store, was gone also, but under the ground rather than out of town.

Dre came out now and walked toward Henry Petroski's car. "You're not afraid of me?" said Henry.

"I ain't afraid of no one," said Dre, attempting to scowl but failing.

"No?" said Henry Petroski. He unlocked the car door. Dre stopped. "Not even if I come out there and beat your ass?" Dre was done smiling now; he was all tensed up and testing his weight on the balls of his feet.

With a roar, Henry Petroski kicked the door open. Dre turned to run. "No!" said Henry Petroski. No? thought Robert. What was Dre supposed to do? Hang back to get beat? But Henry Petroski had seen what neither Robert nor Dre had: the Impala speeding north. It hit Dre hard, right at knee level. His legs buckled, and it looked like he might go under the front wheels, but then the force of the car launched him into the air, where he flew a dozen brutal feet and landed in a heap.

"Oh, God," said Henry Petroski. He moved fast for a fat man. "I was just kidding around. I wasn't going to hurt him." He knelt down and touched the top of Dre's head. But there was no top, and his finger went right on through to spongy brain. "Oh, God."

Robert's mama told him that when a body dies it becomes music. He made himself believe it. He believed it for his cousin Shay who was taken two years before by flu, for his grandmother Beebee who died in bed, and for his father, who had passed when Robert was only three. But most of all he believed it for Dre. The day of the funeral he was sitting in the kitchen with his mama and Lucas. Lucas was so quiet he was loud, and every once in a while he would wipe his eyes with his hands. Robert sat there in his seat, but his ears left the room, went roaming through the halls of the apartment building: They heard voices, furniture scraping, and finally they heard a radio, the Orioles warbling "Walking by the River." Robert settled there. The song filled him and saved him, a little. That night, after the funeral, he replayed the song in his head, first like he heard it on the radio, then like he thought it needed to be. He saw something small and dark just off the riverbank, something that seemed to give off heat although the water was cold. He reached for it and the vision burst, and though he shut his eyes and burrowed deeper into the blankets and the sheets he could not bring it back. Finally he stopped trying with his mind and started trying with his mouth. "Walking by the river," he sang, "feeling all alone. I don't have a single thing to call my very own." And suddenly, he did.

SIDE ONE: COUNTING OFF

Robert
Boston 1963

Every time Robert's nose stopped bleeding it started again, so Carl insisted on driving him home in the cream-colored 1959 Fury that he called Plymouth Rock. Most days, Carl didn't let any of the other band members ride up front. Today, though, Robert got shotgun without any hassle on account of his nose. Carl had busted it, Carl was making amends.

"You okay?" said Carl. He asked like he didn't really care about an answer.

"What do you think?" said Robert. "My nose is bleeding like a fucking faucet."

"Man," said Carl, "I wish you wouldn't talk that way so much. One of these days you're gonna slip and say something onstage."

"Onstage?" said Robert. "Don't think so. Not going to be onstage with you anymore." He held the handkerchief to his nose. "Blue Velvet" oozed out of the car radio, and something from the backseat smelled like rotten food.

The day had started with promise. In the morning, while he was having coffee with Lucas, Robert had heard a song on the radio that he thought the band should add to its set, a ballad called "Pledging My Love" that was a hit for Johnny Ace right after he died. "You know how he died?" Lucas asked. "He put out his own head during a game of Russian roulette. You want to hear the click. He didn't. What do you think he heard instead?" That was just like Lucas, to take a piece of news and try to turn it into a lesson; everyone called him the Preacher on account of the deep, measured way he talked, and what he talked about. He had been in a band, too, but he left to return to the church, and then left the church but didn't rejoin his band. He had an old lady and a kid now and it was hard to imagine that he'd ever get back to his music. It was a shame: He could sing as beautifully as anyone Robert knew, and he played a mean bass with those big hands of his.

"I don't care what he heard," Robert said. "I care what I can't hear, and that's this song, because you're talking." Robert wanted the band to do the song faster, hop it with a Bo Diddley beat, and when he finally managed to tap it out for Lucas on the kitchen table, Lucas's face went wide with a smile. He heard it, too. "Carl's going to like it," Robert said. "I'm sure." But Carl didn't, and not because of the speed or the drums. Carl didn't like it because Robert wanted to do it in rounds, and Carl was very clear on being the only singer in the band. Robert played guitar. Doug played piano. Don played bass. Fudgie drummed. If someone else was singing, there was nothing for Carl to do but stand there and look supportive, and that wasn't what Carl did. The way Carl put it was sharper. "Fuck, no," he said. "Band's mine." At that time Robert's nose had felt fine, and it certainly hadn't been delivering his blood in a steady stream.

They drove. Boston was gray, like it always was when Robert felt this way. Just past Kendall Square, they went by a tall girl decorating the doorway of a beauty parlor. For a second Robert lost sight of the red of the blood and the gray of the city and thought only of the color of her dress, which was an unripe-apple green. "Hey Paula" was on the radio now, and Robert whistled along. If it had been a movie, the girl would have turned to him in slow motion. Her name might even have been Paula. But they were in the real world, where Carl kept on driving, his face set in a frown, and Robert never found out her name.

Robert counted backwards, there in the car with the handkerchief on his nose and blood on the handkerchief, to the day that had started it all, that summer Saturday two years earlier in Big Cyril's Music Shop when he had picked up his first guitar. He had considered the trumpet because of Miles Davis, the piano because of Ray Charles, and even the bass because of Lucas, but then his hand came to rest on a guitar.

Not a guitar, even, but a guitar string. The thinnest of them, the barely present E. He plucked it, looked around guiltily, and moved across the neck toward the thicker strings. Gradually he became aware of the guitar itself, which was covered in cracked red lacquer and was smaller than the rest. "I've been trying to get rid of that one for a while," said the salesman, coming across the room. "I'll let it go for ten dollars." Robert took it in like you would a puppy. The sound wasn't anything to remember, but his fingers fit the neck well, and within the month he could play along with the radio. That was all that mattered. By the next summer he was sitting in with any band that wanted him. And a few wanted him: the C-Necks, the Wonders, the Harborcoats. He made a little dough to go along with the other bits he got from working as a stock boy in a grocery store. He felt like he was teetering on the brink of something, even if he didn't know which way time would tip him. Then he got a chance to join Carl Chandler and the Tremeloes.

The Tremeloes were major, mostly because of Carl. Carl had the look, and Carl had the drive, and Carl had a cousin named Theo who managed the English House, one of the hot clubs in town, and Carl even had a record out, a thing called "Hiding Place." When Carl's guitarist Walter decided to leave the group, Robert got the high sign from a girl he knew. "The Tremeloes are looking for someone," she told him while he was unfastening her dress on the ratty couch in her mama's house. "You should go to the English House Thursday morning and make a case for yourself." He was so grateful he unbuttoned faster.

Ten was the call time, but he was there at nine thirty, dragging his argument behind him: a new Sears guitar and tinny little twenty-five-watt Ampeg Rocket amp. Carl was onstage, crouched next to the microphone stand like a stone lion. He was dressed down raw, in an undershirt that left his shoulders bare and showed a white-pink scar that went across the right one like a second mouth. Robert had heard of this scar: Carl got it in a knife fight. They said that sometimes he sang so hard it bled.

Carl was doing battle with a strip of black tape that ran across a wire at the front of the stage. He tugged at it, cursed, strained until he threw the veins in his forehead into relief. Finally he ripped it up with an angry cry and turned to face Robert. "You here to see me?" Carl said.

"Heard you were looking for someone."

"Step into my office," said Carl. Robert laughed, but there actually was an office, a gaudy and heavy back room paneled with at least three different kinds of wood. Carl shrugged on a jacket over his undershirt and sat down behind the desk. "What do you know about the Tremeloes?" he said.

"That you're top-notch," said Robert. This pleased Carl, who nodded. "That you just lost a guitarist." He nodded again. "I can play pretty good, and I'd like to join up."

"You want to show me?" Robert took out his guitar and when Carl started to hum "Continental Walk" he stepped right in, strumming the rhythm. Then Carl switched to "Little Egypt," and then to "Quarter to Three." The fourth one tripped him up. "That's the Bristol Stomp," said Carl. "If you're going to join, you need a mind like a jukebox."

"I got one," Robert said. "I just ran out of nickels."

On the way out, Carl introduced Robert to a thick-featured man who was sitting by the door with a glass in his hand. "Cuz," he said. "This here's Robert Franklin. He's a guitar player. Robert, this here is Theo. He owns the joint. This may be the last time you see him, or it may be the first of many." The next day Carl called him back to offer him the job. He played his first show the following Friday, and his second later that same night, and his third and fourth the next night. He met the other members of the group and watched as they took him in: this skinny kid, not too tall, not too handsome, a thin, dark face with pronounced cheekbones and a big nose. But he was one of them, and the band, which had been nothing to him just days earlier, was suddenly everything. How did something like that happen? It was a kind of love. He loved the tone in his voice when he had to tell the grocery store that he couldn't come in anymore, or when he unhitched Lucas, after two minutes of talk, saying, "Gotta go, cuz. Got a gig." He loved standing behind Carl and watching the way the motherfucker flowed, all cool and sharp in his sharkskin suit. He even loved the dress-down, when Carl would hear something wrong in a song and snarl at the player who missed his spot. Robert could hear his playing improve with each lecture. And when his playing improved, everything else did, too. The girl who had told him about the job used to see him only once a week or so, but she started coming around more regularly. She said that he was bigger somehow.

If Robert was bigger, others were getting smaller. His mama had always been small but now, if there was a shadow in the room, she would fall into it. Sunday nights were hers, had been as long as he could remember: The two of them would sit at her kitchen table, eat sandwiches or something equally simple, drink beer—she had let him ever since he was fourteen—and talk about her life. She told the same stories dozens if not hundreds of times: her youth in Mississippi, her daddy's store, the way she and her sisters would court boyfriends with skillet bread. That's where she had met Robert's father, who had said he loved her, who had meant it, who had brought her to Boston. "The first time I came here," she told Robert, "I felt like my heart was going to stop. But it was starting. I was just too young to know the difference." Robert would pat her hand, refill her glass of beer. As the memories grew distant, she needed stronger stuff to bring them back to her: The beer gave way to gin, the gin to more gin. Some nights she'd end up falling asleep in the kitchen chair and Robert would help her to bed. When Robert joined the Tremeloes, he promised himself he'd keep Sundays with his mama, and his promise held up until the third week, when Carl told the band that they had been hired to play a party fifteen minutes outside of Boston. "I'll drive everyone except you and Fudgie," he told Robert. "You go with him: He has the car but without someone smart to ride alongside him, he'll end up in Delaware."

"Where's that?" Fudgie said.

"Exactly," Carl said.

Sunday afternoon, Robert told his mama that he'd be missing dinner. "For a job," he said. "I'm getting paid." She didn't say anything at first, then she went to the cabinet and took out a glass and a bottle of gin. She filled it for herself and then, as an afterthought, waggled it in Robert's direction as a question. He shook his head. She sat down and began to pull on the gin. "Have I told you about your father, and how tall and strong he was?" she said. "He was a handsome man. But more important, he was a good man. He treated me right and provided for us, even left me a little money when he passed on." When he was little, Robert didn't have any questions after she described him that way.

The gig out of town went smoother than anything at the English House, more swing, less sting; Robert was impressed to see how Carl took to it, and for that matter how the rest of the band followed along. Don played like he was to the lounge born, all tinkly runs, and even Fudgie eased off on the kit and smiled at the host. Robert wasn't sure he could see the line, let along fall into it. But there was cash paid out at the end of the night to Carl, who counted out bills for Don and Doug and Fudgie, and then for Robert, and suddenly he had twenty-five reasons to set his pride aside. Fudgie dropped him off around one and when Robert came through the door he found his mama sprawled in the chair by the window, the bottle of gin nearly empty. He tapped her until she woke. "Good boy," she said, the fumes of the drink blurring the words. The fact that Robert himself was a little high only made things worse. How could he be his mother's keeper if he was kept in the same place, by the same poisons?

The next day he went to the apartment next door and told his Aunt Ida about his mother. She was a woman who liked to judge and so he expected she'd get her wig pushed back by the news, but she just shut her eyes. "I've been praying," she said. "Lord knows, my sister needs strength." Robert hoped she knew someone underneath those shut lids who might be able to help.

Clubs weren't churches. Clubs weren't home. Clubs were only barnyards, where the older chickens stood with their eyes fixed on the younger ones. Sometimes they took you under their wing. Sometimes they just pecked at you to show you the order. Robert got pecked by a guy named Lee Bosier, a slick motherfucker with a Quo Vadis who played piano and sang with a group called the Yellow Jacket Generals. "Sounds like a gang," said Robert.

"It is," said Bosier. "But not the kind you think." He reached into his pocket for a handful of pills. "Meet my lieutenants," he said.

"What are they for?" said Robert.

"You mean who are they for," said Bosier. "For you, my man. Got yellow, of course. Got red, blue, purple. What's your favorite color?"

Robert liked red. The pills were the size of a watch stem, and they wound him up. He saw sharper. He slept less. When Robert popped pep, he could fly. "Listen to what I think we need to do," he told Fudgie. "I think we need to change the group's name. I think we need something tougher, like the Rip-Chords. And maybe we have to wear hats onstage, all of us."

"You want the rest of your burger?"

"Take it. I ain't hungry. But I'm taking your water." Robert coughed drily. "Listen to my ideas, man. I think we should sell the Fury and try to buy a bus."

Week two, Robert switched from red to blue, and his mood switched with him. He was still happy in the band. It was still his dream come true. But he remembered that dreams were like cream, that they could sour, and he went looking for a reason not to expect too much.

Soon he had one. "Carl's strong, but he's weak," he told Fudgie.

"What?" said Fudgie.

"You know what I mean," said Robert. Carl was weak because falsetto had hexed him. "Lover please, please come back," he sang. "I want you to be my girl," he sang. "Fools rush in," he sang. Robert couldn't stand the lay of the land, It was all top notes, all hills. Where were the valleys, the riverbeds, the sinkholes? He didn't mean the bottom in thick-syrup voices like Roy Hamilton, but soul bottom. Robert heard it in Brother Ray, whether he was singing country or jazz. He heard it in Gladys Knight, who sang like she was dragging the last parishioner out of church. He heard it in Solomon Burke. He heard it in Ike Turner. And he heard it in himself.

Brave from a stew of purples and blues, Robert strode into rehearsal one day and told Carl that he thought they needed to do different kinds of songs. "Who's the horse and who's the rider?" said Carl. "Get back in your stable, and don't come out until I say."

About once a month, Lucas invited Robert over for dinner, which was a proper-like meal, chairs at the dining-room table and a mess of potatoes, corn, and chicken that Lucas's old lady Adele cooked up.

After dinner Adele went to put the baby down—his name was Reggie, and he already looked like Lucas, square head, serious eyes—and Robert and Lucas sat around and listened to records. Lucas had a hot on for James Brown's Apollo show, Butane James wringing every last drop out of "Lost Someone." "You know who's got the bass on that?" said Robert.

"Can't say that I do," said Lucas.

"Hubert Perry," said Robert. "He also played with Bill Johnson."

Lucas laughed. "Well, now. You know all those names now that you're in the business." He ducked his head and came back up. "You know, I've been playing a little bass again myself," said Lucas.

"No shit," said Robert.

"Just keeping in practice."

"I hear of any spots, I'll let you know," said Robert. Then he nodded his head back toward the baby's room. "And you let me know if you hear of any fine women."

"You just hush," said Adele, appearing at the doorway. "You're going to embarrass me." Lucas just set his head back and roared.

But Lucas didn't mention any women to Robert. He didn't need to. The band brought them by the truckload. Eventually he picked a little chickadee from Tennessee named Emily. She was standing in the corner and he came up to her. "Baby, I'd give you Prussia if it could be bought," he said.

"Would you guide a missile?" she said without even blinking. He was impressed enough to stick close to her the rest of the night, and she was impressed enough to let him. They were inseparable for weeks. "You in love?" said Fudgie.

"Don't think so," Robert said. But his bed was full, and what was filling it kept him charged up. And that wasn't the only charge. Carl ordered some new suits, single-breasted plum-colored sharkskin jobs. And Lee Bosier, bless his heart, brought around some new magic to match.

Robert watched a girl run her fingers through her hair in the park. "Charlie," she called. "Charlie." She was a short white girl with a black girl's body, big on top and big in the back, and he watched her with interest. When her clapping and whistling failed, she walked over and clipped a leash onto Charlie's collar. Slavery, thought Robert, and silently wished for the dog to wheel, jaw flashing. But the second the leash went on, the dog heeled meekly. The girl petted him on the head, as if it were an even trade.

Robert kept thinking about that dog all afternoon and all night, and the next day, too. He kept thinking about that dog because he felt he was that dog. Never mind that he was a better singer than Carl. Never mind that he was starting to write his own songs. Robert knew that Carl would never unclip the leash, and in some way he didn't even blame him: Carl was used to being the master.

The year was like an evening: The longer it went, the darker things got. Medgar Evers got killed, and then the world seemed to go down into Alabama and it wouldn't come back out. One day it was some crackers cooking a church in Birmingham. Then it was the blues cracking heads of peaceful marchers. Then it was the governor blocking some colored kids from going into the university. Bull Connor, no honor.

August had a little light in it, mainly on account of King's dream, but the fall just fell apart. Busted, just like Ray'd say. The few bright spots were on the radio. "Pride and Joy," "Fingertips, Pt. 2." "Mockingbird." One Saturday in late November, Carl invited the band to his house. For about an hour they just hung loose, blowing gage and eating watermelon with black pepper. But then Carl got it in his head to start a practice. "Tighter," Carl said to the rhythm section. "Faster, too."

They emerged, eventually, into the afternoon sun to find that people were crying, leaning against lampposts, parked in their cars in the middle of the street. Fudgie guessed immediately. "Someone musta died," he said. But it wasn't someone. It was everyone, a little. Robert went home and watched the news with his mama. Dallas was a black spot on the map, and the rest of the country was dull with grief, too. "What a good man," she said. "What a shame."

That night, the radio played songs of grace like Curtis Mayfield's "It's Alright." Robert sang along, then sang his own words: "Something is missing / I thought I was kissing / You / But it's not true / Something is dying / I know that you're lying / Oh / Where can I go?" He played it for Fudgie. "I think you should finish it, and that the group should play it," he said. Robert was going to finish it the next night, and the night after that, but every time he sat down with his guitar his heart flew away from him. Didn't matter. He knew Carl would have said no anyway.

In December, the Tremeloes got booked into the English House for three weekends. The steady money was good and Robert bought himself some shoes, thirty-dollar Stacey Adams with a white string around the sole. Fudgie got a new hat, a black homburg that was years out of style even for a fat man, and Carl got a French-styled houndstooth topcoat with raglan sleeves. The new threads seemed to grease the skids a bit. Things had been tense before but now they were moving along as smooth as ever. Carl's leads were beautiful, the band was tight, and Robert had his eye on a little honey in the front row who didn't seem sold on holding hands with the guy next to her.

During rehearsal one night, Robert dropped a chord.

"What's the matter?" said Carl.

"I'll tell you when I know," Robert said.

Two days later, he knew. He and Carl were having a drink with Theo. "I've been thinking about the other night," he said.

"Yeah," said Theo. "I'll bet. I saw you looking at that front-row girl. You were goofed after her."

"I don't think he's talking about getting his shoelaces popped," said Carl. Robert was grateful, but when he looked up and saw Carl's stony face he felt a little surge of fear.

"Well," said Robert, "like I said, I was just thinking. When we play a song, we play it like it sounds on the radio."

"Cause that's what the people want to hear," said Carl.

"Hey Jim," said Theo, "you dim?"

"I just think that sometimes you have to try something different—take an uptown number and make it down and dirty, or come back up the other way."

"You're thinking too much," said Carl.

"Yes you are," said Theo. "The ladies especially love hearing what they're hearing. They come across for the boss."

"Take Chuck Jackson," said Carl. "You think you're going to hear change of pace from him? No way. But keep him where he's at, and he's a beautiful cat."

"And that's all you want to be? Chuck Jackson?"

"You can say what you want. The way I see it, life is like a record: Turn it over, and there's another side. That seems like a good deal. But think about it. That's all life is, two sides. No side three, no side four. So you make the music you can as long as you can. No use dreaming of what ain't and can never be." Carl turned his head and smiled like he was smiling through his shirt at his scar. Robert felt his own arm. There wasn't a mark on him.

The stage was being set up. There were two guys moving amps, a third tapping and testing the microphone, and a fourth plugging and unplugging instruments. They were at the Atlantic, a club in Somerville, and the manager, a short Greek everyone called Jack, was yelling into the phone.

Jack came and stood by the table. There was a napkin in his hand and he twisted it until Carl looked up. "No one yet," he said.

"It's early," Carl said. "The rest of our group isn't even here yet."

"Go and eat," Jack said. "Come back."

They came back and the place was packed tight with bodies. Carl went to find Jack and returned with his mood shot rotten. "This is bullshit," he said. There was a sheath of rage around him.

"What is?" said Fudgie. Robert was glad he had asked. He didn't want to have nothing to do with Carl when he was in this mood. And he wasn't in such a fine mood himself; the night before, Lucas had called to tell him that he and Adele were probably moving out West, to crib up with Adele's cousin in Oakland. Oakland: It sounded like another country. He didn't know why Lucas had to go anywhere.

"He's cutting our fee," Carl said. "Says we're late."

"But he told us to go."

"Goddamned right he told us to go. I have half a mind to jack-slap the shit out of that Greek bitch. I'm certainly not going to set a foot on that stage."

But Jack made them play. All he had to do was wave the contract in their faces. Paper scared Carl worse than anything. But he was mad, so mad he spit the words, even when they were "love" and "baby" and "heart." "I Can't Stop Loving You" sounded like a beating.

Afterward Robert was washing his hands when he heard Carl say "tire iron," and then Carl had a tire iron, and he was swinging it. "Come on, you motherfucker," he said. The muscles in his neck were corded. Jack stood behind the bar, right next to the door that led into the office. When it became clear Carl wasn't going to stop swinging the tire iron, Jack opened the door like he was going in, but instead three guys came out, and they walked across the room, pounding their fists into the flats of their palms.

No one had a knife. No one had a gun. It was fists and boards and whatever else they could find.

Robert backed into a corner. To the right of Carl there was a big man with a hammer in his hand. Robert saw the man's arm coming down and called out, turning Carl with his voice so that the hammer missed his head and struck his shoulder. The tire iron fell from Carl's hand. The big man swung the hammer again.

Robert could see Carl's back rippling through his shirt. He could almost hear the scar on his right shoulder screaming. But the big man didn't know about the scar. He didn't know a goddamned thing about Carl. So when Carl moved at him with bare fists the big man kind of sneered, and he was still sneering when both of Carl's arms shot out alongside the man's head and then clapped together over his ears. The noise and the pain must have been a motherfucker because the big man dropped down howling. Then Carl pushed the man into a stack of chairs.

Carl was straightening up with a king's look on his face when another man came out of nowhere and cracked a pipe across his leg. There was a sound like a muffled gunshot. The man swung a second time, and a third, both times striking the leg he had broken with the first swing. The fourth hit caught Carl on the head, which he was no longer protecting. The man turned slowly, then strode out, cool as January, right past Robert, who was back on his heels like he might lunge forward but didn't.

There was a change in the balance of power after the fight. Carl spent a week in the hospital, lost money, lost faith. When he came back to the band his leg was set in a cast along its entire length, and he couldn't even stand without breaking into a sweat, so he reluctantly surrendered the microphone to Robert and went back to guitar. This seemed to kill something in him. He mumbled instead of talked. He wore sunglasses. He slunk into rehearsals late, slunk out early. "Man," Robert said to Fudgie. "Cat's got his own tongue."

In shows, Carl didn't look like a man who wanted to be where he was. He didn't look like a man who wanted to be anywhere. He just went slow on his guitar and slow off it. But then, one night, Robert pointed at Carl in the middle of a song, expecting another dose of tired shit, and Carl exploded into his solo with a fire Robert had never heard before. In terror, Robert grabbed the mike and sang. The show went by in a blur, and afterward he walked right up to Carl with a smile on his face. "Motherfucker," he said. "You trying a short con? I thought you weren't the man you used to be."

"I'm tired," said Carl dully. "Going home." But the next night he was something else again, putting solos where solos weren't, adding rhythms where rhythms couldn't be, and Robert had to rise to meet him. By the end of the set, the audience was as hyped as Carl was drained. Robert thought this might snap Carl out of his drag-ass mood, but it didn't. He stayed home most days, and he was starting to get a night tan, his skin ashy from the absence of sun.

"He's dying so that the band can live," Robert told Fudgie. And he was right. But then he was wrong. Carl's limp slowly healed, and he got some color back on his skin, and his playing went back to being a collection of slick licks. "Hey, man, glad to see you up and around again," said Robert. But the lie left a bad taste in his mouth.

A healthy Carl meant boot-camp rehearsals again, and it also meant that the rest of them had to step to the back of the line. Robert wasn't ready to step. That's how he got to jaw with Carl about "Pledging My Love."

"I know that song," Carl said. "You think I don't know it?"

"I think you do know it. I just hear it a little different in my head, that's all."

"Oh, so you the one with the special motherfucking ears now." Carl spoke flatly, with no question mark and no exclamation. Then he decided to punctuate. He drew his weight back and grimaced. The leg was still sore. But whatever pain he felt fed right back into his arm for the punch. Robert saw it coming, tried to duck or block, couldn't, caught it square on the bridge of his nose. He grabbed a letter opener off the desk and mad-dogged Carl, tried to stick the point in his side, in his leg, but caught only the tops of his fancy-ass Italian shoes.

After Carl drove him home, Robert slept it off. But the next day Carl was still angry. "You wanted out, you got it," said Carl. "I've already replaced you," said Carl, and he had, with Lee Bosier. "You can go make your own music in your own image. Make it all you want. See who's going to come see some little shit-colored mother-fucker who looks like a rat."

The next night, a Sunday, Robert sat at the table with his mama and ate while she drank. "Your father was a good man," she said. "He ran his store honest like he ran his life." Robert put her to bed at midnight and came back to the kitchen to throw away the empty bottle of gin. The next night, he went to see Lucas and Adele, who cut things short because Reggie was fussing. He didn't tell Lucas that Carl had let him go. He told his mama the next Sunday, and all she did was nod. He couldn't tell if she was disappointed or relieved. The next morning, he woke up, tried to leave his room, and failed. After a few hours he came out, sat in the kitchen for a few minutes, and went right back, sanctum sanctorum. He went into the room for keeps. He had no taste for playing guitar so he played records instead. The world outside was all Beatles, but he reached back for Ray, settled on "You Are My Sunshine," cued the beginning over and over again, marveled at the way the brass shuffled, at the slide and glide, and then the high punch of the trumpet. But what put the record over was Ray's vocals: "The other night as I lay sleeping," that was something, but the *whooaaa* that followed, that was everything else.

He had dreams. But those dreams fit under the bed, and after he put them there he was too tired to bring them out again. Instead he brought out his pills and shook a yellow one onto his palm. It was supposed to help him feel better, and he placed it on his tongue. Then he poured a glass of water. It was cloudy, and he drank it fast, before it could clear up.

Robert
Boston July 1966

Long and lean, hair blown out, Robert squinted against the sun. He was twenty-two, like a gun, and he was out dayhawking for college girls in Harvard Square. He shined on them as they passed, gave them a piano of teeth, hummed to himself: *When you smile all the gloom turns to sunshine. If I had it in my power I'd arrange for every girl to have your charms.* He was about to follow a brunette down the street when he picked up on the conversation of the group of kids next to him. They were three white kids, dressed and pressed and fresh from lunch: a thin girl with a red bow of a mouth and two boys, one tall and one short, both with glasses. The short kid was talking basketball, Russell versus Chamberlain, and Robert leaned in and listened. "I don't think Russell's the same without Auerbach. He bit off more than he could chew." Robert didn't care what the short kid thought, but he thought he knew the tall one. He thought it was Tony Clemente, a guy he knew from the neighborhood and then from the clubs. Tony had been into music almost as much as Robert; when Robert had gone off to join the Tremeloes, with that drill sergeant Carl Chandler, Tony had been in the Bluewings and the Sparrows. Tony knew the words to every song, and what they meant. But maybe he was wrong: This kid had longer hair than Tony and he was wearing a blue blazer that Tony wouldn't wear on a dare. Robert stared down at his feet, then over at the group. Now that he wasn't grinning, some of the passers-by detoured around him. Once, downtown, an older woman had caught him looking at a younger woman with too much pepper in his eyes, and she wrinkled up her nose like he was something that had a stink. Had your fill, Emmett Till?

The little kid was wailing the Cousy blues now, how he could still tear up the league if he was playing. "He'd be almost forty now but he could run circles around Monroe. He's coaching over at BC now, you know, but I'll bet you he's planning a comeback." Robert let out his breath. Motherfucker was going to kill him with talking. He stepped in and said, "Tony?"

"Hey," said Tony. Then recognition uncreased his brow. "Robert Franklin," he said. "Long time no see."

"Yeah," said Robert.

"What going on with you?" Tony was soft and smart, like Robert remembered. But the motherfucking blazer was an obstacle.

"Nothin'," said Robert. "Walkin'."

"Carl still hitting it at the English House?"

"Don't know, man. I split from that scene. It's up, up, and away."

"Cool," said Tony.

"Cooler than cool," Robert said. "I'm thinking of starting my own group." He didn't know he was going to say it until he said it, and then he didn't know why he had said it. Maybe to see the glow that appeared in Tony's eyes, which was more warmth than light.

"Really? An R&B band?"

"No," said Robert. "A rock and roll band."

"A colored rock and roll band?" More glow.

"I'm not colored," said Robert. "I'm kissed by the sun."

Tony laughed. "It's not a half-bad idea," he said.

"And anyway, not all colored," said Robert. "White boys allowed."

"Here in Boston?" Robert wished Tony wasn't so interested. But the questions were making him answer.

"Why not?"

Tony laughed. "Not sure if Boston's quite ready for something like that." He tugged on his blazer like it was suddenly too small on him. "I think California's the place to do it. I was out at North Beach last summer and you wouldn't believe it. It makes Boston look like the worst drag on earth."

"Really?" said Robert. "My cousin Lucas moved out to San Francisco."

"Wasn't he a player too?"

"Yeah. Hell of one. Bass. Now he's got a family and what they call a complicated relationship with the church. Hard to bring him back from that."

"Tony," said the small kid. "We got to go."

"We're seeing a movie," he said to Robert, apologetically. "Catch you later. Maybe out in California."

Robert went out to the Charles and watched the boats cut the river, razorlike. At his feet, leaning up against the rail, he saw a paper cup half-filled with milky coffee. He kicked at it, launched the coffee into the river, where it hit the surface and disappeared. He turned and headed back into Cambridge, where he took up position outside the movie theater and waited. The movie was *Othello*, with Orson Welles: Robert didn't remember the book well but he knew it was about a black dude and a white chick. Finally the crowd began to emerge, and Robert caught sight of Tony. "Hey," he said, and motioned him over. "Let me get your phone number. Just in case." Tony wrote out his phone number in a matchbook in a neat hand while Robert waited, dropping a dark eye on the bow-mouthed girl.

The phone number went into his jacket pocket, and the jacket went onto a hook on the wall, and the wall stayed right where it was, and he didn't think much of it for a while. He settled back in, hung with friends, went into his room to practice guitar, took girls on long walks, now and again managed to make them.

Then he was killing an afternoon, eating a sandwich and watching TV with the sound down so that he could listen to the radio. Slim Harpo was on, singing "Baby Scratch My Back," and he was singing along when he saw a picture of Ted Williams on TV. He didn't care about baseball very much but something made him turn up the volume. The newscaster squared her papers on the desk and cleared her throat. "In his Hall of Fame induction speech today," she said, "the Red Sox legend made a plea for the great players of the Negro Leagues to be extended baseball's highest honor." Extended: Robert liked that. It was like a branch going out. Next, the anchor threw it over to a reporter on the street who asked fans about Williams's speech. Two of them nodded, but the third man shook his head and scowled. "Why not put the guys who drive the bus or the grounds crew?" he said. "The Splinter is wrong. Animals shouldn't be next to people. It's not dignified." Animals next to people: Robert laughed, but he felt a pressure behind his eyes, and that's when he realized he was crying. "Motherfucker," he said. "Why you have to go and get me like that?" He picked up the telephone and dialed Tony's number.

"Hey," he said. "It's Robert Franklin."

"Robert," said Tony. "Hold on." Robert heard the TV through the phone. "You see what Ted Williams did?"

"Watching it right now. This what they mean by color TV?"

"He's half Mex, you know. I think he has a vested interest. But I can't stand that now people are going to turn against him. That's why I'm so happy I'm going out West."

"Well," said Robert, pausing just a second before leaping. "That's why I'm calling. You got room?"

"I do if you do."

"It's your car."

"I meant in the band you want to start. Do you need a guitarist?"

Tony was doing it again, asking questions until the thing became real. "Yeah," said Robert. "I got room."

"Your parents okay with you splitting?" Tony asked.

"My father's dead," Robert said.

"Oh," Tony said. "Your mother?"

Robert could hear her in the other room, coughing. Her bottle clinked as she set it down on the table. He knew that when it came time to say goodbye, she wouldn't be able to lift her heart enough to even look at him. She was certain the world was out to take everything from her. "She's fine with it. So long as I get famous."

"Well, then," Tony said, "let's not disappoint her."

How do you square away a life, especially one you haven't started living? You kiss some girls goodbye, shake some hands, drive by a building or two. You pack your bags. You tell your mama, and tell her again to make sure she understands. Then you wake up early one morning and sit by the window, waiting for the car to pull up, and when you see it—a '65 Chrysler New Yorker hardtop, black with rust spots on the hood and doors—you run downstairs, slowing to a cooler walk only when you're spotted. "You ready?" Tony said.

"Give me a minute," Robert said. He went back upstairs, to his mama's bedside. She was knocked out loaded, smelling like last night's whiskey. Robert slipped a letter under her pillow; he had written it a few nights before, when he wasn't mad, when he didn't feel pity. It told her that he loved her and that he wanted her to be proud of him, and when he was there, at the side of the bed, it was all true. He even had a tear in his eye when he got into Tony's ride.

For a while they took turns behind the wheel, but in the middle of Pennsylvania, Tony started driving, because he was better at it, and Robert manned the maps. He wanted to sleep, but he didn't trust Tony to stay alert, so instead he asked questions about whatever he could think of: music, sports, girls. Tony told Robert about skiffle and Robert told Tony about doo-wop and then they agreed that they both already knew plenty about both. Tony said that he was reading through the complete works of Shakespeare. "That's why I was seeing that movie the day I ran into you," he said.

"I remember," Robert said, and told Tony about the way he had given a hot eye to the pretty little girl in honor of the play.

Tony laughed. "Things don't turn out so good for Othello in the end. Though I think your luck with her would have been about the same as his with Desdemona. She's a real ballbreaker."

"Got both of yours?"

"She did, and not in a good way."

Tony told Robert about his family: His father's father had come from Abruzzo to Endicott Street. "When he started dating my mother, his parents were down on the idea because she was Sicilian."

"Italians discriminate against other Italians?"

"Sure," Tony said. "You think racism is just about color? We're smart enough to have our own idiotic prejudices." Tony's mother was a teacher and his father was a judge. "All fathers are, I guess," he said.

They were through to Ohio before Robert knew it, but then the wide middle of the country seemed to widen and there were long stretches where neither of them had anything to say except for pointing out a cherry car or a dead animal. They tried not to come off the road, because coming off meant looks from old men in shirtsleeves and thick glasses. In Indiana he was stepping out of a bathroom when a young guy in a mechanic's uniform brandished a wrench at him. He got back to Tony and the car quick. In Illinois a little girl even pointed and scowled, and her mother, rather than reprimanding her, took one look and whisked her away to safety. Robert felt a chill until he turned and saw Tony smiling grimly, and he smiled grimly in fraternity. "Rednecks," Tony said when they were back in the car. "You'd think they had never seen two fags before."

Robert laughed out loud and in all directions. He laughed at the top of his lungs. He laughed to the tips of his fingers. He wanted to hug Tony but he thought it would be read ironically. "Man," he said. "You just put all the poison out of my head."

"Poison's bad for mileage," Tony said. "And it's bad for me."

Robert went to sleep now. He had all the trust he needed. He dreamed dreams he would never remember except in the broadest sense: dreams of open spaces, of cool temperatures, of palms facing up. In Kansas Tony got his guitar out of the back and played along with the radio. It was Donovan singing "Sunshine Superman." "Shit, man," Robert said. "You forgot the harpsichord."

The morning of the third day, in Nebraska, Robert climbed out of the car, blinking into the flame of the afternoon. He looked past Tony, past the car, past the diner, into the endless fields. Dust rose in clouds at his feet. Robert started walking, and he didn't turn around when Tony called after him. Why should he? He wasn't walking away from Tony. He was walking away from himself. The way he figured it, Robert Franklin could try to leave Boston, but as long as he was Robert Franklin a piece of him would never leave. He had two choices: remain or rename. It was simple and elegant. He did not know why he had not thought of it sooner.

During Robert's turn at the wheel, there were storms in the distance, lightning bolts stabbing the broad hills. The soul station was breaking up so Robert retuned to the news, which was rehashing the Charles Whitman case. "Thirteen dead," the man on the radio said.

"Unlucky number," Robert said. "For everyone."

The next station had an Elvis song, and Robert switched it off. "Not for me," he said.

"That's where you're wrong," Tony said. "He's for everybody." He had skipped Elvis at first, too, he said, because he thought he was too square. He went to Gene Vincent for a little while, but then had come to think that the path to enlightenment involved sitting in his room with girls and playing them Kinks songs. One time he was trying "Til the End of the Day" and his father came home in a rage from work. He burst into Tony's room and told him that the whole house was filthy, raising his voice so terribly that the girl Tony was sitting with burst into tears. Tony couldn't imagine where his father had learned to raise his voice. He had always been a kind man who was called Captain by the children in the neighborhood because he called his car the S.S. Clemente. Tony sent the girl home and cleaned his room in surprise. Afterward he was walking down the hallway when he heard music coming from somewhere else in the house. He followed it to the basement and saw his father in a big leather chair. Elvis was playing on the basement phonograph. Tony stood there and listened and watched as his father's head bobbed almost imperceptibly and his fingers twitched in time. His father either didn't know Tony was there or didn't care. "It was a point of contact," Tony said. "Maybe the only one. But enough. You know that feeling? When you have maybe one thing in common with another person but it's enough to bind you?"

"Do I know that feeling?" Robert said. "I'm having it now."

The soul station was coming in strong. "We got it now, coming at you," the DJ said. "Junior Walker and the All-Stars with '(I'm a) Roadrunner.' What kind of fish or fowl are you?" The song was on, and though it moved, though it grooved, something about it left Robert cold. The sax squeaked. There wasn't enough bottom. But the DJ's question got up into him, and then he happened to look in the mirror, and that's when it hit him. It wasn't a rat or a mouse he looked like. It was a fox, quick and brown. Maybe that was where his name should come from. Fox. He would jump over the lazy dog. Robert Fox? No. Too much like some old-time white actor, or a baseball player. But what if he added another X, for Malcolm and for that other cat, Charles Foxx, the one who did "Mockingbird"? Then he had F-O-X-X, F-O-Excess. But he would have to drop Robert, too. He moved the name through his mind. Black Foxx? Dr. Foxx? Fleetingly he considered Andre Foxx, but put the idea down when it began to tighten a fist around his heart. Rock Foxx? Yeah. That would do: for the music, for the hard heart, for the very sound of it.

Wyoming was everywhere. At mile marker 158, he saw a sign for the Continental Divide. He pulled over on the shoulder of the road and poked Tony awake. "Ow," Tony said. "Where are we?"

"Opinion is divided," Robert said. "I'm getting out of the car."

"You're hyped, Robert."

"I'm not. Not hyped. And not Robert." He stepped out of the car and walked to the sign. Then he jumped back and forth across its shadow. "Franklin, Foxx, Franklin, Foxx."

"What are you doing?" said Tony.

"Crossing over to see myself." He jumped again and didn't come down for years.

"Crazy like a Foxx," Robert said to himself in the car mirror, then in the window of the first shop in San Francisco, and again as he stood on the beach and took a step into the Pacific Ocean. "Crazy like a Robert," Foxx said in reply.

At first the names teamed up: Each on his own wouldn't have known what to do with San Francisco. First of all, there were the girls. They were everywhere, staring out from behind their bangs in the Mission, pressed against the sides of doorways in the Haight. They were white. They were red. They were yellow.

But it wasn't just the girls. New smells popped like corn. The light was lighter, the sun sunnier. Even clothes weren't what they had been. One afternoon Robert rode the vibe, went out in a fishtail parka. "These clothes don't fit me," said Robert. But no one listened to Robert anymore.

The first few days there, Foxx and Tony slept in the car, or under the stars in the green midriff of Golden Gate Park. During the day they set up an open guitar case in front of them and played soul songs in delicate duet fashion. "We're salt and pepper," said Foxx. "We're yin and yang," said Tony. Foxx let it go at that. He had noticed that Tony seemed to need the last word sometimes.

Near the end of the first week they looked at a rooming house on Geary, a subdivided Victorian with an upstairs room to let. "Come upstairs and see it," said the woman who answered the door. It was nothing special, a small space jammed with old-fashioned furniture and stained scatter rugs. There was one bed, one sofa, and one chair. The whole place wasn't much bigger than the car. "Do you like it?" said the woman.

"I likes it okay," said Foxx, putting on whitey by putting on black. "How much it cost?"

She surprised him with a broad, generous smile. "I'd give it to you if I could. I don't need the room."

"You'll give it to us?"

"I can't," she said. "I also need the money. But how about fifteen dollars a month?"

"Robert," he said, holding out his hand.

"Jeannine," she said.

It turned out that Jeannine had been born in Providence, and during their first few weeks in San Francisco, Foxx and Tony traded news with her, East for West. She told them about the Hip Job Co-Op and Cedar Alley. She told them where to go for shoes, and where to go for food, and where not to go to stay safe from dealers and pimps. Finally, she told Tony where he could trade in the New Yorker, and he went away one morning with the struggle buggy and came back with an ash-colored Volkswagen that smelled like hot rubber. It needed paint, and Tony took care of it, paying twenty dollars to some viejo in Vallejo to make it red. Foxx asked Jeannine if he could paint the room the same red and nail a basketball hoop on the back corner of the house. He and Tony played some afternoons, or played around, dribbling and shooting. Foxx was Oscar Robertson or Hal Greer or Sam Jones. "You can be Rick Barry," he told Tony.

"No way," Tony said. "It's Cousy or nothing."

"It's nothing, then," Foxx said, and pulled up to take a jumper over Tony. The ball clanged off the back of the rim. "Swish," Foxx said. "Summertime and the living is easy."

It was easy: There were park meadows that smelled like new grass, girls who walked across the green expanses in miniskirts and fishnets. Foxx and Tony sang five days a week in the park. They cleared enough to pay Jeannine rent and help out with food, and they were even getting a little reputation. They saw the same people and the same people saw them. One Friday a cat in a leather cap put a dollar bill in the case. "Thanks, man," Tony said.

"Thank you," the man said. He introduced himself. His name was Bill Something—Foxx didn't catch the last name, or rather he caught it and dropped it—and he worked for a record label. "I appreciate what you two are doing. Always looking for the next big thing." He had a wide mustache and a shirt that was two sizes too tight.

"Look no further," Foxx said.

"At the moment, I'm not," the man said. "Hey. I have a question. Want to come out to Candlestick to see the Beatles next week? I know a guy who knows a guy who knows Tom Donohue over at KYA."

"Really?" Tony said.

"Sure," the man said. "Horseshoe reserved. The best seats they've got. It's not selling like wildfire, so I can get a pair easy."

"What do you think?" Tony said, looking at Robert.

"I already have a mop," Foxx said.

The man laughed. "The next big thing doesn't want to see the last big thing?"

"Forward thought's the thought I've got," Foxx said.

"I'll go," Tony said. That was good enough for Robert. Anyway, he knew what Tony would report back: that the crowd screamed, that the band was out of shape and out of sorts, that John Lennon made a joke that no one else understood, that the earth didn't move the way it should have. He also knew that Tony would tell him that Bill Something tried to make a move, invite him back to his pad for joss sticks. "I know what kind of stick he wants to smoke," Foxx would say.

While Tony was at the show, Foxx was making a girl he had met at the Carousel. Her name was Mary, and she went round. The next morning he took her back to Piedmont, where she lived, and on his way back he stopped in to see Lucas, who was living with Adele and the baby in a little house in East Oakland. As Foxx pulled up in the Volkswagen, Lucas was pulling up, too, in a 1961 Chrysler Newport whose passenger door was rusted near to out. "Nice ride," Lucas said.

"Nice beater," Foxx said.

"Runs fine," Lucas said. "There's a guy down at work who has a '66 Imperial LeBaron, and this boat can go by it like it's standing still."

"You can get a '66 Imperial on what you make?" Lucas was working as an orderly at Oakland Hospital.

"I can't," Lucas said. "A doctor." He led Robert inside the house and popped the tops off a pair of beers. "You should come by someday," he said. "They're hiring."

"Slow loot, man. And as square as a square meal."

"Don't tell me you're going to try to make it with your band," Lucas said. "The odds are a million to one."

"But I'm the one, baby. I'm the one. You think I'm gonna spend my days sweating for a nickel and then the next one after that? You know me better than that, man. I'm gonna get me some stone vines, an El Dorado, and a big bright ring to go on my big black finger."

"Kid killa pimp," Lucas said, laughing.

"I ain't no fool," Foxx said.

"Could have fooled me," said Lucas, still laughing. "Come back when you have something to report."

He didn't see Lucas for a while. Instead he saw the Charlatans at Sokol Hall. He saw Sopwith Camel at the Firehouse. He saw Dan Hicks in the street, talking to an older guy, both of them appearing angry until he got close and saw that they were laughing. He saw Grace Slick sitting in a new Cadillac holding a glass of wine that was so big it was like a soup bowl. One night he saw the Righteous Brothers standing in the entrance to a closed restaurant, looking all around, like they had nothing better to do. He tried to go everywhere, until Mary explained that everywhere was nowhere, and then he just tried to go somewhere. Change—real change, not the word, but the thing—was in the air, and he breathed deeply until the air was in him. But change had its limits; he split up with Mary when she invited him to sleep in a tent in the park. "Never happened, never will," he said. "I need a real roof over my head."

"Angels can see the sky," she said, by way of argument. Mary spent the night with a guy named Dean, but she was back to see Foxx the next week. "I think I caught a glimpse of you up there among the stars," she said.

"Told you," he said.

One morning, early, before the fog burned off the city, Foxx was sitting on the steps of Jeannine's house looking at a handbill. There was a new band named Moby Grape that had splintered off the Airplane. Everyone said they were going to make it big. "Blues, country, rock, jug, and tons of drugs," a girl had said to him, beaming, like they had just cut a key to her heart. Foxx imagined what the music would sound like: It was a game he played with himself when he first heard of bands, and more often than not he was right. He lit a cigarette, held it for a while, and ground it out without taking a drag. Two of the guys who played with the Alligator Clip were coming up the street, obviously stoned. "Jack," Foxx said, stepping toward them. "Neil."

"Hey, hey," Jack said. "Not too close, man. Stop Tom Lynching me." He wasn't quite smiling.

"I just wanted to tell you that I saw you guys play with Duncan Blue Boy, and it was cool."

"Get your own band, man."

"I'm starting one," Foxx said, with surprise.

"Sure you are," Neil said. "My kid brother is, too. And my grandmother, and the little girl down the street. You all are. One day it's going to be nothing but bands, with no one left to see them. We call that day the Future." They giggled and moved off down the street.

A few nights later, he and Tony went to see Andrey Voznesensky at the Fillmore. "A poet in a concert hall," Tony said. "If this isn't the new world, I don't know what is." Everyone was shoulder to shoulder, which was fine with Foxx because it meant that he could put his arm around the blonde girl next to him. She smiled and focused on a point somewhere in the distance. The poet made some remarks in Russian, the Jefferson Airplane played for ten minutes, and then Lawrence Ferlinghetti read translations of some of the poems. "They're like pop songs," the girl said, but she was wrong: The energy was steadier, with lower highs and higher lows. In one of them, the poet was waiting on a roadside for a friend of his. "Anticipation lightens our lives," he said. Foxx saw the words as if they were written in the air in front of him. But he didn't see things the same way. Anticipation didn't lighten anything. It was a weight, pushing down on him, and everything would be crushed but what escaped. By the end of the show, the blonde girl was focusing on a point nearer to them, and she was even returning Foxx's pressure, but he gave her a smile and moved off into the departing crowd.

"Why didn't you go for it?" Tony said as they were walking home. "Or at least you could have let me try."

"I have something else to do," Foxx said.

"You mean Mary?" Tony said. "I thought you were finished with her."

"I mean the band," Foxx said. "We need it now." He told Tony about how the guys from the Alligator Clip had mocked them.

"So you want to do it because they made you feel bad?" Tony said. "Why don't you wait until it seems right? It's a big world. We'll find a place in it."

"Let's get so big that the rest of it seems tiny," Foxx said. "Let's be the thing that other people look up at and wonder how it got that way."

"Rhetoric precedes action unless it replaces it," Tony said. Foxx assumed this was a line from one of the poems that he had missed while he was putting his arm around the blonde.

A few weeks later, Foxx had an idea for a band, or at the very least a name. "How about Dig?" he said. "Just the one word." He and Tony were stopped at the corner of Sutter and Van Ness, picking at the remnants of burritos. There was a tall Chinese girl in a purple coat on the other corner, and Foxx made sure that she stayed in his eye line.

"Because we dig what's going on?" Tony said. "Or because of the Diggers?"

"Watch your mouth," Foxx said.

"No," Tony said. "You know. The group here in the Haight named themselves after English radicals from the seventeenth century."

"You reading those books again, Poindexter?" Foxx said. "That's history, and I don't care about history. My now and then is in the future. Dig?" The girl across the street was talking to another cat now. "Hey," Foxx called to her. "Want to be in a band?" She turned and smiled, but didn't answer.

"And what kind of music would Dig play?"

"Say 'we.' That makes it real."

Tony sighed. "What kind of music would we play?"

"Music music. You know."

"So you don't know either."

"Man, we'll just play. Didn't you tell me that you met a drummer the other day?" When Foxx went out, he tried to take in the music; when Tony went out, he took names and numbers.

"Yeah. This guy named Pete who has played some shows with the guys in Mystery Trend."

"Bring him over one night."

"And you think that all of a sudden we'll have a band?"

"I don't think. I know. Dig?"

Pete was older, maybe thirty, and he had an endless list of questions about what his guarantees would be if the band ever made it. "You have an awful lot of confidence in us," Tony said. They were sitting in the front room at Jeannine's drinking longnecks.

"You don't understand, man," Pete said. "Almost every player out here has been in ten bands that failed. That's not unusual. What's unusual is that they're all the same bands: Oxford Circle, Grassroots, the Elementals, Capstone. The bands that make it, well, they're the rocket to the moon. If this is one of them, we need to make sure that we're all together in it."

"Okay," Tony said. "I'll have some papers drawn up. But in the meantime, let's make sure you're right for this thing, and that this thing's right for you." He took out his guitar. "I play lead guitar. Robert sings."

"Robert?"

"Me," Foxx said.

"What's the sound?"

Tony looked over at Foxx, frowning a little bit to show that he was curious too.

"You know how the Beatles and the Stones took songs from Little Richard and Muddy Waters?" Foxx said. "We're taking their songs and putting the black back into them."

"Jagger's pretty black."

"I'm prettier—and blacker."

Pete laughed, but he was listening, too. He had his sticks with him, and he tapped out a beat on the tabletop. Tony started in on "You Won't See Me," and Foxx started to sing, moving a little toward the way Otis might have done it, backing off when it sounded too close. Foxx liked the way it was going, everyone keeping themselves in control. He could picture them onstage, and the picture wasn't blurry.

"Works for me if it works for you," Pete said. "Who's your bass player?"

"We're waiting on a guy, but he's holding out," Tony said.

"We're not waiting anymore," Foxx said. "My patience stretches only so far before it breaks."

"While you're waiting, I might have someone for you."

"What's his name?" Tony said.

"Her."

"A girl?" Tony said. But Foxx was saying "perfect" at the same time.

Her name was Gretchen, and she looked like what Foxx thought a Gretchen should look like: tall, Nordic, a little mannish. She could play the bass, though, and moreover, her father knew the guy who owned the Matrix. Foxx couldn't tell if she was Pete's girl, or one of many, or if Pete was one of many guys for her. She did look at Pete like they had a secret, though, and sometimes whispered things that Foxx and Tony couldn't hear. "Annoying," said Tony, who wanted to make her, and Foxx agreed.

They put her out in front, right next to Foxx, dressed in tall boots and a short coat, both white leather. They practiced more than Foxx thought they needed to, past where the songs were second nature, but they didn't sound like first nature so much as they sounded unnatural. When Foxx tried to explain, Tony frowned, so Foxx stopped. The night of the first gig, he felt his stomach for what he hoped would be nerves, but it was like a steel box, sealed off, and he played that way, too. It was nothing special, except for the fact that they went for an hour, and the girls in the front screamed, and one of them came backstage afterward and sat on Foxx's lap and kissed him while she slipped his hand inside his shirt. "You're going to be all there is," she said, and he believed her even though her pupils were as big as nickels.

When Foxx lay awake in bed, he tried to see it, but he couldn't force his imagination. He painted a marquee, bricked a record-store wall, designed a poster that looked like it came straight from the Print Mint, but Dig wasn't there. He woke as the only thing in an empty room.

The gigs were going well enough. Pete was playing hard, and he was starting to have ideas: Most weeks he drove down to see his old lady in Pasadena and brought back music. Most of it Foxx passed on, but he added in Love's cover of "My Little Red Book." As it wound down, Foxx would set his back to the crowd. "You look her up in the little red book," Foxx said. "You call and then what? Engaged tone, that's what." He turned toward the crowd, Pete crashed his sticks down, and the band tore into "Off the Hook."

Pete was high from the medley after they came off stage. "You know what we should do?" he said. "We should have Gretchen wear a snake."

"No way," Gretchen said. She stood up and sat back down. It was Gretchen at her most interesting.

"But we should do something to bring you more to the front," Tony said, walking around behind her and putting his hand on her shoulder.

Foxx left them talking and went walking through the Mission. On Valencia and sixteenth, a voice hissed at him from an alleyway. Foxx stiffened as a man came out of the shadows, a large figure that took away what little light there was. It was Lucas.

"What you doing in this part of town, cousin?" Lucas said.

"I could ask you the same thing." But he couldn't, really, not so long as the light in Lucas's eyes was strange this way. And it wasn't what he was doing. It was who: a small Nicaraguan girl who was hanging on to Lucas's arm and smiling like the world was a place of divine perfection.

"We should hang one of these nights. You can come out across the bay."

"Or the city. Otis is at the Fillmore next week."

"You going?"

"I'm going to stand outside and see if I can get someone to give me tickets for cheap."

"Even cheap should be too rich for your blood. How you making any scratch anyway?"

"Tony and I have a band now. I told you. I'm just coming from a gig. We have a real stiff playing bass. When you joining us?"

"I got something else to tend to at the moment," Lucas said. Foxx didn't answer, and Lucas hovered another minute in the alleyway and then started to slide backwards as if he was on rails.

Tony's conversation with Gretchen about the snake had worked well; the two of them started seeing each other, and Gretchen came by the house the night that Reagan was inaugurated. "I know people don't trust him," she said. "But he reminds me of my father."

"I thought your father ran around on your mother," Tony said.

"He had his good points."

Tony nodded like he was catching on, but there was nothing to catch on to. Foxx concentrated on the TV screen, where the governor was getting sworn in. Just before he put his hand on the Bible, he turned to George Murphy, who was standing at his side, and said, "Well, here we are on the late show again." Foxx liked the line enough that he tried it onstage a few nights later. Most of the crowd didn't laugh, and so he turned his back on them and called for "It's Not Easy." Tony churned the first few notes, and Foxx sang just one line: "Just a big bed and a telephone." He repeated and repeated it until it made no sense, and then all the sense in the world.

Out at the Polo Grounds in the park, at the Human Be-In, he broke the news to Tony. "What's that?" Tony said. The Airplane was playing far away, but loud enough to interfere. A girl on the other side of him was tickling between her breasts with a feather. Beyond her there was an old man with finger cymbals and a Chinese flag.

"I said that's it. Time to bury Dig. I'm done with it."

Tony pulled himself up to full height, which was a half head taller than Foxx. "You're ditching us?"

Foxx laughed and sat down. "Not you, man. You're coming with me."

"Where to?"

"Everyone's going heavy. Have you heard Big Brother and the Holding Company? I want to go lighter and brighter."

The first gig was in February. Gretchen was still playing bass, and she got the band into the Benefit at the Fillmore for the Council for Civic Unity. They were replacing some cats from the League of Sexual Freedom. "Not that I'm against it," Foxx said.

April flowers brought Howlin' Wolf at the Matrix, a man in an oak's body. Then back to the blur, with Fluxfest one day and a big peace march the next and a concert honoring Ali the next. Foxx had a small sense of history being made: There were too many bands, too many names, for it all to be forgotten. The Dead and the Airplane and the Holding Company and a whole lot more. The Foxxes were starting to become a little part of it as well. That was the name now: the Foxxes. He had written it down that way on a handbill and Tony hadn't objected at all, even laughed and said, "Cool." Foxx wrote a little song in celebration and sang it to Tony, and then to Gretchen: "You're a peach, you're a peach / In the tree out of reach / You're a pear, you're a pear / Hanging sweet way up there." Tony had nodded appreciatively and started to work out an arrangement on the guitar. Gretchen unbuttoned her shirt, all the way down. It wasn't the first time she had come on to him but it was the first time he had noticed. "Want to go with me to the Straight Theatre to see Neal Cassady?" she said. She pulled out one strand of hair and ran a finger along it like it was a violin string. "The peace torch is coming from Hiroshima."

"That's hip."

"It's not." She placed her hands on either side of his face and kissed him square on the mouth. "Hip is dead. There's no hip anymore."

It was midday. Foxx and Tony were drinking bottles of Coke and sitting down on a stoop. A tall, thick-set man with a goatee and a peacoat came up the street, checking his watch every few steps. He turned toward Foxx; Foxx braced for the scowl but there was a smile instead.

"Excuse me," the man said. "I have to meet my daughter for lunch and I don't know exactly where I am." His accent was not quite British, maybe Australian.

"None of us do, man."

The man laughed. "I'm supposed to be on Russian Hill."

"It's close, but it's steep. Follow me."

Tony's car was parked just up the street, but they went on foot and the man followed. "Thank you," he said. "But it's really not necessary. You could just point me."

"We'd hate to point you and then see you rolling back down," Tony said.

They went up the hill. Foxx's breath was coming shorter and shorter, but the older man went along briskly. "What do you two do?"

"We're musicians," Foxx said. He and Tony hadn't talked about it since the Polo Grounds. He liked this man and wanted the story believed. "We have a band, the two of us."

"What's it called?"

"Rock Foxx and the Foxxes," he said.

"Are you the leader?"

"Well, it's just like it is now," Foxx said. "He starts out ahead but I make sure the people understand."

"I'm the people?"

"Aren't you?"

The man did a little hop on the incline. "Maybe I am," he said. "Though am I your people? I grew up with different things. Morecambe and Wise? Have you heard of them?" Foxx hadn't. "No loss," the man said. "But when I hear your things, I like what I hear, and the more I hear, the more I like. It seems like there's something happening to people." He whistled a bit of "Ballad of a Thin Man."

They huffed up the hill. Once Foxx had to stop and lean on a tree. He pretended like he was retying his shoes.

At Filbert, the man stopped and tapped his watch again. "Five minutes early," he said. "Thank you both very much." He reached into his pocket. "Can I give you some money?"

"No," Tony said. "We're Samaritans."

"And we're pretty good at it," Foxx said.

"It's a shame my daughter's not here. I had hoped you might meet her."

"She single, man?" Foxx said.

"I'm afraid not. She's married to a banker."

"You don't sound thrilled."

"Yes. I'd prefer someone more like you."

Foxx laughed, high and hard. But the man didn't even smile. He just lifted a finger. "I have taste, you see."

Foxx and Tony walked down Union away from the man, saying nothing at first. The sun was in their eyes. "I liked him," Tony said finally, and Foxx wanted to hear it as artful understatement. But Tony went on. "You don't expect that broad a mind from a man in his fifties." This was the point, but it felt small now that it was out. Foxx silently forgave Tony.

At the intersection of Jones and Union, they stopped. Tony must have noticed the expression on Foxx's face. "You look like you're about to cry."

He pointed back up the hill. "We're going up there," he said. "It's a steep climb but I've seen the mountain."

"What does it look like?"

"You know. We get rid of Gretchen. We get Lucas. Those are the pieces that need to switch. And then we're forward."

"I got to go," Tony said. "Make a plan."

Foxx saw a movie instead. A man, a gun, a horse, a shot ringing out in the narrow canyon, a bird skimming over a dusty plain. He didn't remember anything else about the movie, because there wasn't anything else to remember. At the corner, there was a man about the same age as the older man, with the same kind of beard, hunched over into the shape of a question mark. There was a woman next to him, upright and nicely dressed. "Come on," she said to the man. "We have to go."

The man picked up his head to show wild eyes. "To me I'm a fabulous character," he said. "When I'm near me, I glow." He had an accent, too, from somewhere in the Deep South. He pulled himself unsteadily to his feet and collapsed again.

"Can you help me get him up?" the woman said.

Foxx put a shoulder under the man and lifted. He expected the man to smell of alcohol, but he didn't. Instead there was another smell, both hotter and sharper. "Oh," Foxx said. "It's dope."

"He's just tired," the woman said, so brightly that Foxx knew even she didn't believe it.

"Man," the man said. His breath was surprisingly clean. "Man, oh, man. You're hex backward in your skin," he said. "And you don't even know what shape you're in."

"Stop it," the woman said. "You don't even know this young man." Righted, the man shook himself off and went on down the street.

About a month later, Foxx spent the night with a girl whose apartment overlooked the bay. There was a husband who worked in the financial industry. He was out of town. She had the faintest accent and he imagined that this was the daughter of the Australian man, and that her father's wish had come true. On his way out in the morning, he thought he saw the Australian, and he raised his hand to wave, but it was only the junkie, who waved back energetically.

Robert was watching a black man across the street light a cigarette. Trying to light it, rather. The man was older, maybe forty, but his hand was at least seventy, and he couldn't get a steady grip. A girl walking by told Foxx the guy was a famous artist. "Is that Little Richard?" he said. "He sure looks like he has the heebie-jeebies."

"He's a painter," she said, crinkling her nose. "Nonrepresentational."

Foxx thought about trying to make the girl—she was short and cute, probably half Chinese—but he saw Tony waving at him from down the block. "Hey," he said, running up to Foxx. Tony was out of breath and sweaty. "I found us a party for tonight. You in?"

"To win," Foxx said. "Just show me the way." Tony pointed east and then let Foxx lead. While they walked, Tony talked excitedly about a song he was writing and something he had discovered by listening closely to Herb Alpert. They got to the party, which was on the upstairs level of a corner house. The sun was just going down; it looked like it was headed for the second floor too.

Robert smelled the party before he saw it. Sit in the corner, Mary Warner. He was ready for it, too—a smile for a little while—or at least he thought he was until he walked in and took a measure of the room. On the near wall, there was a chick who was telling a guy about her recent liberation from her parents' values, and how California was helping her come to terms with her true identity. On the far wall, there was a guy who was worried that the girl he was talking to wasn't going to take him into the bedroom. So many people, so much pain: It was hard to tell where one thing ended and the other began. "I forgot something," he said to Tony, and headed back down the stairs. He sat out on the stoop and smoked a cigarette and listened to the radio from the party, which went from "Going to a Go-Go" to "I Thank You." He imagined that he was upstairs, among people, unlonely.

Foxx felt a hand on his shoulder. He turned to tell Tony he'd be up in a minute, but it was a beautiful girl, deep black, with skin that looked purple under the street-lamp. "You got a light?" she said.

He took out a match and struck it.

"Got a cigarette?" she said.

He laughed and blew out the match. "Why didn't you ask that first?" he said, handing her a lit cigarette.

"I don't know," she said. "It lacks imagination." She indicated the upstairs window. "You here for Lulu's party?" She cupped her hand over the cigarette and got it going. Every time she took a drag, the orange light went a little way toward showing Foxx her face. He was grateful.

"I'm not sure whose party I'm here for. My friend Tony brought me along."

"Tony Clemente? I know that guy." Tony went up a notch in Foxx's estimation. "He's in a band, right? You in it with him?"

"I am, or he's in it with me. Depends on who you ask and when."

"I'm asking you now."

He dragged long on his cigarette, then dropped it onto the stairs and ground it out with his boot heel. "In that case, we're in it together."

"What kind of music you play?"

The radio upstairs was playing "You Send Me" now. "Not that," he said, and then, seeing the girl's face harden slightly, regretted that he had said it. "I just mean it's newer than that."

"He's beautiful," she said. "Is your music beautiful?"

"He was beautiful," Foxx said. "No more."

"I know," she said. "I don't like to think about it, so I pretend he's still alive. When I sing, I try to sound like him."

"You sing?"

"You think I'm talking to you about your music because I want you to feel good?" She dropped her cigarette and tapped him on the wrist. "Want to head into the party?"

Foxx pulled himself up and played brave. "After you," he said. It was everything he had expected, and no more. A short girl with a big bouffant offered to take him home for some Romilar and whatever came next. Tony was having luck with a skinny chick who turned out to be a teacher. After an hour, Foxx couldn't stand in one spot any longer, and he was losing the will to move. "Let's go," he said to Tony. On the street, he told Tony about the girl from the stoop.

"That's Yvette Washington," Tony said. "She's a friend of Lulu's. Her dad was a jazz player, a little famous. I saw her at the party. I have her number, but she's unimaginable."

"She's said she's a singer sometimes," Foxx said. "I wonder if we should have a girl singer in the band."

"You're thinking on your feet," Tony said.

"And you're thinking of getting her off of hers."

"Like you're not."

Foxx laughed wickedly. He didn't tell Tony about the touch on the wrist, and about all the things he hadn't felt. There were girls you were hot for and girls you should have been hot for, and it was a shame when the most beautiful ones fell into the wrong basket. Tony was still talking about Yvette. "Trailing her, inhaling her perfume," Foxx said.

"A foolish heart, that I leave here behind," Tony said.

"You're in San Francisco," said Foxx. "You can leave your heart here, but it's a cliché."

Boom. Shake the room. The new year sealed the old year in a tomb. Tony called Yvette, who agreed to go out with him if he let her come by the house and sing some songs. She wasn't bad, either: not much power, but her voice was as sweet as her ass. She sat with them afterward. "Did I pass the audition, Mr. Goldwyn?" she said.

"Don't call us," Foxx said. "We'll call you. In fact, Tony will call you tomorrow."

"Good." She chuckled. "I worked as an actress for a little while. Didn't like it. But I never thought I'd get back into the music business."

"Back into it?" Foxx said.

"Well, I grew up in it."

"Yeah," Tony said. "I looked up your father."

Her eyebrows rose. "You did?"

He blushed. "Well, I happened to be at the library taking out some books on accounting, and…"

Her eyebrows came back down but now her mouth spread out in a wide smile. "You happened to be taking out some books on accounting? I thought I'd heard every line there was."

"He's telling the truth," Foxx said. "Behind every great man there's a stack of numbers and a good man making sure they don't fall over. Tony takes care of all the nuts and bolts. When we make it big, he's going to be the one who's on the phone with Los Angeles and New York and Moscow."

"Moscow?" Tony said.

"We won't discriminate. The Reds need to get their kicks too."

"Tell me about my father," she said.

Tony sat down and peered at the back of his hand like he had notes written there. "Roy Washington, right?"

"So far, so good."

"Piano player in and around Saint Louis, worked with lots of singers: Betty Carter, Carmen McRae. Made a few records with small groups. Appeared on a famous late Billie Holiday single of 'Fine and Mellow.'" He turned his hands palms up. "That's all the book said."

"The rest isn't much of a story," she said. "He got hooked on junk, stabbed a man, went to jail, cleaned himself up, realized he didn't love my mother anymore, left her, got hooked again, died poor. It'll probably be in the next edition of the book." She looked at Foxx evenly, but when she turned toward Tony her face went shy. "You do this much research for everyone you try out for the band?"

"At least," Tony said.

"At most," Foxx said. The only other hire was a drummer named Kevin Moore, a fat little man who was deep into drink and more but could thump harder than thunder bumps a stump. He was married, and his wife was expecting, and he needed the gig bad.

"Well, this library sounds like quite a place. You should take me there sometime."

"Band trip," Foxx said.

"We can talk about it when I'm in the band." She stood to leave, got halfway to the door, corkscrewed around. "Call me tomorrow," she said.

Tony called her. Then he called around. He got them a Friday-night gig at the Insider and a Saturday late slot at Stern. The sets were covers and standards, Otis and Smokey and Little Richard's version of "By the Light of the Silvery Moon," and though they were starting to weave a new sound, Foxx was ashamed of the old threads. At night, at home, he went through Jeannine's record collection, learned what he could about Julie London and the Everly Brothers, architectural Spector and icy Miles. His favorite, though he couldn't bring himself to admit it to anyone, was Sinatra. He loved those records, the way Frank drew a portrait of every word. "Once I laughed when I heard you say that I'd be playing solitaire, uneasy in my easy chair," he sang to himself, almost choking on the sadness. He went out to the porch and tried to write his own songs, but he was like a little boy trying on a man's clothes. The words sat there but they wouldn't stand up.

Lucas trudged up the walk. He looked like a pack animal, or something equally mistreated; there were white rings on his blue shirt where the sweat had spread and dried, and he winced every time his shoulder bag bumped his hip. He was coming from the community college, where he was taking night classes after his shift at the bank let off. He had left his job as an orderly after a supervisor called him a dumb mule. "Hey," said Foxx, who was sitting on the stoop smoking skunkweed. "Welcome to the welcome wagon."

He handed Lucas the joint and Lucas pulled on it. "Thank you, brother." He pulled a lollipop out of his pocket and tossed it onto Robert's lap. "Even Steven." He always had lollipops on him these days; the bank used them to placate kids dragged along by their parents. This one was cream-colored, with a whorl of sunflower yellow. Foxx put it in his pocket, and they went inside and Lucas took beers out of the refrigerator.

"Listen, L. I got a gig for my band. The new one."

"Great."

"But I ain't got a bass player for the gig. Not a real one. We have a guy filling in, but he's not long for it."

"Too bad."

"Too good for you." Foxx tried to keep his voice light, but this was the heaviest thing he'd done in recent memory, trying to move Lucas from where he was rooted.

"I told you, man. I ain't been practicing. I ain't been listening to nothing new. My chops are shot."

"Reload them, then."

"I need to make some bread."

"Then follow the baker," said Foxx. "There's a way to feel fine, Ranger Nine." He steadied his voice so he couldn't hear the kid in himself, the eight-year-old begging

Lucas to come outside and toss a ball. "Come on, man. You haven't even seen us play. You'll get the spirit in you. In two years, we could clear the same as in thirty years of break-the-back bullshit."

Lucas sipped his beer. "Something's gotten into you," he said.

"Everything has gotten into me," Foxx said, spreading his hands out in front of him, palms up in appeal. And it had. There was the war, always the war, and though he didn't like it, he didn't like the people who didn't like it, either. He and Tony argued about that. Tony said that peace was a substance, and that people were needed to produce it. "I thought the people were the government," Foxx said. "The whole thing doesn't hold water." In April King spoke out against the fighting, and Foxx listened like everyone else, but he didn't hear it like everyone else. Foxx let the speech wash over him and when it went back out with the tide, all he had were a few brilliant phrases. "I have moved to break the betrayal of my own silences," King said. "Somehow this madness must cease," King said. "We need to get on the right side of the world revolution," King said. Foxx pledged allegiance not to the ideas, but to the way the language carried them. He would release language from bondage and let the people follow. This is how he'd do his part.

Then, a few weeks later, he felt a finger of God on his spine when he heard Curtis Mayfield sing "People Get Ready." He was at a party, moving up on a short redhead with a low-cut blouse, and somebody outside the window had a radio going loud. At first it was a nuisance, but then it played "Pretty Little Baby," and it was a comfort. And then he heard Curtis, and it just stopped him cold. He didn't notice the redhead or what was in the blouse. Here was a falsetto that had top and bottom and all the rungs of the ladder in between. It was the church come out onto the street, a ribbon in the beak of a dove. "Faith is the key," sang Curtis, "open the doors, unbar them." *Unbar.* The word was astonishing. It took the prison of the mind and dissolved it. It was what happened in Revelations. Later that night, thinking about the war, thinking about the world, Foxx sang it to himself on the edge of sleep. "People get ready," he sang, and slipped into the most peaceful slumber. He explained this all to Tony. "For me, a group of people is a problem, not a solution. The only thing that works to fix it is music. I know that it's what will unbar the doors."

"That's faith," Tony said. He looked pensive.

The next night Foxx had bad dreams, and while he was still awake. It was the heat, but it was more than that. What if everything he had done, everything he was doing, was lost? He was seeing a girl named Ola, and she was there, in his bed, using a damp washrag to wipe between her breasts and under her arms. He got up and walked to the window. There was a melody in his head, and he couldn't get it out.

He pitched his voice high at first, sang nonsense lyrics. Then he picked up his guitar and switched to something real. "What good is time when you ain't got a minute? / What good is an oyster when there's no pearl in it? / Love has no point / It's a circle / Not a square / Someday a body will wake up / And find there's nobody there."

Ola came up behind him. "Is that the new song you've been working on?" she said. "That it is."

"I think you're going to go far," she said. He laughed. "What?" she said.

"Nothing,' he said. But she had given him an idea. He strummed hard, and belted out the chorus: "Gonna go fast / Gonna go far / Gonna go away in my highway car." Ola flopped down on the bed, closed her eyes, drank in every note. When he was finished, she reached for his hand and squeezed it, and he had to pretend he was thinking about her when he squeezed it back.

The Foxxes were drawing bigger weekend crowds now, and the pressure to make a record was mounting. With uncharacteristic shyness, Foxx played "Highway Car" for Tony, who responded with uncharacteristic enthusiasm. They called Kevin, who was sleeping off a Tuesday night, and Yvette, who was presleeping her Wednesday night. They roped in a studio bassist named Winkie. And then they cut a single, "Highway Car" on one side and a stepchild song called "One More Day" on the flip. Foxx turned the wax over in his hands, and it was like a movie trick: In the time it took to complete a full circle, the platter mattered. Girls were starting to scream for it at the shows. "Gonna go fast, gonna go far," he sang, and they pressed closer.

Then a local DJ jumped on, started playing the record whenever he could, and all of a sudden the single hit. Airwaves: What were they, exactly, and how did they move things along? Labels unholstered their weapons, placed them on the table. Foxx shot back with Jerry Lemann, a local lawyer who had a second trade in repping bands. "Don't touch that," said Jerry. "Don't touch that. Touch that." He pointed at Turn Records, a San Francisco label that was offering a one-album deal, good bread up front, control retained by the band's two principals. Jerry brought the Turn brains around, two cats named Clary and Dunn who had deep pockets and bags under their eyes to match. They made their pitch: They were handling a Latin rock band named Dark Arts and a girl singer named Hannah Lewis. They had scored hits for both, and they thought they could do the same for the Foxxes. "We don't think it," Clary said. "We know it." Hands shook hands. Tony signed his name while Foxx watched. Then Foxx signed his name, and Robert Franklin's name beneath it. The lawyers demanded this doubling up.

The song was on the radio, and Foxx's heart leapt whenever he heard it. But then his heart sank back down with unfinished business. He took Lucas out near Stow Lake, where they sat on opposite park benches and drank cheap red wine. The wine shined them up after a time and then they were mirrors of one another. Every time Foxx leaned forward, Lucas leaned forward too. When Lucas stretched out his legs, Foxx stretched also. Neither was leading and neither was following. At first it was a coincidence, maybe, and then it was a silent game. But then Lucas wouldn't even answer Foxx when he was spoken to, stopped saying anything at all, in fact. Foxx couldn't see Lucas's expression exactly, but he could sense it, more watchful than careful, lofty, not quite loving.

Foxx's head was swimming from the wine. "The light divides the darkness from the darkness," he said. Lucas didn't answer. "Let the darkness be gathered together in one place," Foxx said. Still nothing from Lucas. Foxx thought of the flood, of Noah: six hundred years old, told to run for his life, given the secret of staying high while the rest of the world was brought low. He thought of a cartoon he saw once: Noah by the ark, slick lion approaching the door, walking on his back legs like he was a dude, wearing shades like he was a spade, has three or four lionesses with him like he was the hippest cat coming, the shit, the man. Noah had a surprised expression on his face. The lion smiled broadly. "Hey, Jack," he said to Noah. "You try to pick just one." Noah stepped aside. The lion strode into the ark. The lesson: Let sleeping lions lie, especially when they're getting some tail. Outside of the ark the darkness prevailed upon the earth.

"Eyes red with wine, teeth white with milk," Foxx said. He stood and crossed the grass toward Lucas, thinking strangely of Dre. Where was he now, after years beneath the earth? Where was the man he would have become? When Foxx reached the bench, Lucas was not there. "Hey," Foxx called out. "Brother, where you gone?"

No answer. "Tell me where," he said, "you black Jesus. Tell me where, Lucas 1:1. Tell me where, you pious motherfucker. You won't join my band? You're too good? Or are you just afraid you're nothing?"

All of a sudden he felt a shadow on his arm in the dark and his insides went liquid. "Cousin," Lucas said, "I told you not to profane that way." Lucas was holding the wine bottle, which was mostly empty, and like a joke, like a judgment, he swung it at Foxx and caught him just above the eye. The clink of glass on bone brought Foxx's hand up immediately. "Fuck," he cried.

Lucas had a soft hum in his throat that turned, by degrees, into words. "Divine justice," he said. "You'll be fine." He lifted the bottle of wine like he was going to drink it and then deliberately poured it out all over the ground. Then Lucas reached out and touched Robert's face.

The next day, on the way to rehearsal, Foxx saw a big black floppy hat floating down the street. He stopped and stared. It looked like Lucas, but it couldn't have been because that sorry-ass motherfucker was off guarding America's money with a lollipop. But it was Lucas, so big the bass in his hand looked like a violin. And when he plugged in he was suddenly twice the size. He had been practicing, too, no matter what he said: They tore through "Can't Turn You Loose" and "Dancing in the Street" and "You Threw a Lucky Punch" and "Hit the Road Jack" and even "Highway Car," which he had heard maybe twice.

"Where'd your reasons go, Joe?" Foxx called out to him. Lucas didn't answer. "What about your family?"

"They're still there," Lucas said.

"What about God?"

"He's here," said Lucas. Then he thumped out a fool-around version of "Cake Walking Babies from Home."

"Get rid of the big guy," Tony said in the brassy accent of a New York know-it-all. "He's dragging us down."

Foxx laughed. "I told you."

"That you did, my brother. That you did."

Foxx walked across the cold bare concrete of the rehearsal-space floor, conscious of all the eyes on him. When he got to the front of the room, he put his arms straight out and smiled. It was a smile of power, not of pleasure. "Once upon a time in Boston there were two boys," he said. Polk Street was stretched out behind him like a punishment, abandoned cars dead against the curb, junkies doing junkie choreography, weaving left to lamppost, right to shop window, now and then tipping a hat to a passing businessman. There was color out there, but no one was making anything happen with it. "Now those two boys are here. Once upon a time is now."

The band murmured, mostly in assent. Except for Kevin. "Why do you have us wearing these costumes?" he said. "They make us look like faggot garbagemen."

"It's garb, not garbage," said Foxx.

"Smooth, my man," said Lucas, laughing. "You're a politician if I ever saw one."

"It's the art of the possible," Foxx said. "Write that down." He had given up his name for another name. He had given up his city for another city. He was less himself and more himself, all at once. "Me and Tony are going to wear fancy-looking clothes, British shit with cuffs. Yvette's wearing U.S. Army. Kevin, you're going to wear a zoot suit. But you have to do something about that goat of yours. That wispy piece of red-blond shit is putting a strain on my vision. Color it black. It'll look good with the suit."

"Can I dress up like a priest?" said Claude. Claude played horns, and was also hitched to Cheryl, who played horns, too. Claude wasn't real friendly and didn't smile much, and his playing left something to be desired, if that something was energy. But then there was the small matter of his family: His father was one of the largest landowners in central Louisiana. The first night he was in the group, they all went to dinner and Claude dropped sixty bucks without blinking. The van Foxx drove them all around in needed upkeep, and all of a sudden there were wooden benches in the back, and new speakers too. He could play okay? He could play great.

"You and Cheryl are in white," Foxx said. "Wedding colors. I'm telling you. That was the problem at the Council for Civic Unity show we did in February. No bright eye. When people in the audience see us, they have to see it all at once. We got to learn to get down in these getups. And I'm also going to get some medallions made. Big gold motherfuckers with words on them: Love, Peace, Light, that kind of shit. Everyone will wear those. I will, Kevin will, Tony will. And Lucas...well, as usual, Lucas goin' do whatever the fuck he wants." Lucas gave a deep, rumbling laugh and mock-saluted Foxx.

"I ain't walking through the Potrero in no zoot suit and medallion," said Kevin. "I'll get collared as a pimp."

"Who told you to live in the Potrero anyway?" said Tony. "Come to Richmond."

"I ain't got the money to live in Richmond."

"Why you saying 'ain't' so much, college boy?" said Foxx. "You trying to sound tough? Well, it ain't working. You ain't no ruffian and you ain't no pimp. You a drummer with a zoot suit, if they make them in fat little man sizes." He moved to avoid the drumstick sailing through the air toward him. "Ain't so quick, slick. Anyway, I got to get out of here. I got to go meet someone."

"Who?"

"A real pimp," said Foxx, and everyone laughed. But he was serious then, and he was still serious an hour later, when he was waiting outside a bar on Castro Street for fifteen minutes, wipers keeping the rain off the windshield of his new Thunderbird—it was a '63, but it was new to him, and as cherry as the day was long—as "Ruby Tuesday" played on the radio. He sang along, but sang "Rudy Thursday" instead, because it was Thursday and he was waiting for a man named Rudy Bannacourt. Finally Bannacourt showed, stepping out of his new Cadillac and showing off a yellow silk shirt open at the throat, a blue-and-green-striped cap, red gabardine pants and a red gabardine coat, and black wing-tipped shoes. His hands were even louder: On his right hand alone he had three gold rings, one with a huge red stone, one with a three-quarter-carat yellow diamond, and one in the shape of a dog's head with two sapphire eyes.

"Hey, man," Foxx said, opening his door and going up onto the curb with a rolling walk, shoulder over hip, hip under shoulder.

"Foxy foxy," said Bannacourt. "You cool?"

"Cool as I am," said Foxx. They went inside the bar and took a table near the back. Foxx left his jacket at the table and went to get beers; while he was away from the table, he knew, Bannacourt was putting a bag into the jacket's inside pocket. When he got back to the table, he handed Bannacourt a beer and a hundred bucks. "Here's your change," he said.

"Damn," said Bannacourt. "I should have gotten two." He made the same joke every time.

Foxx patted the pocket. He wouldn't even put his hand in there until the next morning. He was using like he was drinking coffee: just enough to start the day.

There was a jukebox in the bar that was loaded up with crooners. Jimmy Scott was on now. "Yeah," said Bannacourt, imitating. "Don't he sound like one of those little birds?" Bannacourt did some singing himself. "Hey," he said. "I been down in

Los Angeles for a few days." He pronounced the *e*'s as long. "I'm probably going to move my central operation."

"You got a problem with San Francisco?" said Foxx.

"Less green to be seen. And that's the only problem I need to have."

Bannacourt drank another beer and then left, and Foxx stayed and listened to the juke. It was music from another era, which was just fine with him. If he listened to the competition too much, he'd start thinking that time was on some other motherfucker's side, and then his mind was liable to cloud over with anger and greed and other dark thoughts. Foxx had read an article about a chess prodigy that said that the mark of a genius was that he attacked with multiple pieces at the same time. That's what he heard in his band: They were attacking with ballads like "Something Is Missing," with up-tempo shit like "Fill Me Up," with slinky snake-funk like "She's So Bad She's Good." Foxx had written them all. He had a ritual—into the bedroom with two pieces of paper, one to roll into a joint, the other for writing down the lyrics. Then onto the porch with his guitar and a tape recorder. Then back inside to present to Tony. He had the process down pat, but what he didn't have was another hit. "Highway Car" had put a dent in things, but it hadn't broken through. A true hit would clear away everything in its path. A hit would light up the sky. Foxx located the bag that Bannacourt had sold him. He snorted up a line and prayed that it was pointing him in the right direction.

It happened in a hurry, one crisp afternoon. The band wasn't at full strength: Yvette was out taking one of the long walks she called air baths. Claude and Cheryl weren't there either, which was Foxx's decision; he liked adding the horns after he had a song nailed. So it was just the boys, Foxx and Lucas and Tony and Kevin, along with some studio musicians left over from somebody else's session earlier in the day and a few girls who didn't seem to have anything to do except sit around and look fine. For a while they worked on a jam Foxx had brought to the session, trying to fit some words to it. Foxx had a chorus: "I don't want to tell you again / You don't know when to say when." It didn't sound like love and it didn't sound like a party either. "Maybe it's a protest song," said Tony.

"Whatever you need, Jimmy Reed," said Foxx. He was bent over his guitar and not really listening.

"I have those lyrics I've been working on," said Tony. "You know the ones?"

"I can't say that I do," said Foxx.

They started up again and were well into it when someone in the booth said "Stop," and then, "We're out of tape." They went into the lounge and smoked a joint with some of the session musicians. One of them was a wiry little white guy who wouldn't stop talking about how he almost got to play guitar on the new Beach Boys record. "It's a hot, hot record," he said. The three girls who were still there were arranged in a row on the couch. One of them was small and sexy. She was the old lady of one of the session bassists, and she asked Foxx who the bass player for his band was.

"The big man," he said, pointing to Lucas.

The other two were tall brunettes in matching red dresses. "Backup singers," said Tony under his breath, and that's exactly what they were. One walked right up and looked at Foxx, who gave her the twist-eye in return.

When the tape was fixed Foxx didn't want to keep going with the jam. He had another thing he wanted to float. He bent over his guitar and picked out a seven-note melody. It could have been a fanfare, or an organ riff you hear at a ballgame. *Dum, dum-dum-dum-dum, dum-dum.* He went through it a few times slow, sped it up, slowed it back down.

"I like it," said Tony. But Tony was wrong. It was too chewy, crust when it should have been filling. Foxx asked Lucas to copy the riff on the bass, and that solved the problem. He and Lucas played together until Kevin and Tony locked in; when the band was in the cut, Foxx stepped back and made alterations. "Kevin, stop fucking that hi-hat and get on the tom-toms. Cousin, on the second verse, drop the end off of what you're playing, just the last two notes. Tony, I need a ring."

"A ring?"

"Yeah, a fast bell near the end of it." Foxx went over to show him. "Here," he said, and strummed quick, almost flamenco.

"Oh," Tony said. "You mean like at the end of 'Papa's Got a Brand New Bag.' Just say so."

They rode the groove for a while and eventually Foxx started to pick up the words he found bobbing on the broad wave of the bass. "I asked my mother / I asked my friends / On what exactly / Their happiness depends / You know what they said? / A roof and a bed / And a place for ourselves in the sun." That's where he wanted Lucas to play the riff, slow and low. "Just keep it in style," he sang, pausing so Kevin could tap out a tattoo. "Make the music worthwhile. And go to that place in the sun." Then he waved his hands and they stopped for another smoke.

"You write that just now?" Tony said.

"Yeah."

"Not bad," he said. "Not Shakespeare, but not bad."

They did about an hour of tape and then went to the lounge again. This time the girl who had asked about Lucas told Tony that she and her bassist weren't really married. "We're nomos," she said. "Meaning we used to be married but we ain't no mo'." One of the backup singers shook out some West Coast turnarounds into Kevin's hand, and he said he was going to get something to eat. "Me too," said Lucas. Lucas went to the restaurant; Kevin went to his car with the backup singer.

If Foxx had to guess, he would have said that he and Tony worked in the booth for an hour, adjusting levels, splicing a drum part here and there. Two hours he would have believed. But four? No way. And yet there it was, midnight and then some, when Kevin and Lucas returned to the studio. "Traitor," Foxx said to the clock. "We got rolling," he said to Lucas. He had written the horn charts and added a funky little bridge. He would just rap over it. "White or black, dog or cat, Republican or Democrat," he said. "Everyone is everyone."

"Cool," said Tony.

He had another idea, too. The jam they had started off with would stay an instrumental except for the chorus chant. "We can name it 'James Meredith.'"

"Who's that?" said Kevin.

"Who's that?" said Foxx. "You know Vivian Hood? James Malone? Tay Ninh?"

"No," said Kevin.

"Man," said Foxx. "Someone should have told you the newspaper's for something other than putting over your head when it rains."

"I'm about through for today," said Kevin. The backup singer he had taken to his car was putting on new lipstick.

"Let me just sing the horn part so that Claude and Cheryl can play it later," said Foxx. All of a sudden Tony saw it and Lucas did too. There was magic in the song. Foxx went through it again, snapping his fingers, trying hard to keep the grin off his face. Play it cool, fool.

"We All Need a Place in the Sun" was Billboard's hot debut the first week, and it hit the top twenty in its second week out, which happened to be the week that Ali got jailed for failing to show up at his induction hearing. This stung Foxx. Motherfucking government. And his song even had a motherfucking line in it about staying in the ring: "Get knocked, get hit / Don't stop, don't quit / Fight for your place in the sun." Two joints and a line took the edge off it, though, and the chart was warm like a hearth fire.

The wind smelled like sunshine and the radio had everything on it including a new Freddie Scott that got Foxx dancing in the bucket as he went through Carpinteria. That's what geniuses did: dance in the bucket. They also finished records in record time. With "We All Need a Place in the Sun" still shining on the pop charts, Foxx counted seven more songs either in the can ("Highway Car," "James Meredith," "One More Day," "You're a Peach") or just a fix or two away ("She's So Bad She's Good," "Fill Me Up," "Something Is Missing"). Then, in one afternoon, he wrote a ninth ("Man in the Street") and then reversed its melody to get a tenth ("Links in the Chain"). He had a title, too: *A Place in the Sun* and an idea for the cover: the white band members standing in the shade, the black ones standing in the sunlight. He told Tony and Tony just broke out in a broad smile.

It was Friday and Foxx was celebrating, heading down to Los Angeles to hang with Rudy Bannacourt. "One oh one," he sang, "is nothing but fun." He got into L.A. at around five, picked up some dinner out on Manchester Boulevard, and then drove back to the hotel. Bannacourt was right where he said he'd be, in front of a huge potted plant. He had put on some weight and his hair was marcelled and smelled like process. "Arbee," Foxx said. "Looking good, my man."

"Let's go to the bathroom," said Bannacourt. "Then we can have a drink."

In the bathroom, Bannacourt left a bag on the counter like he was forgetting something and Foxx picked it up like he was remembering. "Thank you, African mailman," Foxx said. Then they went down the street to a darkened lounge to meet the girls. One was black, small, beautifully built, and wearing a white leather overcoat and a white hat. The other was white and like a doll, beautiful but stupid and expressionless. She was not as well built as the black girl, but neither was anyone else in the room.

"The good girl and the bad girl," Bannacourt said. "Only I know which is which. What will you have?"

"A beer," Foxx said, lifting his hand to a passing waiter.

"You know what I mean. What's the matter? You don't trust my girls? They're fucking primo." He spoke with a nasal Latin accent that was probably something he had picked up from the TV.

"Beer's fine."

"Suit yourself, man. You working on your record?"

"Just planted a flag in that baby and claimed it for me."

"Ever need any singers?"

"If you want to come up to the studio and sing on the next record, just give me a call."

"Yeah?" said Bannacourt.

"Brother," said Foxx. "But not next month. We're going on tour. National."

"Before you push off, push in," said Bannacourt, pointing toward the black girl. "She's not my best, but what woman is?"

"You're quite a salesman."

The girl turned toward Foxx with her lips open. "He's a bastard," she said. "But I put up with it."

"Because she's a whore."

"Both of you are whores," the white girl said.

"Who the fuck is talking to you, bitch?" Bannacourt said.

"Fuck you," she said.

"Don't be foul," Bannacourt said. "We're just two friends and two beautiful ladies having a drink on a beautiful evening."

They sat there and the girls lit up cigarettes and Foxx smoked a joint; no one seemed happy except Bannacourt. The black girl was drunk and she slumped back against the booth blowing a stream of smoke and turning her face to catch the red light of the room and shifting her weight so that the warmth of her thigh hummed next to Foxx's. She pulled off her hat and Foxx saw that she had an immense Afro.

"I bought you that hat," said Bannacourt. "Can't you show it some respect?"

"I don't like it," she said.

"Can't you at least get a wig? You look like shit with your hair like that."

"I love it," she said. "It makes me feel right."

"You think you're some African princess."

"It's my natural hair. That's more than I can say for you."

"You best be nice to me or you can just forget about the powder and the paint," said Bannacourt.

"You've got some blow, don't you?" she asked Foxx.

"The customer is always right," he said. "The customer is always me. Am I right?"

"You got enough for me?"

"Rudy?" said Foxx.

"I don't care," said Bannacourt. "I'm not running these bitches mainly. You do whatever you want."

"I'm getting tired of talking," said the black girl. "Let's go upstairs." She stood and reached for Foxx's hand.

"I'll get to you about singing," said Bannacourt.

"You do that," said Foxx. But he knew he never would.

Yvette was a certain kind of girl. "She's not shy with her affections," Foxx liked to say, but that was a polite way of saying the true thing, which was that if you hit her head, her legs would fly open. This was no problem so long as she steered clear of Tony, who loved her and might get the wrong idea. For that matter, Foxx wanted her to keep it on the shelf around the rest of the band, and she did without being asked. There were plenty of men who worked for clubs and theaters, for the label, for hotels and booking agents.

Then, just before they were scheduled to go out on the road, Yvette fucked Kevin. Foxx walked in on them at the practice space on Polk Street. Kevin was on his back on the floor, and Yvette was riding him. Her face was somewhere else, and she didn't even notice Foxx staring. There was plenty to stare at—her smooth throat, her long legs, the way she had shaved her bush to a point. She was back and forth between this world and the next, and then she decided to stay over there, and her body went tight, and then it went loose. Foxx beat a retreat from the doorway, went to his bedroom, rebuilt a picture of her in his head. He remembered their first meeting, the way she had touched him on the wrist, the fact that he had felt nothing except sister-love. It didn't keep him from knocking one out in her name, but it kept him from falling too far.

The next morning, he asked Yvette to hang on for strategy. Ever since she joined the band, he had been pressuring her to give up her old-time music for some new style. Act your age, Satchel Paige. He played her "Love Is a Hurtin' Thing." She sniffed. He played her "Got to Get You Off My Mind." She smiled but faintly. He played her "A Sweet Woman Like You." She looked at her fingernails. When he got to the new Brenda Holloway song, "You Make Me So Very Happy," that caught her up. Foxx wasn't crazy about it—he thought the vocals were mixed too low, that it didn't have the fire that her other songs did—but he needed Yvette pulled into the present, and any rope would do. "You should write a song like this for the band," she said. "By the band I mean me."

"I will," he said. "On one condition. I need you to keep clean, if you know what I mean." Yvette frowned and resumed her inspection of her nails. "I ain't fooling. You got to keep it locked down. I know you may not be Tony's girl, but Tony doesn't know that. It makes a man crazy when he and his neighbor are cooking with the same gas."

She leaned forward and touched his knee. Still no spark: He gave thanks. "You mean Kevin?" she said. "I wish he would learn to keep what's private quiet." Foxx didn't tell her that he had borne witness with his own eyes; no harm in a little distrust between friends. "Anyway," Yvette said, "that's just drugs fucking other drugs. And it was only once."

"But Kevin? Why not just roll a barrel?"

She laughed, but when she spoke she was dead serious. "The world hurts me, and I keep trying to find something that makes it better. You should try it."

"No thank you," he said, holding up his hand. "I know where you've been."

"Well, I never," she said, exaggerating her sense of insult so he'd imagine that there was some. She took a little pill bottle from her bag and shook him out one. Then she took two.

"Jack and Jill went up the pill," he said.

"That reminds me," she said. "I have to go and fetch a pail of water. Then I'm going to listen to 'Bumble Bee Blues.' You probably never heard of it."

"That stings," he said, and she laughed. And, as she was walking away, he called after her: "Stay skinny, Memphis Minnie." She refused to show her surprise but Foxx could tell from the way she slowed way down for one step. How you ever going to finish if you're not reading all the time?

Then it was back to the road, where there was music in the corners of every room and women everywhere. There was the quiet-until-she-was-loud high school teacher who slipped backstage in Detroit, the sweet-as-a-drop-seat redhead in Hartford, the black Amazon in Pittsburgh, the Filipino biker chick in D.C. Foxx told them things he couldn't even tell Lucas and Tony, and the good ones listened. The bad ones looked at him like they were listening but he saw that their eyes were bright with thoughts of what hadn't happened yet, the sex and the drugs. One nineteen-year-old in Atlanta extracted a bag from her snatch. Foxx had no problem with a good high, and he smoked with that girl, and he joked about putting the bag back when he was done. But he didn't like the way that drugs were operating on the band. Mainly it was a question of competition, and specifically Kevin's competition with everyone else. If Tony took a thousand mikes of LSD, Kevin took two thousand. If Foxx was smoking a joint, Kevin would smoke one dipped in something that smelled like cleaning fluid. Foxx had a talk with Tony about the situation, and Tony said that he had a difficult time not supporting another man's freedom. Foxx started to laugh but then he saw that Tony was serious. "Another man?" he said. "I'm talking about Kevin."

The women and the drugs were only amplifiers, and the sound that they amplified was the sound of the show. Lucas and Kevin went out as advance scouts, always first, finding a foundation. Then Yvette began to stroke the melody softly, singing a wordless stream. Foxx would be waiting, listening for the deep shudder of the bass in the arena's innards, and when he heard it, he walked out. No. Foxx didn't walk. Foxx strode. The crowd went wild. By the time he got to the microphone, Lucas and Kevin had reinstated time. The chaos had ordered itself into waves, and Foxx rode the waves, which grew higher as the band stormed louder. "Music coming to you, rhythm going through you," he sang, and each time was better than the last, sharper and more electric. Thunder's just a noise, boys.

Philadelphia was something, and Cleveland was something, too, but Boston was something else, because Turn rented a proud-mama limousine that stopped at Tony's parents' house and Aunt Ida's house before pulling up, triumphantly, in front of the apartment house that seemed so distant now to Foxx that he wondered if maybe he had seen it in a movie about another man's life. Foxx's mother had been in the hospi-

tal, and they gave her dry-out orders, but she was so happy—and he was so happy to
see her happy—that he didn't say anything when she poured herself a scotch in the
stretch. "I wish my Andre could be here to see this," Aunt Ida said.

"Mama," said Lucas, "if he was here, he'd be in the band."

"That's the heavenly truth," said Foxx. He was high enough to wonder what
each separate word meant—heavenly? truth?—and straight enough to realize that
they meant nothing, jumbled in the jaw of a mortal man. He dreamed of Icarus,
but in his dream there was no wax in the wings and the boy went straight into the
heart of the sun.

In the tour's second week, the band rolled into New York City. Foxx did some blow
off the bathroom counter before he went downstairs for his press conference: not his
usual thing, but it was hard to tell what was usual in an unusual land. He gave the first
question to a reporter in front, a young thing in a tight gray miniskirt.

"Your birth certificate says Robert Franklin. Why did you change your name?"

"Ma'am, what's in a change?"

She smiled at this, so he let her ask a follow-up. "Did you get in trouble when you
were a kid?"

"No," he said. "Not much. Did things I shouldn't have done, but who doesn't?"

A gray-haired man who said he was with the *Times* wondered aloud about the
racial makeup of the Foxxes' fans. "Does anyone have a question for the band?" said
Foxx in a white voice, and the crowd laughed.

"Yes," said a thin, dark woman, stammering a bit as she stood. "How do you
write?"

"With a flashlight and a knife." There was more laughter. "I don't want to be a
drag, but people don't care about this."

"Your fans do."

"My fans care about the same things I care about. The world and the things in it,
and how to get something out of them before you get out of it. Next question."

"Do you believe in revolution?" This from a fat man in the front row who waved
his hand like a whale fin.

Foxx stroked his chin, pretended to think. "Revolution? We got our own revolution. It's black and you can buy it for a dollar." The crowd laughed a third time, right
on schedule. He had them in his palm, in his pocket.

The whale frowned, kept coming on. Foxx squinted. Wasn't there a book about this? "You've made some statements in support of Malcolm X. Were you a follower of his?"

"I don't follow anyone, exactly. But I had great respect for Brother Malcolm." A flashbulb popped.

The whale frowned. "How can you say you respect a man who believed in complete separation of the races when your band is the opposite?"

"Does anyone remember when Malcolm came back from Mecca? There were reporters there. Maybe even some of you. He said the white man wasn't his enemy. A man continues to grow. A man continues to learn."

"That's something," conceded a woman up front.

"No," Foxx said. "That's everything."

The whale still wasn't satisfied. "But..."

Foxx raised his hands, slowly, like a pope. "You know I'm not trying to cause a scene. I'm just trying to go from here to there, and to stay straight while I do it. That's the way to save us all some time. But whether you're Malcolmized or King-sized, you have to see what's being shown us. We have a country that's black and white and all torn up. It's torn up in Cincinnati. It's torn up in Kansas City. It's torn up in Tampa. You people read your own newspapers? Yesterday a black cab driver got roughed up by white cops over in Newark. John Smith. That's a name that should warn you. It can happen to anyone. As one color goes, so the other one goes. Look under your nose. Look under your nose." The reporter in the miniskirt smiled like she was keeping Foxx's secret. Afterward, he asked her to go to the bar for a drink. "I have to file my story," she said. He invited her up to his room, and she filed from there.

The next day, while the band was doing star time at a TV taping, Newark erupted. A crowd protesting what had happened to John Smith had gathered around the Seventeenth Avenue precinct house in the early afternoon, and when rocks and bottles started to fly the police streamed out of the building with nightsticks raised. By midnight there were fires in the streets, looters, pigs packing and buildings lit up.

The papers credited Foxx with predicting the riots; one column said, "Would that he had prevented them." He heard a version of the same story on three different taxicab-radios and finally asked the fourth driver to turn off the news. At the Thursday night concert, there were several fights in the audience. "Stay cool," Foxx kept saying, but the room just got hotter.

That night there was no party. There were no girls. Foxx, Tony, and Lucas stayed in their hotel room, smoking weed and watching TV. National guardsmen and state troopers marched into Newark. Trash barrels burned with the rage of the rioters; a TV-news close-up showed a baby doll melting on top of a heap of blackened papers. Friday night's show was a subdued affair, with a newly added cover of "A Change Is Gonna Come." Across the river, the cops shot ten people dead and wounded a hundred more.

Foxx started Saturday's show with a speech. "You know what the troops are doing?" Foxx said. "They're shooting into black-owned businesses. And you know how the troops know they're black-owned? Because they tried to protect themselves by writing 'Soul Brother' across their storefronts. They say that the black man gave the blues to America, but America gave the blues to the black man." He counted off "one, three, two" just to show how wrong it all had gone, and the band lurched into a thirty-minute version of "James Meredith" and then stormed offstage. For the encore, Foxx came back out with just an acoustic guitar and sang a slow-burn version of Percy Sledge's "It Tears Me Up." Simple and plain, Shirley MacLaine.

The tour dragged along. The thrill was gone. Detroit went up like a candle with riots worse than Newark. At press conferences the questions got blinder and blinder, like people were looking right into the fire. Foxx tried to rise above, succeeded. When he looked back earthward to try to spot his possessions, he was possessed mainly by the drive to go even higher, and the things on the ground shrank away until they were no more than a point, punctuating a sentence he hadn't read yet. The last show was in Los Angeles, at the Whisky A Go Go. "Soul army," Foxx said. "Soul army. All the soldiers put their hands up!" said Foxx. But the soldiers were tired just like everybody else.

SIDE TWO: B/W

Betty
January 1968

They were yanking the theater seats like teeth, breaking down the Coliseum Ballroom after the show so that the place could host an Alton Kelly show the next night. Kelly's posters were all stashed against the walls, facing outward, and the closest one was a yellow-and-black ad for a Grateful Dead show. Later, that's what Betty would remember, the yellow and black, because it reminded her of a bee, of getting stung, and of honey.

She wore a narrow gray skirt and a sky-blue top, and her hair was tied back in a chignon. She was there because her roommate Elena knew a girl named Opal who used to go with someone connected to the Airplane, and usually Opal gave Elena tickets to whoever was playing: the Santana Blues Band, Dan Hicks, Sweet Rush. Betty went along when she could, each time laughing when Elena asked her if this was a change of pace from Chicago. But then Elena's boyfriend Fred got drafted, and immediately after that Elena got a flu she couldn't shake. "Take my tickets," she said to Betty, holding them away from her as if they had an odor. "Chuck Berry is opening. I can't think of going when I'm this worried about Fred. There's even a backstage pass in there. You go." Elena seemed to take a certain pleasure in her melodrama.

Betty took the tickets, put them in her purse, promptly forgot all about them. When she remembered to look at them, it was only hours before the show, and she had no one to go with her, so she went alone, stopping beforehand at a little Italian restaurant for pasta and a glass of wine. During Chuck Berry, she was quiet, but as soon as the lights in the house went down for the Foxxes, she started shrieking along with the rest of them. It wasn't her style, but that was the thing about the Foxxes: They changed your style. She told that to the boy next to her, who smiled like he knew just what she meant. After the show she walked to the small black door to the left of the stage. It was unlike her, but it seemed like that was how the day was going: She was a little bit out of herself, a little off-center. "Yeah?" said the man who pulled it open.

"I'd like to come backstage," she said. "I'm a friend of Opal's."

"Let me see your pass." Fingers wormed through the crack. "Come in."

At the end of the hall there was a big man with a gold medallion around his neck. Betty must have been staring a long time because he laughed at her, a deep laugh, and walked over. "Hello," he said. "Have we met?"

"Betty Cobham," she said, extending her hand.

"Lucas Sanders," he said. "Can I get you a beer?" The medallion, she saw, said POWER.

"Sure," she said.

He ducked around the corner and returned with a bottle. "Cold," he said.

"Thank you."

"So," he said. "You dig tonight's show?"

"Loved it."

"Glad to hear that," he said. "There's not enough love in the world. We have a new record coming out soon. We just got back from Paris. Played some of the new tunes there, knocked the French out. Have you ever been to Paris?" Betty shook her head. "Man, it's something else. Buildings so beautiful you don't miss the trees and parks so beautiful you don't miss the buildings. You from around here?"

"No. I mean, I live here now, but I grew up in Chicago. I work in a medical library. And I sing a little bit, too."

"Really? Cool." Lucas gave her a strong smile, all teeth, to show that he was a fine brother, which he certainly was. Betty started to pick up on his glow, and he was picking up on hers. "You want to go meet the rest of our entourage?" said Lucas. She nodded, and they walked on down the hall, went around the corner. "That's Big Morris," Lucas said, pointing to a heavy man with a delicate mouth. "He's security." He moved on to a small man with angry features that looked like they had been carved. "That's Small Morris, who drives. We call them Boris and Smorris." A beautiful woman she recognized as Yvette Washington was lying down on a green couch. Then they went by a room whose door was mostly shut; inside, Betty could see a short man tying a rubber cord around his arm. "That's nobody," said Lucas. "He plays drums."

As they got near the end of the second corridor, Betty heard a voice. "Shit, cooyon," the voice said. Then she walked by a door frame and was blinded. Rock Foxx blasted out from a bathroom, a rolled-up magazine in his hand. He was taller than she thought he'd be, and he came across the floor like a fire across a forest, his face serious but also smiling. He was wearing a blue leather jacket cinched at the waist and a blue leather stingy-brim hat. His medallion read BE.

"Lucas, my pillar of strength," he said, looking only at Betty. He was high but he was beautiful and even though Lucas's hand tightened on her arm she felt him slipping away. "Introduce me to the lady."

"This is Betty," said Lucas. His voice was smaller than it had been a minute ago.

"Betty," said Foxx, bowing like a courtier. When he straightened back up, he stood funny, his knees locked back like an archer's bow. "I was just on the throne, reading about how President Jive is becoming a master at talking out of the hundred sides of his mouth. And every month, thousands of boys get carried and buried over in Viet Nam."

"My roommate's fiancé just got drafted."

"He black?"

"More than me, less than you." She was like coffee with cream, her cousin used to always tell her.

Foxx shook his head. "It ain't right, Charlie Musselwhite. Lucas and I know a brother or two from back home in Boston who joined up, and I keep dreaming I'm going to see them in a box. I know that the white boys are dying, too, but the numbers seem like they done tripped and fell. I just wish I could get with the protests, bunch of college kids who are looking for a righteous vacation." The telephone in the hallway rang. He reached for it. "Start talking," he said. "Hey, baby…. Not yet, not yet. Tough enough.... Why don't you do what flowers do, and grow.... See you in a while.... Peace, my sister." He hung up and turned back to Betty. "You ever do any modeling?"

"I bet you say that to all the girls."

"We do say that to all the girls." This was from another guy—white, tall, and skinny, with striped pants that made him look skinnier. "But not the way you think," he said. "We're taking pictures of our fans. We're going to pick a hundred to use for the cover photo. We're calling the record *Get the Picture*." He extended his hand. "I'm Tony. I play guitar."

"We don't have time for shaking hands," said Foxx. "We have to see what develops." He pointed to a chair positioned in front of a camera, and Betty sat down. While Betty waited for the picture, she prepared her speech for Elena. Girl, you will not believe what happened. Yes. That's right. And it wasn't just the concert. I met them. I watched them. I talked to them. The flashbulb popped, and Tony pointed Betty toward the corner. "If you'll just come over here, we need you to fill out some forms."

"Forms?"

"Permission for using the photograph." He thrust a piece of paper under Betty's nose, and she carefully lettered her name, her address, and her phone number, and then signed. Girl, they asked *me* for an autograph.

"We're all going out a little later," Tony said. "Would you like to come along?"

She looked around. Foxx was on the telephone again, saying "baby" again. "Oh," she said. "No. I think I'd better go on home. My roommate is sick."

"Okay," he said. "Maybe next time." He handed her a plastic badge, red with a sticker of a medallion on it. The medallion said IN. "This is for the next show. It'll let you back here."

"Thank you," said Betty. "Thank you very much."

As she was leaving, Lucas called her name. She turned, but it wasn't Lucas. It was Foxx, hand cupped over the telephone. "Where you off to?" he said.

"Me?"

"Yes, you. No one leaves until I say so." He must have seen a disturbance on her face, because he laughed. "I bet I say that to all the girls," he said. Then he turned, and all she saw was the back of his jacket, blue with rhinestone lettering. STAR, it said. She laughed despite herself and went out through the theater, where they were still yanking out the seats.

The phone rang, maybe for an hour, but Betty just heard the tail end. "Hello?" she said. There was silence on the other end, then a series of mechanical noises. "Hello?" she said again. The line went dead.

Betty swore, just to hear herself do it. "Asshole," she said. She rolled herself out of bed and into the shower. The day was bright, and the water was perfect against her face. It was the kind of day that made a poor man rich and a fat man thin. She was late to work, but only a little late. Nothing to worry about. She got out early and made it home before the sun set. She sat outside and had a cup of coffee. Then the telephone rang again. Betty made her voice flinty and hard, and then she made it deep and ripe. "Asshole, asshole."

The third time, Betty snatched the receiver up in a hurry. She heard the same noises, metallic scrapes and pops. Then she heard the sweet voice of a horn. It took her a minute, but she recognized it: Miles Davis, playing soft and slow. She had been about to hang up the phone, but you didn't just hang up on Miles Davis. "What record is this?" she said. It was a silly question, but the only one that fit.

Kind of Blue, said a gruff male voice. "Like my jacket."

"Who is this?" she said. But she already knew, and that meant that they were already dancing.

"Betty Cobham, please," he said.

"Speaking," she said.

"Yes, ma'am. I am calling on behalf of Mr. Robert Franklin. Alias Smith and Jones, alias President Lyndon Spades Johnson, alias J. Eldridge Cleaver. Most of all, alias the Rock Foxx. I am calling about the matter of your photographs."

"My photographs?"

"Ah, *yesss*." He held the hissing end of the "yes" for a long time, passed by the place where it sounded like a snake, went toward the place where it was an invitation. "The photographs I speak of were volunteered by you, or a woman claiming to be you, at a rock show—that's capital R—about three weeks ago in the lovely Bay Area town of San Francisco. That's capital S, capital F." His voice was prissy, mincing, purposefully white.

"Oh. I think I do remember something about some photographs." Betty sat down on the edge of the couch.

"Well, I am regretting to inform you that there's a problem with the pictures. A terrible, terrible problem."

"I'm so very sorry to hear that."

"And I'm sorry to have to be the bearer of this bad news. The thing is that we can't use these pictures."

"No?"

"No. I'm sorry. Regulations prohibit us. And if we try to break regulations, there are other regulations that prohibit us from doing that. It's quite impossible, I fear."

"Could you tell me why not?"

"Of course I can. Let me look at the paperwork. Please hold." He went away from the phone, and *Kind of Blue* came back on. It bodied toward her like a tide, and she was ready to let it carry her away when Foxx returned. "Hello, Miss Cobham? It appears that there's a black mark on your file."

"A black mark?"

"Yes. A stain. Our records show that you refused a dinner invitation from a Mr. Robert Franklin, alias Smith and Jones, et cetera, et cetera." Now the black in his voice broke through, wonderfully grainy. But he recovered the white. "And as you know, refusal of dinner invitation is cause for rejecting the photographs."

"Well," she said.

"Well, indeed," he said.

"The thing is," she said, "that I didn't refuse any dinner invitation."

"Really?" he said. "But our records clearly show that…"

"This is what I'm saying," she said. "Mr. Smith and Jones never extended an invitation."

"I see." He paused. She could hear Miles Davis again, which meant that he was holding the phone away from his face. She thought she heard the faint sound of laughter. "I think I may be able to help you."

"You can? Well, that's just great news."

"I can help you, that is, on one condition. Would you be willing to accompany Mr. Smith and Jones to dinner?"

"Well, tonight I'm busy."

"Not tonight, no. He's busy, too. He's in Detroit. And then next week he's in Atlanta."

"When, then?"

"Let me check his calendar. It's hard to say."

"Well, then it's hard for me to say yes."

"But you're not saying no."

"No. I'm not."

"Well, I think that in light of the circumstances, we can erase that black mark on your file."

"That would be wonderful."

"All right then. Thank you very much for your time, Mrs. Cobham. Or is it Miss Cobham?"

"It's Miss."

"So there is no Mr. Cobham?"

"There is not, no."

"All right then. Goodbye then."

Over the next few weeks, she got a handful of calls just like the first, always at odd hours. He was a DJ on the telephone, cutting songs off in the middle of verses, replaying, fiddling with the volume. By the sixth call they didn't even bother with the conversation; she just hung on the line while he played her a jazz version of "I Want to Hold Your Hand." All the while she watched her own feet, amused that she was doing so. They were longer than she had remembered, more elegant. Did feet grow on into adulthood? "Who was that?" she said when the song was over.

"Grant Green," he said, in his normal voice.

"Beautiful," she said, and hung up. The next day, he called back and played a Frank Sinatra song, "I Concentrate on You." She came to count on the calls; once, she picked up, said, "Miss Cobham here," and was surprised to hear her mother's voice. She and her mother talked for an hour—about her cousin Charlotte, who was on her third pregnancy, still with no husband; about Elena, who was spending all her nights with Fred now that he was back from the war; about her mother's health, which was holding up—and all the while, Betty kept her eye on the clock. When she hung up, would it be too late for him to call from wherever he was?

Then he was back in town. Just like that. Just like magic. When that call came in, she could tell from the ring that it was something different. "Betty, please," he said.

"Speaking," she said.

"Hi," he said. "It's the Rock Foxx. Would you like to come to our concert at the Fillmore next Friday, and then afterward maybe we could go grab a bite to eat?"

"Okay," she said. "That would be nice." It sounded to her like her voice was coming from a great distance. How could he be so strange one moment and so normal the next?

"I'll leave your name at the stage door," he said. "Just come on back afterward."

"I have a pass that Tony gave me," she said. "The red one with the gold medallion on it."

"That and a dime will get you a dime," he said. "But like I said, I'll leave your name."

She was fussing with her hair and the dress wouldn't lay right. Then she worried that the jacket didn't match and had to dig another one out of the back of the closet. She was late to the show. The Foxxes were just finishing their first encore. She went right to the front corner of the theater, near the part of the stage where Tony and Yvette were standing. She had brought the pass, just in case, and it poked at her through the lining of her pocket.

The night before, Betty had told Elena that she thought it was an accident. "I mean, he must have me confused with someone else," she said.

"No doubt," she said. Elena was happy again because Fred was home, and he was talking about getting married. "Maybe he thinks you're Diana Ross. Or Dorothy Dandridge come back from the dead."

"Betty, you is my woman now," said Betty.

"Is he sending a car to pick you up?"

"No, he's not sending a car to pick me up," said Betty. "I'm taking the bus."

"Doesn't he have enough money to send a car?"

"What do I care?" said Betty.

"Do you?" said Elena.

The show ended, and Betty tucked herself inside a notch right next to the door. After five minutes, she knocked, and this time the fingers that appeared were not grimy but gloved. They were attached to an elegant young woman who took Betty's name, disappeared, and then returned to open the door. In the meantime, a dozen girls had collected behind Betty. None of them got in.

At first, it was just like the Coliseum. The first person Betty saw was Lucas. He was just as friendly as he had been before. "Hey," he said. "Robert told me he invited you."

"Robert?" she said. "Oh, yes. He called me."

"Great." He walked her to a lounge where the walls were painted red. The rest of the band was there, along with some girls who were chatting with Tony. Betty shook Yvette's hand, which was as soft as a feather. Up close she was even more beautiful than she was onstage, with skin so dark it made her look like an African carving. The band sat there, smoking joints, wiping their faces with towels. Tony offered Betty a beer but she declined. "I'm going to the bathroom," said Kevin.

She waited. People disappeared into a small room at the back of the red lounge: a white man drinking straight from a whiskey bottle, an angrily beautiful Hispanic woman who announced to the room that she represented the Brown Berets, and a husky black man in a cap someone told her was Bobby Seale. Finally no one else was going into the small room, and Foxx came out, wearing a black suit with a white turtleneck. She imagined an envelope in her mind, took a snapshot of his outfit, and slipped it into the envelope. Foxx brushed by the girls who had made a half circle around the door and went straight for Betty. "Hi," he said. "Do you want to get out of here?"

There were many fancy cars in the garage near the arena. Foxx was walking a little too fast, but she was afraid to ask him to slow down. "That's a Ferrari," he said. "Miles Davis has one of those. Might even be that one. That's a Porsche. And this," he said, stopping in front of a little black sports car, "is mine. It's an MG." He ran his finger over the hood, stopped to look at himself in the side mirror that stuck out like a stem. "It goes from zero to sixty in five point three seconds," he said. "That's faster than me." She didn't know whether he was making a joke about his walking or about his driving, or about something else entirely. But he drove the car slowly enough, stopping on the way to the restaurant to point out all the streets where other rock stars lived.

When they sat down, she couldn't look him in the eye yet, so she studied the menu intently. It was a Mexican restaurant, which made her ask about the Brown Berets. "They're a Chicano group down in Los Angeles," Foxx said. "They just had about ten thousand kids walk out of the schools in an organized protest. The East Side blowouts."

"Why was she at the show?"

"To meet with Bobby Seale."

"So that was him. I thought so."

"Yeah. Bobby's cool. He likes to drop by sometimes. Not so much since Huey got arrested. He's been busy."

"Are you in the Panthers?"

"Not in, not out. I see what they're doing—jobs, free breakfast for kids."

"Do you think they're violent?"

"Not from what I've seen."

"You always see them with guns."

"For self-defense. Someone going to knock a head, best that it not be yours. And anyway, anything that the government hates so much can't be all bad. They keep putting them in jail because they're afraid: Huey, the Rage."

"The Rage?"

"Eldridge Cleaver. Deep guy. Cool. Ice, like his book says. But he can't shine the light on every pig and politician." He refilled her sangria. When the food came she ate hungrily, watching her plate as she ate. The sangria was beginning to calm her down, enough so that when she went to the bathroom she knew that when she returned she would be able to look at him, and when she returned she did. Robert—it was easier to think of him as Robert—was a handsome man, deep chocolate brown, with fine white teeth and a broad, intelligent forehead. The most striking part of his face was his eyes, which didn't seem to have pupils—or rather, they seemed to have nothing but pupils. They were guarded but they were capacious; they could take in a whole room at once without letting anything go, and now they took in Betty. Sometimes when he smiled he looked cruel.

"So," he said, smiling. "Lucas tells me that you're a singing nurse."

"Not a nurse," she said. "I work in a medical library. And I don't really sing. I mean, I do, but just for myself."

"Well, whatever," he said. "Either way, it's cooler than a singing nun." He rubbed his nose. "Are you any good? Be straight but not plastic. Don't go all Pat Nixon on me."

"I'm pretty good."

"How did you start? Church choir?"

"Oh, no." Betty laughed. "My mama's good with God, but she ain't exactly the church type."

"My mama neither," he said. "But Lucas's mama is a church mouse. Where you from?"

"Chicago."

"We were there just last fall," he said. "Didn't get to see much except the hotel and the theater. Looked good from the airplane, though."

"Well, I go back there all the time," she said. "Next time you should come along."

He laughed. When he laughed he never looked cruel. "Next week we go on tour again," he said. "Seven more shows, two opening for the Rolling Stones. And then in about a month we put out the new record."

"Really?"

"Yeah. The one that we took your picture for. It's done but the lawyers are spending their time worrying over it. I could play you a copy but it's probably illegal."

The sangria pitcher never emptied, no matter how many times Robert tilted it and poured. Betty could look at him without any difficulty now, and she noticed smaller things, like the fact that he had trimmed his beard so that it ran in a line right along his jawline, and the fact that he was wearing three rings on his left hand. Ruby, diamond, emerald. Like a stoplight. She collected these facts and placed them in the envelope in her mind.

She took some things out of the envelope as well. She told him about her mama, who was blind, and her cousin Charlotte, who couldn't stop having babies. She told him about the men in her life, the ones who had loved her, the ones who had hurt her. One had done both: She told Robert about him, too. "He was a cop in Chicago. A sweet guy. But then he got some other girl pregnant and thought he should be with her. I'm sure he did what he thought was right," she said, hinting something.

Foxx picked up on it. He was good that way. "White boy?"

"Yes," she said. "And a white girl, too."

Robert put his hand on hers. "Step back," he said.

"What?"

"You know that old rhyme: If you're white, you're all right. If you're brown, stick around. If you're black, step back."

She didn't, or didn't think she did.

"All I'm saying is that ain't the bag you should be in."

They went from the restaurant right back to the car because the mist was thickening into rain. In the car Betty turned on his radio, and it was Smokey Robinson singing "You Really Got a Hold on Me." "I was going to play this for you on the telephone," he said. It was the first time he had mentioned their phone calls, and it was the right time. Suddenly they were kissing. "You know," she said, surfacing, "I should be getting home."

"And I should be getting you home."

Twenty minutes later she was still supposed to go, but they were still sitting in the car, kissing. His hand was between the buttons, then inside her blouse. "Really," she said. "Robert."

After he dropped her off, she called for Elena, who wasn't home. Then she took a shower with her eyes closed and reassembled the evening from the contents of the envelope. The phone was ringing when she got out of the shower. She picked it up. She waited for the tone arm to come down. Then came piano, then ragged harmonies, then Mick Jagger telling her not to worry about what was on her mind, telling her not to hurry because he could take his time, making her an offer she could, just barely, refuse.

Robert
February 1968

Foxx meant to write to Betty. That's why he had a pen in his hand. They were backstage in Atlanta after the show, and the freaks were all laying raps on him, talking erotic astrology and Thich Nhat Hanh. Next to him Claude and Cheryl were playing the first Velvet Underground record. He liked the second one better—he wasn't much for the tone-deaf German girl—and he had said so several times, but Claude didn't seem to care. They were cool, though, cooler than they had been the week before, when Claude had told Tony that he couldn't be in a band with Kevin. "I can't stand to see him doping up all the time," said Claude. "I don't mind a little weed, but he has marks on his arms. I asked him about it, and you know what he said? 'Spike-o-analysis.'"

Foxx promised Claude he would have a talk with Kevin, but you couldn't talk to Kevin. Right now he had a gorilla mask on and he was running around the dressing room, clowning everyone in sight. "Watch me," he said. "I want you to watch me." At least he was honest. He fell to his knees and pushed his head under one of the girls' skirts. "Tastes like banana."

"Man," said Tony to Kevin. "You must have some worm in your monkey brain. I told you not to eat without washing your food." Tony was in a bad mood—during the show, someone had thrown a bottle onstage and it had hit him in the foot. He had a bag of ice on it.

"Your problem," said Kevin, surfacing, "is that you never eat unless you've washed your hands for an hour."

Suddenly, a voice at Foxx's left startled him. "Hi." He jumped. It was a slip of a girl. "I came down here because I got in a fight with my mother," she said. "She looks young. People think we're sisters."

"You look just like sisters to me," Foxx said.

"You know my mom?" she said. "She'll be happy to hear that." He closed his eyes for a change of scene and when he opened them she was gone, replaced by a tall blonde. Up on towers of heels, glinty earrings dangling, she pushed her hair to one side of her shoulder and then the other. Both options looked spectacular, but she was satisfied with neither. "I'm Astrid," she said. She leaned into him and moved his hand to the bottom of her miniskirt. Foxx touched her leg. Now turn the record over and play the other side. He remembered Betty in the car, the way she had put her arms on his neck while she kissed him. He took his hand back. After all, it was his hand. "Baby," he told the blonde girl, trying to sound weary. "It's crazy in here. I'm about to go back to the hotel and get some sleep."

"What's the matter? You married?"

"Do you see a ring?"

"You could have taken it off."

"But I wouldn't have."

She corrugated her brow and pursed her lips. She was tottering on the brink of an insight, but she regained her footing just in time. "Okay."

"I'll leave you with an associate of mine," said Foxx. He called Kevin over.

Foxx went back to the hotel but he couldn't sleep, so he went down to the lobby and watched the nightlife trickle in. A dapper older gentleman in a tuxedo led his much younger date in by the arm, after which he turned and yelled at her for some invisible sin. Men were cowards, even in small things. Foxx knew it and it shamed him up to his room and into his bed, where he smoked a joint and went to sleep.

Atlanta, Miami, Baltimore. What was Friday night in Philadelphia? Jack the Peach and law and order in the air, y'all. Everybody rose to the rock and soul. Afterward the mayor came back with two thirteen-year-old girls who had won a newspaper contest, and the three of them took pictures with Foxx.

And then came Detroit and the first date with the Stones. Tony and Kevin wanted to meet the band before, but the Stones' people wouldn't allow it. Only Yvette got an invitation. "Can you stop her from going?" Tony said.

"No," Foxx said, but he made sure her stage clothes weren't delivered until late and then he barked at her that she was going to miss call time.

The snow was falling just before showtime, and the kids were bundled up in their stadium coats, making hobo jungles in the parking lot. Foxx watched them from the window of the stadium. He wondered if he could move among them as Robert Franklin, crouch down and cup his hand around a joint. But instead he got fixed in Foxx, went on before the screaming crowd to deliver a short set, some of which he cared about, and afterward was honored to take his turn with the 35-mm film can filled with cocaine that went around the room like a party tray. An opening set was short and left them wanting, so they sat backstage listening to the Stones rip new holes in the Detroit night. Tony even got up and danced to "Paint It, Black." Foxx didn't: song sounded like it was some rich white massa trying to get a new coat put on his house.

When the Stones came offstage, they stepped right into the wall of radio interviewers and journalists. Mick started talking immediately; he was a skinny motherfucker just about Foxx's size, and with the same size lips. "I went to the London School of Ecologics," he said in response to a question about the band's politics. He giggled on the last word. "Economics, whatever. When I was there I cared about politics. I was passionate. I beat on tables. Now we're professionals. We make music." He took another question about drugs and another question about women, but after someone asked about the Stones' blues influence, he waved his hand in boredom and the lights snapped off. That was as close to the Stones as Foxx thought he'd ever get. The next night, in Cleveland, though, he got even closer. "That 'Highway Car,' that's a tough one," said Keith, stopping him between their two sets. "I'm thinking of nicking the riff." Then he passed Foxx a joint. It was wet with juice, though, so Foxx didn't drag on it. Keith stood there, calmly appraising Foxx, and Foxx looked back at Keith. Foxx was still taking that in when he saw Allen Ginsberg, who materialized backstage. "You're the most wonderful band," he said, pumping Foxx's hand.

"I just heard you saying that same thing to Mick," Tony said, laughing.

Ginsberg gave them a beatific Buddha smile so wide that you could have driven a Cadillac into it, if you believed in Cadillacs. "One day we'll all be dead, you see, and I don't like to speak ill of the dead. I'm just carrying that to the extreme."

An hour later Foxx was coming through the hotel lobby when he saw Yvette sitting at the bar in a T-shirt, talking to one of the Stones' techs. He took a spot a few seats down. "It's not band policy, exactly," the man said. He had big muscles and a short mustache he kept pushing up and down. "I just know that it would be easier if you saw things our way."

"And what way is that?"

"Horizontal."

Foxx knew that she could handle herself, but he was in a chivalrous mood. He slid his stool closer to them. "Hey," he said. "Good show tonight. If the Pips ever bounce Gladys Knight, you should make a bid."

"You again?" Yvette said. She scowled to show that she was grateful, and he saw from her glassy eyes that she was more in the bag than he thought. Maybe she couldn't handle herself.

"It's late," he said to Yvette, "and you'd better get dressed. Party starting soon."

"Why is everybody always telling me to get dressed?" she said.

"I doubt that's what everybody's always telling you. I know I've never said it."

"Did you have something else in mind?"

"I might. If you can make the time, I'll produce the clock." He took a fistful of peanuts. "I'm easy, you see. Not a hard nut to crack."

"I'm Jack," said the man with the mustache.

"Good to meet you, Bill," said Foxx, staring right through him. "I think we've been introduced."

"You want to take off?" Jack said to Yvette.

"I think I should stay," Yvette said. She jerked a thumb toward Foxx. "My boss."

Jack pushed out his stool and lurched off, trying for a gunslinger walk, hips wide, but only looking drunk.

"Thanks for the rescue," Yvette said. "Bill there was trying to convince me that I had to fuck him to get to Mick."

"He say that?"

"Not exactly. But I got the drift."

"That's how things work in this band, too," he said. "You want me, you got to do your time with Tony."

"And if I don't?" She pushed back her stool and stood behind it unsteadily.

"Selfish, selfish." Foxx paid for the drinks, including the ones that the man with the mustache had neglected to buy. "You really do it for him, you know."

"Who?"

"Tony."

Yvette sniffed. "Good to know it's there if I need it."

"What if he needs it?"

"Everybody is out high-hatting," she said, waving her hand in front of her face. Even though his room was right next to hers, Foxx asked to use her bathroom. There was a bag under the sink, just like he thought, a little black canvas thing. He went through it, expecting to find a rubber hose or a syringe. Nothing. When he walked back out, Yvette was watching the local news on TV. "See you at the party?" she said. Now she seemed focused, like maybe the earlier wobble had been an act. He shut the door because it was easier than opening his mouth. You can only paint the town red so many times before you begin to bleed.

He was still thinking about Yvette an hour later, at the party, when he stepped into a side room and let one of the girls who came with the Stones take him in her mouth. "Professional advancement," he told her, and she murmured something indecipherable in return. That girl, too, was among the clouds on some combination of powder and paint. Foxx tried to catch his image on the inside of the window. Who was he looking at, exactly, and was there any point in reflection? When people thought about the lives they led, were they really leading?

After the girl had finished with Foxx, after he had spotted Mick disappearing with a Chinese girl onto the balcony, Foxx and Tony ended up sitting on a bed, looking out across the city, where lights flickered in what Foxx was sure was code. Foxx felt closer to Tony than he had in weeks, but he wasn't sure why. Maybe because he had blood-brothered him with Yvette. "Man," Tony said, "One of these days we need to talk about business." He was whispering. "Just to get everything straight, to make sure that what we're promised—and what we're promising—on this tour lines up correct."

"To be sure, Victor Mature," Foxx said. He helped Tony to his feet, the two of them found Keith and shook his hand, and they went off down the hallway of the hotel, leaning on each other because they had to. Foxx dropped Tony off and went back to his own room. In the bathroom he heard noises so he pressed his ear to the wall. "Yeah," Yvette was saying. "Oh, yeah. That's good right there. You don't even have to send for Mick."

"I wouldn't even if you told me to." It was Jack, the guy from the bar. "Tonight this is all mine."

"And this is all mine," Yvette said. "Pass me the kit." There was a pause in the moaning. "I'll do you if you do me." Foxx listened for a little while longer and then left the bathroom and turned off the lights. "Not a hard crack to nut," he said.

Indianapolis. Milwaukee, Lincoln. Days gone forever in Des Moines. In Kansas City, Foxx decided to keep at least one full day in his pocket, not let the motherfucker fall to the ground and shatter. He went to the art museum, hung out on the broad green lawn in front of the building, then went inside and snuck down stone corridors. He ended up parked in front of a painting of a woman, her skin milk-white, her dress washing over the red bench like a tide. He tried to work back to the time when the woman was alive, when she had eyes that watered, arms that moved, a pulse that throbbed gently in the hollow of her throat. He couldn't do it, couldn't make her more than a ghost even when he prodded himself with thoughts of heat and voice, of skin and trim. She was just a picture of a girl he wasn't sure had ever breathed. Betty breathes, he told himself, consoled. In the Chicago airport the next day, he confirmed it with a phone call. "You breathe," he said. "That's lovely."

She laughed. "I'm not breathing on the phone for you, if that's what you're asking."

The Foxxes closed in New York. By then the band was getting tight onstage again, especially Lucas and Kevin, but Foxx was out of step. "I think you're just worn out," Tony said. "Sounds like you're dragging a little on the fast numbers."

They were sitting in the bar of the hotel, back in street clothes. A baseball game was on the TV. "I'm dragging on all of them," Foxx said. "By the ninety-ninth time the words have no meaning."

"That sounds like the first line of a song," Tony said.

"Always looking on the bright side," Foxx said. He didn't tell Tony that he was afraid that the next batch of songs would be that bad or worse, that he worried he was tapped, that the competition that was appearing in record stores each week would go right by him. You ever hear the one about the band that made a big splash and then went down to the bottom of the lake? Tony probably would have listened and offered sympathy, but that was more than Foxx could bear. "Hey," he said instead. "Let's talk turkey. And by turkey I mean that for which we give thanks."

Tony brightened. Next to guitar, money was what he liked to talk about most. "We said we'd pick up half the cost of the lighting rig and that the Stones would subsidize transportation," Tony said. "When we go on without them, though, that means assuming the full cost of the bus, so we're going to have to make up the difference. I was thinking about the concession in a few of the cities, and also seeing if there's payment for radio appearances."

"Will that work?"

Tony scratched the back of his head where a bald spot was already showing and gave Foxx the only answer he understood. "I'll figure it out." That night, someone invited the band to a fancy formal in a hotel ballroom, filled with young lawyers and older authors. Foxx ended up in a corner untying a knot of wives. Most of them were wide and soft and sparkled; it was as if their husbands had bought all the jewels first and then bought the wives to hang them on. One wife wasn't wide or soft. She was tall and hard, wearing a short red dress, and she kept on him with a clearly rehearsed speech about how her husband had more money than King Farouk but couldn't get it up to save his life. "I'm going back to the hotel," she told a man who claimed to be her husband, and he nodded. Slick. Foxx took her up to the suite and listened patiently to her talk about her charity work and her trips until she took off her top and thrust one tit in his face. That was his cue to suck for a few minutes, bored, and then retreat to the bathroom to smoke a joint alone. When he came out ten minutes later, Kevin was in the room, burying his face in the woman's pussy. Foxx sighed, sparked another joint, and closed the door. When he opened it again, both of them were asleep. She was snoring lightly and Kevin was rolled to one side, eyes closed and a faint grin on his face. "Dream a little dream," Foxx said, and rolled him back into the woman's lap.

Betty
March 1968

Robert was Betty's secret, and she kept it as best she could. She told her mama, of course, who clucked her tongue and said that she hoped the young man, whoever he was, knew what a jewel he had in Betty. She told one or two friends, but painted it as a friendship. At work she found she had to say something, so she asked a sturdy black nurse what she thought of the Foxxes. "I don't think rock and roll is what we need to be hearing," she sniffed, chin thrust out. "It's not a pure music—it uses the white man's language and the white man's logic." Evelyn listened only to jazz.

"Man," Robert said when Betty told him, "don't let that go too far into your head. Those jazz cats are cool, but most of them aren't making much of a difference to anyone anymore. We're ten years after. Tell that girl to get in step."

The next time Robert invited Betty to dinner, she brought along a present. It was a legal pad in a leather case and a fancy jet-black pen. Robert took it, turned it over. She smiled through the whole inspection. That was what she did now: she smiled.

"What's this for?" he said finally.

"It's for you."

"Not who's it for. I know that. What's it for?"

"I want you to use it to write songs."

"I use a guitar."

"But when we were talking on the telephone, I started to hear songs in almost everything you said."

"Like what?"

"One time," she said, "you were talking about Frankie Lymon and how he was too old to die young. Do you remember what you said? You said, 'Pick up on what I'm putting down.'"

"Yeah. That's an expression. You know, like dig what I'm saying to you."

"Well, it should be a song." She reached for the bread, tore off a piece from the heel.

"Can I fill this pad with letters to you?" he said. "In Atlanta it occurred to me that I should be engaging you in a kind of romantic correspondence but there was only hotel stationery, which is highly impersonal." The white voice again.

"No," she said. "Write songs."

"The thing is," he said, "that's not really how it goes. I go in with the band, and the songs come out of what we play."

"Okay, okay," Betty said. "Sorry."

"No apologies. You want to dream that I'm that kind of hero, go right ahead, especially if it helps you sleep at night. I'll tell you something: In Boston once I went into a room and came out with a song. I'll tell you something else: I wrote the band's new song that way. One of those things is true."

"Sing it for me," Betty said. "The new song. I want to hear it."

"It's the single. It's coming out in a week. Go to a store and buy it."

She clenched her teeth, pretended to be angry. "Sing me the song, fool."

"Okay." He started deep, stopped after two words. "This is Lucas's part. That's why I'm foghorning it."

The world was dark then you came along
You turned on the sun and got me singing this song
Next morning I woke up to find you weren't there
The dent in my pillow still smelled like your hair
Make it better, babe
Make it better, babe
Don't leave me here like this
Please answer my letter
Make it better

For years I was lonely and had no way out
Then you came along and defeated my doubt
When I had a dream it was you that I dreamed
But things turned out different than things used to seem

While he was singing, his guard dropped, and parts of him began to flow out through his eyes. Light came out of him in a thousand ways, each one rare.

Betty put her hand on top of his and squeezed. "We really should go," she said, but she didn't say where or when. Robert squeezed back, but he couldn't match her strength, not in that way. "Next time," Betty said, "you'll sing when I tell you to sing." Robert exhaled whatever was left of his resistance.

Robert
March 1968

The rain was coming down like there was a jailbreak in the clouds. Songs were coming down, too. There was one in there now, a shoot that had grown from the seed that Betty had planted. He had fussed with it and not much had happened, but now he saw how it could work, how he could shout out "People," and then Yvette could sing "pick up," and Lucas could finish with "on what I'm putting down." He had to pull over and call the Tienda Publica and tell the engineer to hold a reel-to-reel near the telephone. The engineer sighed and did what he was told.

He hopped back into the car and sped over to the hospital to meet Betty. She was there, talking to another girl, but she pretended not to see him. He honked and she turned around. He waved and she waved back. He revved the engine and she ran toward the car, laughing.

The restaurant was in the Castro, and while they ate he told her about "Make It Better." It was running aground on the outer banks of the top twenty, and he was worried. "It's the strongest song we got," he said. "So if nothing happens to it, I don't know what that means for the rest of the record." They walked for about an hour afterward before she leaned up against a streetlamp and suggested that he take her home. At first he thought she wasn't having a good time but then he looked at her face and it was clear what she meant.

Betty's apartment was the third floor of a little building in the Marina. She unlocked the door and went in first, flicking on a light switch as she entered. The lamp didn't do much. The room was small and mostly beige and filled with fabric of all kinds, pillows and blankets and rugs. The windows had heavy plum-colored drapes over them.

Betty went into the back to change. Foxx flopped down on a couch and put his feet up on a small black coffee table. He rolled a joint, lit it, and smoked while he watched the second hand sweep around the dial.

He could hear her now, opening and closing dresser drawers. He imagined that she was undressing for him. Rather than look at the clock again, he went to find her.

Betty's bedroom was in the rear of the apartment, next to a small bathroom. Foxx was about to go into the bedroom, but then he heard the sound of water running in the bathroom. He pushed the door open slightly. Betty was there, standing in front of the sink, and she was naked, scooping water onto her face. He took time to consider her body, which was less girlish than he had thought, wider in the hips and thighs. Her breasts were small but high, with broad, dark nipples.

The house betrayed him. Something creaked, and Betty's eyes swung his way. She caught sight of him through the crack of the door. For a second he thought she might scream. Instead she smiled, and motioned for him to come into the bathroom. Then she stripped him like somene peeling fruit.

In the shower, with the water beating down, Foxx let his hands wander over as much skin as he could find—his, Betty's. At some point, she led him to the bed and crouched on top of him.

On the road, the girls were often pretty, sometimes beautiful, always willing. But they were easy and he wanted to stay hard; he couldn't count how many times he'd been in love with a piece of one-two only to feel something shift behind his eyes and lose the taste for it entirely. But when Betty told him to keep his eyes open for her, her face was like the first map of a place, before it was all motherfucked up with lines and names.

There was something miraculous about the sex itself, too. Usually he had to do most of the work. This time, the pussy worked him. He felt embarrassed to think that of this girl, who he could look at from across a table when she was reading a book or talking on the telephone, but facts were facts. She had her eyes closed, she had her hands on the tips of her breasts, which were swinging. She was riding and she was bringing him along for the ride. He tried to clear all the ugly words out of his head: He cleared *fuck*, he cleared *cunt*. He focused on a short scar on her right shoulder, just above the seam of her armpit. Finally, with a throb, he drained, and all that he had in his consciousness was a single shameless thought: that he deserved her.

With her arms around him he started to doze off immediately. This, too, was a miracle. Usually he was up like a shot, zipping out right after ripping out. The bed was small and the room was too cold. But here he was, going gently into sleep.

He was only vaguely aware of Betty after that. She moved around him, straightening blankets, disappeared to the kitchen where he heard the clanging of a teapot, and made her way back to the bed to bend down and kiss him gently on the forehead.

Betty
March 1968

Elena was in the apartment. She had moved out but now she was back, and she was speeding through a six-pack of beer. "I don't understand," she said. "I don't understand."

Betty was sitting on the couch Indian style. Elena was slumped in a chair, the same chair she had been in when she told Betty that she and Fred were getting married. Now she was telling Betty that she and Fred weren't getting married, because she had caught him cheating on her with a woman who worked with him down at the post office. "Just a sneaky little Mexican bitch," she said, but a queen would have made her feel just the same. Fred's affair meant nothing. He still loved Elena. He wanted things to work out. All of this came from the horse's mouth. But Elena didn't want to hear from the horse. "I am going back to Seattle," said Elena, and to prove she was serious she felt around in her purse until she found her plane ticket.

Betty wasn't sad to see Elena go. She felt terrible that this was true, but it was. Ever since Betty had started seeing Robert, Elena had done nothing but pry. "What kind of car does he drive?" she asked, and, "What kind of shoes does he wear?" and, "How many people does he have working for him?" At first Betty tried to explain. "He's not a spaceman," she said. "He sleeps seven hours a night like me and you. He has people he cares about like me and you." But the more she had to explain, the more she felt wrong saying "like me and you." Compared to Robert, everyone else existed at a slight remove. Twice, Elena had asked Betty to bring Robert to one of Fred's parties. The first time, Betty didn't even mention it to him. The second time, she did, and he said what she thought he would say, what she would have said if she was him: "If you want me to, I'll do it, but you don't want me to."

That weekend, Betty drove Elena to the airport. It wasn't her car—it was Robert's MG —and the whole way there Elena kept talking about how much she thought it cost. Betty didn't say anything, and when she let Elena out at the airport she gave her a hug but no kiss. Then she got back in the car and went to pick Robert up at the studio and they went up into the hills for the afternoon. Betty sat next to him in the front seat and watched in the rearview mirror as the city disappeared behind them. Off to the right there was a meadow, and over it the mute shapes of mountains. She leaned to see out of Robert's window, but he leaned forward to obscure her view, and when she leaned back, he leaned back, too. They stopped up by Round Top and Robert pretended that he couldn't see Mount Diablo. "Where is it?" he said. "I can't quite make it out. Seriously, baby, don't fool with me. Where'd you put the mountain?" On the way back, they pulled over into a meadow and he took a bottle of wine out of the trunk and opened it with a corkscrew. While he was slamming the trunk shut, the key ring fell out, and they both had to get down on their knees and search for it in the tall grass. Betty found it, but she wouldn't give it back to Robert until he poured her some wine. "The cups are in the trunk," he said. Betty said she couldn't be tricked that easily, and drank straight from the bottle. "Can I have the keys now?" he said, and she still wouldn't give them to him. She turned on the car radio and they lay down on a blanket in the grass and kissed and listened to music. "Lady Madonna" was first, and then "Just Dropped In (to See What Condition My Condition Was In)." "Yeah, yeah, oh-yeah," sang Robert. Then it was the Delfonics singing "La-La Means I Love You," and Robert matched the falsetto perfectly. "Do you know their names?" he said.

"No," she said.

"There's two brothers named William and Wilbert Hart. Is that the stupidest thing you ever heard? Two brothers, and the mama can't think of names more different than that."

"I have a sister named Elizabeth," she said.

"You don't," he said, and rolled over on top of her, laughing.

"No. But I know a girl at work who has twin boys named Andrew and Andre." Robert stopped laughing and rolled off her. "Really," she said.

"I believe you," he said. He lay on his back, face up. "You know, I had a cousin named Andre. Lucas's brother. He was the same age as me, more or less. He died when we were kids."

"How?"

"We were playing in the neighborhood. Just hanging out by the junkyard, banging shit. And there was this big ox who worked for the local mob. He used to sleep out in his car. Me and Dre snuck up on him and started pranking, and he started yelling. It was just to scare us, but we didn't know any better. So we started running like hell on wheels. We went down the street and ran smack into a car."

"Were you hit?"

"Grazed," said Robert. "I got up and dusted off and went over to where Dre was lying. His eyes were closed. I thought he was playing a game. But when I called his name and he didn't move, I touched his head, and my hand came away wet."

"That's terrible."

"It almost ruined his mama, Lucas's mama. She came back from that, though, and started being an old Bible girl. The worst kind. And some of that got into Lucas, too."

"How about you?"

"No way," he said. "How you gonna tell me there's a God when my best cousin got knocked into the next life before he had time to be a man?"

They lay there for a while, not saying anything. She squeezed his hand but he didn't squeeze back. Then she put the keys in his hand, and he got up and put the glasses and the wine back in the trunk. "We're not leaving yet, are we?" Betty said.

"Why? You want to stay?"

"We can go in a little while. But let's play the Greatest first." This was a game they had invented during their drives. One of them would name two singers, and the other one would try to say which one was better. "I'll start. Smokey Robinson or Jackie Wilson?"

"Smokey. Because sometimes when I listen to his songs I remember things I love, and I forget the things that are around me. You know what I mean?"

"No," Betty said. But I agree. Your turn."

"Rolling Stones or Beatles?"

"You want me to say Rolling Stones, but I'm saying Beatles."

"I want you to say what you feel."

"Beatles."

"You're wrong."

She laughed. "Wynonie Harris or Roy Brown?"

He affected a British accent. "My dear, you're positively historical." He rubbed his chin. "Wynonie, to be sure. You know that song, 'Keep on churning till the butter comes?' Filthy, filthy, filthy. I wish I had written it."

The game went on as the sun sank and then washed out against the larger game, which was a version of hide-and-seek where you were found every time. Robert drove back and Betty asked him up to her apartment, which was the one place she was still shy with him, and she put him in her narrow bed and pushed up close to him. "Will you sleep here with me tonight?" she said. "Just sleep. I want to see if we can do it."

"If it's what we want to do, we can do it," he said. And he stayed in her bed, his eyes closed, his breathing regular, but she noticed that his hands moved while he was sleeping like they were around the neck of a guitar or a man.

Robert
April 1968

He carried Betty's things up the stairs all morning. "Special offer," he told her. "First day in a new house, your man's your mule." Ten times he came across the lawn feeling the frown of the neighbor lady: gray, charmless, and with a diamond-shaped birthmark on her face. "You moving in or out?" she said, idiotically, as she stood on her porch with a thick frown on her face.

"I'm robbing these fine people," he said, and gave a seething grin. Everything was in the house by noon, except one brown motherfucker of a dresser that looked to weigh a ton at least. "What's in here?" he said. "All your hopes and dreams?"

"My gratitude," said Betty. "And my shoes."

"One pair, I'll bet," he said. "Big-ass feet."

It was a new house to Foxx, too, a Victorian he bought with cash, partly because Jerry told him that real estate was a good investment and partly because Tony, who was standing behind Jerry at the time, nodded. The appliances were new, and he closed his eyes when he ran his hand over the surface of the refrigerator, stopping at the warts of the magnets. They were presents from Betty: two little bread loaves of men, one playing the guitar, one singing. He sat at the kitchen table and suddenly missed his mother. "Man of the house is calling," he said. "He needs a sandwich, quick."

"That I can do," Betty said. It was ham and cheese and a clean spring breeze, and Foxx ate it in his new house and watched the light come through his girl's dress. He thought, I've got to get me some of that. Then he thought, some of that is mine. He took her upstairs and claimed it.

The next morning, they stayed in bed and Foxx did what he had been doing more of lately, asking Betty about her life growing up in Chicago. He liked the story about how she made her mama throw out new shoes because they were ugly and the one about the drunk in the local bar who could name every song on the jukebox. He liked hearing about the preacher's son, Sparrow, and the grade-school teacher everyone called Cigarette Tree. But his favorite stories were the ones that reminded him that Betty wasn't some innocent flower, but a woman who had seen plenty of the world, even from her little corner of it. "There was this girl in the neighborhood who was a little loose," she said. "She needed to be screwed in, is what I mean."

"You'll make me blush," Foxx said.

"Can't see it," Betty said. "Anyway, one afternoon in the middle of winter, I walked by this alley, and I saw her down on the ground, underneath what looked like another body. She looked like she was struggling. Her legs were all over the place. Her shirt was pulled up over her head. And she was making a funny noise. I went closer. And you know what I saw?"

"I have some idea."

"No," said Betty. "Do you know who I saw?"

"I don't believe I do."

"Her brother Thomas. They were fucking." Foxx didn't like to hear her say the word, so he loved it. "Yeah," said Betty. "She was with her brother, and not completely against her will. He went off to the army after that, and he got killed. Most of the people thought that he probably did it himself."

"And what happened to little Lorena?"

"She went away."

"She's probably one of those girls down in the Tenderloin. Brother, can you spare the time?"

Betty laughed, too. Then she stopped. "Don't you think it's sad? That poor girl."

"I think," he said, "that things have a way of working themselves out."

They went to bed again, tried to fit themselves into this new space. The small high window in the bedroom was so perfect that it made Foxx sad. Could he fly right out of it? "You my sister," he said, grabbing Betty around the waist. "Stop that," she said.

In the evening, he drove down to the studio. He had heard something in a Julie London record, of all places, that he wanted to tinker with, a little backflip of bass and organ at the beginning of "Show Me the Way to Go Home" that he thought could be remade as a beautiful threat. He recorded himself on keyboards, then added in the bottom. "Got it?" he said to the engineer.

The cat came out from behind the board. It was one of the new guys, a tall kid in a baseball cap who was tripping on peyote. "I got it," he said, but then he forgot it and started in on a monologue about Foxx's potential as a communicator. He held up the syllables of the word one after the other, like fingers. "Have you heard your own records?" he said. "It's like they're covered in roses and ashes both." Foxx laughed the kid off, which was easy to do on account of his sideburns. The second take was sodden, and during the third the phone in the studio rang and the kid left the board. He clicked in a minute later. "It's for you," he said.

"For me?" Foxx said. "You shouldn't have."

It was Lucas. He said Robert's name, waited, said it again. His voice sounded choked.

"Where are you, cuz? You sound so far away." There was silence on the line, and Foxx had a moment of sudden terror. Had something happened to Betty? Was this what love turned out to be? Worry in a hurry? "Lucas? You there?"

"You haven't heard?"

"No. Heard what?" Lucas dissolved into tears. Through them, he managed to explain. King was down. Shot dead in Memphis. "This isn't what the Bible says," Lucas said. His words were shattered by heaving sobs.

"Fuck," said Foxx. It was all he could think to say. Lucas couldn't stay on the telephone, which was good, because Foxx couldn't stand to listen to him this way anyway. He wasn't sure how to deal with a Lucas who was vulnerable. Not down on himself, or pretending to be down to keep Robert up, but really vulnerable. When he heard the breakage in Lucas's voice, he wasn't even sure that he believed it. Was this Foxx's failing or Lucas's?

Foxx drove straight home, walked through to his new kitchen, and threw up in the sink. Betty came and stroked his hair. She had been crying, too. "Stop," he said. Her touch was too strong for him, even when she tried to ease off. There had been sad moments before for the country and the parts of it that he loved: when Sam Cooke got shot, when Ray Charles got pinched for dope at Logan. But this was larger. This was the world and then some. He stayed up with his notebook on his lap, flicking the TV on and off. He wrote "no" on the legal pad, then ripped off the sheet of paper and burned it in the trash can. Then he wrote "o" on a second sheet and burned that one too. He went out into the street and watched the blue light flicker in all the other houses on the block. In the morning he was still too raw to speak, and he squinted tightly against the sun. What business did it have coming up?

Motherfucker who killed King was trying to make the world whiter. But the murder just blackened everything, and it was left to the gods Foxx wasn't sure he believed in to send a little light. Tony called Foxx to tell him about James Brown keeping the peace in Boston. "He had a concert," he said. "Not only didn't he cancel it, but he let the city show it on TV to try to cool things down, keep the kids at home instead of out in the streets.'"

The assassination also pushed "Make It Better" up the charts. Foxx figured it was the healing message, the easy melody. But then Tony told him that a DJ in L.A. had noticed that the second verse had the phrase "I had a dream," and started playing the record alongside a recording of King's famous speech. "That's ironic," said Tony, who explained that King had copyrighted the speech. "Once," he said, "he actually sued a record company for using a piece of it. And it wasn't like it was a white company. It was owned by brothers." Foxx related the story to Betty. "What does it matter?" she said. He saw her point. Black or white, vinyl or lead: Any way you sliced it, King was dead. Then Little Bobby Hutton got done in cold blood by the Oakland cops just a few days later. Pigs, Cong: Everything was wrong.

As the weeks went on, Foxx tried to see the bigger picture, tried to learn to take the credit and let the cash go. One morning he chewed up some Heavenly Blue morning-glory seeds and waited until he saw the Valve. It was open, and everything was pouring out of it and into it at the same time. "So much rushing can be crushing," he wrote in his notebook. Then, beneath it, he wrote, "Right, right. Bright pinks are inky black at night." He stared at the notebook. The words were swirling. He called Tony to see if he thought the lines would make for a good opening verse. He found himself needing Tony more these days: He was the kind of friend who confused Foxx into being calm, with all of his small, careful steps toward big ideas. But Tony wasn't around. He called Kevin up instead. "Come over," Foxx said. "I got something to show you."

When Kevin got there, Foxx showed him the notebook, but Kevin was more interested in the morning glory. They got in the car and drove down into the Mission, stopping at a diner across the street from the R. Crumb mural, spics and spades and tailor-mades. The waitress who took their order was young and pretty and had a black eye on her white face just like the brown stain on her white uniform. Foxx thought that maybe she had fallen but then he heard the chef yelling at her and that's when he knew that she had been hit, not once but several times. When she returned there was shivering everywhere, in the plates, in the glasses, in her apron. Foxx wanted to tell her that she didn't need to be afraid, but he couldn't because in his heart he knew she should be afraid of them all. The rest of the meal he was quiet, fanning out his fingers and then closing them again to stop the sun from coming through. That was the name of the song now, and he had a verse to go with the title: "Morning lingers / On your fingers / It's sad to see you, too / But it can't stop the sun from coming through."

On the way back, Kevin made him stop off at the beach for a swim. There was a man fishing off a boulder; a fish hit and curled back the top of his rod. Death was always trying to tug life away. They'll tell you that you're going to a better place, but it's just the air above the water. Easy to choke on all that heaven. Underwater, Foxx held his breath. Too much was happening. He couldn't catch up. He didn't know where to go. Lucas always said self-knowledge was a journey, but Foxx saw it differently. Journey meant travel, and to get to the self, you had to give up travel. It was all about agreeing to stay put until the haze cleared and you could see the series of crazy ladders leading upward from the man you were to the man you wanted to become.

He surfaced, temporarily saved.

In the car, Kevin was starting to return to normal, talking about going back to the diner and taking the waitress home with him. Foxx rolled up his pants. There was a small, swollen leech dangling from the knob of his ankle. He couldn't believe it. His heart raced. He felt dizzy. He breathed more and more slowly, until he could no longer hear his pulse in his ears, and then he pinched the thing between his thumb and forefinger and solved his problem.

Betty
July 1968

The strange thing was how quickly the house changed her. She didn't expect it to happen the way it did. Back in her own apartment, the one she shared with Elena, she had routines. She ate apples naked. She took baths at midnight. Then she was in Robert's house and she was someone other than herself. One time she was getting ready to take a bath—after dinner, not late, already a concession—and Robert told her to wait because he wanted her to come and watch the Smothers Brothers. She told him that she didn't mind if he watched without her. He told her he wanted her to come sit with him so she did. Then after, she was on her way to the bath when she changed her mind and invited Robert into the shower with her. "It was fun," she told Elena. "That I have to admit."

"But it wasn't what you wanted to do in the first place."

"Not exactly," Betty said. "But I compromised."

A few nights later she tried to take a bath again, and Robert tried the same stunt. This time she said no and went off to the bath herself. Elena was proud of her for that. "You have to hold your ground."

The best nights were the ones that Robert took her out. At first he wouldn't go to parties. He would turn down invitations two or three weeks in a row. Just sat in front of the TV or went into the small studio he had built in the house. Sometimes wouldn't come out until after Betty went to bed. Then Betty said that she wished they could go to a party sometime. They were in the shower again, and he was scrubbing her back, and he wasn't really scrubbing her back anymore. He said, "We can go to a party on one condition." So she crouched and felt him moving into her, slowly at first and then faster. Finally he was done. He was the same temperature as the water. She told Elena only that they were kissing and even then Elena sucked in air through her teeth like she didn't want to hear any more.

They started going to parties all the time and wherever they went they were the guests of honor. Drinking, she got used to quick. A joint now and then didn't faze her much. And sometimes Kevin or Yvette would slip her a pill that made the world bloom. At one party Robert went off to talk to someone and she ended up dancing with Lucas, who had thicker arms than Robert and a deeper voice and eyes that always seemed like they were listening. She kissed him at the end of the dance, and he told her he was happy Robert had found someone like her. She felt ashamed. Had she forgotten herself? She kissed him again, quickly on the cheek like she would kiss a friend, to erase the first kiss. Then she went and danced with Tony and even Kevin, to put camouflage around what had happened with Lucas.

She knew what would happen sooner or later. She had a ring she was supposed to put in but there were plenty of times when she and Robert came in drunk and she knew that sooner or later it would slip her mind. One night they were in bed and she was steering him into her and she remembered that she had forgotten to put it in but she didn't think to stop him. Who would stop him? She held on tight. She felt his breath on her neck. The next morning she was pretty sure what had happened. Three weeks later, she definitely knew. She decided to wait before she told Robert.

Elena asked her if she was sure she was ready. When she answered she chose her words carefully; she didn't want to seem too certain because that would make her seem too young. "I don't know if anyone's ever ready, but I feel like the baby's ready to come to us." Elena made a noise, either like she agreed with Betty or like she disagreed.

On the map, Cincinnati seemed far away, but Robert sounded close on the phone. "Hey, Baby B," he said. "Guess who I met?"

She guessed wrong on purpose. "Yeah," he said, laughing. "That's right. Old Mildew Nixon. We're pals now. Me and him and Henry Kiss-nigger."

"I wish you wouldn't say that," she said.

"Come on," he said. "Isn't Kissinger always good for a laugh? Guess again."

"I give up," she said.

"Are you sitting down?" he said. "James Brown."

"That's great."

"You're goddamned right." His voice was higher than usual, strained from what she hoped was excitement. "These young cats came to the show, and they were freaks. Players. So Tony started talking to one of them, and he lets it slip, cool as December, that they just happen to play with James. Can you dig the size of that? He runs them like an army. Wrong note: fifty-dollar fine. Wrong step: fifty-dollar fine. One cat is going to leave the band soon, so he took acid just to see what would happen. He told me that the amps started talking to him in Mr. Brown's voice. That's what they call him. Mr. Brown." He sped on. "They asked if we wanted to meet him, or we asked if he was around, and we hopped in a car and drove over to the studio and there he was, sitting in the corner, reading *Life* magazine. He stood up, walked over, shook my hand. I told him that I couldn't believe the things he said in 'Say It Loud.' He told me he liked *Get the Picture* and that he hoped the next record was a motherfucker. And it got me thinking."

"About what?"

"About us."

"What do you mean?" She was worried. Sometimes she sensed such a restlessness in him.

"I stood next to a great man, baby, and I felt great myself. And I realized that there are only two things I love, the music and you. I want them both. I want you to marry me." For a second his bravado failed him, and it almost sounded like a question.

Betty dropped the telephone and started to cry. It was silly, she knew, the kind of thing you'd do if someone was watching you and you wanted to show how overwhelmed you were.

"Those best be tears of joy I hear, 'cause I ain't taking no for an answer," Robert said, his bravado back in place.

"Of course," she said. "I love you."

"Let me play you something," he said. She heard fumbling in the background. "Ready?" There was a whirr, and then the sound of an acoustic guitar. It was picking out a figure like a spider, delicate but deadly. Robert's voice came across the wire.

"Feels right like a flight on the wings of a dove / If anything should happen to our love." She heard more bumping, and then his voice came back on the line. "I wrote that for you," he said. "I'm going to write you one now, and one when we get married, and one on every anniversary and one every birthday. And when we have babies, I'm gonna write one for them every birthday, too. We have a big enough family, I'll put out a double record every year."

Betty held back her news from everyone this time, even from her mama. She wasn't quite sure that she believed it. She looked at the leaves of her tea. Plus, she had news for him, and now the baby inside her was something less than a problem and something more than a blessing. But when Robert came home from Cincinnati, he didn't confirm or deny. Instead he went into the bedroom with a James Brown instrumental called "In the Middle, Part 1," and played it round the clock for two days straight. He came out once, holding the single, to tell her that he didn't understand it. "I'm trying to crack the motherfucker," he said. "I'm trying to get what it has so I can use it. It's so tiny, three minutes only, but it don't seem to begin or end. Maybe that's why he called it 'In the Middle.'"

"Probably," Betty said.

"I don't know. I just don't know. Motherfucker's like a snake. It just comes sneaking in, two guitar chimes and then a little spiral downward. It has horns all over the place."

"We need to talk," she said.

"I need to work." He waved the record in front of him. "I mean it. I'm trying to figure out the secrets of things. I'm trying to make them yield."

Betty could have let him go, let him win. But he wasn't unbeatable. This she had learned from watching the band, and more specifically from watching Lucas. Robert couldn't listen to Lucas without also listening to himself listening to Lucas. Betty wondered if it was because he was afraid, and decided that it was. Then she wondered why he was afraid of Lucas, and decided that it was because he loved him. "Robert," she said, trying to say it the way Lucas would, "you need to put away the record, because we need to talk now. I'm pregnant and I need to know when we're getting married."

"You're what?" he said.

"Pregnant. A baby." She said it slowly this time, bracing for him to raise his voice or to retreat back into his studio. Instead he stepped forward and put his arms around her.

"You know what we need to do?" he said. "We need to get married tomorrow. Let me go put this record away."

They went down to City Hall first thing, with Tony as a witness. Then they went to see *Romeo and Juliet*. "That's us," he said. "Lovers for life."

"They died," she said.

"Life, death," he said. "What's the difference?"

In the car, Robert was quiet. "I didn't mean it," he finally said. "I know what life is. I think I even know what life with you is. I just wonder what happens when you hold a dream near a flame to see it better. Does it burn up?" She held him tight all night and in the morning she went to get the James Brown record so he could start decoding it again.

Robert's overnight bag was by the front door, which meant that he was driving down to L.A. "Going to see some people," he said, which meant that he wasn't going to say any more. The whole weekend she ran a fever, and Sunday morning there was cramping and spotting. The night before Robert was due to come home, she was dozing off, watching the news with the sound down and listening to Aretha on the stereo, when she felt a surge of something warm between her legs. She knew immediately, and called Elena to come over. Betty took lots of Tylenol, but the cramping only got worse and she was passing dark brown clots. She shut her eyes and prayed for the cramping to go away and finally it did. She was on the toilet then, and she felt it slip out of her. She could see it even though the lights were off. She could see it in the blackness. She stood on unsteady legs and flushed without looking.

Betty sat in the kitchen all morning. Robert rolled in around ten. "I'm hungry," he said. "Can I get a big plate of eggs? I'd like six of one kind and a half-dozen of another kind."

Betty didn't move.

Robert noticed the way she was white-knuckling her coffee cup. Then he smelled the whiskey in it. He knew at once. For two days, he stayed out of the studio. He sat next to her with his guitar and played her songs from the new record. Her favorite was "Eyes of a Child." "They see everything they need to," he sang. "They see everything that's real / They see good and they see bad / They see exactly what you feel." When he thought she was sleeping, he stopped playing and lay down on the bed next to her and brushed her neck with his fingers.

The third morning, Betty rolled out of bed and padded to the kitchen. There were old dishes piled up in the sink. At about nine Robert came out of his studio. She hadn't realized he was in there. He told her he loved her, how he would always love her. He told her about how he had heard the new Beatles record, and how there was this talking guitar on the left track of "Dear Prudence" that he wanted for Christmas. She held his hands and felt the current coming through.

Robert
January 1969

Right after Foxx and Betty got married, he married Nancy Sinatra. Some reporter saw his ring, heard a rumor or started one, and there it was, right on the gossip page. At first it was just the guys at the studio ribbing him, calling him Frankie Junior and that kind of shit, and that was cool. He could give the rest of those Rats the stinkeye. Hey Deano, you'd better put that drink down before it falls down. Hey Sammy, it ain't the Black Pack. He even went into the studio and cut a version of "These Boots Are Made for Walkin'," just to keep the guessers guessing. Then he got a phone call in the middle of the night from a hoarse male voice who suggested that it might be in his best interest to set the record straight. "She's a good girl," it said. "She doesn't need this trouble." The voice went on to call him a jungle bunny, an eggplant, and a spare-tire-colored piece of trash. "You ever hear of whitewalls?" said Foxx, but the man was gone. It had probably been a put-on, but he was plenty put off.

"What are you going to do?" said Tony.

"Make a statement," said Foxx, and he did, of a fashion, from the stage of the Hollywood Bowl. "Miss Sinatra and I regret to announce that we are dissolving our union," he said, and the crowd went wild. Betty was there, sitting right up front. Ever since she lost the baby, he tried to bring her around to as many concerts as possible. Sometimes she would beg out, stay home, cry—he knew because he saw the tissues in the garbage. But when he persisted, told her she didn't have to dress past a men's shirt and jeans, told her she didn't have to do anything she didn't want to do, she relented. "You just have to sit," he said, banging the back of the chair. "You're the queen."

"And what does that make you?" she said.

"You know it," he said. At the Hollywood Bowl, after he announced that he and Nancy were through, he brought Betty out onstage for a second. "This is my Nancy," he said, and she smiled tentatively into the crowd's fearsome roar. Her shirttails were twisted up in her hands. "Could someone take the queen back to her throne?" he said.

Foxx was calling the new album *Wreckered* now, because he thought that was the best song they had cut. The sessions were rolling along: They were done with "Eyes of a Child" and "Wednesday Ain't So Bad," done with "Mixing Board" and "Staggering," done with "Get Up and See It" and "If Anything Should Happen to Our Love." They were looking at May to release the finished disc, but Foxx thought that maybe they could get it done for his birthday in April.

"That might be one of my last birthdays," he said to Lucas. "I'm not one of those fools who thinks nothing's going to happen to him."

Lucas shook his head. He thought that Foxx was uncounting his blessings, and he thought humility was better done with faith than with fatalism. "You're going to live to a ripe old age," he said. "You'll get older and older and then fall from the tree one day. No one will pluck you off, cuz, because no one will want to."

"I might want to," Kevin said. He was smiling but showing his teeth, even his canines. The band hadn't been cool with Foxx for most of the year: too many trips down to L.A., too many days when he didn't make it in to practice. But the new batch of songs had turned them back toward him. Take the title track. Claude and Cheryl got to do their Miles and their Coltrane, cool blue tones from the trumpet and red-hot sax behind it. Then Lucas bounced and Tony buzzed, and then Foxx spun the world. He had two verses and a chorus, and all he was looking for was the third verse, which he found as he was driving to the studio the morning of the session:

Wreckered
Player

How it grows
Stretching out
Is all it knows
Come out smelling
Like a rose
I rise
Revolution
In my eyes

"Damn," he said. "Ain't nobody going to top that." Then he went back into the booth to make motherfucking certain. He came home late, head clearer than it had ever been, and slipped into bed next to Betty. She murmured hello and he hugged her from behind and gently pushed between her thighs. She rolled toward him and told him about the dream she was having: There was an earthquake, and the house caught fire, and he pushed her out into the street, where a fireman covered her with a blanket. Inside the blanket she was immediately cool, and at peace.

"You know what that means?" he said. "It means we rescue each other."

"From what?"

"From the world's bad moods," he said. "Natural disasters, tragedies, the clock turned upside down."

She slept with a look on her face that told him that she believed in beautiful things. He couldn't sleep, and fell to doubt. What if the record didn't do the things he needed it to do? What if the world spun away from him instead of on the teeth of his gears? He watched the ceiling and remembered what his aunt would say in Boston, that it was someone else's floor. She was trying to teach humility but it always felt like humiliation. Now he had only blackness in his mind and got up to find some white. He kept a bag in the top drawer of his dresser, the Bannacourt special. The first few times he had done coke, it was recreational: get him sharp before a press conference, shine him up for the tenth take of a song. Then, one winter morning, it was creational. It changed on him all at once, a single snort, and from then on it did something different to him. He knew that there was nothing good could come of it. He counted the times he'd counted the cost. Still, when he weighed the risks against that feeling when the coke lit him up from inside, there was no comparison. To get clean, he'd been running a game on himself, buying shit from Bannacourt and then flushing half of it down the toilet as soon as he got home. Tithing. He laid the rest out on the bathroom counter, snorted two long lines, and went back to bed. Within six hours he had written the best lyrics he had ever written, held the best woman he had ever held, and snorted the best coke he had ever snorted. He was a man who stayed in the rafters. Higher than high, Captain Bligh.

Hugh Clary over at Turn Records had called a face-to-face meeting for nine o'clock Monday morning, but when Foxx got down to the office the meeting had turned into a telephone call. There was a blizzard up in Tahoe, and Clary was trapped in his new half-million-dollar cabin. Foxx knew what Clary had paid because Clary told his lawyer, his lawyer told his secretary, and his secretary told Foxx. Foxx assumed the news was meant to travel, and if that was the case, why not travel with a fine messenger like this one? Her name was Linda, and she batted her eyes—and everything else—while she got Clary on the telephone. Foxx was at a conference table with some cocaine and the newspaper. "I'm on the line," he said, straight-facing it. Linda laughed.

"Listen," said Clary. "I'm worried about something, Robert."

"What is it, Hughie?" said Foxx. Tony had started the Hughie business. "Contempt breeds familiarity," he said, and Foxx felt the wit of the remark so deeply that he followed suit.

"I think that the album is fantastic. But I think you have the wrong single."

"How so?"

"Well, you said the last time we talked that you thought 'Wreckered' was the single."

"That's right, man. It's like nothing you've ever heard."

"What about 'Mixing Board'?"

"What about it?" Foxx liked "Mixing Board." It had velocity and a nice build. But "Wreckered" had teeth that went all around the edges. When he played the finished version for Betty, she cried, and the tears rolled down her cheeks and settled into the corners of her smile. That settled the matter, Mad Hatter.

"People want a song from you that's about coming together," Clary said. "This one's about coming apart."

"You been out in the real world lately?" Foxx said. "Everything's not as rosy as the sunset you see over the mountains. I'm trying to show the world a mirror, and there's only one song capable." He stretched out the word like taffy.

"Let's talk about this when I get back to L.A. I may be snowed in another day."

Foxx did another line. Linda laughed again. The best jokes don't even know they're getting made.

Clary didn't call him when he got back to L.A. Instead Turn's lawyers called Jerry and tried to push for "Mixing Board." Jerry conveyed the message in careful formal terms so that Foxx knew he was serious. "Fuck no," Foxx said, so that Jerry knew he was serious in return. Lawyers were bitches, all of them. Give you a smack for a snack, a raw deal for a meal, and the rest of the hurt for dessert. "The single is what I said it was. End of discussion before discussion begins."

For three weeks, while Jerry made small concessions here and there to smooth ruffled feathers, the masters gathered dust in the Turn offices. Foxx threatened to sue the label unless he got his single released, but he threatened through Jerry, and he wasn't sure that his angry words were ever heard. Finally, they came to an understanding. "No hard feelings, man," he said to Clary on the telephone. "Only hard choices." On the day Turn gave in, he bought himself the most expensive fur coat he could find and went up into Nob Hill telling himself, I got a better coat than that dude, got a better coat than this one. He was able to glide along for twenty minutes or so before he saw a tall brunette in a Jacques Heim brown mouton jacket. He tried to meet her eye but she wouldn't give it. Her prerogative. She had the better coat.

Betty
April 1969

Robert had finished his record, the first record he had made as Betty's husband. He wrapped it in gold paper and leaned it against the lamp on her bedside table. There was a card, too. It said, "To Lovely Betty," and on the inside he had drawn a crude sketch of two faces joined together. Beneath the drawing, he signed his name. Robert.

Betty removed the wrapping from *Wreckered*. The cover of the album was a photo of a car crash. Behind the crash was a boy who dwarfed the two cars, exposing them as toys. One of the cars was white, the other one was black. The boy was black and wore a red shirt.

Betty took out the album, still in its sleeve. There were nine songs. "Pick Up (on What I'm Putting Down)" was first. "If Anything Should Happen to Our Love" was second. She whispered the titles to herself, all the way down to the last song, "Staggering." She held the sleeve up to the light and looked through the spindle hole.

Betty put the record on the record player. Notes tumbled out of the speakers; jubilant organ chords and a bass popping beneath them. Then Robert sang: "People pick up on what I'm putting down / The house on the hill is sitting there still." The organ and bass stopped short. There was a half-second of total silence. Then the rest of the band exploded: Claude went all the way down his trombone's slide while Cheryl punctuated with her trumpet; Tony strummed, quick and funky; Kevin hammered. The sound was a wall and Robert climbed it. When he was up on top he sang again, brasher, brighter, better: "People pick up on what I'm putting down / The man on the screen is starting to lean." He laughed, and the band went off like a firework again. The second song was the ballad Robert had sung to her when he called from Cincinnati to propose. By "Mixing Board," Betty was squeezing her knees together, a laugh spinning in her mouth. When she listened to "Staggering," the laugh froze. Robert's voice was slowed down to a menacing blur. "A racial slur," he had called it. The words emerged as if they were crawling from between the floorboards:

I ain't your boy
I ain't your slave
I won't be digging
For your grave

But when you're falling watch the sky
You'll see me up there I fly I fly

Staggering oh staggering
Mack the knife is daggering
America is flaggering
I'm staggering

I ain't your son
I ain't your Tom
See me fragging
In Viet Nam

The street ain't always wide enough for two
I'm crossing over to take good care of you

Staggering oh staggering
The family dog is waggering
The Rolling Stones are jaggering
I'm staggering

Betty flipped the light off, flipped the record over. She lay in the dark and waited for him. She loved him all over again.

Robert
August 1969

Foxx was afraid of airplanes. Not because he thought they might crash: that he accepted as part of fate. Some planes hung. Some planes fell. He was afraid because when he saw them passing overhead, he sometimes got the idea that they were traveling through time instead of space, that they were going into the future rather than the West, or the North. And he didn't want to go into the future, not just yet. That was why he said no to Woodstock, without even looking at the terms. Jerry was brassed off at first: He explained to Foxx that it was a big show with big acts and that the Foxxes belonged among them. Foxx laughed and said that the rest of those motherfuckers belonged among him. Plus, he said, there were rumors that Bill Graham was scrambling to put something of his own together, a Golden Bear festival with the Doors, Pelota, the Rolling Stones, and maybe even Dylan. "You do what you think you need to do," said Jerry. He was talking softly, but his anger came out in the way he twirled his cigarette lighter. "But missing this is a mistake. You're going to send me to an early grave." But Foxx didn't care. Graves were dirt. Graves were earth. He had the heavens. He was so far ahead, so high above, so great beyond. He saw it all spread out beneath him.

Wreckered had been out three months, and it had made him a giant. The title song went top five, and he was so happy he let Turn put out "Mixing Board," which went to number two. "Staggering" would have taken the top spot if it hadn't been for Zager and Evans. Man has cried a billion tears, and that was just while he was being forced to listen to the song. In July, Foxx had the cover of *Rolling Stone*. In August he had a portable phone, a big talking brick in a suitcase that he had to set up on top of a fire hydrant. Thanks to Rudy Bannacourt, he had all the blow he wanted and glow to spare. And thanks to an open line of credit at the Emporium, he had seven-hundred-dollar shoes and a sense of how to use them: keep them clean, so that the kids fighting to worship at his feet could see themselves reflected back. The Foxxes were sweeter than the Beatles, more filling than Dylan. Tommy James? Tommy Roe? He'd take them both down with a trench broom. Backstage at the Foxxes' shows, he saw people he recognized, and not just local dudes like Applejack and Darby Slick. He saw Jim Morrison. He saw Isaac Hayes. He saw Neil Diamond. Once, after a show in L.A., he came off the encore like a new-crowned king, went with the hip roll down into the bottom of the theater, started looking toward the dressing room and the girls who were already collecting there like moisture. Then he felt a presence at his right elbow, a presence too strong to pass, and he turned and who was it but Miles Davis, sharp as a knife in a charcoal-gray suit, with a drink in his hand and sunglasses darker than a moonless night. Foxx felt a bright blade of excitement go right through him. He held out his hand and Miles shook it firmly but finally, like there wouldn't be another time. "Nice set," he rasped.

It was the only moment when he felt as if he had both feet on the ground. The rest of the time, the world spun faster than his record. "What's it like to have the number-one album in the country?" A girl asked him this, a skinny blonde thing in a short green skirt who snuck backstage at the Fillmore to write a story for her college paper. Foxx made her sit down. He made her look him in the eyes. Then he gave her the answer: "It's like love." She nodded, rapt, told him that she and all her friends dug him. She trembled when Foxx signed her hand for her; he thought she was going to come. Then she left, and left Foxx alone with his lie. It wasn't like love. It was like fucking and dying and falling up a mountain and losing your mind all at once. He called Betty and didn't say much, just listened to the sound of her on the phone until his heart resumed its normal rate.

Before *Wreckered*, Foxx didn't need to shine all the time. He could take off the fringed white leather jacket, take off the yellow suede hat, take off the black boots studded with rhinestones and the red diamond-encrusted eyeglasses. He could also take off his face: Or rather, he could take off the Foxx face, which was a mask that could absorb the heat and deflect the blows. FOXX ROCKS FILLMORE gave him pleasure, but from a distance. FOXX FALLS FLAT wounded him, but only superficially. When he felt the time was right, he could turn the mask around and inspect it for the effects of all this attention, the scars and the touch marks. Then he could send it out to be cleaned.

But after *Wreckered*, it was harder to see how he could do without the mask, even for a day. He heard his name shouted on the radio. He heard it screamed from rooftops. In Berkeley, he was out for a walk, just a normal afternoon walk, when a woman saw him going by her apartment building and launched herself off her porch. A hedge broke her fall, and she got up, her hand dangling limply off a sprained wrist, and stumbled the few steps just to touch the hem of his garment. Crazy, no doubt, but what made her different from the others was only that she jumped.

In Milwaukee he was in the hotel, weed in his hand, Gerald Atkins Show on the TV. Every time he moved to put on his clothes he got a brief pain in his head. He blinked, looked again, got the pain again. Soon he realized that the problem wasn't in his head at all, but in his mind. It was a mental rebellion. He had to go onstage but he didn't know why he had to go onstage. To please the crowd? The crowd could please itself. To make money? The money was making itself. To be seen? He laughed, and the pain came in a rapid volley, popping audibly, like paparazzi flashes. To be seen was impossible when the light was so bright. There was nothing to do but bring everything down a notch, which he did, first with a pill, then with a pinch of powder. Pretty soon he was being warmed by a new calm. It had him in the palm of its hand. It gave him a soft place to land.

The phone jangled. "Hey, baby," Betty said. "You about to go on?" He grunted a yes. "Well, good luck. Remember that I love you."

"That much I know," he said. "But it's hard to remember the rest of it. Like was there a time when I wasn't the most famous cat in the world?" She laughed, taking his tone for playful arrogance. He tried to slow down his heart, which was racing again. In the spaces between the beats, he tried to remember.

Betty
October 1969

She went through a tunnel when she lost the baby and emerged from the other end a different woman, one who wouldn't watch scary movies, who wouldn't ride in a bumpy car, who didn't like to stay too long in a room that was too hot or too cold. And while she still smoked reefer sometimes, she cut out everything else, especially the pills Kevin and Yvette took. They gave her life, but then they reminded her of death, because that's what life did. "You can't be too careful," she said to the empty bedroom, to the empty closet, to the empty space inside her.

"You don't have to go to the office," Robert said. "No wife of mine needs a job." But it was only two days a week now, and it was all she had. Elena tried to get her out in the evening to see a movie but Betty didn't want to see Butch Cassidy or any other kid. Plus, she wasn't really working late. She was reading about miscarriages. The books said that most spontaneous terminations occurred within the first sixteen weeks, that guilt and anger were common emotions, and that she shouldn't have relations for up to a month. The simple sentences flowed down into her like something dispositive. One book recommended making something for her unborn baby, so she took a red crayon, flinching at the color but determined to be brave, and drew a garden. In the garden she drew a little tree. Under the tree she drew a circle with two eyes that she knew in her heart was her baby.

Another book recommended rediscovering your partner. That was the name of one of the chapters, the one after "Forgiving Yourself" and before "Confronting the Future." But this was as impossible as having relations. Robert was down in L.A., scouting some of the new groups and looking for opening acts, and then he was going to New York to meet in Turn's new East Coast digs, and then he was performing in Dallas, and Denver, and Phoenix. If she thought about it, Betty knew that he had women on the road. But she didn't think about it. Not because she couldn't bear the first thought, but because once she started, she couldn't stop. She wanted to ask him all about it: the urgency, the guilt, the pleasure. She thought that his affairs—that's the word she used when she dared think about it, because it was an upper-class word, a word that put a gold edge on things—were for him what her pregnancy had been for her: a hole deep enough to fall into, and dark enough to erase the difference between falling and rising.

Then one day Betty heard Elena announcing that she was leaving early to go see *Bob & Carol & Ted & Alice*, and Betty asked if she could tag along. Afterward, Elena couldn't stop complaining that the movie was too long, and Betty couldn't stop saying, "Tee-tee." She laughed. Elena frowned.

The next night Betty called up Tony and Lucas and asked them if they wanted to drop by the house. They came by again over the weekend, and Kevin came along also, and this time she didn't recoil when he gave her a pill. She wandered deeper into the house and found Lucas and Tony on the couch watching TV. Lucas put Betty under his arm. "I've been having dreams lately that we're all in the movies," she said.

Lucas nodded sagely.

"In the movies, in the audience, and in the movies, on the screen," she said.

Lucas nodded again.

"Can I tell you that the dreams aren't really about the movies?" she said. "They're about the cemetery. I dream that we're in the cemetery, in a grave, and also in the cemetery, visiting a grave. And you know whose grave it is?"

Then she was weeping, and his other arm came around her. She was happy to be in his arms because they were broad and strong. She was afraid that without those arms she would be in the grave. Then she was in the bathroom alone, calling Robert's name. She wondered what was attached to that name, and what else she could attach to it. What if she looked more closely and found out that the name was nothing any longer, that Robert had vacated his body and signed his soul over? Could she love him under another name? Did she want to? There was a pill bottle on the counter and she pushed it onto the floor. She was sick of everyone else doing all the destroying. There was power in ruination, and it was power she meant to have. Lucas came in when he heard the bottle clatter. He reached down and retrieved it. "Nothing spilled," he said. Betty tried to swat it out of his hands. Then she was crying again, touching his face. She felt around for his name, for something to keep her safe. The next morning, she was afraid that she had made a fool of herself but Lucas was too much of a gentleman to say.

Robert
October 1969

What swung like "The Popcorn"? Nothing at all. He was driving when he heard it first, the bell of the guitar, the book of the sax, the candle of the trombone. "Come on," the chorus said as the guitar strings stretched and bent. "Come on." Mr. Brown and Fred and Maceo beckoned. He would have gone anywhere with them.

He pulled his Jaguar into the parking lot, handed his keys to the kid with a twenty-dollar tip, gave the same to the doorman and the elevator operator, and went on up to Bannacourt's pad, where the party was already on.

Foxx didn't see Bannacourt. He wasn't looking. Wasn't looking at anyone, in fact, because everyone was looking at him. The room split down the middle when he came through the door Black Moses-style. Someone put a drink in his hand and someone else passed him a joint. He made for the far wall, where he turned to face the women who had gathered around him. He had a routine by now. He would tune into the finest girl in the room, look her up and down, say "Well, God bless the goods we was given." Had another one, too: "I prayed for a sign and I got one: Slippery When Wet." He wasn't serious about doing anything, but he hung out his lines anyway because they made Bannacourt bag up.

When Foxx walked in they were playing Motown, "I Wish It Would Rain" and "Ball of Confusion," but someone must have noticed him come through the door because they switched the Temps out for Miles Davis. He had told a reporter a few weeks earlier that he was into Miles and Miles alone, and she had printed it, and now everyone thought they knew that piece of him. The girls were still talking to him, but now everything they said had to come through the music first, and most of the chatter wasn't heavy enough to sink in. The music was city lights, busy, cheap, and beautiful. Then someone pulled the plug and the whole scene drained, and at the bottom of it was a bass-and-organ skeleton, Dave Holland and Joe Zawinul knocking out a two-beat and Miles rising up from a hole in the ground and putting the meat back on them bones. It was a kind of treachery, how strong the music was, and all the more so for seeming so gentle. Foxx looked around the room to see if anyone else was getting it. Most of them were dragging on their reefer, pushing up on the nearest cat or chick, talking about the weather or the Weathermen. As for the few who had their eyes closed, he couldn't be sure. He closed his own.

The year before, Foxx had learned quickly. But now he was beginning to pass what was there, to hear things before they happened. He had tried to explain it to Bobby Seale when he came backstage one night in Oakland. But Foxx was a little stoned, and Bobby seemed angry. "While you're unlocking yourself, don't forget the political prisoners."

"Man, being human is political prison," said Foxx. Boris, nearby, laughed. But the more he thought about it, the more certain he was that Bobby didn't have it down. Housing was cool. Jobs were cool. But if you couldn't make people see differently, houses and jobs were just new places to bleed. The Panthers liked to talk about Coltrane, about how he was playing the sound of their thoughts in the months before he died. But Foxx knew exactly what Coltrane was doing, because it was the same as what Miles was doing, and the same as what he was doing. He was making a different music. And the music was making him different.

The new songs were vast deserts that were hard for the Foxxes to get across. "Your problem," said Lucas, "is that you think we don't understand you. Our problem is that we don't." He called up Tony for consolation and the phone just rang and rang.

At Bannacourt's, he singled out one woman, a tall thing from South Africa, and when she started to lay her theory of justice and art down he hooked into it for sport. She pulled and he let her, but then she fought so hard he thought she'd snap the line. "Americans are so naïve," she said. "You live in a bubble, protected, like children." Feigning offense, he turned to go, and she put her hand on his hip purposefully. "Damned if I don't," Foxx said. But he didn't.

An hour passed. The minute hand came to attention again. Now it was some Bud Powell solo piano that was, with the coke, as comically quick as a silent movie; Powell, shitbird crazy, playing from the distant past, tore through "Sweet Georgia Brown" like he only wanted to leave the girl's teeth and tailbone. Someone was passing out tabs of acid; the paper had designs of Lyndon Johnson. Foxx heard the purling of the water in the bathroom sink like it was right there next to him, like it was flowing into his ear.

It was a brook and then it was a stream and then it was a river and then it darkened until he wasn't sure if it was water or blood. Foxx wasn't the only one feeling it. Rudy was on all fours, looking up at the lamp. "The moon," he said. "Turn it off." A girl with long red ringlets was sprawled faceup across the bed, her hands over her pussy. Bud Powell had stopped now. There was no music, only Bannacourt dancing with the lamp. The girl folded her hands downward, the tip of the index finger serving as a descender. Her other hand pulled him in. She was someone important to him. He didn't recognize her.

Betty
October 1969

On Halloween they went to a party at a Spanish-style mansion out on Figueroa. Betty wanted to go as Tina Turner, but Robert didn't think it was funny. "These are music people," he said. "They'll know Ike and Tina. Shit, Ike and Tina might be there." Betty frowned and went as Nancy Sinatra instead: same skirt, same boots, swapped the black wig for a blonde one. She was feeling both obedient and bold—secure, maybe that was the word—ever since she skipped another period. And as much as she hadn't quite believed it the first time, this time she was sure. This baby was coming, and it was a boy. She saw him when she closed her eyes: running in the hallway, clapping in the bathtub.

Robert refused to dress up at all. "Isn't this enough?" he said, waving his hand over his leather vest and leather pants, the snakeskin belt with the buckle that had FOXX written on it in six-inch letters made of rhinestones. She had to admit that it was.

Their whole life was a party, so each party was just an incidence of life. At this one the smoke was thicker than ever; people disappeared into it while they talked in shocked tones about My Lai. Betty hugged the people she knew (Tony, done up like James Bond; Lucas, who was Sergeant Rock; and Kevin, who had greased back his hair and come as Bill Graham) and she shook hands with those she didn't (Gino Rubino, who was wearing a Nixon mask; Grace Slick, who was a witch; and a stooped, gentle producer named Frank Tamborelli, who was working on the Foxxes' next record and appeared to be dressed up as Clark Gable). Robert disappeared almost immediately to work the room, and Betty snuck into a corner with Tony and Lucas. Both of them were stag, so they stood sentinel on either side of her. They talked for a while about the band, about Lucas's kids, about the girlfriend Tony had just dumped. Frankensteins and Draculas drifted by. After a while, Betty spotted a leggy girl decked out in full Barbarella gear. "She looks just like Jane Fonda," she said.

"I think it is Jane Fonda," said Tony. They watched the crowd for other famous faces, but it was hard to tell the difference between the masks and the people wearing them. Then they went out by the pool, where a Richard Burton was being fed grapes by Cleopatra. Off in the shadows, a Louise Brooks in a long gown that had slits up the sides was at the breasts of Marlene Dietrich. "This," Lucas said to Betty, "is Sodom."

"This," Betty said, adjusting her wig, "doesn't bother me. But has anyone seen Robert?"

Tony left her side. He returned in a half hour or so with a man who answered to Robert's name but to many other names also. His eyes were so far back in his head they were on his ass, and she said so. This struck him funny and he fell down where he stood. "Who's the most popular personality?" he sang. "I can't help thinkin' it's no one else but me." But when he got up, he was limping. "Calling all doctors," he said. "My ankle's wrinkled."

"Time for you to go home," Betty said.

He clapped. "Tony," he said. "Drive me to the place this lady wishes." He was up until three, singing, chattering, and sometimes crying. Once when Betty came over to stroke his head she thought she saw a small mark on the inside of his arm and fear gripped her heart.

The next day when he finally came downstairs he wasn't singing. "It's two," she said.

"You been waiting long to tell me that?" he said. "I got a watch." He poured himself a bowl of cereal and sat there in his red and black bathrobe, the one with SUPERSTAR on the back in gold rhinestones. Betty wouldn't look at him.

"It's killing me," she finally said.

"No it's not," Robert said. He smiled a broad smile and Betty had to look. His teeth were straight and white and she was suddenly exhausted and wished she could forget all about it. "It ain't no such thing," he said mockingly. "It's not even killing me."

"You're always telling me you're worried about Kevin or Yvette."

"What's different," Robert said, "is that some people are weak, and some people are me."

"I had a daddy that drank, and then he left. My mother didn't touch the stuff, ever."

"I have an aunt that leaves every cap sealed tight. You know that. It just ain't me." He lit a joint. "See? I sit here for two minutes and already I'm sinning. Save me, save me." He took a drag, held it in, and then exhaled with a sigh.

"I want you to stop."

He barked out a laugh. She took the joint away from him and held it to her own lips, though she didn't take a drag.

"I thought you were a saint," he said. "But a martyr?"

"I'm sorry," she said. "I don't want to get on you for no reason. Like I said, maybe I just don't understand."

"What's to understand?" He began to sing: "A little toot, a little weed / A little something that I need."

"What if I get pregnant again?" she said. "I'm sure it'll happen sooner or later." She felt her stomach. If Robert had been the type to notice, he might have. He would any day. She'd tell him, tomorrow or the next day. He'd embrace her. He'd put on a show. That wasn't in question. But would she believe it?

He stubbed out the joint. "Betty, this is just smoke. It ain't gonna stop a child from coming."

"I'm not talking about weed."

"What are you talking about?" he said. She tapped her arm. "Uh-uh," he said. "No way."

"Robert," she said slowly.

"You mean last night?" he said. "One line. That's not even an arrow. And that's all it is, was, or will ever be." Now he was standing, washing out his cereal bowl. "I swear it to you. So you can stop worrying."

"I can't stop," she said. "And it's not worrying. It's thinking. You should try it sometime." He laughed. "Don't laugh at it. I'm not always so happy to be entertaining you this way. 'The warmth you feel / Can hurt and heal.' You wrote that, didn't you? Maybe you should try to understand it, too."

The baby, or some idea of it, bounded up a bit inside her. Not even born, and he was already trying to get into the conversation. She didn't mind. She could use the help. Robert shrugged his shoulders in his Superstar robe and trudged back upstairs. "Catch you later, Great Dictator," he said.

Robert
December 1969

"Somewhere the cattleyas are blooming," said Tony. Foxx didn't know what cattleyas were, but he sure as hell knew they weren't blooming in the darkened dressing room of the Michigan Coliseum, where he and the band sat, drinking beer and Jack Daniel's, waiting for the arena electrician to rewire the house lights so that the show could begin. "I think it's a jog circuit that got fritzed by the spot-op," said the fat, ponytailed cat who kept wiggling the flashlight beam over the wall. As the tour went along, Foxx sensed the fatigue thickening. At first it was like a film of sweat that you could wash off with a quick blast of cold water and a sliver of soap. But as the days went by it settled over them like a garment.

To deal with it, they hired a doctor to travel with the band. Dr. Phil, who had lost his practice in Sacramento when a patient died. Somehow he had kept the materials necessary to write prescriptions, including the pad, which he liked to call "Tyrannosaurus Rx." Tony and Lucas didn't like him much but they tolerated him because he could get pills and powder for Yvette and Kevin and that seemed safer than making them shop on the street.

At first, Foxx wasn't interested in what Dr. Phil had to offer. After Betty caught him out at Halloween, and especially after he found out that there was a baby on the way, he tried to limit his intake of blow, cut back to weed and speed, cut out the whatever-you-need. But the new health-food diet affected his writing. The melodies were less sweet, the lyrics less sharp, and things that should have moved him left him cold: sunsets, rainstorms, Betty with them hurry-home drops on her cheek. His mind, which once had multiplied the smallest matter, now divided it up, and he knew he was approaching zero. Plus, when he was straight, he noticed how crooked everyone else was. Kevin was a stone criminal, and probably crazy. Tony was sold so deep into Yvette that she could have robbed him blind and he would have apologized that he didn't have any bread left to keep her in clover. And Yvette: Well, she had always been a good-time girl, but recently she had been easy pickings for anyone with a dime bag of anything. Foxx caught her in Minneapolis with a guy who owned a club, and Kevin said that he had seen her in Cincinnati with some punk dealer. Tony didn't see it, but that's because Tony hadn't seen it. Foxx envied him his ignorance. He tried to talk to Lucas about it, maybe come up with some way of helping the girl, but Lucas just frowned and shook his head. "The promises of God are strong reasons for us to follow after holiness; we must cleanse ourselves from all filthiness of flesh and spirit," he said. That was another thing: Lucas may have sounded like holy thunder but he was just scared of the world's shadows.

So one night in Detroit, Foxx went to Phil. "Give here," he said, and the good doctor shook some candy into his outstretched hand. "I hear a symphony," Foxx sang. Two hours later he was flying without instruments, feeling up a slick young chick whose name he didn't catch, listening to "Going to a Go-Go," asking himself how he could take Smokey's drag-uh and stag-uh and stick them to the pieces of the new song that had been rattling around in his head. He woke up the next morning without the girl—he had sent her home with just a memory of his fingers—but with an answer to his question: the sweet-as-a-summer-day "Kicking the Can." They added it into the shows and felt the crowds surge when Lucas thumbed out the opening chords. "Say you can and you can be sure that you will," sang Foxx, waiting for Lucas's response, "Say you can't and you'll never get up that hill." Now Foxx was back on the line full-time. The shit, he said to Tony, should get cowriting credit on the next record.

The bus brakes screeched. Foxx wouldn't have even known what city if it wasn't for the piece of paper folded in his jacket pocket. "If it's Thursday, it must be Indianapolis," he said.

We're here?" Tony said. He had been up the whole way looking over papers filled with numbers and making notations in the margins. "I was just falling asleep. I'm going to be exhausted for the show. Can we play something that doesn't require the services of a lead guitarist?"

Foxx shook a pill into Tony's hand. "Prescription Philled," he said.

"This will wind me up in time?" Tony said.

"It'll wind you up so you can keep the time. The problem will be unwinding after."

"You mean I won't sleep? That doesn't seem like a problem."

"It's not, my man. It's progress in tablet form."

They came off the bus squinting and went to check in. The room clerk was a middle-aged man with a blank name tag. Foxx laughed at the joke, blinked, saw that it said "Gary." He blinked again, but he couldn't get the blank to come back.

Upstairs he shook a pill out for himself. It was a Placidyl, which was supposed to take the brightness of the blow and spread it around in his mind. Even distribution. He sat on the bed but couldn't think of why he was sitting there. He went next door and knocked at Tony's room. No answer. Maybe he was in the shower. He knocked at Yvette's room. Tony answered. "Well, hello there, young man," Foxx said, waggling his eyebrows.

"We're just talking," Tony said.

"Remember that a good conversation is give and take." He knocked on a third door, which turned out to be the janitor's supply closet, and then went back to his own room to sit on the bed again. Coincidence or someone else had pretuned the radio to a soul station, and he heard Stevie and then Curtis. "Brotherhood," he said out loud, because there were some cats he just couldn't consider competition. Now it was Jerry Butler singing "Only the Strong Survive." Was everything a message? Betty would laugh to think he was hearing signals in the songs. He laughed a little, but the laugh caught. It was the first time he had thought of Betty all day. He pushed himself off the bed with great effort and went to the window. It was a long way down to the ground. It was a long way up to the sky, too, but that looked like set design. "Don't you let them make you feel like a clown," the Ice Man sang. Foxx did a dance there at the window, a soft-shoe. "Just a little jig," he said.

Betty
December 1969

Betty scrubbed the dishes. On one of the plates, there was a food stain in the shape of a lake, and she worked it until it came off. When she was a child she used to get mad sometimes at her mother for being blind, because it meant that Betty had to do more chores. She remembered wishing that her mother wouldn't leave the plates dirty. Now, though, there was no one in the house except Betty herself. She had dirtied the dishes. She cleaned them.

Betty was the only one in the house. But Betty wasn't the only one inside herself. The baby was in there, growing by the day. She was so big that it was hard for her to get around: hard to stand up, hard to sit down, hard to lie down, hard to sleep and hard to shower. Eating was easy enough, so that's what Betty did. And the television wasn't out of the question either.

The telephone hung on the wall near the kitchen sink. It was a black phone, and it picked up grease easily: from hands, from faces, from the air. Betty didn't like the way it looked when it got greasy, so she was always cleaning it. Whenever it rang, it seemed she was in the middle of cleaning. She told Elena that it was like a genie's bottle, rub it and it grants your wish. Elena was on the other end of the phone much of the time, but she was also over at Betty's place. Betty's mama was on the phone, too, telling Betty how happy she was that she was going to have a grandson. She was sure it would be a boy. "Do you have a name yet?" she said.

"Yes, ma'am," said Betty. "My name is Betty."

Her mama loved that joke, no matter how many times Betty told it. Strangely, Robert never called while she was rubbing the phone. He called while she was watching candles. When she was done watching Carson, she liked to light the candles that were lined up on the bedside table. When the candle was lit, she plumped up a pillow behind her head and watched the flame weave and leap while she sang along to the radio. She imagined that she was singing to her baby, and she sang only baby songs. "It's not the way you smile that touched my heart," she sang. "It's not the way you kiss that tears me apart." "Love is hope girl, love is strength," she sang. "Here's someone standing right beside you who would go to any length." "Oh and I do declare, I want to see you with it," she sang. "Stretch out your arms, little boy; you're gonna get it." Those were the moments Robert picked to call. It was as if he sensed that she was at peace, and wanted to interfere.

When they were first dating, Robert had said nothing, only played records through the phone line. Now he started talking before she could even get the receiver up off the cradle. "Yeah, it's me," he said. "I'm here in Denver, looking out of the hotel window. What you doing? Sleeping? You want to fly out tomorrow and meet me here? Or maybe you can meet me down the line? Not the telephone line. The line of time. If it even is a line. Some people say it's a loop, you know. Betty? You there? Let me speak to my son."

"What if it's a girl?" Betty said.

"Won't be," he said.

On New Year's Eve, Elena had a party. She begged Betty to come, and Betty said she would, but both of them knew that it was politeness and nothing more. Betty napped in the afternoon and spent the evening by herself, watching the news on TV and drinking coffee from a mug so big it was like a bowl. She was alone, finally, but she was never alone anymore; she smiled sadly at a commercial for Playtex nursers. When the baby kicked, Betty kicked back, tapping the tip of her index finger against her belly. Where was Robert? She tried to remember but found that she couldn't find the energy to care. She dozed off on the couch watching *Then Came Bronson* and woke just in time to see the celebration from Times Square. Even the ball looked like a pregnant thing to her, a sister in arms. She talked to the baby, told him that it was a new year, his year, that he'd be along before he knew it. "Hey, hey, hey," she sang. "Baby, baby, try to find, hey, hey, hey, a little time and I'll make you mine."

Robert
March 1970

Foxx told Boris to go deal with the redhead, who was trying to do exactly what she said she wouldn't do: snap unauthorized photographs of the world's biggest rock star, captured backstage in all his white-leather-jacket, brown-leather-boots, spade-who-made-the-grade glory.

"Don't fucking hustle me out of here," she said. Boris put up his hands in a no-offense gesture, and then hustled her out of there.

"Let me get up and see you out," Foxx said. But sitting on the sofa in the dressing room, speaking into the tape recorder held under his nose by the *Rolling Stone* reporter, he couldn't really get up. There was a mirror on his lap and three lines of coke on the mirror. Plus there was the reporter's hand, which was resting on his thigh.

"What do you think about the new groups?" she said.

"Mostly nothing," he said. "But nothing is something, and we all need something. Structure your acceptance, baby."

"When will you have a new record?"

"Soon. It's going to be called *The Exploding Foxxes Inevitable.*" He had a different title every time they asked: *Gone With the Foxxes, Of Foxxes and Men, The Foxx Motor Company.* "But it will be all new, all the time. I won't be one of those cats who cashes in with a live set."

"There are songs recorded already?"

He stroked his chin in a theatrical manner. "There are songs, yes," he said. "They are recorded, yes." This was partly true. There was one song, "Kicking the Can," that they had played live for months, but he was still tinkering with the lyrics, absolutely sure only of the chorus: "Don't choose the fire / Or the frying pan / They say you can't / But can't is just kicking the can."

"Can I hear any of them?"

Foxx held up a finger, then got up and walked to the other end of the dressing room, which was small and had dingy yellow walls broken up by mirrors and washed-out watercolors of Parisian cafés. He picked up a reel of tape and came back to his chair. He pointed at it. "No," he said.

The reporter didn't laugh. "How about drugs?" she said.

"Help yourself."

"No." Now she laughed. "I mean, what about the people who say that the drugs are helping the music? Lennon said that they opened up his mind."

"Drugs have no sincerity. They just *operate*. They just *are*."

She seemed to like this answer, and she put her hand back on his thigh. She was two inches from pay dirt; in his excitement, he split the difference. He considered making her. But he had a son coming, and so he shifted away.

"Almost done," she said. "What do you think about race relations in this country?"

"Oh, man," he said. "I'm tired of playing spokesman. I just run this band."

"So are you apolitical?"

"Ain't no way, Renee. Black man goes down the street, he's political. That's the skin he's in. But it's more like I am where I am. I'm not delivering an address. Notes, not keynotes. Got it?"

Yvette and Tony came into the room. They were drinking out of a paper bag and laughing. That meant that Yvette was teasing Tony again. "I'll bet you're wondering why I called you all here today," Foxx said. The rest of the band shuffled in slowly: Lucas first, then Kevin, then Claude and Cheryl. What was going around? They were. *Wreckered* was on a turntable in the corner of the room. Foxx turned back to the reporter. "One last question."

She squinted at her note. "I just wanted to ask about the spirit of your band, whether it's changing as you get more fame."

"The spirit is still going strong," he said. "Peace, love, and everything, y'all." This was a lie. It had been a lie even before Fred Hampton got murdered, even before Altamont. He knew it the second he saw the sleeve of *Let It Bleed*, the cake atop the pizza atop the film can. It was sweet and it was salt, and it was everybody's fault. On the back, though, it was all fall down, and when he put the record on his turntable and heard the first skidding notes of "Gimme Shelter," he knew what had caused all this destruction. It was evil. He had the same fear for the Foxxes. There was so much frailty in them. Tony had once given an interview where he said that men in bands were like sailors at sea, either sad over what they had left behind or relieved that they could leave it there. Foxx thought he was wasting his eloquence. Far as he could tell, most cats in bands were nervous motherfuckers who threw up before the show, or angry motherfuckers who threw punches at their bandmates, or stupid motherfuckers who got in planes with drunken pilots or sad motherfuckers who went belly-up in their own swimming pools. "No time for games, Skip James," he said, and left the reporter standing there.

Out in the hall, a guard was trying to rough up Smorris. "Move on before you're moved on, mister."

"I'm *supposed* to be here," said Smorris.

"Let him go," said Foxx, coming forth.

The guard didn't. He held tightly to Smorris's sleeve and his face clouded. "Goddamn you. All of you…" He didn't say "niggers." He didn't say "hippies." He didn't say anything.

"Hey, baby," Foxx said. "What's the holdup? Let's get the gold up."

At the end of the corridor, Tony was waving at Foxx. "What is it?" Foxx called back. "We have a situation here."

"We have one here, too," Tony said. "Jerry is on the phone. He says he needs to talk to you."

"Now?"

"Right now," Tony said. He came closer. His face was tight. "Something about the label. They're going to do a new pressing of the record with an extra song."

"An extra what? What extra song?"

"Clary has it in his head that we should do a soul cover of 'Sugar Sugar.' He found a line in the contract about rereleases that gives him the right."

Foxx was down the hall in a minute. Kevin was holding the phone out. His face was grave. Foxx ripped the receiver out of his hand. "The fuck they are," he said into the phone.

"Congratulations," Jerry said. "You're a father." Behind Foxx, Kevin and Tony were laughing. Kevin lit a cigar and handed it to Foxx, who was so surprised he almost stuck the lit end into his mouth.

Betty
March 1970

She was in the cleaners when it happened. There was a skinny white kid by the front window who didn't look more than nineteen but he was talking on the phone like he was a lawyer, fast and low. "If we lose the appeal, we lose, but I want to lose on facts," he said. "Not the judge's prejudices."

That morning Betty had already waited in the garage with the mechanic while he felt under the hood of Robert's Fiat, stood on the front lawn and listened to the gardener complain about late payment, and spent a half hour with a realtor who wanted her to look at some new properties. She had only talked to Robert himself for ten curt minutes. "Sound check," he finally said, and she hung up without saying goodbye. And now the dry cleaner, a middle-aged British man who knew Robert only by the size of his checks, was explaining in an overly patient tone that the shirts wouldn't be ready by early afternoon. "Who exactly will be picking up Mr. Foxx's items?" he said. He said the name like he thought Robert was white.

"I will."

"And you are?"

"His wife," said Betty, irritated. Then something pulsed in her pelvis and she felt a warm trickle going down the insides of her thighs. "The mother of his child," she said.

She called Elena, who told her not to panic. "Just sit tight," she said. "I'll pick you up."

The doctor who greeted her at the hospital wasn't her normal doctor, and Betty didn't trust the way his mustache drooped over his top lip. But Elena made a big show of passing him a dollar bill. "Show my friend here a good time," she said. Elena and the doctor thought this was hilarious. Betty was beyond good cheer; her contractions had begun, and they were earthquakes within, rips in the terrain. "We're giving you gas," the doctor said, and she breathed deep and that was the last she remembered. She was thinking bigger thoughts, thoughts so big that she had to move far away from herself to see them in their entirety. There was a life moving inside of her, and soon it would be outside of her, and then she would be inside of it. There was a new being that was her and Robert, both and neither, living proof and paradox. Every once in a while she felt a tugging between her legs.

Where was Robert? She had lived so long with the question that it had become something familiar to her, and the prospect of an answer seemed distant. She tried to focus her mind to see him. She saw a hotel room, but it appeared empty. She saw a stage, but it was empty, too. She told the doctors to call Robert, and they said they had phoned his hotel already, and she didn't know for sure if she was making any noise at all, or if they were answering her. She was slipping into the folds of a deeper sleep.

When she woke up, the doctor and Elena were standing at her bedside, beaming. "Here you go," said the doctor, and handed her a bundle. She took it from him, certain that it couldn't be hers. It was a tiny raisin of a boy, barely visible in the blanket. His eyes fluttered open, and he twisted to one side, and he had her.

She named him Dewey, like Robert wanted; it was Miles Davis's middle name, which she hadn't known. Betty studied the baby's face, studied it in the hospital and in the car on the way home and in the bed where she pushed up on pillows and put the sleeping baby in the bassinet. Sometimes she couldn't find Robert in there anywhere. Other times he looked just like his father. When he was reaching for something, for example. That brought out the resemblance.

The phone rang that evening when she was watching TV and nursing Dewey. "A new release," Robert said. "Put him on the phone."

She laughed. "When are you coming home?"

"I'm at the airport now. We rescheduled Seattle and Portland. Family business. Be there before you know it."

"Oh," she said. She hoped she hadn't sounded disappointed.

"Gotta go," he said. "Time flies, and so do I."

Betty left the phone off the receiver. When the baby's lips moved to feed, she felt a streak of certainty go through her—certainty that this was her child, that she was his mother, that they were bound for life. When he was done, she lifted him to her shoulder, but not before pressing her lips to his forehead. "The very thought of you," she sang.

Robert
April 1970

Tony was living in the Sunset now, renting a corner place with a wide porch in the front and an orange tree in the back. He answered the door with a beer in his hand. Foxx checked his watch: ten in the morning.

"Delivery," Foxx said.

"But I didn't order a headache," Tony said. He didn't invite Foxx in. Instead he came out and sat on the floor of the porch. There was a glass on a low table and he poured a few inches of beer into it and offered it to Foxx.

"Is this the good stuff?" Foxx said.

"I think it's a '67," Tony said. "It's been in my cellar. So what brings you out to where the regular people live?"

"Man, you're hardly regular. You ready for Monday?"

"New York? I thought Jerry was going with you."

"He is. But you too, right?"

"Jerry can handle it. What else is a manager for?"

"I'm not worried about that. If there are things that need saying, he'll say them. But it's a money and contract trip. That's your bread and butter. Plus, I thought it would be fun to spend a few extra days out East. Catch some bands, maybe. I'm feeling in need of some inspiration."

"I can't make the trip," Tony said.

"You're kidding me."

"I'm not," Tony said. "I need to be in town next week."

"For what?"

Tony said nothing, but on cue, the front door opened and Yvette walked out. She was wearing only panties and a denim shirt of Tony's. "Hi," she said. "I was thinking of making some eggs. Anyone interested?"

"That would be nice," Foxx said. He saw Tony's face fall. "Just joking. I'm about to be on my way."

"When you get back from New York, let's get together and talk about the meeting," Tony said. His tone was all business. Foxx was on Stanyan before he realized that he was still holding Tony's glass.

On the plane, Foxx tried to explain to Jerry why he was worried. He was trying to be a father, trying to be a husband, trying to be a friend, but the combined effort was slowing him down, and other brothers were coming up on him fast, even passing him on the inside. Take Miles Davis. Foxx had called the cat, waited on the line like a motherfucking customer while he heard the phone bumping and dragging. "Yeah," Miles said, rasping like oxygen was ground-up glass. "Let's get together and hang." But they didn't hang. Foxx called again a few weeks later. "Come on over," said Miles the next time he called, but he didn't say where, and then he sped right on past Foxx with *Bitches Brew*. James Brown was on the move too, with "The Grunt," which had that 5-2-2 dynamite where all the horns hit hard at the same exact time. So what was left for him? The songs that were in his head were light and sunny, bits of '69 that he hadn't yet flushed away. As soon as he got something down on tape, he lifted it off again; he was erasing more music in a week than most acts made in a month.

"You're worrying too much," Jerry said. "Turn doesn't care what kind of album it's going to be, not at this point. You just have to tell them that they'll get their record, when they'll get it, and how much they'll have to pay to get it. That's all that matters at this meeting, because that's all that matters to Hugh Clary."

But Clary wasn't there. That meant that Bruce Dunn was in charge, and it also meant that he had his own Dunn at his side, some new kid named Monroe Stringer who was wearing a black turtleneck and a two-day growth of beard. Foxx had hopes for the kid, and he addressed his opening remarks to him. "So we're still riding high with this record," he said. "We're still feeling it. And the touring is taking everything the band has got. I'd like to give the group a pass for the summer and record again in September. Plus, I have a new single on my own label." Stringer looked up dully.

"He means the baby," Jerry said.

Dunn arranged his hands in a cage in front of him and brought his palms together. "We understand the need for time off, of course. It regenerates you."

"That's what they say," Foxx said. "I'm the voice of a regeneration."

"But we do want to discuss the possibility of a platform that would include new material."

"English, baby," Foxx said. "I don't speak suit."

"Fine," Dunn said. "We want a greatest hits collection with an extra song or two." Jerry began to object. "We know that this isn't part of the existing contract, but we believe that the time is right."

"There are reasons Robert doesn't want to do that," said Jerry. "It's not just stubbornness. He believes that it signals a point in a career when inspiration is flagging."

"Plus," Foxx said, "every record I make is a greatest hits. You can get rich just collecting the wrappers."

"Other labels have had great success with collections."

"Who? Motown? They punch out singles like cars. Does it seem like that's what I'm doing?" Not to mention that these days Motown was doing him, for cheaper. He heard pieces of himself in the Temptations, in Marvin Gaye—a tricky horn figure here, a guitar line there. Then in April, he watched Michael Jackson come out, all candy coating and short pants, and rob him blind. He took the Foxxes' music right out from under them, and ended up over them on the charts. One bit of black magic deserves another, so Foxx put a curse on that little boy. He swished some strong coffee around in his mouth and pronounced it voodoo soup. Shango shango, give him great unhappiness in later life.

"Robert," said Dunn. He had taken Clary's habit of using Foxx's first name. Like everything else, it seemed too big on him. "We've heard this new song of yours, 'Kick the Can,' and we think it's terrific."

"Kicking the Can," Foxx said. "And it is terrific."

"But we don't want to sell it as a single only. You know how the LP business is going. It's going up."

"You'll get that album," Foxx said. "I promised, didn't I? My word is my band."

"It'll be six more months, tops," Jerry said. "Let's leave it there for now, and get on with the rest of the business."

Jerry and Dunn pulled out folders and got into the numbers. Foxx watched Stringer for a little while, but it was like watching a clock face with a little beard where the six should have been. He just ticked along, taking in what Dunn and Jerry said, never leaping ahead, never turning back. The regularity of it got to be too much for Foxx, and he looked at the pictures on the wall instead. Turn had other artists, too. Some of them were coming up fast and some were going down slow. But none of them was giving serious thought to doing away with gravity altogether. Under the table he clicked his heels together. He wanted to get home. He wanted to see Betty and Dewey. He wanted to find out what was happening with Tony and Yvette. Most of all, he wanted to hear himself. One of the songs that was swimming around inside him would turn out to be perfect when mounted, a piece of his soul that he managed to capture on tape. When that happened, the rest of it would happen, no matter if he sold a million records or a dozen. And then they'd take down the picture of him in Turn's office and put up in its place a picture of the sun—or better yet, a window so that everyone could see through to the sky and wonder about where, and if, it ended.

Betty
July 1970

Betty heard a baby laughing, and then a man. She woke up and squinted against the light. The sound was strangely doubled, at once distant and close.

Curious, she walked down the hall.

Robert was in his studio, with Dewey on his lap, holding a microphone up to his son's face and fiddling with an expensive-looking piece of equipment.

"Go on," Robert said to Dewey. "Laugh for me one more time." Robert liked to wake up early just to hold his son. He said that Dewey's arms around his neck felt just like love. "You want me to tell you a joke? Here's one: Why wouldn't your Uncle Lucas take aspirin when he had a headache? Because he was too proud to pick out the cotton." Both of them were smiling, and they were showing off their common feature—the way their eyes could light up a room.

Standing there in the doorway, Betty felt like a spy. She shifted her weight but no one seemed to notice. She cleared her throat. Robert looked up first. "Hey, mama." He turned to Dewey. "Should we show her what we're doing?"

"Yes," she said. "You should." She tried to sound disapproving, but the words came out happy.

Robert talked in Dewey's voice. "Daddy's showing me how to use a four-track. He's laughing on two tracks and I'm laughing on the other two." Then he talked in his own voice. "Sing what you heard, baby bird."

Betty listened to the tape. She heard Robert's deep laugh and Dewey's giggle, and they were slowed down and sped up just enough that they had a logic to them. "I'm gonna use that as a percussion track on the new record," he said.

"You gonna be done soon? I'm going to go down and start making breakfast."

"I've been feeding the little man already." He pointed behind Dewey, where Betty saw a jar of baby food with a spoon planted in it.

"I don't think he likes that kind," she said.

"Funny you should say that," he said. "Watch this." He put the spoon in Dewey's mouth. Dewey swelled up his cheeks and spit the food all over Robert. Then he started laughing.

"That baby is an extremist. When he's spittin' out his applesauce, he's spittin' out the world." Dewey was still laughing. "Keep on with that, little man. Let me get that on tape."

Betty backed out of the room. The scene made her warm and cold at the same time. Was it that easy for Robert to bring Dewey around? He was creating with what she had created. She wasn't the first woman to feel this way, and she knew she wouldn't be the last, but there was no solidarity she could find, not at the moment. She remembered the ball over Times Square, and how soundly she had slept that night when there was no one else around for miles. She remembered afternoons when she was a little girl, sitting quietly on the couch while her mama sat in a chair. They were alone together. Betty loved her mama for that. Now she needed to get away, but she had nowhere to go. She went back to the bedroom to practice the yoga that Elena had been teaching her. Mountain, Lunge, Plank, Cobra. It was poetry written with the body.

Robert
August 1970

Foxx had a girl to dress him. Amy. He had another Amy to do his hair, and a third to put makeup on his face. He had Perry, who built the sets, and Lenny, who ran the army of techs. He had Smorris for driving, and Boris for carrying his money, and Dr. Phil for helping him to drop it. Penny, a cute brunette who worked for the label's publicity department, joked that he should hire someone to hold his cock in the bathroom. "Open auditions," he said. "Set 'em up."

Between razor strokes he smoked, dragging on a joint he left humming in an ashtray on the bathroom counter. And while he smoked, he thought about Hamlet. That's what he was reading now. He had started it for Tony's sake, a strange motive and one he couldn't reveal, but it was the truth. The episode with Yvette had put some distance between Foxx and Tony, and he wanted to close the gap. He got stuck at the start, the part where Hamlet wanders out into the woods and sees his father's ghost. Revenge, and betrayal, and poison in the ear. He flicked his own lobe. It was a good speech, but it went on longer than "In-A-Gadda-Da-Vida." It picked up speed after that, especially when Hamlet walked in on Ophelia with his shit all undone. Foxx liked reading it, mainly because he was guessing things before they happened. Like the way he knew that Hamlet was going to drop a blade into his uncle. The higher he got, the more of the stories he could see. He rose like smoke. It was altitude, man. All altitude.

He left a beard behind when he shaved, a goat and a soul patch. He left wide sideburns. He wiped the shaving cream off his jawbone and went.

The book was only part of his new routine. All summer long he had done what he said he would do: stay at home, keep his wife and child close by, keep the band at arm's length. They didn't play. They didn't record. When he met with Tony, he tried not to talk about business or the new act on the radio he had to suffer or abide. Of course he didn't talk about Yvette either, but that was mostly out of concern for Tony; he couldn't bear the thought of a sad tale. Slowly, the balance began to flow back into Foxx's life. He woke up in the mornings without the nagging pains in his shoulders and neck that had plagued him since *Get the Picture*. He reached the evening without the dull headaches that he assumed would be his companion until the end of his days. Sometimes he dreamt that rain would come along and cool things down, and rain came along and cooled things down.

This weekend was an exception. Some L.A. promoters were putting on a big charity event at the Hollywood Bowl for the first-year anniversary of Woodstock. The Foxxes were invited despite that, jammed between the Who and the Guess Who. The MC for the event tapped the microphone and cleared his throat. "Tonight," he said, "history is being made." He didn't say how, and the crowd didn't seem to care. King Kong went on before the Who, and they were loud enough, but the opening notes of "It's a Boy" wiped them from memory. Townshend's guitar was so loud that Foxx just pointed at Tony and gave a thumbs-up. He wondered if Tony was remembering what he was remembering, the way they had driven West from Boston gladdening every time a Who song came on the radio. Kevin dosed himself with liquid courage and wondered out loud if he might be able to borrow one of Keith's sticks. Foxx put his thumb down. There were times to reminisce, and then there were times to get his own troops ready. "No need to borrow," Foxx said. "From what I can hear, it seems to be doing about the same as any other motherfucking stick."

In the limo afterward Foxx did a line off a pocket mirror. It was his first line in about a month, but he deserved it. He closed his eyes and found that he could still see everything—the streets in front of the driver, the bicyclist to the left, the level of scotch sloshing in the bottle in the car-bar.

The concert hadn't gone well. Everyone else there would disagree. They had played the hits, played them hard. But it felt like he was singing through someone else's mouth. And then there was the deal they struck afterward: a small tour at the end of the summer, a half dozen dates as headliners. The money was good—Jerry and Tony had negotiated a big number—but Foxx had hoped against this. He had dreamed of a different music, something that drove people back inside themselves and pulled them out all at the same time. And now Tony had gone and gotten them four more opportunities to reach into the same old bag of tricks.

That night, back in San Francisco, he scooped up Dewey and took him into the studio. Dewey sat on his lap while he sat at the board, thinking. He had thought new blood would change everything, and for a little while it did. But now he saw things falling away even in the baby. "Make sure tomorrow isn't just a lazy today," he said.

The first of the newly booked dates was in Milwaukee. Foxx and Lucas took a car down to the arena early. There wasn't any reason to be there early, but there wasn't any reason to be anywhere else either—the weather was bad and the mood followed suit. Yvette and Tony weren't there but Kevin was, getting smothered in the corner of the dressing room by a big blonde who looked as if she'd come straight from the funny papers. He introduced her as Mary, although he could have been saying almost anything, since he had a nipple the size of one of his thumbs in his mouth.

"Do you ever think that all this shit just gets in the way?" Foxx asked Lucas.

"Every day," said Lucas. "In every way. It keeps you from knowing yourself."

"I ain't so interested in that," Foxx said. "That's too many people to meet, and I'm the shy type. But I'm trying hard to find some way to get us back to the music. And not the same music. I'm trying to get us back to something that wasn't there before."

"I know what you mean," said Lucas. "But the spirit ain't always in what's new."

"Uh-oh," said Foxx. "Is this Jesus coming up on tiptoes now?" Lucas had been back at the Bible with greater frequency ever since a girl on the road had told him she was pregnant. It turned out to be a lie, but the experience had left him grasping for God.

"'I remembered my songs in the night,'" said Lucas. "'My heart mused and my spirit inquired.'" Do you know where that's from?"

" 'I keep falling, but what can I do. I'm too weak to fight.' You know where that's from?" Lucas ignored him. "I'm just saying that it's never just saying. Remember when Martha Reeves put out 'I Should Be Proud'? Weepy little song, her man's over in Nam, dies there, brown bread, she's under the hair dryer when the telegram comes. Even that was too much. Radio stations pulled it. It wasn't a fantasy, cuz. It was true, is true every day."

"I thought you didn't like protestors."

"I don't. But a song isn't a protestor. Protestors stand in one place or march. A song moves in all directions at once."

"And yet, think not that I am come to send peace on earth: I came not to send peace, but a sword."

Foxx held up a single finger, like he was counting reasons not to get mad and couldn't think of many. "It's not about the war, even. Not really. It's about what Martha Reeves can or can't say, or Edwin Starr, or why people need to put other people in groups. It's about why there are schools and camps: Motown over here, Stax over there. What's in the middle? What's around the edges? Everybody tries to make the world assume a pleasing shape. But it's the shape it is."

"You sound confused."

"You're goddamned right I'm confused. That's what helps me see so clearly."

"But God is not the author of confusion."

Foxx stubbed out his joint. No use talking with a man who stood so closely behind God. How were you going to get to him through that? Plus, Yvette and Tony had arrived, hand in hand. They were still at it, though rather than Tony keeping Yvette clean, she was getting him down in the stuff: weed, pep, a little junk. "You think you need to be with that?" he asked Tony, but Tony took it the wrong way, thought that Foxx was criticizing Yvette, and that was the end of the discussion.

The band shuffled onstage. The crowd cheered. Foxx called for "Mixing Board" but told Tony, Cheryl, and Claude to lay off, and asked Kevin and Lucas to carry the weight on their own. Then he started rapping sideways on the motherfucker. He talked about the doubts he had been having, hummed snatches of melody. "What's beautiful in morning," he sang, "at night might end in blood. Get ready to get ready for the flood."

"Put the Foxx in the box," he sang, "and put the locks on the box."

"I can feel it in the night," he sang. "And what you're doing just ain't right."

The cheering died down, although he noticed that the few people still screaming were screaming louder than ever.

The next night was Kansas City, and he did the same thing: jumped off "Wednesday Ain't So Bad" halfway through the chorus and put in new words. "He was sent in to San Quentin," he sang, "for a dozen years or more / On the corner I tried to warn her not to go down to the store." "To the store," Yvette echoed, sweet as peach syrup. In Cleveland he wrote a little Kent State rap. In Chicago it was about the 1968 convention. New wounds, old wounds—what did it matter as long as they bled?

At first the band complained about the changes. But then he had a meeting and asked them if they were content to play "She's So Bad She's Good" in a hall of mirrors, each one looking exactly the same, none of them real. "So if I have a new fill I want to try, I should just do it?" said Tony. Foxx made a gun with his hand and shot it. Copa-motherfucking-cetic.

The critics got it, except for the ones who didn't. *Rolling Stone* dubbed him "The Rapper," after that Jaggerz hit. That was fine with Foxx. He liked it better than "The Preacher of Soul," which was how he was introduced in Denver. "I ain't no preacher, 'cause a preacher's a teacher," he said during a particularly unrecognizable version of "Wednesday Ain't So Bad." "I'm just disrupting the church with a cavity search."

The final date was in Phoenix. "Rise from the ashes," he said. "Fly from the fire. The prize in the sky can learn to inspire." When he returned home, he went to the studio and laid down a song called "Rap." It was a long, low groove, like "King Heroin" or "Public Enemy No. 1," with lots of talk over the top. He started with lyrics that he had used in concert, but he kept changing them to fit in the headlines. "New York chicks / With justice sticks," he sang. "Meet me in Saint Louis, Huey." The studio was better than the stage—cleaner and cooler, better food and better drugs—but it was also worse. With four walls around him, he could feel the movement but he couldn't be sure of the direction, if it he was flying to the moon or working in a coal mine.

"These foolish things," he sang, "remind me of me."

Betty
September 1970

Betty did not rush to be by her mother's side because her mother told her that the doctors were fools. She pronounced it with a push, *foo-ools*, and whinnied the end like a horse to make Betty laugh. But then a week later she spoke to Charlotte, and Charlotte said that it was more serious. "She has something wrong with her lungs,"

Charlotte said. "They have to operate, and either she'll be fine or she won't. I know that she's telling you not to worry, but sometimes I see a look in her eye and I know she wants you here." That was enough for Betty. She bought tickets to Chicago.

"When you come back, I might not be here anymore," said Robert. He said it like a soap-opera character, the woman who is telling her no-good husband that she's not going to be his doormat any longer. But she knew what he meant, because he had been saying it for months. He wanted to move down to Los Angeles. He had his eye on a house that was owned by an actor who had made his money in a series of spy films. "Motown went there," Robert said.

"So what?" she said.

"Keep your friends close and your enemies closer."

She had to admit that the house was beautiful: some rooms seemed powerful and cavernous, others like monks' cells. There was even a private screening room that Robert wanted to convert into his recording studio. All he was waiting on was the money. There was plenty flowing in from *Wreckered*, but plenty flowing out, too— salaries for the band and the crew, Jerry's commission, costumes, transportation, crew, especially the studio time that was leaking them from black to red. "We're in the hole for the next record already," Robert said, "and we haven't even started. That's why I need a real home studio, so there's nothing to pay except the cost of being the boss. You know what I'm saying?"

"I know," said Betty. This was the tenth time she had heard the story, at least, and she needed to concentrate on packing. Three dresses or four? How many pairs of shoes? "Will you help me pick out which skirts to take?"

"Can't believe you're going," he said. "Leaving me home alone." But Robert wasn't home at all. The small August tour had filled arenas, and Jerry had convinced Robert to reconsider his don't-call-for-fall rule. You never know when America's going to stop asking for you, he said. So while America is asking, you best be answering. Now they were heading out for five more weeks. "We'll be in Chicago in early October," said Robert. "I'll get to meet your mama. And maybe I'll even take you out on a date." Then he launched into a gospel-shout rendition of "Surrey with the Fringe on Top."

"If that's not enough to drive me out of town," she said, "I don't know what is."

"Ooo," he said, clutching his heart. "You shot me."

Later that evening, Dewey was standing next to the table, holding himself upright on the seat of a chair, when his grip slipped, and he flopped backward with a puff of breath, landing face to face with a stuffed dog. "Woof," he said. Betty scooped him up, laughing, and took him into the next room to tell Robert. "Your son..." she started to say, but stopped. Robert's eyes poisoned the room.

"What's the matter with you?" she said.

"Not a fucking thing."

"Okay," she said. "I'll go."

He looked up, his eyes apologizing, but his mouth still set hard. "I'm just trying to think my way through this new song," he said. "You never know which one will be the one."

Though Betty left Los Angeles on a brilliant blue day, she landed in Chicago through a layer of haze. She buttoned her jacket around her neck and did two extra wraps of the scarf around Dewey's head. He had been an angel on the plane, quiet except for the occasional burble or laugh, happy to grab the stewardess's finger in his fist. Now he was starting to fray, though.

She took a taxicab from O'Hare down to the South Side, amazed at her extravagance. Dewey had taken her suggestion and was sleeping.

The streets started to look familiar, then started to be familiar, and then she was turning down her block. Her cousin Charlotte was outside of the house when the cab pulled up. "Well, well, well," she said, standing. "If it isn't the queen of England." She stepped forward to hug Betty, and Betty saw that her belly was stretched out.

"Again?" she said.

"Again," she said. "This time with Lonnie again. I think we're going to stick it out."

"Well, that's cool," said Betty.

"Aren't you going to introduce me?" said Charlotte, reaching to touch the bundle.

"Sure thing," Betty said. "Dewey, this is your cousin Charlotte."

"Aren't I his aunt?" said Charlotte.

"I don't think so," said Betty. "If you were my sister, you would be."

"I'm not your sister?"

"Have it your way," said Betty. "Dewey, this is your aunt Charlotte."

"Give him over," said Charlotte. She took Dewey from Betty. "I think he needs burping," she said.

"He hasn't eaten in a little while."

"No, but I can tell," she said. In a second she had him up on her shoulder. And sure enough, he needed burping. "When you get through three or four of these things," said Charlotte, "you become a kind of genius. You can tell just by looking. You'll see." Dewey gurgled in assent.

If Charlotte had one kind of magic, Betty's mother had another. Betty heard the music of rearrangement when she knocked, the bent note of a chair creaking, the shuffle-beat of feet coming across the floor. Charlotte had prepared her: "She looks older than when you saw her last." But that's where the magic came in: the woman who answered was her mother exactly, not a wrinkle more, not a hair grayer. "You look good," Betty said.

"I told you what those doctors were, didn't I? *Foo-ools*." She stepped back so Betty could come through the door. "Hold on," she said. "I smell baby."

"I'm going to hold him up so he can kiss you," said Betty.

"You must be Dewey," her mother said. "Nice to meet you. You know what's funny, Dewey? You look just like your grandfather."

The first week in Chicago was all bright sunshine slanting in and the spur of coffee in her nose. She and Dewey bundled up and walked through the park near the house. Charlotte introduced them to the army—that was what Betty's mama called Charlotte's sons—and told the army to play nice with their cousin. "I'll make sure," said James, who was the general at six. Lonnie, the father of the youngest boy and the one to come, was as kind a man as Betty could have hoped for her cousin. "I'm lucky to have her," he said. "And I haven't always been lucky." He worked as a janitor in the local high school, and he was taking night classes in mathematics. "I got started while I was up at Joliet," he said. "Lots of time to count."

As the days went on, Betty saw what Charlotte had meant about her mother. She was older, slower. Her legs, especially, seemed to defy her; joints would misbehave at odd moments, and she would have to struggle to regain her balance. But her mind was as sharp, and she still knew how to work a room. "It's cold," she said. "Why don't you pop that baby of yours in the oven?" Another time she got on the telephone and started calling around for prices on a new color TV. "I'm sick of this old black-and-white set," she said to Betty, adding in a stage whisper, "It *is* a black-and-white, isn't it?" At night she told the children stories. "You know when they went to the moon last year?" she said. "I was in the ship."

"No you weren't," said James.

"Are you calling your grandma a liar?" Betty's mama said. "I was right there, in the bottom of the spaceship. I got out onto the moon, and it was the strangest thing. When I was up there, on the moon, I could see. See everything. The mountains and the rivers and the oceans. I ran all around up there, looking into every corner. Then the astronauts called me and said it was time to go back. I got back here, and I was blind as a bat again."

"Let's go to the moon so you can see me," said James.

"We'll go tomorrow," Betty's mama said.

One night, Charlotte and Betty took Betty's mama for a walk down the street. The night was cleanly cold, and on the way back they sat on a neighbor's stoop. "You know what I miss?" Betty's mother said. "I miss hearing you sing."

"I still sing," Betty said.

"Maybe so," her mother said. "But I haven't heard much of it in years."

"Yeah," Charlotte said. "Do you remember how you used to stand in the bathroom for hours and make yourself into a radio star? Instead of becoming one, you went and married one."

"And now," Betty's mother continued, "you probably got it in your head that a song ain't a song unless it's on record. But I'm blind, girl. I can't tell the difference. Sing away." So Betty did. The next day, while Dewey ate breakfast, she sang "A Natural Man" and "Smackwater Jack," "You Keep Me Hanging On" and "Hey Jude." She sang loud enough that her mama, who was in her recliner in the other room, could hear her.

Then the month was halfway gone. Betty knew this because Robert was in town. She had pulled up to her mama's door in a taxicab; he did her one better, gliding up in a gleaming ivory limousine, letting Smorris—in a top hat—open the door and stepping out as if he was the morning sun. He was wearing purple leather boots, a red coat, and oversize yellow glasses. Betty watched him from the second-story window. He didn't look up, just checked his reflection in the limo window. James was running out to play with the other boys, but the sight of Robert stopped him in his tracks. "Who you, little man?" Robert said. James mumbled his name. "Well, I'm looking for pretty Miss Betty. You know where I might find her?" James nodded. "You want to go get her for me?" James nodded again. His eyes were the size of apples.

"I'm up here," said Betty. By now the street traffic was starting to clot with people who knew who Robert was and people who had no idea. "I'm coming down to get you." By the time she got downstairs, Robert was already trapped in the midst of the thickening crowd, signing autographs. "Come see the show tomorrow night," he said. "My driver has some tickets for y'all." That distracted the throng for a minute, and he squirted through to Betty. "Hey, baby," he said. "All of a sudden this trip makes sense."

Upstairs, he shook hands with a dumbly grinning Charlotte and a speechless Lonnie. Then he kissed Betty's mama. "You're even prettier than I thought. If Betty looks half this good when she's your age, I don't know what I'll do with myself."

"Go on, now," Betty's mama said. "You talk that sweet all the time and you'll get cavities."

That night, Robert took off his glasses and his jacket. After dinner, he put Dewey on one knee and James on the other. "You're big, little man," he said. Then he leaned out the window and told Smorris to bring up his guitar. "You want me to play something?" he asked James. "Okay. But tomorrow night I have to do all my own songs. So tonight I'll do something even better." He twisted a chair sideways and strummed out the opening chords to "What'd I Say." "Miz Cobham," he said, killing the chord with his right hand, "do you mind if it ain't church music?"

"You see any pews?" Betty's mother said. "I don't."

He laughed. "I see the girl with the red dress on." He taught James to do the "hey" and the "ho."

They ate ice cream out of coffee mugs. Then he and Betty went to the spare room. "You want to come back to the hotel?" he said.

"No."

"You inviting me to stay?" he said.

She kissed him, and the pants and the boots came off, too, along with the brocaded silk shirt. In nothing but plain white boxers, Robert leaned out of the front window to send Smorris back to the hotel. He curled up next to her in bed, one arm stretched across Dewey.

"I love how you are here," she said as they lay awake in the dark. "You're so different than in California."

"You know what I am?" he said.

"No."

"I'm mercurial."

"You're mercurial?"

"That's right. Characterized by rapid and unpredictable changeableness of mood."

"You been reading the dictionary?"

"And not just. 'Music for a time does change my nature.' That's Shakespeare. You ever heard of him? Tall cat, good with a knife. I think he's from Denver."

"You're a strange person," she said.

"Please," he said. "Mercurial."

The next morning, Dewey was coughing, and Robert kissed him on the forehead. "You best stay with him tonight," he told Betty. "Don't worry about coming out to the show." Lonnie and Charlotte went instead, and came back with the wide eyes of converts.

"He couldn't hang around with us afterward for too long," said Charlotte.

"Baby, you know he's busy," said Lonnie, as if he had known him for years.

Robert's car pulled up around one in the morning. He stood on the sidewalk and stage-whispered "pebble, pebble" at Betty's window. She leaned out and put a finger to her lips. "Quiet. The baby will wake up."

"Come down here and let me in."

She did. "Much thanks, m'lady" he said, taking her hand and kissing it. "Can we proceed into the residence now?" She could tell he was high from the way he articulated everything so precisely. Upstairs he tried to climb on top of her, but she pushed him off, playfully, she thought. "What the fuck are you doing?" he said. "You know how a man feels when he's denied the company of his wife?"

"There are other people to think about," she said.

"That's where you're wrong," he said.

"How did the show go?" He didn't answer her. "Don't be mad," she said. "I just feel weird in my mama's house." Still nothing. He was asleep. The next morning, the car was back to get him before breakfast.

Robert
January 1971

Foxx missed his family. He wanted them around because they reminded him not to slip or slide. But he also missed them like a missed connection. The weekend Betty came back home to pack up the house, he was in New York doing radio spots. And when he got back to San Francisco, she was gone again to Chicago to see her mama, who had taken a turn for the worse. She didn't ask him to come along. He would have said no, that he wanted to but couldn't, but she didn't even ask. On Dewey's birthday Foxx made sure his present got delivered: a miniature black leather tour jacket and miniature black leather boots that he had custom-made in Nashville. He made sure he was at a phone when he knew they'd be there, getting ready for dinner. Betty's mother answered. "Hello," she said, and then some other things he didn't register. Jokes, maybe, but he wasn't in the mood.

"My son there?" he said, trying to keep his voice light.

"Dawa," said Dewey.

"You trying to say your own name?" Foxx said. "It's Dewey Franklin Foxx. Big name for a little boy." The next weekend, Betty came home again, but he was down in L.A., looking at the house. And then he had to fly straight to London, where the Foxxes were co-headlining a benefit. Foxx was supposed to meet Eric Clapton, but he didn't show up right away, and Foxx got sidetracked by a woman named Marie who insisted she was royalty. "You the queen?" he said.

"Of course not," she said. "I'm a duchess."

"What a coincidence," he said. "I'm the Duke of Earl."

When she laughed, her breath whistled through the gap between her two front teeth. Foxx noticed this only in time; at first he was more concerned with the bag of white powder in Marie's hand, and the wisps of reddish hair under her porcelain arms.

After they did a few lines, he forgot all about Clapton and followed her home, to a mansion on a hill above the Thames. She had lace curtains that were unlike any curtains he had seen, with lacework that showed pictures of cherubs and harps. They fucked for four hours in the canopy bed. Her pussy was shaved to the shape of a diamond. He came once and was starting to get going a second time when she produced a cigar box from her bedside table. "Cubans?" he asked. But when she opened the box, it had no cigars in it. Instead there was a syringe, and a spoon, and a small gas lamp.

She set up the lamp on the side table, lit it, and sterilized the needle over the flame. Then she shook some of the white powder from the bag into the spoon. It looked like sugar. Her hand was trembling as she lifted the spoon to the flame. "Start fucking me from behind," she said. He did, and she drew the liquid through the needle into the syringe. Then, gripping the spike in her right hand, she banged herself in the vein of her left arm. After a few seconds, her head drooped and Foxx felt something loosen inside her. He stayed up after she dozed off, watching her stomach rise and fall. Beyond her, on the table, the point of the needle glowed in candlelight.

In the morning, Foxx took a walk in the garden, which was so perfectly arranged that he couldn't keep himself from trampling a flower or two. A distinguished older gentleman materialized from nowhere. "Sir," he said, "please do not destroy the flowerbeds." He seemed to be in a great deal of distress.

"Who you?" said Foxx. "Marie's father?"

"No," said the man, in even greater distress now. "I am house staff."

Foxx howled. "Lady Luck wishes me to have the run of the place." But Lady Luck didn't want anything except another four hours with him under the canopy.

After England, something happened to Kevin. Lucas said that he was grieving for his father, who had died while they were abroad, but Foxx knew it was something more than that. Fundamentally, Kevin had gone wrong. The appealing things in him had scattered and left a hard core, like a rock in rice. In Saint Louis he knocked Tony down during a dressing-room dispute, and did it again in Pittsburgh. And he was shooting up more than ever: From arm to leg, there were marks on him like the tiny crosses that show a ship's progress across a map.

The worst came in Philadelphia. Foxx was sitting on the toilet with the door cracked open, reading the newspaper headlines out loud. "Jesus," he said. "Nixon's trying to fuck us for his Minutemen." If he leaned one way, he could see Tony and Yvette on the couch; Tony was tickling her back and the base of her neck while she absently stroked the bone of her own wrist. If he leaned the other way, he could see Claude and Cheryl, their two sets of headphones plugged into the same stereo and their music leaking—it was Beethoven again. Maybe there was too much love in the room, and it was divine balance that brought Kevin in right at that moment. He heard the door open, and Kevin came into the room. "Ay, mates," said Kevin. He had picked up the accent in England and some days he wouldn't put it down. "I said, 'Ay, mates.'"

"We heard you," said Tony.

"Would be nice to show a little respect, then, instead of fucking the band whore."

"Please," said Yvette. This was her belle voice, the one that begged for delicacy and usually got it. But Kevin was halfway down the fuse already. "I can't sit idly by and watch this. After all, I'm a married man," he said, preposterously, holding up the hand with the ring that had, days before, dented the cheek of a girl in Milwaukee.

"Go away," said Tony.

"Go away? You can't fucking tell me to go away. I'm here forever. You go away!" Kevin's accent was gone now. Foxx saw his shoulders knotting under his shirt.

"Hey," said Foxx. He pushed the door open. "Kevin," he said. "Cut it the fuck out."

At that moment, Lucas entered the room. His instinct told him that she needed protection, and so he went immediately toward Yvette and stood in front of her. That's when Kevin decided to rush right at them. Later, Foxx thought that some nasty shit must have been running through his head. Why else would he have tried for Lucas—Lucas, a man, a *mountain*? Lucas knocked Kevin back three steps without even the slightest effort. Kevin's lip was bleeding, but he wiped it off and gave Lucas a crazed smile, the red smear on his cheek like lipstick. "And a good day to you, too, sir," he said.

"Go on," said Lucas. "Get." He wasn't smiling, and the room was suddenly freezing.

Foxx woke up that night with a stomachache. He went down to Tony's room and knocked until Tony came to the door. "I'm going down to the bar," he said. "Come sit with me." Behind Tony he could see Yvette, dark against the sheets.

Downstairs, Foxx flirted with the barmaid, a pretty blonde with owlish glasses. "That Kevin," Foxx said. "He's so fucked up he doesn't know which way to turn."

"What if he had come back at Lucas?" said Tony.

"That would have been the end," said Foxx. "Lucas would have hit him so hard it'd still be happening."

Tony rotated his drink on the bar. "You know," Tony said, "I have a question for you."

"Shoot."

"Do you miss your family? I mean, you have a baby now."

"He's a man," said Foxx. "Little, but a man."

"Do you ever just want to cash this all in and spend your time being his daddy? Being Betty's husband?"

"Naw, man."

"Really? This all doesn't seem hollow to you sometimes? I mean, when we started this, did you think it would go forever? What happens next?"

This was the old Tony, the one who used to ask him questions until he could feel the grill marks. Foxx reached for some peanuts. "You got what we are?" he said finally. "We're superstars. You know what that means?"

"I think I know what you think it means. But there has to be a life after this."

"Why? Even if there is, this is the life before the life after this."

"I forgot how much you like to talk in riddles."

"Riddle me this," Foxx said. "Why are you so worried all of a sudden? You thinking of settling down? Cutting out? Thinking of a change?"

"I don't know," Tony said.

"You don't know, or you don't know because you know?"

"I don't know."

"Tony," Foxx said. He tried to say the name like he would have said it in '67 or '68, clean, unloaded. "If you decide to do that, we should probably have a talk."

Tony laughed. "What are we having now? Meditation?"

"All I'm saying is that if you're serious, let me be serious with you."

Tony pushed his chair back and stood up. "I think I'm going to go upstairs and get some shut-eye," he said.

"Okay," Foxx said. "I think I'm going to go upstairs and sleep with one eye open."

When the tour went through New York, Foxx booked them into the Record Plant and tried to get some new tracks started. But after three hours, Yvette still hadn't shown. "Fuck," said Foxx, but then he saw Tony's expression. "It's no thing," he said, and canceled the session. Later that night, Jerry hosted a celebration for the release of "Kicking the Can," which they were putting out as a stand-alone single. They invited some radio people, some models, some hangers-on. Foxx performed a stripped-down version of "Rap," just his vocals, Tony's guitar, and Lucas's bass. "Shirley Chisholm—heal the schism," Foxx said. "Stokely Carmichael—just part of the cycle."

Lucas joined him for the chorus: "The soul's on a roll, that's a natural fact / I'm putting on whitey by putting on black / She went into her head though I said it's a trap / Stay out here, babe—put your ear on my rap."

The women in the room were swaying for him, along with the DJs and the freaks and the kids. "Foxx," they screamed. What bothered him were the executives. They stood at the back of the house, silent and sullen, stares of gray in this field of brilliant color. He had the whole world in his hands. If he dropped it, would it bounce?

Betty
February 1971

Betty pulled up to the new house in a new car, stepped out onto the street wearing new shoes and a new dress, and felt the same old doubts. The place seemed too rich for her blood. There were spaces she feared she would never fill. She hadn't lived in San Francisco long enough to decamp for L.A. She and Dewey moved into a corner of the first floor, the corner with the kitchen and the den and one of the guest bedrooms. Every day workmen were there when she woke up, and they were still there when she went to sleep.

"I know it's a hassle, but I need a studio," Robert said. "How else am I going to catch lightning in a bottle?"

"I'm sure I'll get used to it. But for now I'd rather be back in Chicago with my mama and Charlotte. At least there Dewey has other kids to play with. At least there I'm not alone all the time."

"Invite Charlotte to bring her kids to California."

"And what about Lonnie?"

"Lonnie? Who's that?"

"Charlotte's boyfriend."

"Oh, yeah. Put him on the payroll. Can't a big motherfucker like that work security for me?"

"He has a job, Robert. He wouldn't take charity." But she knew Lonnie would if she asked him.

"Okay," Robert said. "You decide what to do. But you work it out. A fountain's just a waterfall when it begins to bore me."

Betty wrote a note to herself to call Charlotte and left it in the middle of the huge kitchen counter in the huge kitchen in the huge new house. Her writing looked tiny on the page.

That night, Betty dreamed of a future without Robert. It wasn't apocalyptic, or even melodramatic—it was a slow dream of Betty sitting in a garden with Dewey on her lap. They were the only two things in the dream that moved—the background was like a painting—except for the peacock that strutted around the cement path on the garden's perimeter. In the dream, Dewey was already talking. "Where's Daddy?" he said. He had a sweet voice. Daddy? Betty said. Daddy's still on tour. "When is he coming back?" said Dewey. Not so long, said Betty. "Is that Daddy?" Dewey said, pointing at the peacock. No, said Betty, but then she looked at the hundreds of eyes and the fan of feathers and she wasn't sure.

When Robert got back from tour, he stayed with them at the new house for a weekend. He was kind and loving, but eventually they fought because he wouldn't take off his sunglasses. "You already made me take off my fur and all my rings," he said.

"Because you're at home," she said. "Not out working the streets like the other pimps."

"Baby," he said. "I shine. That's why I got to wear these glasses—so I don't blind myself."

"Get over yourself," she said. "If you can jump that high."

"I can jump higher."

"Seriously," she said. "This is a stupid argument. I can't even see your eyes."

The next morning, he went back up to San Francisco. "Does this make any sense?" said Betty. "When we lived up there, you were always coming down here. So we moved down here, and now you're going back up there."

"It's one weekend, woman," he said. His tone mock-angry, the way it was whenever he was in the wrong, but he leaned too hard on it. "Just trust me," he said more gently. "I'll be back Monday."

Monday came and went, and he wasn't back. Tuesday night he arrived without warning. "Sorry I'm late," he said. He was still wearing his sunglasses. "I got to show you something." He opened a briefcase on the kitchen table. Inside was a reel-to-reel tape recorder. "*Man from U.N.C.L.E.* shit, huh?" he said.

"What's it for?" she said. "Didn't you just spend tens of thousands of dollars on a home studio?"

"I did, dear Betty, but different pleasures call for different measures." He flicked a switch and the briefcase began to hum. He tapped a ring on the table. "Go get Dewey," he said.

"He's sleeping," she said.

"Wake him up."

She brought Dewey downstairs. He was plump and warm, a dinner roll. "Listen," said Robert. He flicked another switch and the suitcase began to rattle. Then she realized that the noise wasn't a rattle. It was a rhythm. "Sounds like a clock rolling down a hill, doesn't it?" Robert said. "I need you and Dewey to sing for me."

"What?" she said.

"You remember before we got married?"

"No," she said. "My life started at the wedding."

"Ouch, baby," he said, laughing. "You got to soften the blow so the bruises don't show. I'm asking you if you remember what I said I'd do." He hurried on, as if he was afraid of her answer. "I said I'd write a song for you every year. Well, I thought of a better idea. You're going to make a song. This is a track I wrote called 'Cause.' It's just the drum and the bass now. I laid them down myself. What I need you to do is to sing at the chorus."

"You talking to me or to Dewey?" Betty said. She meant it as a joke, but Robert didn't smile.

"Both of y'all. And don't worry about extra noise or nothing. I'll bury this shit deep in the mix. I just want a girl's voice." He rewound the tape. "Right there, at the chorus, see, sing 'Just 'cause.' Sing it any way you want."

"What about Dewey?"

He seemed to have forgotten. "Oh yeah," he said. "If he makes noise, just let him run. It's beautiful. It's reality. Anyhow, I got to go do something in the other room."

Robert produced a microphone from the briefcase—it seemed to have no bottom—and left the room. Thirty seconds later she heard the car pulling out of the driveway. Gone the whole weekend, back for five minutes, and gone again. "Why is your daddy such a fool?" she asked Dewey. Betty put the microphone down. She'd be damned if she'd do what she was told.

She went to the studio, to the corner where Robert kept his records—they were still crated up, as if he was unsure if he belonged—and started to go through them. She complained to the records as she flipped through them, no, wrong, won't do. She finally settled on the new Eddie Holman album. His voice was high and sad and didn't remind her at all of Robert's, which was the point. The singers that sounded too much like him flipped a switch inside her, and lately it was going from light to dark. She sat sideways on a chair, listening to Eddie Holman sing "It's All in the Game," trying for peace and quiet. Dewey was sliding records out of their sleeves and leaving them on the ground. Finally she picked up the microphone and started the tape. The beat stuttered and faltered, almost fell apart, but held on by a thread. Near the chorus, the beat surged. "Just 'cause," she sang. "Just 'cause."

Robert
March 1971

The house was done. Everything was pristine: paint, furniture, equipment. Foxx spent the morning taking pictures: Betty on the new leather couch, Dewey underneath the huge glass drops of the chandelier. He got dressed up just to walk around. That was what kings did, and he was the king, and the kingdom went from the front door past the walk-in closets into the dressing room with the concealed lighting out through the louvered patio doors around the pool and back inside again. The glow of wealth and fame was everywhere, but it was brightest in the studio, where he paused before his prize jewel. "I could knock over a chair and it would sound like Sgt. Pepper was knocking it over," he said.

He got right down to work, laying down instrumental tracks. He prayed for the day to hang, but it jetted; the eight hours vanished before he could get his hands around them. He couldn't get a likeness of what he saw in his mind, and that was just the basic keys and drums, the sketch he'd need the band to paint. The same problem happening with the vocals. "You just need to get used to the place," Betty said, but it was more than that. He knew he had a perfect song in him and the thought excited him so much that he couldn't sing over the pulse in his throat. He sometimes took bennies until he was swimming in his head a little, thinking that if he made it to shore he'd have what he wanted. But there were always interruptions. One morning he was starting to roll when Betty came in to tell them it was an urgent call from Monroe Stringer.

"Urgent? " said Stringer, his voice soft. "No. Of course not. She must have heard me wrong. We just wanted to tell you how excited we are about the new record. We're crossing our fingers for another *Wreckered*." This was the fourth call Foxx had gotten that month, and he hung up fast. Motherfucker had it coming, anyway; when the white man said "crossing" he meant "double-crossing," and when he said "fingers" he meant "singers."

Plus, Foxx didn't care about hits anymore. He was writing poetry. "Back," the first piece, was about Fred Hampton, and it kicked off strong: "It's true / What follows depends on who is leading / It's you / Holding up the gun while I am bleeding." There was another song called "Lost," which kept repeating the line, "Your color makes you free." Foxx wanted Yvette to sing that, first brassy like Bessie Smith, then whiter and whiter until she was trilling it like Melanie. From black to white, from white to black. Two terminals, terminally ill. He was even using Kevin to sing on some tracks: ugly wasn't pretty, but the truth had the potential to achieve beauty.

Foxx wanted to name the record *Bleached Black*, after a cover picture he had in mind (he wanted Yvette, in a blonde wig, doing Marilyn with the rest of the band under the grate, on their backs, like buried corpses) or *Fade to Black*, after another poem he had written ("O Holy Moses / Why you striking poses / Like the Joker in the pack? / Fade to black"). He had told Jerry that he wanted to produce it himself, but Jerry advised going with Turn's pick, Frank Tamborelli, and Foxx gave in. Now he was sorry he had. Frank was a prince, always on time, always polite, but he came from a dying tradition that Foxx wanted to hurry up and get dead. He was always cutting sessions when they came off the beat, telling the band to take it from the top just as Lucas began to get into something righteous. "Tambourine," said Foxx. "You got to let the motherfucker breathe. And let us put the needle in the red. I want Tony's guitars to have some hair."

"Okay," said Frank. "We'll run it again."

"I still say we should name this one *Carrara Marble*," said Tony. "Because it sounds like there are songs in there struggling to get out."

"Kevin," said Foxx. "Get in here. I need you and Yvette to sing that part."

"What part?"

"'I've got the whole world in my hands.' That part."

"Let me warm up," said Kevin. He cleared his throat. Kevin was always a headache, but for the last three weeks he had been a headache times ten. This time, the cause was simpler to find: His wife had left him. For several days there was no sign of her: no telephone call, no postcard. Kevin was wild with grief. Then someone pointed out that the guy who owned the Chevy dealership was gone also, and then Kevin was wild with anger. One day Tony threatened to call the cops because Kevin was all over a teenage girl who had hung out at the studio. He was giving her rough timber in the hall by the bathrooms, knocking her white-eyed. Now he reached for a wretched high note and stayed with it: "I'm going away soon / I'm going straight to the moon / I'll get there sooner or later / Then I'll take a shit in a crater."

"Not bad," said Foxx.

"Let me sing it myself," Kevin said. "I don't want that minge in here with me."

"You're a prick," Tony said.

"And you're a bee sting," said Kevin. He pantomimed a scene of Yvette with some unknown suitor, dick to jaw, dick to jaw. Tony winced. They had been split up for a few weeks and he was terrified that she'd start seeing another guy.

"Hey," Foxx said. "Let's not start."

"If I start with him, I'll finish him," Tony said.

"Leave it where it fell, William Tell," said Foxx.

It should have gotten easier. It didn't. Yvette didn't show the next day. Then Lucas had to miss two days of session time to meet with Adele and a judge. Foxx didn't ask why, and he knew it seemed like he didn't care, and he supposed that was because he didn't. Man wants to play like he's close to his Lord, man should act like he's close to his Lord. Lucas had been catting on the road as much as any of them, but he always insisted it wasn't him, not in truth, not in God.

Tony came to the studio. He always came. He arrived early and sat on the counter playing the chords to "Lost" on an acoustic guitar Foxx had gotten as a gift from some hippie rocker who admired the Foxxes. "Good thing you got this new studio," said Tony. "You don't have to pay for time."

"I'm paying," said Foxx. "It's just a new way to pay."

The next week, the price went up. Foxx came into the studio, joint in his hand. The first thing he saw was Tony, standing hand on hip, in the middle of the room. Off to the right, crouched on top of a chair, was Kevin. He was holding a knife. No, not a knife: a letter opener. But he was holding it like a knife.

"Fuck you doing?"

Tony answered for him. "We're having a friendly conversation." He spoke slowly, like a lion tamer.

"We were talking," said Kevin, teeth chattering, "about how a band is more than one person, and about how this band seems to be only one person."

"Right," said Tony. "And I was explaining that it's the papers that make it seem that way. Because they care mostly about the singing and the songwriting. They don't know shit about drumming, or playing bass, or guitar." He turned and stepped toward Foxx, a plea in his eyes. Fuck this, thought Foxx, and he was about to say so when he saw the red spot on Tony's left side, just under the rib cage, spreading.

"Yeah, man," said Foxx. "Tony's right. Sometimes I start writing a song, and I can't even think of finishing before it reaches the rest of you. Without the drums, 'Lost' is nothing. It's a nursery rhyme." He talked slowly while Tony took a long loop around Kevin's back. "It's like I was telling the reporter from *Creem* the other day. I may be in the spotlight, but I got lights behind me that are even brighter than that."

"You said that?" said Kevin. Tony had almost reached him now.

"Yeah. Most of the time I write the songs thinking of the way you'll play it, or the way Yvette will sing it."

"Yeah," Kevin said. Tony brought both hands down on Kevin's wrist. For a second, Kevin tensed, but then he surrendered the blade with a sigh. "I'm no good with a knife," he said, suddenly deflated. "I'm better with a gun." Then he collapsed.

Foxx rushed over. "You okay?"

Tony rolled his shirt up so Foxx could see where Kevin had cut him. "Yeah. I mean, it hurts, but it was pretty shallow. He just fucking freaked out on me. I guess the reds and blow and booze and smack and whatever else just blew up inside of him."

Foxx moved Kevin to the couch, smelling his fear and the whiskey that had come through his pores. "I'm better with a gun," he said again. Foxx didn't know what he meant but then he had it. In '67, they had driven out to Virginia City to play a dance party in the Red Dog Saloon. They hung out all night with the girls, had their fill of cream and peaches. But the next day it got boring, and they borrowed some guns from some guys and drove out into the desert. Tony put beer bottles on rocks, and Foxx and Kevin shot them off. Kevin was a crack shot. He got every bottle. "My calling," he said. "Call me Marshall Dillon." Foxx hadn't been a good shot. He didn't remember how many bottles he hit. He remembered something else: that the guns were little, and after they were shot a bunch of times, they got hot and had to be set down. That's why the gangsters called them heaters. That's what being a star was like. After a bunch of shots, you had to take a break. It just got too hot.

Betty
March 1971

"You see what I mean?" Robert said. "I need to know that where I'm going is the promised land, instead of straight back into ordinary life. Right?" He was in the bathroom, with the door cracked slightly. She could see a sliver of him, brown against the white tile.

It was March, and Los Angeles was surprisingly humid and clammy. Betty was wearing Robert's pajamas to keep herself warm. She rolled over onto her side and listened to him run the water. The sound brought back an aching image of the time when they were new to each other, the way she would turn toward the noise and feel an intimacy swelling up in her. Then came a time when she took it for granted, and then a time when she resented his passage through her space. These times were crowded tightly together. It was not easy to know where one ended and the next began. Is that what life was, in the end, a series of somewhat unknowable bands of experience that could not be differentiated from one another? Robert came back into the bedroom but not back into the bed. He sat at the foot of the bed and bounced the mattress with his hand. The bands Betty was picturing in her mind dissolved. Keeping her thoughts when Robert was near was not her strength. "Hey, girl," he said, "why don't you wake up?"

"Because I can only sleep for a few hours anyway, and these are those hours."

"I got energy drops if you want."

"I don't want pills."

"Fine and dandy, Mandy. But wake up anyway. Come downstairs with me. I want to show you something."

She could have said no, rolled back over, returned to sleep. But taking a stand against Robert's desires: This was not her strength either. Sometimes she heard old women talking about how much they loathed their husbands. They found them boring, odious, laughable, impotent in mind and in spirit. Betty did not have those problems, at least, and so she followed Robert downstairs through the house, careful not to trip over the too-long legs of her pajamas. There were still too many shadows, too much dark that might have strange bodies moving through it. The ground floor was better. The kitchen light was on. But then they went through into the studio, which was as dark as the stairs had been, a black sheet broken only by the tiny red and green lights of the control board. "Robert," Betty said. Her voice sounded frightened to her.

"Shh," he said. "Don't say a word. I want all the air in your lungs for something else." He punched two red buttons and a green one and the booth suddenly filled with sound. It was the song Robert had brought home in his suitcase. Robert fitted headphones over Betty's ears, and she tried to disappear inside them, lowering her eyelids until her eyes were almost shut. Through the slits she could still see the red and green lights. "I need you to do some more singing," Robert said. "You know how I had you singing 'Just 'cause' before?"

"Yes," said Betty.

"Now I need you to sing 'Why?' Just the one word. Ask it like a question."

"Isn't Yvette still in the band?"

"Not that question."

"No. What I mean is why am I singing instead of her? How many girl singers do you need?"

"I know what you mean. I want your voice on here. It's a different thing than hers. It has more footholds, and that's what I'm trying for. I need something that the people listening can climb to the top of."

He pressed another green button, and two more red buttons, and the tape wound itself back to the beginning, where it waited with an impatient high-pitched squeal. "Here goes," said Robert. "You're going to hear me singing 'oh,' and after that, right after, just give me a high 'Why?' Give it a little rough-and-tumble, and hold it for about five seconds."

"How many times?"

"Twice."

He played the tape. When she had heard the song in the kitchen, it was a skeleton of bass and drums. Now it was fleshed out, with a percolating organ and a sharp guitar line. And there were words, too, sung slow and low by Robert.

They resist with a raised fist
I'm great, bent or straight
Don't argue with the absentee rate

Then came a swell of piano, and then Robert sang "oh," a long and mournful "oh" straight out of Ray Charles. It hung there in the air, then died out, and Betty sang, "Why?" She held the note, sustained it, turned it up at the end, and just as her vibrato began to break the bass burbled up again. "Yeah," said the Robert in the studio.

"Yeah, baby. That's the way to make my day." The Robert on the tape was singing again.

They defy with a hot eye
I'm alive, shuck or jive
The article is in the archive

They oppose when the wind blows
I'm on guard, striped and starred
The warden's dressed in plainclothes

Then there was a break and Robert, on tape, exhaled another "oh." This time, Betty reached down as deep as she could, tried to match him, and ripped out her second "Why?" She could feel Robert's eyes on her in the dark. Why did he look at her now, but never in the light? Why did he spend all his time away? Why didn't he hold his son more? Why did she hate him as much as she loved him? Why? The question didn't answer a thing.

Robert switched off the tape right after she finished. "God damn, kilogram" he said, laughing. "What the hell was that?"

"You told me to do it rough-and-tumble."

"Did I say to knock down the rest of the song? Spare me your talent, woman."

Betty took off her headphones. "Give me one good reason."

He kissed her.

"How did we ever meet?" she said. She wasn't being romantic. She really wanted to know.

"Fate," he said. "The force you love to hate."

"Let's go outside," Betty said. She was thinking they might swim, but it was too cold, and instead she took him by the hand and led him around the side, where the short stone wall ran along the driveway. Robert lit up a joint and passed it to her. Los Angeles was spread out before them, every little light an unchecked impulse. "City of Angels," she said.

"I can't see them," he said. Then he looked at her, grinning. "Except one."

"You seriously think you can talk to me like you're in a movie?"

"Like we're in a movie," he said. "Don't think I'm appearing in it alone." But that was exactly what she thought. She was sure of it. Still, they made love right there, up against the stone wall. She was slippery and her breathing was becoming ragged. "Damn," he said, tugging at her pajamas. "Those motherfuckers are silk."

"Then take them off me," she said. But he didn't. He just kept on going, and he came, and she almost did, and that was good enough.

"I just don't know what I'd do without you," he said, pronouncing every word clearly like it was dialogue. "You're my baby, and you made another baby for me."

"He's beautiful," she said.

"Gets it from you," he said. But he couldn't resist. "And from me, of course."

They went back inside and stood at the foot of the stairs. "Come to bed," she said.

"Not yet," he said. "Got to make another song."

"You're not serious." She stopped and put a hand on her hip. She was posing now, like her mama used to do, and the thought amused Betty, though the circumstances did not. "You are not staying up to work."

"What I'm not doing is arguing." He started to tell her about the song. "It's called 'Brown,'" he said. "I had some lines I couldn't fit anywhere else: 'What we once believed we'd leave behind, we burned / There's no contradiction, just conviction overturned.'"

"Do you listen to the words, or just write them?" She heard the anger in her own voice, and she thrilled a little as she raised the volume. "Be in bed in an hour, or don't come at all."

The next morning, she found Robert in the studio, dozing. He had his hand right under his cheek. It was the same way Dewey slept. She went back upstairs and stood over his crib, imagining that he was not hers, but something she was watching in a movie. "Sleep, baby, sleep," she sang, "until there's nothing left to keep." When she leaned in to kiss him, he flinched. Sometimes he liked to fake it, but she could tell from the way he reached up to fend her off that he was really gone, in a place where a kiss was the same kind of threat as any other unexpected touch.

Robert
April 1971

"Stringer's nervous as shit about the record," Jerry said. "He keeps calling me to tell me that Dunn keeps calling him. He thinks Clary is leaning on Dunn. 'The honcho,' he keeps calling him."

"Isn't that John Wayne?" said Foxx.

"That's Hondo," said Tony.

They were out by the pool, on the elevated deck that gave him a view of the other pools down the hill—Barbra Streisand's, Richard Dawson's, Lance Marker's.

"Do you remember those motherfucking Apaches?" said Foxx. "Didn't one of them try to pour hot coals on Hondo's chest?"

"Yeah," said Tony. "But I think that was in the TV show. And that wasn't John Wayne. That was that other guy."

"Stringer says Clary is dying of anticipation."

"Let him die a little," said Foxx. He lay back in his chaise, hands pressed flat on his chest. On the table next to the chair was a copy of a new *Rolling Stone* and a blond-wood box filled with pills. The magazine had a story about the band: WAITING ON THE SECOND COMING: HAS AMERICA'S TOP ROCK STAR OUTFOXXED HIMSELF? The wooden box had an answer to the question. Foxx watched a point of light on the wall that wiggled when he wiggled and stayed still when he stayed still. At length he realized that it was reflecting off the tiny spoon that was resting on his chest and had, a moment before, been held just beneath his nostril.

"I went into the Turn offices with Jerry this time," said Kevin. Ever since Kevin broke down, Jerry had been showing him favor, and Kevin was like a son whose father had returned from overseas. "You go in there, and they're slick and nice to you, but you know all they want is to take the fucking master tapes and never see you again. They don't even think of you as a person."

"Yeah," said Foxx. "And I'm so much more. Anyway, how much they offer us?"

"Three hundred grand," said Jerry. "If it's in by August. Another hundred if the record is delivered by the end of next month."

"Well, we can kiss that money goodbye," said Tony.

"We don't have to." Jerry withdrew a piece of paper from his jacket pocket. "Not if we agree to a *Greatest Hits.*"

"I'm not agreeing," said Foxx. "No motherfucking way. And what if the record's not in by August?" He fingered the spoon, moved it from side to side until the little point of light that was its reflection appeared on Jerry's arm. White light on a white man. "I can't always tell how long it might take. It's a process, baby."

"What's a process?" said Kevin.

"Watching your dumb cracker ass fog over and then imagine we're going to re-wind just so you can join us," Lucas said sharply.

"What's with him?" said Kevin, stung. Foxx wasn't sure. Maybe it was because of the recording session the previous day. Lucas had brought a song, a midtempo anthem called "We." Foxx listened to it twice, liked it fine the first time, liked it less the second time: lots of bass, not much grace. "We need to force things forward," he had said. "This is walking in place." Foxx shut off the monitor. He didn't look up. They were in the studio, and out of the corner of his eye he saw Lucas's jawline tighten. Now, out by the pool, the jawline wasn't tight any more, but the words were.

Tight. That's how Foxx was measuring everything these days. There was tight when it came to money, tight when it came to pussy, and tight when it came to music. That's why he had fired Frank Tamborelli from *Pitch.* It wasn't that Tamborelli was doing anything wrong, exactly. He had produced Blood Sweat & Tears and Chicago and he got them tight in one way, but not in the right way. For the drums, Foxx was using these new Linn drum machines and had session guys drum on top of them. The vocals were the trickiest. He had dubbed and overdubbed so many times, the master tapes were stretched. Sometimes they sounded hollow, sometimes hazy. That harmonized with the songs: There were love songs ("Held") and anthems ("Cause"), but the best way to get the mood of the thing was to close your eyes and let the hurt come through. He added punctuation: in "Lot," a distant tambourine that sounded like slave chains banging; in "Brown," a warped guitar solo, fuzzed and furious, over a chant of "We are dying, we are dead / Put the needle in the red." That was tight. But the tightest motherfucker was the title track: "Pitch" was "We All Need A Place In the Sun" slowed down to half-speed, a pulse of the darkest light. Everything around him was white, the powder and the power. Foxx needed a little black back for himself.

"Anyway," Lucas was saying, "this is a perfect incentive to get back to the studio, don't you think?"

"What do you mean?"

"Tony and I were talking. If the band finishes the record on time, we figure that everyone can split the extra cash."

"Oh, do you?" says Foxx. "Do you figure? I don't figure that exactly."

"What?"

"Do you know about the slave days, cousin? Do you remember how we worked in the fields? I don't like Dunn running around acting like a cross between Lincoln and Stalin."

"I don't see the connection between the two of them, or either of them and Dunn."

"That's because there's a hidden connection."

"No," said Lucas. "That's because there is no connection. You don't want to use the money as a way of getting the band back into the studio because you don't want the band back in the studio."

"You got to trust me, man."

"Do I?" Lucas said. "Come on, Robert. I don't want to hear that our livelihood is all part of the master's master plan. It reminds me of a song: 'Critics, cameras, reporters / The knife comes at closer quarters.'"

"Hey," said Foxx. "I wrote that."

"And I'm fucking living it," said Lucas. He was standing now, talking louder than the loudest cars on the street. "All this talk about freedom. Man, this is the freest prison I've ever seen."

"Let's settle down," said Jerry.

"No," said Lucas. "I'm sick of it. Sick of the tantrums, the games, and the rip-offs. Let's not settle down. Let's settle up."

"You're just burned up over Adele," said Foxx.

"I have trouble in the marriage, true," Lucas said.

"You're not doing an interview, man," Foxx said. "Who do you think I am? Who do you think you are? Do you feel like you get asked that question often?" He split the word and spit the *T*: of-ten.

"Shut up, bad-luck bird," said Lucas. He turned and walked away.

"I'm going to write you the prettiest song, cuz," called Foxx, mockingly, to his receding figure. The words should have bounced off his back, but they hit and stuck. It was almost like you could see them.

Betty
July 1971

Back when Betty first moved in with Robert, she learned that she could count on him to do one thing right but not two in a row. If she asked him to pick up some milk and some eggs, he would get the milk but forget the eggs.

She tried to be understanding, then, when he seemed to forget Dewey. It wasn't that he didn't know he had a son. Rather, it seemed to slip his mind that he needed to talk to his son, to hold him, to feed him. "I love him," he said in his defense, as if love was a separate account.

He was downstairs in the studio, where he spent almost all his time. Twice that morning, Betty had gone to talk to him, but he had shooed her off with a shake of his head. He was busy. She noticed the bottle next to his elbow. He was drinking too much, from what she could see. She supposed there were also things she could not see.

The third time, she ignored his protests. "Oh, shit," he said. "You're going to fuck up my session." He pounced on the control board and slid two levers as far down as they would go. "I lost something," he said, exhaling heavily. His breath was stale.

"What is it?" Betty said, her voice sweeter than her eyes.

"That Chuck Berry record. *Berry on Top.* I haven't seen it since we moved. Did you put it somewhere?"

"No," she said. "I don't touch the records. You know that." But he wasn't looking at her anymore; she had been able to get his attention, but not to hold it for longer than five seconds.

"I'm going back upstairs," she said, hoping that would matter to him. He gave a single wave, south to north, a dismissal.

Robert distracted and half in the bag wasn't a dream come true, but it was better than Robert hot, with the bag at his feet. One day Kevin came by with Lyle Pence, a young singer who happened to live down the street. Robert took an instant dislike to Lyle. "Peckerwood names," he said, "got peckerwood brains." Betty thought Pence was pleasant enough. She brought him a beer and he told her that he liked her dress. "Very summery," he said.

"Thank you," Betty said, and went back to tickling Dewey on the chest and shoulders, where he liked it. That was the full extent of her relationship with Lyle Pence. That's why she was shocked when Robert, less than an hour later, kicked the door open and demanded to know exactly what had passed between the two of them. "Every last fucking word," he said.

"I brought him a beer and he said he liked my dress."

"And that's all?"

"Yes."

Dewey, stunned into momentary silence by the door, was now bawling.

"No," he said. "That's not all. Do you know what that motherfucker did? He came out and said that he had talked to some girl out in the house."

"Oh." She wasn't sure what Robert meant.

"Do you hear me, girl? It's like he thinks you work here. He thinks you're the cleaning lady."

"That's ridiculous." She held up her hands in a show of logic, but Robert wasn't looking. He dropped into a chair behind the desk in the corner and fished a pen out of the drawer. "What are you doing now?"

"I'm going to show that motherfucker what I got, Shirley Scott." He wrote Pence a note, which he then read aloud to Betty. "If you're going to be my guest, so be it. Otherwise, let's Stagolee it." Then he stormed out. Ten minutes later, Betty came back through the room and saw the note still sitting on the desk. She folded it up and put it in an envelope. She would give it to Jerry to give to Lyle Pence. No point in disobeying Robert. It would only make him angrier. And she didn't want him angry around Dewey. You never knew when he might decide to make time for the boy.

Robert
September 1971

How long did it take him to finish *Pitch*? Twenty-eight years, plus however long it took. But it was done, or nearly so. What was done? He hadn't forgotten. He just didn't know what the word meant. *Done.* He stared at it until it broke into pieces. The *o* rolled away. He had emptied out his soul and refilled it with finer things. He had repeated this process until what was in him was more precious than he could have ever imagined, and then he had poured it all into *Pitch*. It was a kingdom called by many different names, a crown with all its jewels glinting. Glinting? No. That was wrong. Nothing glinted. Nothing shone. Pieces of songs drowned and resurfaced in other songs. Stillbirths got the same treatment as the songs born bawling. The record seemed fathomless—any bottom was a false bottom, and any light you poured into the motherfucker ran right out.

Foxx stayed awake long after he had sent Betty to bed. He lit up one joint, then another, then a third, trying to see new sounds in the curves of the smoke. For about a week he was all about the bass, and he worked the tracks he had until Lucas's instrument sounded like it was walking on a wire. Then he thought better of Kevin's drums, and he loosened them up so that they rattled. There in the middle of the night, in the middle of the studio, with his reefer pinched in his hand, he was happy, or close enough to happy that he felt the tail of the *y* tickling his neck. "Free and clear," he sang. "Free and clear. No one else round to hear." He remembered playing guitar in Boston. What was it, eight years? Ten? Time passed with a changed cast.

He was so high on the record that he got low everywhere else. In late September, just a few days after Attica, he sat backstage in the Fillmore, his eyes filling up with tears he couldn't explain. Was he losing his mind? "All right," a stagehand said. "Almost time." The band fell into formation: Tony shouldered his guitar, Kevin did that superstitious thing where he turned his hand palm-up at eye level and rubbed his wrist against his nose. But Foxx didn't move. When he wrote songs, he tried for the music that was the most alive, for lyrics that were the most alive. When he talked to Betty, he tried for the conversations that were the most alive. Shouldn't he operate under the same laws here? And if he should, the thing to do, indisputably, was to refuse to take the stage. To refuse to sing "Highway Car" or "We All Need a Place in the Sun." A tear fell to his lap. A tear in his lap: Was this another song? Maybe the record wasn't done.

"What are you doing, cuz?" said Lucas. They had made up after the fight by the pool, but things were still tense between them. "Everyone else is standing. You feel okay?"

"I feel fine," said Foxx in a dull monotone.

"You want me to get on that microphone and tell everyone that you're backstage but you refuse to come out?"

"You do what you need to do," said Foxx, still riding the monotone. "No more, no less. It's a philosophy, not a fad."

Lucas stared long and hard. Then he walked out onstage. Foxx pulled the curtain back and watched as Lucas announced that Foxx was sick. "But we're going to start," he said, "because he's not that sick. Maybe he'll get better soon and join us." A cup of beer came through the air and landed at Lucas's feet. "Hey," said Lucas. "Stop throwing."

"Yeah," said Tony, stepping to the microphone. "Cut that out."

But they didn't cut it out. A shoe followed the cup, and a bottle followed the shoe. Five minutes later the arena was in full riot. Foxx, still watching from the wings, saw a girl pushed down in front. If he walked right out and took the microphone, would it all stop? He did. It did. Afterward, he cried again.

That night, he snuck down to put the finishing touches on "Lost," the next-to-last song on the record. He had nine songs now, including the half-speed remake of "We All Need a Place in the Sun." He needed a tenth. He sat down at the piano. What was space? It was a place to feel. What was time? It was a way of stretching that place where you felt. What was Attica? It was chickens coming home to roost. What was America? It was a poem written by history. What was history? It was the marriage of time and space. What was marriage? It was love looking at itself in a mirror, as vain and as foolish as it was proud and hopeful. What was love? It was something that pulled you up. What was up? He took a look, just as his fingers came down on the piano. A major chord went through him, full, strong. "Up," he sang. "Sometimes I'm rising in my mind / But how far up is surprising." He sang hunched over so that his chin touched his breastbone. His voice came out in a ragged croak, off-key, off-beat. It was way off the mark. It was right on the money.

The mountain is tall
It goes up before me
And a fountain's just a waterfall when it begins to bore me
The airplane has wings but not a feather
Up in the clouds they'll tell you wind's just heavy weather
Up is a deception, even though they promise that it's the right direction

I tell you, up has a nasty smile
Oh, man, high time is gonna take a while
Up insists on hoping
But to me it's only joking
Up

He reached to stop the tape. The tape was already stopped. A cold chill seized his scalp. Had he forgotten to run it? He began to sweat, and lit up another joint to calm himself down. He rewound the tape, hit play. The button went down like it was pressing into his heart. But then he heard his voice. He climbed upstairs and snuck into bed next to Betty. He slid nearer to her until he fit into the seam of her ass. She murmured and turned. "Baby," he said. "I'm sorry but I can't. You're not going to get any heat from this meat. Not tonight." She kept working him, with her hands and her mouth, but he had given at the office, and there was nothing left. Still, there were worse things in the world than lying in bed while your beautiful wife kissed the tip of your cock. He stared at the ceiling and started to make a list of them.

Betty
January 1972

Robert had finished his record, the second record he had made as Betty's husband. He gave it to her as a gift, wrapped it in black paper and left it on the table beside the bed. There was a card, too. It said, "Lovely and Dark / Meet Me Out In the Park," and on the inside he had drawn a crude sketch of a tree with a tangle of a couple beneath it. On the trunk of the tree, he had written, FOXX WUZ HERE.

Betty removed the wrapping from *Pitch*. The cover of the album showed a thick black substance pouring out of an overturned bucket. The spill looked vaguely like a map of America.

Betty withdrew the album, still in its sleeve. There were ten songs. "Back" was the first song on the record. "Lot" was the next one. All the titles were single words, right through to "Black," the closer. She held the sleeve up to the light and looked through the spindle hole.

Betty put the record on the record player. The first song, "Back," started with a horn line that sounded like it was underwater. Then Robert's voice came on, soft but also hard, like a man waking up from a dream and not liking either what he had seen or what he saw:

It's true
Who follows depends on who is leading
It's you
Holding up the gun while I am bleeding

Drums surfaced from the depths of the song, made a noise, sank back down. Robert's vocals groaned, creaked, and wailed. And he was the only voice around for miles: All the backup vocals, including the ones she had recorded for "Cause," were gone. She didn't miss herself, and she damned him for making her feel that way. After the final notes of the final song, "Black," the first notes of "Back" played again faintly, like a ghost haunting the record.

Betty flipped the record over, went back to the first side. She lay in the dark and waited for him. She loved him all over again.

Robert
April 1972

Dewey was starting to talk, or trying to anyway, bleating out half-baked phrases, preaching to his toys. He gave a warning to a lion. He praised a crocodile. Foxx, who was stretched out on the floor, smiled up at him. But his smile was painted on, and paint curled in the sun. Dewey started to cry and tripped over Foxx's feet. He went down. "Get up, little man," said Foxx.

In the last few months, he had learned that lesson himself. "If there is a better album this year than *Pitch*," *Rolling Stone* wrote, "it's not coming from this planet." Other critics agreed. "It's nice to hear," said Jerry, "but we need the people to weigh in. The proof is in the pudding." Foxx was ready. He checked the charts. But the people wouldn't put their lips around the spoon. The album rose into the top ten only briefly, and three weeks later it was fighting to stay above Beverly Bremers. "Wanted to be the first to tell you," said Jerry, who liked to drop the "I" when he was bearing bad news. "Record's twelve and probably heading south."

"Saints get thinner," Foxx said to Tony. "That's how you can spot them." Tony had moved down to L.A. now, too, and was renting a bungalow, and the afternoon sun was coming down hard as the two of them ate lunch on the patio.

"I guess they'd rather have their Brandy and their Candy Man," Tony said.

"Who stole the soul?" Foxx said.

"They didn't steal it," Tony said. "They moved it. You saw what Gamble and Huff got from CBS? Two hundred million."

Foxx hated the admiration in Tony's voice. "I heard Billy Paul's new one the other day," he said. "Version of that Elton John song that made me want to scratch the record sideways."

"An acquired taste, I guess. But lots of people are acquiring it."

"I'm not in acquisitions." Foxx frowned and narrowed his eyes. "Mixed-up, shook-up world."

They were just finishing sandwiches when Foxx saw the bird. It was a black bird, fast, on the small side. As it came overhead, the bird stopped flying. And when it stopped, it stopped cold. It didn't glide. It dropped. Two seconds later, it hit the patio with a thud. Motherfucking thing just fell right out of the sky, lay there with the shadows of the patio rail on it like prison bars. Tony gasped but Foxx laughed. "I know just how he feels," he said.

Up in Seattle, Foxx took the band through a short set of hits and then closed the door on the crowd after "We All Need a Place in the Sun." "Are we going back out there?" said Lucas when they came backstage.

"Fuck, no," said Foxx, and knocked the bass out of Lucas's hands. Tony took a step toward them and froze. Lucas just shrugged and walked away. When the band started to pack up their things, Foxx went out by himself and closed the show with a solo piano rendition of "Lot." He leaned on the sharps and flats; they were keys you could play blind. A couple in the front row scowled. The smiles on the women behind them erased those scowls, just as the scowls erased the smiles. What was left behind? Nothing. Foxx sang hard, sang loud: He liked to watch the crowd climb down into the well of that black thing.

He slept on the plane, slept in the limo, tried to sleep in his own bed for the first time in weeks. Betty was gone, like she always was. She was with Dewey at a play group. Foxx made a phone call to Penny, the Turn girl he had been seeing sometimes after hours. "Find a Penny, pick it up," he said. But Penny couldn't get off work. "Then you can't get off at all," Foxx said, and lay in the vast middle of the bed. He was hungry. Five years before, he would have known exactly what to do. He would have gotten up and eaten something. On the road, he had help, more help than a man knew how to handle. He needed help to help him tell the help what to do. And when that help disappeared, he was helpless. He reached for the top drawer of the bed stand, found another joint, smoked it, and then went into the bathroom and sat with a straight razor pressed against his throat. He didn't think he'd pull it, but you could never be certain with this kind of thing.

Rolling Stone was rolled up and jammed between the toilet and the sink. He opened it to the article about the tour. There was a photograph of him at the press conference, standing in front of a poster of himself that was an enlarged version of the sleeve of *Pitch*. He was wearing sunglasses, but the huge face that loomed behind him wasn't. Betty was always saying that you couldn't see his eyes. The fuck was she talking about? Of course you could. They were right there, larger than life.

Tony relayed a message from Lucas. "He wants us for a band meeting," Tony said. "I think it's some kind of surprise for your birthday."

"I feel like the happiest girl in the whole USA," Foxx said. As he drove over to the restaurant, he had an unfamiliar feeling in his stomach, and it wasn't until he pulled into the parking lot that he realized it was hope. Everything had been so tense since the start of *Pitch*, particularly between him and Lucas. Maybe they could be six arrows again, all sailing toward the same target.

When he walked in, the band was sitting at one of the long booths. Lucas looked tired, Yvette sad, Kevin out in orbit as usual, Claude and Cheryl shoulder to shoulder and set apart. Only Tony looked like he was happy to see him. When the waitress came, she recognized only Foxx, and that didn't help matters any. Kevin ordered a scotch on the rocks. Everyone else had coffee. Then Yvette had to get out to go to the bathroom, so Foxx had to get up to let her out. While she was gone, they made small talk about Kareem Abdul-Jabbar. Then Yvette came back, and Foxx had to get out again.

They ate, mostly in silence. Foxx listened to the radio overhead. "I Saw the Light" was playing.

Lucas said, "You know what really bothers me?"

He was looking right at Tony, like he was asking him. But Tony didn't answer and no one else did either. The forks kept moving, plate to mouth to plate. Finally Kevin said, "What?"

"Sometimes there's a piggishness in man."

Foxx looked at Lucas and noticed that he wasn't eating anything.

"What I mean to say is that sometimes mortal man doesn't know when he's got enough. He keeps taking, not caring who he hurts or how."

"Should we have said grace?" Foxx said. Lucas scowled at him, but wasn't joking. Foxx couldn't take the temperature of the room.

Claude stopped eating and set down his fork. "Is it time already?" he said.

"Time for what?" said Tony. His fork was down now, too.

"Yeah," said Foxx. "Time for what?"

Lucas stabbed a greasy potato, lifted it up in the air, and inspected it. "Time," he said, as if he was talking to the potato, "to have the talk we should have had six months ago."

"No one said a thing to me," Tony said. "Not six months ago, not yesterday, not this morning when we spoke on the telephone. So what's going on?"

"Time to have the talk," said Lucas, who never minded saying anything again. "Some of us have been meeting, and now I need your attention." His voice was soft, and it wavered a bit. He looked at Foxx. "For about a year now, there's been trouble in the band. I'm not talking about the little bits of ego that fall out when we're playing or the jostling for position in the studio. I'm talking about serious problems." He turned the potato so that its cut end was facing Foxx. "Some of them are ego problems. Some of them are creative problems. Some of them are problems with what people are putting into their bodies, or what they are keeping out of their souls. There comes a time when the problems are bigger than the promise. That time has come." He clasped his hands in front of him. "And it is time to go."

Foxx opened his mouth to respond, but he didn't have the words yet. Instead it was Tony—careful, analytical Tony, who would give you a book with an underlined passage rather than speak to you directly—who led the charge. "This is some cowardly bullshit," he said. "I expected better from you. I mean, I know you have problems with things. But man, this is your cousin. And this is an ambush, besides."

"It's not an ambush," said Lucas. Foxx looked around the table quickly, thought he saw a grin just slipping off of Kevin's face. "This is the only way it could happen. It's been months since we had any real conversation."

"Who's in on this?" said Tony.

"There's nothing to be in on," said Lucas. "There just is what is." Foxx heard the swell in his voice, that preacher's pride. "As a band, we have seen our better days. This life and the way it's being lived, it claims victims, and I don't want to end up that way, and I don't want anyone else to either." He lowered the potato back to his plate.

Then Foxx jumped in himself. But he jumped in by jumping out. His voice was even quieter than Lucas's. "Fine," he said. "Go. All of you go. I'll stay in hell and you can go to heaven or wherever you think it is you deserve to be. You can tell them I sent you."

"Cousin," Lucas said, evenly, without any venom in his voice, "you'll cool down soon and see that this is the right decision. I'm not the only one who thinks so."

"Kevin?" Tony said.

"I'll stay if there's still a band," Kevin said.

"So it's not everyone," Tony said. "Yvette?"

"I got asked to join another band," she said. "As a backup singer." The color left Tony's face. "I said no, but I'm wondering now if I should have said yes. One never knows, does one?"

"If it's Lucas saying it's the end and me saying it's not and two other people who aren't sure, then what are we talking about?" Tony turned to Foxx. "Do you still want to lead?"

"Depends on who's following," Foxx said. He wished he had a more direct sentiment in him, but what he meant was bent.

Claude cleared his throat. "I think that Cheryl and I are through, too. We're thinking of starting a family. And if we did, this wouldn't be our life. Obviously."

Tony pushed his plate away. "I can't eat." But Foxx wouldn't say anything more, wouldn't even look at anyone directly, and one by one everyone else left. Lucas went first, then Kevin, then Claude and Cheryl. Yvette stayed, whispered something to Tony, kissed him on the forehead, which was both a comfort and an insult, and excused herself for the bathroom. She didn't return.

Foxx finished eating, paid the bill, and headed out to the parking lot. Tony kept within two steps until they got to his car. "Wait a minute," he said.

"One minute," Foxx said. "That's all I got. Then I have to get home and explain to myself why I don't have a band anymore."

"I swear to God, man, I didn't know anything about this," he said.

"Yeah," said Foxx.

"I'll get them back."

"Not Lucas. The motherfucker's stubborn as a mule, and it's not worth fighting him to the death. I got his blood in my veins. I don't need it on my hands, too."

"I'll settle Kevin down, then. I'll take care of Yvette."

"Your call."

"I can't believe they did this on your birthday," Tony said. He looked stricken. "I even got you a present." He opened up the car and took out a box. Inside was a new Wilson basketball, a Jo Jo White signature model.

Foxx took the ball out, tried to palm it, couldn't. His hands were slippery. "We'll play," he said.

Betty
May 1972

"I'll book a ticket today." Betty's mother was sick again, then better, then sick again. A few days before, she had sounded like a young woman. Today she sounded like she might not make it through the weekend.

"Don't be silly," her mother said.

"My heart is there with you."

"Better to send your lungs," her mother said, and coughed for effect. "Anyway, your husband needs you. It doesn't sound like it happens very often, so make the best of it."

When Robert told her that the band was taking a break, Betty thought it might smooth the creases out of everything. But after three weeks, Betty realized that they were only deepening. Robert wasn't around any more than before, and when he was he just sat in the kitchen drinking beer or led Betty into the bedroom. "Afternoon delight," he said, but Betty didn't see what was so delightful about it. He was nearly silent throughout. His eyes tended to focus on invisible points somewhere over her head.

One afternoon Betty went out to sit by the pool with *Gorilla, My Love*. Robert was there too, wearing a bathrobe and a fur-felt Stetson. "Hey," she said, and he grunted. His eyes were closed and his hands were folded over his chest.

She started to read, went through the first paragraph twice without getting traction, set the book down on the table beside her. "Robert," she said. "Can we take a vacation?"

"Take a vacation where?" He put his sunglasses on to cover the bloodshot eyes she had already seen. "I been around the world and it's been around me."

She pushed forward: swimsuits, suitcases, snapshots. "We could go to the islands," she said. "Or to Europe."

"I'm on vacation right here. From the band, from the road."

"And you're like a tourist at home," she said. "Do you live here or not? Dewey looks at you like you're a piece of furniture."

"I'm a chifforobe, baby. Is that why you're busting me up?" He sighed. "I'm just getting back near music that I can use. Did you ever notice that it's all music? The sprinklers, even."

"What?"

"The sprinklers. Someone back there is running theirs." He waved a hand toward the rear of the yard. "I don't think it's us. Is it? It sounds like Philly Joe Jones."

"My apologies," she said. "Maybe you do need a break." She tried to follow him where he went, but there were too many times that he blocked her path. Now Betty heard the sprinkler, and she almost heard what he meant; that was one more noise she wouldn't be able to filter out. "I just worry that things are slipping away," she said. "We're not getting any younger."

"How much younger do you want to be?"

"I just want to feel hopeful."

"I don't want hope as much as I want truth. It's probably the age difference. You may be twenty-four, but I'm a million."

"You think it's the right time for your stories?" she said. "When I married you, I didn't plan on trying to talk you into living a life with me. There's no future in sales."

"Good, good," he said. "I should write that one down. Could be a song."

"I didn't sign up for this."

"No one signs up for anything," he said. "In my million years, I've learned that." Betty wanted him to take off the sunglasses and see her. If that was impossible, she at least wanted to see him. But he wasn't even there. The body in the chair was only a technicality. "Salt peanuts," he said. He folded his hands on his chest again and went to sleep.

"Dewey, dinner." Betty said.

She was chopping vegetables.

"Dewey," she said again.

"Okay, Mama," he said. He was closer than she thought, right on the other side of the counter, in fact, and his voice startled her. The knife in her hand slipped and sliced the tip of her finger. She squeezed out the blood onto a paper napkin. It made a shape. Robert would have pursued the likeness. He would have opened every door until he found a match. To her it was only a cut, and she threw the napkin out.

Robert was already at the table, still in his bathrobe, his Stetson, and his sunglasses. He took the plate from her and began to eat. "Do you like it?" she asked.

"Thank you," he said. "Thank your mama for her cooking," he said to Dewey.

"Thank you, Mama," Dewey said.

But that wasn't what she had meant. She didn't want to be thanked, not only. She wanted the things she made to mean something. Robert had unlocked that secret. Why couldn't she?

Dewey looked at her face. He was always looking. He could tell she was sad. He finished up what was on his plate. "Can I have seconds?" he said.

"You can have minutes," Robert said.

Dewey laughed.

"Hey," Robert said. "I'm not a clown."

"Well, you've cleverly disguised yourself," Betty said.

Robert laughed, and Betty joined him. "Oh," she said. "You should see the way you look." Then she excused herself and went to the bathroom, where she cried, because the bathroom was too big and the house was even bigger; because she had gained weight she wondered if she'd ever lose; because she couldn't take a trip; be-

cause even if she had taken a trip she would have found herself in a place that reminded her of her marriage, all narrow streets, crooked and old, and signs no one
could read; because it was only a matter of time before everyone she knew would
pass from the earth—her mother, her family, herself; because all human beings were
insubstantial except insofar as they belonged to the solid memory of God; because she
wasn't sure she believed in God anymore; because she had cut her finger; because she
had not cut it worse; because Dewey would soon be sleeping happily but he'd wake up
soon after that; because most days she felt boiled down to her bones.

Robert
July 1972

"Bang," Foxx said to the screen in Washington D.C. "Bang, bang."

The movie was a Clint Eastwood flick called *Dirty Harry*, which Foxx had wanted to
see since it had come out. "Months and months of waiting," he told the ticket girl, who
couldn't have cared less. It opened with a woman being shot dead in a rooftop pool in
San Francisco. "Been there," Foxx said to himself. "Hell of a party." The killer, Scorpio,
left a note that said he was going to kill again, and that he was going after a brother and
a priest. Clint got the case, even though he was trouble: He put a slug in a rapist without
doing the things that cops are supposed to do. He stumbled into a robbery and ended up
standing over one of the guys, Magnum pointed down while the guy pointed a rifle up at
him. Clint wondered out loud how many bullets he had left. "You've got to ask yourself
one question, 'Do I feel lucky'" said Clint, cold as a motherfucker.

Foxx got up and went out into the alley, where he smoked a joint. He came back
to a cat-and-mouse game between Clint and the killer. Later, Clint started drawing
conclusions along with his weapons. When he got to the huge cross at Mount Da-
vidson, Foxx began to feel a little homesick, even if it was for a city of cops and kill-
ers. Foxx slumped back in his chair, and something clattered in his coat pocket. He
reached down to see what it was: a pill-bottle, almost empty. He moved it to the other
pocket for safety's sake.

Afterwards, Foxx stood in front of the theater, studying the posters. There were
movies he didn't know, mostly, but then he came to *Shaft*. Now there was a movie: hot

pieces of ass, black as black could be, and a brother who knew how to wear a leather coat. Just a few nights before, in Philadelphia, he and Tony had been trying to convince Kevin that he needed to see the movie. "Round-tree," Foxx said, making two words out of one.

"Maybe I'll go," Kevin said.

"Come on," Foxx said. "You a man or a drummer?"

Ever since Lucas quit the band, Kevin had been like that—easy to rattle, no fun in a battle.

Foxx felt a pain in his stomach at the thought of Lucas. When he quit the band, he quit California, too, got on a plane and went on back to Boston. Adele called Foxx for the first time in years, crying her eyes out. The split was one thing, but a continent of separation was something else. "Don't worry," Foxx said. "He'll be back. He's confused, but that only means he'll need to clear his head." But then just like that he had a new band (named King's Way) and a new wife (named Kathleen), and before Foxx could swallow that, Lucas had a hit—with "We," no less, which went on up the charts, twenty-five to twelve to five. That was exactly how "Highway Car" had moved. Coincidence? Maybe. But sometimes things rhymed, like in a verse, and some other things repeated, like in a chorus.

And sometimes things went on, like in a jam. Claude and Cheryl had gone where they said they'd go, to the chapel, and were living in a ranch house in Mill Valley, but the rest endured. "Kevin stayed for Tony," Foxx told Betty. "Tony stayed for Yvette. Yvette stayed because she likes the attention." He wasn't sure if it was true—maybe Tony had stayed for him, too, and Yvette never did anything for a reason—but he liked the way the sentences lined up. That was where he was: Trust what looked nice, because sometimes it was all you had. He got what looked nice into the studio to cut one new song he had written, "Jar Bug." The arrangement was sparse from necessity: just Tony on guitar, Kevin on drums, and Foxx and Yvette singing. Bare bones, not trombones.

The Foxxes were playing a short set at a festival in Baltimore, and Foxx had come down into D.C. dressed against success, just a no-count in jeans and a cap, to catch a movie. What was the name again? He took his ticket out, squinted against the sun, fished his glasses out of his pocket, put them on, walked off down the street. The few last pills were still noisy in the bottle, in his pocket, and he leaned up against a government oak to swallow them. Now the bottle didn't make a sound. Silence was golden.

Half a block down, there was a circular park with a fountain rising out of the center and ringed by a knee-high concrete wall. Foxx sat on a bench about twenty feet away and watched two black girls who were huddled together in conference. One of them was facing him; the other was turned away until she sensed his eyes on her back, and then she turned to face him, too.

Foxx got up and walked once around the fountain. There were more girls on the other side, but they weren't as fine as the girls on his side. A bum approached him for money. "Hollywood," said the old man. "Hollywood, Hollywood, Hollywood, Hollywood." Foxx went back around the fountain the way he had come. The two girls were still there. Now they were looking at him. He raised a hand and waved and they erupted in giggles. One of them was what Kevin liked to call Chocolate Cake, wide where it mattered, pillowy lips, hair a tight mat on the top of her head. The other was lighter by two shades and longer, as was her hair, which hung down in braids. They started to walk toward Foxx, who was suddenly nervous. Shit, he thought. Nervous about what? He sang under his breath: "You're a pear, you're a pear, hanging sweet, high up there."

The girls stopped short, maybe three feet from him. "Hey," the tall one called out.

"Hey," he said.

"You someone famous?" she said.

"Depends," he said. "Who you?"

"You are," she said. She turned to the shorter girl. "I told you," she said. "It's Marvin Gaye." Then she turned back to Foxx. "What do you sing again?"

Foxx didn't say anything. What could you say to that? He smoked a cigarette and a sherm and leaned on a tree longer than he thought he'd need to.

In the TV studio, Yvette was whistling "Temptation Eyes" to herself. Kevin was shooting speed into fruit. "I'm preparing them," he told Denny, the bassist. He had replaced Herb, who had replaced Sammo, who had replaced Lucas.

"For what?" said Denny.

"For fame," Kevin said. One of the production assistants, a tall blonde who had always hung on Lucas, came backstage to give them a ten-minute cue and lingered to talk to Denny. They were in New York, taping for Gerald Atkins. The first time Foxx had been on the show, it had thrilled him. His voice, America's choice. The second time he had tried to rattle a young actress who was making her first appearance.

"Don't look at Atkins directly, but don't look away," he said. "That's the best advice I can give you." The third and the fourth time it was old hat, but now the hat wasn't in fashion anymore, and he felt conspicuous.

"Hey, you," Foxx said to Yvette. "What say you?" She wore a fringed shawl she had bought in Mexico, where she had gone on vacation with a man who owned a string of car dealerships in Los Angeles. Tony was hoping it was nothing serious. "No," Foxx said, when what he meant was yes, yes, yes. If Doctor Foster has got her you know you're through; he's got medicine and money too.

"I say nothing," she said. "You should know that by now."

"How was Tecate?" he said.

"Tijuana," she said. "It was hot. But easy."

"You must have blended right in," Foxx said.

Across the room, a famous actor and a famous actress were deep in discussion about something. The actress looked disapprovingly at Foxx and wrinkled her nose. The wrinkles moved across the room, a smell in reverse.

"You seen Tony around?" Foxx said.

"No."

"Me neither. You know why? Because he's not here. I talked to him twenty minutes ago, and you know where he was?"

"Tecate?" she said.

"Funny. No. He was in bed." Foxx paused to let the word sink in. "Tony. Reliable Tony. In bed the day of a live TV performance. What do you have to say to that?"

"Well, hello," she said.

"What kind of answer is that?" said Foxx. But then he heard Gerald Atkins's voice at his back, and turned. Tall as always, suit crisp, face aglow with the rich man's tan America saw on TV every night, Atkins came across the room with his hand out. He and Foxx had seen each other up in the Hollywood Hills, Atkins driving his Alfa or his MG, Foxx putting his Benz to the test. Foxx had heard on good authority that Atkins liked blow as much as the next man, and that he preferred the company of young girls. Sometimes there was accounting for taste. "Hey, hey," said Foxx, soul-clasping Atkins's hand.

"See you out there in a few minutes," said Atkins.

"Right," said Foxx. He sat down again. "See you when I see you."

Kevin brought Foxx the telephone. "It's Jerry," he said. "Some problem with the label."

"I didn't even know I was expecting," Foxx said into the phone.

"Just want to let you know that Turn's going to give you a shadow," Jerry said.

"I have a shadow," Foxx said. "I'm looking at it right now."

"They're attaching someone to the band," Jerry said. "A junior executive who reports directly to Stringer. They want to make sure they understand what you're doing."

"You mean they want to make sure they control what we're doing."

"Not necessarily," Jerry said.

"You in cahoots?"

"Yeah," said Jerry, impatience binding up his voice. "I'm in cahoots. All I'm saying is be ready for this guy. I think his name is Leon Brisbane."

"Okay," Foxx said. "I got to go out and meet the press." He hung up the phone. "You have to stay in here and wait for Tony," he told Yvette and Kevin. "When he gets here, tell him fifty-dollar fine." He stood, and Kevin came to his feet without thinking. The unpunctured apples tumbled to the floor.

Atkins straightened his tie while a short black woman brushed his hair and another one worked on a spot on his shirt with a hair dryer. Then the women disappeared and a light went on over the camera. "A warm greeting," Atkins said, "for our old friend, Rock Foxx."

"If I knew it was warm," said Foxx. "I wouldn't have worn a jacket."

Atkins led the crowd in laughter. "Tell us about your new single, 'Jar Bug.'"

"People think it's a dance," said Foxx. "It ain't a dance. It's a documentary." His head was buzzing. Atkins nodded for him to go on. Foxx nodded back. "You see, Mr. Atkins, there's a certain kind of man, a certain kind of American, who is in a jar. He can't get out, but he can see out. He can see that everyone has what he don't have. He can see that everyone's moving freely while he's stuck. How does that make him feel?"

"Bugged?"

"Yas, yas, yas," said Foxx.

"'Light up, firefly / America first / The best of the best / Meets the best of the worst.' Some people have said that you're inciting a race riot."

"I ain't inciting nothing. I'm in-sighting."

"You've also taken the unusual step of releasing this new song right on the heels of another record."

"Right on the Achilles' heels," Foxx said. "People might not have gotten exactly where we were going with the other record, so we wanted to offer what you might call an amplification."

"Is that why you've brought amplifiers?"

"Quiet," Foxx said. "They might hear you."

"Do you have a message for the young people who listen to your records?"

"Be good at what you do."

"Are you good at what you do?"

"I most certainly am, my good man."

The show broke for commercials. Atkins leaned back in his chair and cleared his throat. He cleared his throat again. Foxx was watching the bank of monitors, where some blonde chick was washing her hair with Breck shampoo. There was another monitor that showed the hallway. Foxx saw that Tony had arrived, which was good. He also saw that Yvette was avoiding him, standing down a good long way and talking to Kevin, of all people. Oh, well. He couldn't heat up everyone's heart. Atkins stood, cleared his throat a third time. This time Foxx looked at him. "The lower back," he said. "It's hell to pay on the racquetball courts." Then he hopped across the front of the stage, flapping his arms like wings. Sing what you heard, baby bird. "We're right near each other," said Atkins. It took Foxx a few seconds to realize that Atkins wasn't talking to his earpiece, but that he was talking across the chair, at Foxx.

"I know," Foxx said. "I can see you."

"No. Our houses. We have the same mailman. You should come up to my place sometime. In fact, we're having a barbecue next weekend. Bring the family."

"We're just coming off tour," he said. "They've probably had their fill of me."

"No, no," Atkins said, laughing. "The actual family."

"Oh," said Foxx. Who was that, exactly? He and Betty weren't talking except in clenched half-sentences. When he spoke to Lucas, it was only to be judged. His mama was in an assisted-living facility where she enjoyed a comfortable and dignified lifestyle that recognized her limits while at the same time preserving her desire for independence. The fancy language cost him a thousand dollars a month.

In desperation, he looked around for a rescue crew. He got lucky: Denny came down the hall. He was out on the line as usual, rapping to the pretty assistant. "Did Picasso and Matisse sit together and chill?" he said. "Did Jesus and Buddha? Did Ali and Patterson? No, man. But me and the Foxx, we friends. To say the least, he's the most."

"Will you look at that?" said Foxx.

"I don't care," said Atkins, and now he was talking into his microphone. He held up a finger and smiled. When the show came back on, Atkins flipped through some picture postcards with Foxx: missing Woodstock, the Nancy Sinatra rumor. "You're going to perform in a few minutes," said Atkins, "isn't that correct?"

"Yas, yas, yas," said Foxx.

"And will you be playing your new song?"

"I don't know," said Foxx. "I can't wait to find out." That wasn't true. He already knew what he was going to play: a six-minute version of "Let's Go Get Stoned."

"You serious?" Tony said. He had just arrived and was wiping his brow with a towel.

"As mud, blood, and what got lost in the flood."

"Works for me," said Denny.

"No," said Foxx. "You work for me."

He counted off and dove in. Tony looked as if he hadn't slept in a week but he could still spin pretty riffs. Yvette could still cast a high shadow over Foxx's vocals. And Kevin found the groove that made it move. Atkins watched from his chair. Everyone else played the part of distant moons: the crew, the studio audience, the motherfuckers catching the show on TV. "You know my baby, she won't let me in," he sang. "I feel pity; I'm gonna go buy myself a bottle of gin."

"You know I work so hard all day long," he sang. "Everything I try to do seems to turn out wrong."

"Ain't no harm to take a little nip," he sang. "But don't you fall down and bust your lip."

"Yeah," he sang. "Everybody."

Betty
October 1972

The flight to Chicago seemed short sometimes, and other times it seemed to last a lifetime. Maybe that was because she wasn't sure whether she was going home or leaving it. She had been to Chicago three times in the last month, each time more worried that her mother was slipping away, and each time she had returned to Los Angeles shocked by her mother's quick recovery. Betty's mother said that the visits were responsible. "Miracle cure," she said. Betty didn't believe it, but she couldn't explain the improvement. She tried to talk to Robert about it, but he was in one of his moods. "Baby, baby, don't get hooked on me," he said, and locked the studio door from the inside.

Dewey, too, had his moods. He liked to walk in Chicago, bundled up, cute as a bug in his puffy coat and puffy pants. There were children playing in parks so he played in parks, too, and the wind got inside his hood and made him cry. He ran back to her, making poor time on his short legs, and buried his head in her hair. Spring was a long way off and he seemed terrified that it would never come.

The cold was no friend to Betty's mother, either. "Sometimes just breathing in this icy air hurts me," she said. But she seemed in better spirits ever since the doctors had removed more of her lung. "You know what I think about cancer?" she said. "That it's kind of like God."

"What do you mean?" said Betty.

"If you don't believe in it, that's when it hurts you the most." She smiled. "But I believe." Her mother patted the cushion beside her. "Come sit."

Betty sat.

"You know," her mama said, "with all this sickness here in the house, we never get to talk about you."

"Oh," said Betty. Then there was a pause. Sometimes pauses were pregnant. This one was carrying twins.

"It's just that it doesn't seem fair to ignore a girl who went and married someone famous, does it? A girl like that probably wants some attention, don't you think?"

"Maybe," said Betty.

"So, how are things back at home? Pretend I'm asking just like a friend. We meet after a few months, and I tell you about my life—no-good husband got laid off, but the kids are doing great, Janie loves chess club—and I ask you about your life. How are things?"

"Tough," said Betty. Just saying it made her ten pounds lighter. So she said it again. "Very tough."

"You'd say that to a woman you haven't seen in months?"

"I think so."

"Well, then." She coughed, but this one sounded more like punctuation than sickness.

Betty had watched scenes like this in movies or on television: the young wife confessing her fears to her wise old mother. They always struck her as contrived. Even now she wasn't sure. Her mother sighed and patted her hand, and Betty knew what was coming next: a lecture about how men were not to be trusted, or how men were to be obeyed, or how men were to be controlled. But that wasn't what came next.

"He's a doper, right?"

Betty was astonished.

"Come on," said her mama. "You think I'm blind?" She didn't even pause for a laugh. "I can smell it on him a mile away. I can tell from the way he says hello." She gripped Betty's hand with sudden violence. "With a man like that, Betty, you got two choices. You can stay or you can go. I'm not saying that you have only one choice. But if you stay, you're going to have to let him be who he is. Some people will tell you times will get better. They won't. They'll stay this mix of good and bad, and for some people that's good enough." It was more on this matter, or any other matter, than her mother had said in months, and it seemed to have exhausted her. She was motionless for so long that Betty's heart lurched fearfully. But her mother restarted with a snort, and there was more.

"There are lots of big issues with a man like that," she said. "But mainly it comes down to the little one."

"You mean Dewey?"

"I mean exactly Dewey. Women are strong enough to deal with the up and the down. But women know that their babies aren't always strong enough. That's why sometimes they make the choice."

Robert answered the phone with a grunt. "I've been thinking about you," she said. The phone cord was wrapped tight around the top knuckle of her finger, making a grape of the tip.

"Yeah," he said. She could hear him fiddling with dials and slides. "You know, murder is against the law."

"Robert, listen to me," she said. "No jokes. I want to tell you that I love you. That I really do, still."

"Okay," he said. He stopped fiddling. "Why are you telling me this?"

"Because I want you to know it." She lifted the grape of her finger to her mouth. "No matter what happens." He didn't say anything. The silence thickened. "Robert," she said again, and this time his name, ripping through, came away with tatters of the silence still hanging from it.

"Yeah," he said. Static crackled on the line. "B?"

"Still here."

"You know that I think of you, don't you?" He rushed to explain. "Not like that. I mean when I'm making the record. I've been using that book." For a minute she didn't understand. "You know," he said. "The one you gave me. The blank pad with the leather cover."

"From when we were first seeing each other?"

"Yeah," he said. "I found it about a month ago. I hadn't seen it since *Wreckered*. I wrote down all the *Pitch* lyrics. I thought it might make me feel better."

"Did it?"

"It did," he said. "Peace at hand." She chuckled: Kissinger was always good for a laugh. "And I'm putting all the new ideas down in there. Not just ideas for songs. Things I can't say directly to myself. Things I can't say directly to you." He paused the length of three breaths. "Are you coming home soon?"

"Soon," she said. "I promise. And we'll talk."

"We will," he said. He sang her a new melody. "You'll get a look at my miracle book." Then he sang an old one: "It's all too beautiful."

Robert
March 1973

Tony was thirty, and to prove it Foxx bought him a huge cake in the shape of a guitar. His name went up the neck in cherry gel. The candles flickered down by the whammy bar. "Hey old man," Foxx said. "You should get some help blowing those motherfuckers out."

"Let 'em burn," Tony said. Foxx passed him a cigarette but held it high up in the air, so Tony had to look up when he took it. After years of staying mostly clean, Tony was using hard. It was Yvette, of course. She had convinced him to stay off junk, and then she had broken up with him again, which sent him straight into it. Tony wasn't shooting—he was too afraid of that—but he had been snorting regularly for about two months. His eyes were watery. He sniffled. And he had a new look, long hair and a mustard-colored mustache drooping down on either side of his mouth. He looked closer to forty than thirty.

Along with the cake, Foxx was giving Tony a party in the back room of a fancy restaurant in Los Angeles. Betty, dressed as hot as she could go in a short red dress, had helped arrange the party, bought the present, driven there. Foxx leaned over and covered her mouth with his as they pulled into the parking lot. "Careful," she said, smiling. "It's a school night."

"School's out forever," he said. And the party proved it. Jeannine was there, and Boris, and Smorris, who was Mahmoud Akbar Ali now. Yvette was there, keeping her distance from Tony. Lucas had been invited but he didn't show because he was touring with King's Way. There were girls whom Foxx knew by sight, and other girls he knew by touch, and a few girls he didn't know at all, one of whom seemed to be Kevin's date for the evening. "That's Heather," Tony said. "Her old man is one of those guys at the record label."

"Who? Clary?"

"No. The other guy."

"Bruce Dunn? Kevin is fucking Bruce Dunn's daughter? This is some sweet revenge indeed."

"She's a lawyer for the label," said Tony.

"Oh," said Foxx. "So she's fucking us right back."

"You're in a fine mood tonight," Betty said. "Something agrees with you."

"I agree," Foxx said. "With you." He left Betty talking to Mahmoud Akbar Ali and went into an even smaller area at the back of the back room to do a few lines with Kevin and Yvette. James Brown records were coming through the door as he told them about the new songs he was writing. "These are mountaintop," he said.

"All of them?" Kevin said.

"Each of them," Foxx said. "You can't deal with songs in a mob. You have to handle them as individuals."

"Will you sing me one?" Yvette said, sliding onto his lap.

"Can't," he said. "Classified." But he told them the titles: "Rays," "Radiant," "Gravity." The real motherfucker was "Pop Pop." "Shit starts out as bubblegum and ends up with muscle in its mouth," he said. "It's all head."

"What do you mean?"

"I mean it's a head. It thinks. It sees. But I cracked it open, laid the top half on the table like a bowl, and stirred in pieces of other things, a little bit of 'Midnight Train to Georgia,' little bit of 'I Believe When I Fall in Love with You It Will Be Forever.' Then I let the whole mess dry into a kind of plaster. Then I broke the plaster into powder. Then I tested the powder." He did another line to demonstrate.

"Come on," Yvette said. "Sing a little. I miss it. I'm lonely without it." She had her head on his shoulder.

"Okay," he said. "You twisted my arm. But just the first verse."

> *Too much rushing turns the day into a nightmare*
> *Pop pop—It ain't fair*
> *Oh, well, the ghosts are mostly trouble when they dare*
> *I score, they scare*

> *Before I wake I'm sure to take my daily dosing*
> *Pop pop—Peace to the pill*
> *My second cousin brought a dozen, now I'm grossing*
> *Pop pop—Follow the bill*

"You wrote a song about pills?" said Kevin, a smile spreading over his face.

"You're sharp," said Foxx. "Sharp as a motherfucking circle." Then he sent them out of the little room, sanctum sanctorum, and told them to send in Betty. She came in, drenched from dancing, and stood close to him, almost over him, like a wife. "What you need," he said, and passed her a joint.

"What you think I need," she said, and pretended to refuse. But she was loose and sucked the smoke down into her lungs. "Did you miss me?" Betty said.

"Why? You think I sent Yvette and Kevin to get you?"

"No," she said. "I mean all the other times."

He closed his eyes. "I think that you're a good girl, Betty."

"I ain't no girl, fool."

"You know what I mean. A good woman." His tongue dragged. He was gone a little bit, the weed colliding with the coke, the beer sloshing around in his stomach.

"What are you saying?"

"I'm just saying."

The chair creaked. Betty's foot slid within reach of his hand. He brushed her ankle with his fingertips. Then she sighed, not a high sigh but a sober one. "Robert, Robert, Robert," she said.

"So nice they named me thrice," he said.

"I thought about this all the time in Chicago."

"About me? I'm flattered."

"I thought about Dewey, mainly."

Foxx closed his eyes tighter and saw Dewey in the darkness, a point of light that grew, or got closer, until he could see that it had arms and legs and a little nappy head and eyes that were themselves each points of light. "I love him," he said.

"I know you do," she said. "I want him to have a chance. A good chance."

Foxx tried to talk but his throat filled up with something that was sweeter than sorrow but saltier than relief. Finally he could speak, and then he did. "Goddamn, woman," he said. "You gonna come back here with big questions for me?" His eyes were still closed. He couldn't bear to look.

"Or big answers," she said. Her voice was tender and hard at the same time.

"All I'm saying is that I see a red dress like that, and what I expect is walk, not talk."

"So you don't mind if I change the subject?"

"Depends what you mean," he said.

"This is what I mean," she said. He opened his eyes and saw that she had shed her dress and was standing over him in nothing but her bra and earrings. "Goddamn again," he said. She laughed, throatily, wonderfully, easily. "Whatever happens, remember that there were plenty of times you made me happy," she said, and, lowering herself onto him, repaid the favor.

"Let's have a meeting about that," Foxx said to Betty as they emerged from the back room. "I'll have my people call your people."

The party was breaking up. Heather Dunn had gone home with Kevin. Tony sat in a chair alone in the middle of the room, a plate of cake in his lap. "I thought you left," Tony said.

"No way," said Foxx. "We're twins, man. That means that your birthday is my birthday too."

Smorris was leaving. He waved, and Tony stood up to wave back but he couldn't keep his balance. "*Oof*," he said, coming back down onto the chair. His right hand fell into the cake.

"Man, let's just sit for a second," said Foxx. The three of them sat. "Today, my son, you are a man," said Foxx.

"I am a soldier, sir."

"A soldier it is, then. And as a soldier, do you promise to defend this band with your life?"

"With my life, sir." Tony saluted stiffly.

"We have suffered heavy losses lately. We lost men. We lost ground."

"Understood, sir," said Tony.

"And then there's this bean counter who is supposed to hang over us like an awning and steal our motherfucking sunlight."

"Yeah," said Tony. "Jerry keeps talking about him. What's his name?"

"His name is motherfucking mud. Are you with me, man? I mean, soldier."

"Yes, sir," said Tony wearily. "For what it's worth, I thought that *Pitch* did everything it should have done. It's an act of bravery."

"Glad you liked it. Sad you couldn't convince the others."

"Funny you should say that. Because I happen to know that Lucas thought it was a fucking brilliant record."

"Now I know you're high."

"He did," Tony said. "He only lies to you. A few months after it came out, he was driving through Compton, and he looked out on the street, and all he saw was *Pitch*."

"You mean cats were playing it?"

"No. They were living it."

So Lucas went out and saw some street-corner bloods with identity crises hanging round their necks: black crosses and albatrosses. The truth was always a noose. "But what next? What if it tapped me out instead of tapping me in?"

"I'm not worried." Tony sang Foxx the first verse of "Pop Pop," word for word.

"Kevin remembered that shit? I didn't think he could remember his hat size."

"No," Tony said, blushing a bit. "Yvette sang it to me."

"Really?" said Foxx. "Well, Happy birthday, Mr. President."

"You still think I should stay away from her?"

"Follow your heart. I hear that's what it's for."

"Remember when she came to audition? We were where? Tienda Publica?" He trailed off. "Permission to go home and sleep, sir?"

Foxx looked at Tony's mustache, which had too much in it—powder and bits of food—and at Tony's eyes, which had too little in them. "Granted," he said. "And you don't have to call me sir, son. Stand down. In fact, stand down and away. All this talk of the past gets me down, and I need to be up. There's a war to be fought, son."

"Yes, sir." Tony raised his right hand. It came out of the ruins of the cake, and it was clotted with darkness.

Betty
May 1973

The car was new, and she breathed in the smell. Then she rolled down the window and breathed in the air, which was new, too. "And if we live to be a hundred years old," she sang. "If you ever let that spring turn cold."

"Sing the other one, Mama." Dewey hung his arms over the front seat. "The one that you and Daddy made."

"Which one?"

He scrunched up his forehead in a parody of concentration. "The rainbow."

Betty laughed, just as she had laughed when Robert had told her that he planned to cover "Over the Rainbow" on his new record. "It ain't no motherfucking joke," he yelled. "And I want you to sing it with me." He lit up a cigarette, and it shook in his hands, which were shaking also.

They were shaking because he was kicking. He had come to her at night, when she was half asleep, and asked her in a level sweet voice if she would mind waking up and talking to him about something important. With Tony the way he was, Robert said, he couldn't be the way he had been. He had to change. Drugs, he said, were sometimes just about change, and going straight was enough of a change to last him a while. He didn't promise anything permanent.

Betty answered with a story about her childhood. There was a junkie in her neighborhood. He was incoherent, sometimes violent. He rarely remembered to zip up his pants. He was Betty's reference point, and when she thought about users she thumbed down the corner of the page on which he appeared. But then she met Robert. "You confused me," she told him.

"Zipper always up," he said.

"No," she said. "You could do it all. You could make things."

"That's nothing to be proud of," he said. "It's in me, and all I have to do is let it out. I think that's why I put so much else in me, to feel like I had some say over what was there."

They had walked together down the hall, stood over the crib, and watched Dewey's small fists clench and unclench. They had embraced like parents in a movie. The next morning, she went to join Robert in the shower but had to jump out because the water was like ice. "It's my cold shower," he said. "And then I'm going to have some cold potatoes to go with my cold turkey."

If Betty had been confused by Robert when he was using, she was even more perplexed when he quit, because the shifts in mood she had attributed to the drugs remained. People, places, amusements still went abruptly in and out of favor. And he was still the master of microscopic unkindnesses. "Give," he said, withdrawing his hand from hers in a movie theater.

After he told her he planned to cover "Over the Rainbow," he led her downstairs with feet that seemed uncertain on the stairs. But when he pushed her into the booth and slid in behind the mixing board, all his confidence returned. "I have a new arrangement," he said. "Warm organ and some faded horns. I need you to sing duet with me on the chorus."

"Where's Yvette?"

"Who the fuck knows? She's missing. Tony's ripped up about it. At his birthday party he thought he might have a chance with her again. But now it looks like she's down in Tecate again with some rich dude."

"So I'm the substitute?"

"You look pretty tall but your heels are high," he said. "Now let's go." He rolled the tape and the song came on, slow, seductive. If Betty didn't know better, she would have thought it was a soul ballad. "And the dreams that you dare to dream," Robert sang, his vocals slurred but beautiful, "really do come true." "Okay?" he said. "I'm going to rewind it. And when I get to the chorus, the 'Somewhere over' part, I want you to sing for me."

"Heard that before," she said.

She felt the beauty of the arrangement and tried to match it. "Good," he said.

"Too loud," she said. "Let's go again." The second time, she kept the vocals low. Robert played them back for her, and they were dreamy, mystifying, like tides at night. "Let's do a few more like this," he said.

Now, in the car, it was Dewey making the demands. "Sing the rainbow song," he said again. "Lullaby."

Robert took her to the couch in the studio after they recorded. "Hey," he said, kissing her neck. "You want to know why I took you off the song all those years ago?"

"I know why. Because it wasn't good enough."

"Wrong," he said. "Because you made the song beautiful and it needed to be ugly." Robert slid from her neck to her shoulders. "These songs need to be beautiful."

"You say that now. But what about when you erase me in three months?"

His tongue dragged across her belly. "If you could see the things I'm writing, you wouldn't say that."

"Can I see them?"

He was between her legs. "One more thing," he said. "As long as you're here, you got to look me in the eye. I got rid of the sunglasses, and you have to honor that."

"It's kind of hard at the moment."

"You know what I'm saying," he said. "You don't have to waste your time if you don't want to be a friend of mine."

"Those aren't the words to that song," she said.

"They are now," he said softly. He stopped kissing her. She knew before he spoke that his voice would be icy. "You done slipped and fell, Tammi Terrell." He stood and left the room. She could see him through the window, shoulders in a slump. He punched the wall but she wasn't sure his heart was in it.

"Mommy," Dewey said in the car, "sing the rainbow."

"I'll sing you another song instead," she said. "Little bitty pretty one, come on and talk to me. A-lovey-dovey-dovey one, come sit down on my knee."

Robert
June 1973

In Maurice's, Foxx took a table by the window. "Coffee," he said. "Black."

He was waiting for the new Turn guy, whose name was Leon Brisbane, probably after the city he came from in motherfucking Australia. The label seemed to have an endless supply of these stiffs, with the same tight assholes and striped ties. Foxx checked his watch, which was running behind the clock on the wall. The motherfucker was delayed. He drank his coffee, ordered a lemonade.

From his seat he had a good view of a soul sister at the bus stop. She was as fine as the next girl, if the next girl was Pam Grier. He watched as a series of men approached her and checked her out. Each was sent away. Then a short dark dude stepped in and began to make his case. He was something, dressed like a character from TV—long suede jacket, stingy brim—and he walked with the swing of a pimp: shoulder dip, hip roll. The woman laughed like she had just heard her favorite joke and the cat in the hat put his hand on her arm. Then the little man took a notebook out of his back pocket, jotted down something the woman was saying, tipped his hat, and headed straight for Maurice's. He came through the door, devoutly cool, and his eyes settled on Foxx. "Leon Brisbane," he said, extending his hand.

"No shit," said Foxx. Brisbane was strong for such a little guy, and when he smiled there was something familiar that happened to the skin around his eyes. "You want a lemonade?" he said.

"Sure thing. Although," he said to an approaching waitress, "you know I got to get me some meatloaf."

"On the house, baby," she said. "Any friend of Foxx is a friend of Mama."

"Well, all right, then," said Brisbane.

When they were settled in, Foxx squared himself at the table. "Tell me," he said to Brisbane. "How's a dude like you end up working for Turn?"

"I'm part of NITO."

"What's that?"

"The nigger-in-the-office program." He showed all his teeth but didn't laugh. "It's like that old saying: One good turn deserves a nigger." Teeth again. "Okay. Now ask me again. I done used up all my material."

"How'd you end up at Turn?" said Foxx.

"My old man used to be a janitor there, and he was the only one who didn't steal. So I gots cred with whitey. As a matter of fact, that story bears some relevance to our meeting." He reached into his pocket and took out two envelopes. "This one, we'll get to in a minute," he said, tapping the top one, "but first I want to show you what's in this one." He opened the bottom one and slid out a photograph. "This is a picture of me and my old man and some other dude." He slid it to Foxx. Foxx looked at the picture, saw a squat man who looked like Leon and a little shorty who looked like Leon minus twenty years. Then he looked at the third figure. It was Ray Charles. "Yeah," said Brisbane. "They told me that you had a thing for Brother Ray. Dude is everything to everything, you know. They say he can smell the pretty ladies."

"You seem to do have a nose for news yourself," said Foxx. "I saw you out by the bus stop."

Leon laughed again. "I got one more picture to show you," he said. This one was of Little Richard, and he had Leon on his lap. "More into the pretty boys than the pretty girls, but there's no denyin' that he was flyin'."

"You heard all the outtakes of his from Specialty?"

"No," Leon said. "You got 'em?"

"I do," Foxx said. "Come over sometime and I'll play them for you."

"You still living where you were? I heard you split from your old lady."

"Hard to tell. Or hard for me to tell. Maybe she knows for sure. But she's with her mama in Chicago, so I'm at the house most of the time."

"Cool." Brisbane put the photographs back in the first envelope and slid the second one forward. "You know what I got here?" he said. "Orders from Monroe Stringer to keep a close watch on your black ass."

"Oh, yeah?" said Foxx.

"Yeah," said Brisbane. "Those boys over there, they are stupid times ten. Let me read you a bit. I think you'll enjoy it. 'Mr. Brisbane'—that's me—'is entrusted with ensuring the delivery of said album.'"

Foxx snorted. "Said album."

"Sez them," said Brisbane. He picked up a piece of cornbread. "They plucked me out, like a black eye from a black socket, and sent me over here to see what I could see. I just got one question for you. Why on earth would they think that my loyalty was with them? I mean, shit, man, you think they ever even listened to *Pitch*?"

"They must have," said Foxx. "Why else would they go out of their way to call me and tell me that it was a piece of shit?"

"They did not." He let go a long, low breath. "What they do, they smile in your face."

"What they said, exactly, was that given its performance, they didn't expect to break even on their outlay."

"They don't usually talk about money directly," Brisbane said. "There's a word they like to use. *Viable.*"

"A word is dead when it is said, some say," said Foxx.

"A word is what you heard just yesterday," said Brisbane.

"Brother," said Foxx. Cat quotes from "Jar Bug," cat gets a point.

"So look," said Brisbane. "You have a new record, right?"

"It's about half right so far."

"How about I keep them off your back and you go and do what you got to do? What's it called?"

Foxx didn't know, and then he knew. "*Revolution,*" he said.

"Yeah," said Brisbane. "I hoped it would be something like that. And how long you think it has left in the oven?"

Foxx coughed. "Two months," he said.

"Cool," said Brisbane. "I think they're worrying over much smaller potatoes."

"Being whitey does that to you."

"Hey, man," said Brisbane. "You're talking about my esteemed employers." He went back to the letter. " 'Mr. Brisbane will also shepherd the band in its dealings with the press.' "

"Does that make me a sheep?"

"Black shepherd for a black sheep," Brisbane said, and fired off a loud laugh.

"What help do I need with the press? They love me like a brother."

"I saw an interview you did with *Billboard* where you told them that the band was all cleaned up from drugs."

"True."

"True that you said that, or true that the band's all clean?"

"True that I said that."

"But it's not the fact of the matter, is it?"

"It's not a fact. Does that matter?"

"Not to me," Brisbane said. "But if evidence surfaces to the contrary, well, some people who like to keep track of you might view it as hypocritical."

"Hypocrisy is the only privacy of the famous."

Brisbane laughed again. "Who said that?"

"A wiser man than I."

"Who?"

"Me, yesterday."

"Ask yesterday, and it says 'Try me tomorrow.'" Brisbane said. Cat quotes from "Jar Bug" twice, cat gets two points. "Which reminds me: I have to jet. I'm going up to Seattle tomorrow and I have to get my house in order. You heading out too?"

"Yeah," said Foxx. "Let me ask you a question."

"Anything."

"You get a number from that sister at the bus stop?"

Brisbane unleashed another laugh. "You know I did. You want it? I'll give it to you along with mine." He took out a business card, wrote on it, passed it across the table. "Just seven numbers could straighten out your life," he said. He even sang a snatch, a little wavery, but with a nice hold on the melody.

Foxx drove home high as a kite, and he hadn't taken any pills or powder in hours. With Leon, he could hold Stringer and the other motherfuckers at bay. He could get on that highway car and ride again. He wasn't sure who else was riding with him, exactly. Tony, probably, but Kevin was one slip away from slipping away entirely. And Betty was the worst of them all: She had told him that she was heading to Chicago again, and that she didn't know how for how long. Foxx let her go. See you soon, Daniel Boone. But he needed troops. He needed a battle map. And he needed to know that when he gave the order to fire, he wouldn't feel the bullets in his own back.

Man in his corner, man on the move. Brisbane called him most days from payphones around town. "Would you ever work with Tower of Power?" he would say. Or: "Some folk chick wants to cover 'Wednesday Ain't So Bad.' Should I give her permission?"

"You never in your office," Foxx said. "Why you need one?"

"So I have a place to put all the shit I done stole," said Brisbane, and blasted the line with another screeching laugh.

Betty
August 1973

Robert had finished his record, the third record he had made as Betty's husband. He mailed it to Chicago. There was a note, too. It said, "Read this now" on the outside. The inside was written hastily, with angry loops on the letters. "You know that plane you took?" Robert said. "You know that miracle book? When you left, you left me with my notebook, and I put myself into it. I already got six songs for the record after this one. And they *move*. Meanwhile, take a listen to this motherfucker. I hope it puts tears in your ears."

Betty unwrapped *Revolution*. The cover of the album was a blue-tinted picture of Robert sleeping. He looked so peaceful that way. Betty withdrew the album, still in its sleeve. There were nine songs. "Rays" was first. "Radiant" was second. She whispered the titles to herself, all the way down to the last song, "Over the Rainbow." She held the sleeve up to the light and looked through the spindle hole.

Betty put the record on the record player and listened to it. The first notes sounded like a concerto, solo piano rising and falling like a tide. Then there was a flute, then a violin. And then Robert began to sing. "You know I try, baby, try all day long / I got nothing to show for it except for this song." This was "Rays," but it was sadder than she had ever heard it, a handkerchief with bluesy organ riffs stitched around the edges. After the first verse, Robert started to let more energy creep into his vocals, into the arrangement, and on the edge of the chorus Betty braced for the explosion she knew would come. And it did: "The days are the nights, the nights are the days," he cried. "I'm working so hard, baby, I need a raise." The second song, "Radiant," was entirely different from the version Robert had played her just a few months before, with a new guitar part and new lyrics ("Poison," he sang. "America's a cage to keep the boys in"). When she got to "Pop Pop," which now had nothing but a drum machine and horns, she turned on the light next to the bed and studied the cover for clues. "Moved along, I'm getting strong—or is that faster?" he sang. "Pop pop / Ain't nothing sadder than the brink of a disaster / Hey mister, remaster." It was a riddle, more devious than any music he had ever made, which made her suspect that it was more straightforward. This time, her backing vocals had made the cut, and Robert had even credited her, as Betty Cobham. Was that the message? "A map of the world / Unfurled / It went up in flames / Places, names," he sang. Maybe that was the message. A lonely guitar played four notes that sounded like the beginning of a country-and-western song, or the end of an era. Was that the message? She lay on the bed, decoding everything, understanding nothing.

Betty was trying to cut him off clean: no phone calls, no letters. She told Elena, who had a baby on the way. She told Charlotte, who had recently split with Lonnie. But she didn't tell her mama. She couldn't. Every time she thought about it, her heart lurched. Telling her mama would make it gospel truth, and she wasn't ready for that.

But her mama knew. The sicker she got—and this time, it was real, so real that she wouldn't even joke about it—the more she seemed to know. One morning, she told Betty that it would start to rain at ten thirty, and at ten twenty-five on the dot, the clouds began to mass in the same sky that two minutes before had been as clear as glass.

"Betty," said her mama. "You can stay here as long as you want. I like to touch my little Dewey's hair. I know that Charlotte likes having you around. You're like a sister to her. And you're like a daughter to me." She laughed.

The longer she went without talking to Robert, the more Betty started to think of him in pieces. Not broken, exactly, but the camera in her mind started to give her close-ups of different parts of his life: his guitar leaning in a corner, his hand stubbing out a joint in an ashtray. The one picture that kept returning to her was a picture of Robert writing in the legal pad. She liked remembering him then. She wanted the book to prove that he was like that once.

"But he told you that you could have it, right?" said Charlotte.

"When he's dead," said Betty. "Very melodramatic."

"From what you told me about the way he does that dope, maybe you won't have to wait that long."

"That ain't right to say. I don't want to talk about it anymore."

"Fine," said Charlotte. "You coming out with me tonight?"

"Not sure," said Betty. "I'm supposed to see Lucas."

"Oh, ho," said Charlotte.

"No 'oh, ho.' He's in town for a radio appearance. I may not even see him. I may just talk to him on the phone."

"Oh, ho," said Charlotte. "I saw him on TV the other day. He was on the *Midnight Special* playing that new song of his. He's fine." She stretched the word: *fi-i-ine*.

"He's with someone."

"So what?" said Charlotte. "So are you."

Betty went back to her bedroom, the same bedroom she had slept in when she was a girl, and lay down in the bed with Dewey. "I like you and love you, mama," said Dewey.

"I know," Betty said.

She put Robert's new record on the turntable. She picked the next-to-last song, "Gravity," which had a Stevie Wonder-type synthesizer riff and some high horns that stayed up in the rafters of the mix. "I took a rocket to the top of the moon," Robert sang, "with a watch in my pocket and a silvery spoon." He shifted to a bass growl. "Feel my soul tumbling, tumbling down," he sang, breaking off a piece of the Stones' "Tumbling Dice" and rolling it alongside a piece of Aretha's "Going Down Slow." And for the chorus, he switched again, went all falsetto, like Curtis Mayfield:

> *Oh will it break or will it splash*
> *Thirty-odd pieces or the fifty-yard dash?*
> *Sixty seconds till impact, crash*
> *Does it have a minute*
> *In it?*

She thought of Robert when she met him, rounding the corner backstage at the Coliseum, his teeth shining like the sun, his skin like the sky at night. She thought of Robert at the kitchen table in Los Angeles, the white bird winging through his eyes. Five years before, she had just met him. Would she know him five years from now? She saw Robert's vocals in her mind. They were a thick line that went up even when his voice went down, even when he started shouting, "Gravity! Gravity!" She went up with them, floating, like she was drunk or a little high. Robert's voice filled the room, but the way that darkness filled a room rather than the way light did. "Yeah," he shouted, like a stone from a slingshot. "Yeah," he moaned, like a snake down a pipe. Betty heard the sound of faint crying, tried to locate it in the mix, realized that the noise was coming from Dewey, who was right there on the bed. She gathered him up.

Robert
January 1974

Floyd Hughes was a barber in Annapolis, Maryland. He cut heads and listened to the radio, and in the early sixties he formed a barbershop quartet with some cousins of his. "A barber who's actually in a quartet," he liked to say. "Imagine that." The group was named the Anchormen, and they sang around Maryland dressed in matching striped shirts and straw boaters. Around 1965, Hughes turned the Anchormen into an R&B vocal group; he took the middle, like Robert had back in Roxbury.

Then came the late sixties, and the draft, and Hughes's cousin Allen, the tenor in the group, went to Nam and died on his belly in Bho San. At around the same time, Hughes started dabbling in acid. The Anchormen weren't getting bigger or better, and Hughes was discouraged. He rechristened the group Anchor, set aside doo-wop for funk, and started recording cracked, trippy epics that put bass in every corner of the place. Their biggest hits were all over the charts by late '73: "(For Rich, For Poor) Get Your Feet on the Floor," "Climb Up a Tree and Visit Me," and their anthem, "Anchor What?"

Some people dismissed them as an echo of the Foxxes, but Hughes didn't mind being accused of imitation. Foxx knew this because Hughes told him. Hughes told him because Foxx asked. Foxx asked because he was curious. Foxx was curious because Hughes had some primo toot, laid out in neat white lines right on the back of Seals & Crofts's *Summer Breeze*. "At least it's good for something," Hughes said. "And I certainly am blowin' through that jasmine in my mind."

They were goofing and white-roofing in Foxx's den on a bright Saturday night that proved that the stars still shone. Leon Brisbane, who knew both men, had made introductions. Hughes had his band massed around him—he had renamed them after the parts of an anchor, Ring Lee, Stock Miller, Fluke Johnson, until he ran out of parts, and then he just gave them normal nicknames. "I'm easy that way," he said. "Easy the hard way. What do I care if people tell me I imitate you? Does the color black imitate the color black? Both are made in the shade."

"That's the truth," said the man right behind him. This was Shank Brown, the guitarist.

"Original is how you stink, not how you think. If you follow the right people, you'll get to the promised land."

"Say it again," said Shank Brown.

"You dig what I'm saying? We got to Canaan and found out that the green meadows and the rolling hills were just your lawn, man."

"Uh-huh," said Shank Brown.

"We ain't nothing but a little music from the house next door," said Hughes.

"Well, you have my blessing, neighbor," Foxx said. "Carry the torch from the field to the porch."

Penny was there. Penny was always there now. She wore Betty's clothes, which seemed to fit her perfectly. Shank put "Basketball Jones" on the record player.

"That's giving me a headache," Foxx said. "Shut it off."

"You heard the man," Brisbane said. He flipped on the radio, which was playing "Call Me," that new Al Green track.

"This is some serious feel-it-in-your-heart shit," said Hughes.

Foxx nodded, but he didn't feel it in his heart. He felt it in his fist: butter-throat motherfucker getting over on his charts. "Let's keep spinning the dial," Foxx said. "Around the world." Next they got "Break Up to Make Up," which Foxx loved, but getting the song also meant getting Penny singing along, unstylistically. "Someone hear a crow?" Leon said.

"Kiss my ass," she said.

"Then I'd be out of work," Foxx said. Penny kept tuning until the radio landed on "Frankenstein." "Stop here," Foxx said, mainly because it had no singing in it.

"You see this dude?" Hughes said. "He so white he's black."

Foxx felt good, not just high. He had his court around him, Leon and Penny. He had a prince at his side to prove that he was king. And, for the moment, he had his kingdom back: *Revolution* was number three on the Billboard big board, and not coming down. In fact, Turn was so hot on the band that they had sent Leon to find out about a new single. And Foxx was so relieved that *Revolution* was charting that he had agreed. "Sure, man," he told Leon. "I can get them a new single in the next month or so."

"They say they want a positive message."

"It'll be number one with a plus sign."

Penny sat on Foxx's lap, slid her hands underneath her own ass to feel him. "Rock steady," he said.

Much later, after Hughes and Brisbane were gone, after Foxx had pitched a Penny, he got up off her and went to the kitchen. He sat at the counter and fingered a G-rock. He looked at his reflection in the toaster. Something was etched into his face. It was longing. He wanted to hear someone sing better than Penny. He went to the telephone and took a chance, his fingers burning each time he spun the dial.

"Hello?" said Betty's mama. "Who is this?" It was always her mother.

"Is Betty there?"

"Who? I'm hanging up unless you tell me who this is."

Now her voice sounded younger. Maybe it was the cousin.

"It's Robert," he said. His voice shocked him with how it sounded: gentle, pleading, a voice in need.

"Robert who?"

"Robert Robert. Betty's husband."

"Betty who?"

"Who is this?" he said.

"Shannon," she said. Now her voice was even younger, and hard.

"What number is this?"

She told him. He was off by one in the next-to-last digit.

He hung up the phone and put the coke back up his nose, where it belonged.

The next day, Yvette was back at rehearsal. Tony had located her. You could always count on that; he was driven by love, and whatever else was falling down in him, his instincts remained pure. Yvette looked thin and tired, and she had a bad cough. "Just under the weather," she said.

"Well, you shouldn't have left it out in the rain," Foxx said. The band was practicing out in Carmel, in a converted furniture warehouse. It was like their first practice space back on Polk, except a hundred times the size. "Did you see this?" said Tony, waving *Creem*. He flipped if open and read. "Rock Foxx has pulled off a masterful magic trick with his last studio record. But can his band still deliver the goods onstage?"

"I have an idea," said Kevin. "I know no one believes that I have them, but I do. I think we should push Yvette further out in front."

And he was right. Right as Rufus. Yvette's voice had always been pretty, but these days it had a touch of ugliness in it too, and was more beautiful as a result. It worked at rehearsal, and in the first show back, Robert let her take lead on "We All Need a Place in the Sun," and she climbed the melody like she was shimmying up a tree, and the top of the song opened up for her, and she stretched out inside it.

Then Foxx came on. For the first verse, he sang off-key, missed notes, bulled ahead into the wrong song. He did it on purpose, to feel the pity of the crowd upon him. He wanted them to think that he had lost it. Then, just when they were going to give up on him, he ripped into the song with all his heart. He wished Betty could see him, even though he knew she would have disapproved of the deceit.

Foxx wanted to take the band for food after the show, but Tony bailed. "Head-ache," he said. Kevin went off with a girl he had met.

"I'll go," Yvette said. "If by food you mean drink."

"Special food for a special flower," he said. "Special power for a special hour."

"Is that a line from a song?"

"Now it is," he said.

Foxx and Yvette went to a bar on Division Street, where Foxx told way-back tales about Carl Chandler's band while Yvette drank whiskey. "Keep going," she said.

"Story or whiskey?"

"Both," she said. "Clink, clink, another drink."

After a half dozen, Foxx looked at his watch. It was too dark to read the face. "What time is it?" he said.

"It might be time," she said. She leaned in close enough that he could see the tiny hairs on the back of her neck. "Should we go finish that song?"

"Which one?"

"Special flower, special petals, special steam from special kettles. That one."

"Terrible," he said.

"Make it better."

"Special sons and special daughters," he said. "Special smoke on special wa-ters."

"That's better?" Yvette said. "Take me home."

He drove slow, pretending to show her the sights. They parked outside her house. Yvette touched his hand, and then his face. His hands were sweating. His stomach would not settle. The light from a streetlamp spread out against the windshield.

"What's the matter?" Yvette said. "Can't I do something for you?" She started to do something for him. He thought of Betty, which made him sick and then he stopped thinking of her, which made him sicker. He opened the car door and climbed out.

Inside, he put Yvette in her bed, fully clothed. He sat on the foot of the bed and asked her to sing for him. She sang Joni Mitchell, went from "love came to my door" to "glory train passed through him" to "fallen angels." He stood to go, was drawn back again, tried to make sense of her beauty. But beauty made no sense. It was the universe's way of writing poetry. He thought of Betty again, started to feel sad. It ain't pretty, Gordon Liddy.

Yvette was sleeping now, and he went back to the car and drove over to see Penny. Because she didn't make him sad. Because he didn't love her. Because she would come when he called.

Two girls were on the TV, fucking each other. One had her face between the other's legs, which were opening and closing quickly, beating against the ears of the first like wings. Foxx had the volume down because he wasn't really looking. He wasn't really looking because he had seen it before, and also because he was looking at something he hadn't seen before: one of his records perched atop the Billboard charts the same week one of his singles hit number one. "It's like stars aligning, if by stars I mean me," he said. It was a line he meant to use in the morning's radio interview; he was due to go on in a half hour with an Atlanta DJ. But he had a bit of business to conduct before the interview. He hummed the chorus to "Rays" under his breath, picked up the phone, and dialed.

"Hello."

"Betty, please."

"Is this Robert?"

"Yes, ma'am." It was her mother again. He had tried the house late at night, early in the morning: The old woman answered every time. "Can I speak to your daughter, please?"

"I'll tell you what I told you two days ago, and four days ago, and every other time you've called. Not until you decide to do what you have to do. You know what that is."

"No," he said.

"What's that?"

"No, ma'am?"

"I'm not telling you what to do, but I'm telling you what to do if you want my daughter back. And your son."

"There are rules now?"

"Don't think of them as rules. Think of them as demands."

"Tell her I called."

"You know I won't."

Tony was up, reading *Rolling Stone* and smoking some grass. Denny was wolfing down room-service eggs. Yvette was watching cartoons. Kevin wouldn't come to the door of his room. The road manager, sighing, went to get the bellboy he had just sent away. Foxx and Tony went into Kevin's room, which was empty, and then Foxx went into the bathroom. Kevin was balled up on the floor. "Fuck," said Foxx. The mother-fucker was turning purple.

"Get Dr. Phil," said Tony.

Dr. Phil came in with his bag and told everyone to stand clear. Foxx backed off quick. The body spooked him. Dr. Phil took out a needle.

"Jesus," said Tony.

"This is adrenaline," Dr. Phil said, and injected it into the webbing between Kevin's toes. It was like watching a baby being born: Kevin got color in his cheeks, then opened his eyes, then started bawling.

Foxx had someone call and postpone the radio interview. By noon, they had Kevin sitting up and taking sips of coffee. The web of skin where Phil had jabbed the needle was a violent pink; Foxx had to go into the bathroom and do a line himself just to calm down.

"You know," Dr. Phil said matter-of-factly as they waited for the elevator. "He's going to die sometime. Maybe tomorrow."

But he didn't. Not the day after, or the day after that. Foxx and Tony made sure of that, shadowing him everywhere he went, card games, strip shows, long evening drives. The tailing had two effects: Tt kept the band close, boys being boys and all that, and it started to turn Tony around.

In Detroit, it was warmer than it had been in weeks, and Foxx and Tony woke up early the morning after the show, borrowed a basketball from the hotel, and went down the street to shoot hoops at a high school. "My wrist hurts," said Tony.

"Excuses already?" said Foxx. But then Tony started sinking shots from every corner of the court. Foxx was tired, had nothing moving in his blood, so after the second game he waved his hands. "I'm through, McAdoo," he said.

On the way back, Tony decided to invite Kevin and Yvette down to the lobby for breakfast. "Just the four of us," he said. "It'll be good for the band."

Kevin answered his door in his underwear and asked for ten minutes to dump the piece of ass that had ended up in his bed. "I hope Yvette's alone," Tony said.

"Now it's more than your wrist that's hurting, isn't it?" said Foxx.

"You know," Tony said. "I think I'm still in love with her. It's something that follows me. Buendía's blood."

They went up to Yvette's room. The door was open a crack. Foxx laughed. Bitch was probably so stoned that she forgot to close it before she went to sleep. But Yvette wasn't sleeping; or rather, she would never be doing anything else. He knew she was gone the second he saw her face. It was like a volume knob turned down to zero on a song you wanted to hear the rest of.

The cops said that she died from the purity of the smack; for weeks afterward Foxx heard talk on the street that sales were up because of it. Buy the shit that buried Yvette Washington. Sick.

The band pulled off the tour, canceled the remaining leg. Jerry met them in Seattle, where Yvette's mother lived. Foxx barely saw him, even though they were sitting right next to each other. He barely saw anyone except Yvette's mother, whose face was a leathery mask.

The next night, Foxx went to a place near the airport with Tony and Kevin and suffered through a dinner where no one said a word until Tony said, "I'm thinking of moving to Florida," and Kevin said, "Well, that ruins my plan to move to Florida." Someone made a noise that was half laugh and half relief.

They shook hands and hugged and Tony got on one plane and Kevin got on another one. Foxx knew that wasn't all there was to it. The chords would resolve. Chords always did. He stood alone in the hotel and tried to catch a look at himself in the mirror. He looked insufficient, too little and too late. Later that night he risked a call to Betty. "She knows about Yvette," Betty's mama said. "She's very sad about it, but this is all the more reason she can't talk."

The next week, he and Jerry took a plane to New York to see the label bosses. But the bosses couldn't make it. Clary was in Europe. Dunn was in Florida. Even Monroe Stringer had something better to do. The room was filled with men like the one who was talking to him, scrubbed sub-veeps who didn't dig his music and never would. When they got up in the morning, they didn't put their pants on. They put themselves on. "We're so sad about the personal tragedy that has befallen the band," the man said. "But at the same time, we're so happy with the performance of the last record. We just want to make certain that we supply your audience with more of what they've come to expect."

The meeting was as smooth as a baby's face. Jerry agreed that the band would deliver a new single within the month. "Positive message," Jerry said. "We can dedicate it to Yvette's memory." A solo record was to follow. "We think that we can supply that by October, which would let you do a January release," Jerry said. The vice president spoke some numbers and Jerry nodded.

At the end, everyone stood and the men on both sides of the table flowed toward Foxx. He shook hands with them all. "We just want to protect our number-one artist," one man said. "Your first record was the first record I ever bought," another said.

The old man who worked the elevator said hello to Foxx. "You going up?" he asked.

"Straight down," said Foxx, and meant it.

Betty
May 1974

"That a new single?" The boy talking was seventeen, maybe, with a big blown-out Afro that looked like a tornado.

"I never heard of it before." The other boy was taller but younger.

"But you heard of him, right?"

"Sure. That last record is cool. But a girl in the band died. I think they split up."

"Like I said," the older boy said. "That a new single?"

Betty turned to look. The older boy must have thought that she was checking him out, because he returned her stare. She moved off down the aisle to pick up what she had come for—"Rock the Boat," for Dewey, who had heard it on the radio and asked for it by name—and then, when the boys were gone, she moved back. They had been standing by a cardboard display of Robert. In the picture he was grinning broadly and hugging a big rubber ball that was painted like a globe. The title of the single, "Smile and the World Smiles with You," was printed underneath. On the back of the sleeve there was a small picture of Yvette, with her dates beneath it in parentheses. Robert was in that picture, too, in the background, pretending to read a newspaper.

Betty hadn't seen Robert for six months and hadn't talked to him in more than five. "Be brave," her mama said.

"Never afraid," she said. But she was afraid, mostly for Dewey. He was asking about Robert more and more, and her answers weren't stalling him like they used to.

When she got home, she set him up with his present on the small record player in the kitchen and went into the spare bedroom to play the record she had bought for herself.

Robert's song was a short pop confection about positive attitude. His vocals were cheery, almost candied: He sounded like he was standing on top of a birthday cake:

Bouncing back
Getting back on track
Learn before you learn to burn
Get wise before you criticize
What they say
Isn't just a style
It's true
Smile and the world smiles with you

Betty had higher hopes for the flip side, "Blink of an Eye," but the false cheer was thick there, too.

Blink of an eye
Keep your head high
Wade through the water
Like you ought to

Where was the man she knew? He wasn't in these songs. They were child's play. Betty was ready to take the record off the turntable when, midway through the B-side, there was a drum crack as loud as a gunshot.

The music came back up as a slow, funky brew: spidery guitar, distorted tack piano, muffled drums, flat synthesized horns. The music had a spin that Betty hadn't heard since *Pitch*: it was elusive and a little mean. But it was the lyrics that chilled her, near-whispered vocals reprocessed through filters and gates. The words were barely audible unless you leaned in close to the speaker:

Settling down
Settling up
Who's been drinking
From my cup?
Two birds flying
One falls down
I wonder what he found.

After that, it was all outro: Robert leaning on the organ and singing just a single couplet: "There's always something moving when it starts / What will grow can also break apart." He sang it over and over again. He sang until it was over.

This was a little piece of him, and from it she regrew the whole man. She remembered his fingers moving quickly over piano keys as if he was a blind man who was reading something already written. She remembered his love for melody, the way he'd move notes around until they assumed a pleasing shape. She remembered how he couldn't sleep without drugs, and how he couldn't wake up without them either.

She wandered into the kitchen. "Don't tip the boat over," Dewey said.

She went through to the living room. Her mama was sitting in the dark. Betty lowered herself into a chair. She stretched out her feet and took a deep breath. She thought about Robert. Her heart changed shapes: ramp, funnel, spear.

Robert
June 1974

The first thing he saw was the shadow of a guitar stretched across the ceiling. He heard a funny rasping noise, which he soon realized was his own breathing. The paint on his side of the door was blistering.

Fire. He breathed in sharply, then breathed out in panic. He rolled off the bed onto the floor. Stay low. He crawled, back hot, out of the room and down the hall. The end closer to the studio seemed clear, and he ran toward it and looked in. A poster for his new single, "Smile and the World Smiles with You," hung by the door, charred along one edge only, otherwise miraculously spared. The record had come out a week before. Sales were promising. Monroe Stringer had called him personally. But the telephone Foxx had used to speak to him was melted on the counter, and the space beneath the board was a tangle of melted wires and thick smoke.

Foxx went down the hall again toward the front door. He couldn't remember who else was in the house with him. He guessed no one from how lonely he felt. At the end of the corridor, he found that in his confusion he had crawled the wrong way. He wasn't near the front stairs; he was at the back of the house. The other end of the hallway was engulfed in flame.

He ducked into a bathroom and wet down his hair and his face. He rushed back into the hall, took a left turn and another left, half-rolled down a short staircase, and finally came to a window that faced the front lawn. Next to the window, there was a bust of Ray Charles that Leon had given him. He picked it up and heaved it toward the glass.

And then, like a miracle, he was out. The grass was wet under his face. His lungs were taking in new air. His right hand was bleeding, and his left arm hurt like someone had cut it open from elbow to wrist.

A woman across the street was standing on her walkway in a bathrobe, her hand over her mouth. "Call the fire department," Foxx said. Then he went off down the street, cradling his hurt arm with his bloody hand. He walked past a school and past a small park. It took a few minutes or forever. The houses were big like his, then smaller. None of them were on fire. Soon he came up on Penny's apartment building. "You got me up," she said. "What time is it?"

"I need to use your telephone," he said. The operator told him the fire had been reported. "Did they save my house?"

"I don't know, sir."

Penny was running a cloth across his face. "Hold still," she said. "The soot's coming off," she said.

"You see any white under there?"

"Quiet." She scrubbed with the rag. She bandaged his right hand and put ointment on the burns on his left arm. None of it was done gently. Maybe she was trying to hurt him. He didn't care. He couldn't sleep, and when he did, he didn't sleep for long. He had cold sweat on his back, hot points under his arms. A band around his chest tightened until it was breaking him.

The sun was a bitch. The white sheets were a bitch. Everything was wrong, too bright and too dim at the same time, and Foxx rolled over on his stomach and pressed his nose into the pillow. He was chasing peace, what little of it remained. The sun was in his eyes, though, like it meant to stay there. He turned over and sat up. "Close the curtains," he said. No answer.

Foxx pulled himself up to his knees and took a pack of cigarettes from the night table. He lit one and dragged on it. He was supposed to go to his lawyer's office, if it was Tuesday. But maybe it was Wednesday. Or maybe it was Monday and he had time to spare. Didn't matter, not much, not anymore. He had lost track since the fire. He stood up, found that his legs were weak and tender to the touch, limped to the front door of the apartment, undid the chain and the deadbolt, and leaned down to collect the newspaper. He knew he wouldn't read it. The day was just a prison meant for breaking. He laughed: Was that a line from one of his songs? He couldn't remember.

The plastic bag next to the bed was almost empty. He called for Penny again, but she wasn't in the bathroom or in front of the TV or in the kitchen. That was three strikes instead of a hit. Foxx's nose was running. He was cold.

Foxx went into the bathroom. He stared into the mirror, unsure what he was seeing, dimly remembering another time, another mirror, the same uncertain contents spread out under the silver surface. He reached under the sink and took out the leather bag. He withdrew a syringe. "Shake vigorously," he said, because it was what they said on the instructions for the thermometer. He unwrapped the bandage from his right hand. Then he made a fist with his left hand, held it until he could see a vein near the elbow, just below the burn, and then he buried the needle in the vein. He steadied himself against the sink while the shit raced into him. Suddenly the dimness fell away and the brightness stepped up, straightening every color: the white of the tiles, the yellow of the curtains, the red streak on the wall beside the sink that was the calligraphy of an unclogged syringe.

Before he left, he took the box of old needles out from under the bathroom sink and double-wrapped them in foil. No need to have some garbageman sticking himself at pickup. He wrote Penny a note: "Gone for something funny, honey." Then he slipped on a jacket and slipped out the door.

With the morning light in his eyes, Foxx shuffle-walked down to his car. He had hired a driver, a young kid Jerry knew. He could have driven, but he wanted to show everyone that the fire had hurt him worse than they could imagine. "Get the door for me," he said. Beneath his jacket his left arm was burning.

The fire investigators were two cats named Malawel and Bijou. Malawel was an old motherfucker who looked like he never met a tailor and who coughed at least twice in every sentence. Bijou was a cool Wardell Franklin-type dude who wore sharp, light-colored suits and had a lilting island accent that Foxx thought was put on. The men had already met with him once, the day after the fire, when they led him into a back office at the stationhouse and asked lots of questions about his habits, his debts, the company he kept. Malawel spoke soft, like he was worried about Foxx bolting; he told him he knew about the drugs and asked him not to lie, so Foxx didn't. Then he pushed a picture in front of Foxx that looked like something from a barbecue. It was his studio, or what was left of it. "Wasn't that bad when I saw it," Foxx said.

"Well, then you got a memory to keep," Malawel said. "That's about all that's left."

Today Foxx was meeting the investigators at the station, and then the three of them were going to drive over to the house. On the way over there, Foxx noticed that his knee was shaking, up and down, like he was keeping the beat to a song he hadn't written yet. "Which is it?" he said. "Burned up or burned down? Seems like you need to make up your minds, all of you." Malawel tilted the mirror so his eyes met Foxx's. He didn't smile.

When Foxx walked into the house, the first thing that hit him was the smell, a dense and sickening odor of smoke. The second thing that hit him was the realization that fire ate like a little child: unpredictable appetites, no sense of proportion. It had devoured his bedroom but left the bathroom untouched. It wiped out the den and the studio, but didn't do a motherfucking thing to the kitchen. And while most of his records were melted, the red guitar leaning up against them was still there, in perfect condition save a black finger on the body. The set list taped to its neck wasn't even singed.

Malawel and Bijou were in the kitchen. Bijou called Foxx in. "You know what alligator char is?" he said. Foxx shook his head. Bijou got down on his haunches and touched the molding with two fingers, like he was an Indian scout. "When fire burns," he said, "it leaves a pattern that looks like scales on an alligator's back. The pattern is distinct at the point of origin, where the scales are the smallest and the grooves between them are the deepest. You have your point of origin here, which is very rare. Fires usually go to the upper part of the room. This is called low burn, and it makes me think that there was an accelerant on the other side of this wall." Bijou was a motherfucking treasure mine of good news.

"What was there?" Malawel asked. "Cleaning supplies? Some kind of tape-head solvent that might have been highly flammable?" Foxx shook his head. "No, or not that you know of?"

"Not that I know of. Could have been," Foxx said. "You should ask the house-keeper."

"We will," said Malawel, pausing to cough. "And you sure you have no other idea how it might have started here? Sometimes people light the wick themselves, if you know what I mean."

"For insurance? Man, I don't need the money, and certainly not that way."

"That's good to know," Bijou said. "Also, when people burn themselves out, they usually check to make sure their policy covers the damage."

"What the fuck do you mean?" said Foxx.

"Yours lapsed about four months ago."

"I pay people to take care of that."

"You should pay them more. Or better yet, don't pay them at all and send the money straight to the insurance company."

"Pete," said Malawel. "Hold up. Let's go easy on the man. He just lost his house."

"And all I'm saying is that it's staying lost, because he ain't going to see a dime in insurance."

"I don't want insurance money," Foxx said. "I want my house back."

"Well, unless you can run the tape backwards, that isn't going to happen," Bijou said.

"When tape runs backwards, you get messages no one wants to hear," Foxx said.

"We have to finish our investigation," Malawel said. "Want to stay?"

"Can't," Foxx said. He bounded out the front door, or what was left of it. If he couldn't go back, he would run the tape forward at dangerous speed. He felt a kind of freedom that he hadn't felt since Boston: no chains, white or black or gold.

He walked for ten minutes, then twenty. The day was cool and it was cleansing him. He sang himself snatches of what he hoped were new songs. At an intersection, there was a police car, siren screaming. A cop was crouching at the curb. Next to the cop there was a car that had smashed into a bus stop. A young man was sitting on the curb, blood streaming from his forehead. He looked up at Foxx. He was the very image of his dead cousin Andre, so much so that he almost called his name. "Please step back," said the cop. Foxx did more than that. He jumped back as if burned.

There was another bus stop across the street, and he bolted for it blindly, not sure whether the light was with him or against him. When he got there he sat down and felt his pulse, which was going like a motherfucker. He hummed to calm himself, some Sam Cooke, some Ray Charles, skipping Smokey Robinson because it made him think of the fire.

A truck pulled up at the red light. He was still humming, but he was not sure what song, because he couldn't hear himself over the whirr of the truck motor. The driver was a white cat, maybe forty, and he had the window rolled down and the radio tuned to talk.

Then the light changed and the driver dropped his foot on the accelerator. A noise rose from the belly of the truck, a deep rumble followed by the hiss of the brakes releasing. He watched the truck go around the corner, and only then was he aware of the noise of his hobnailed boots on the concrete. Tap-tap, pause, tap-tap-tap. It was more chatter than rhythm; if there was a beat, he couldn't keep it. He reached down and stilled his feet with his hands.

SIDE THREE: MIXED DOWN

Robert
1976

Rock Foxx owns the street. The street makes a sound where his feet slap down. The Foxx feet are the Foxx beat, which you don't hear enough these days on the ray-dee-oh. Stretch the word. Don't clip the motherfucker. A pig patrol noises by. At the corner store, a man rolls an orange from hand to hand. Foxx stops to look at a headline about a girl in a coma and then he goes, blues and news and run-over shoes. Slap, slap, slap.

It's eight in the morning on a Saturday. The human animal shouldn't be out this early. Foxx checks his watch showily, sniffles, snorts. That morning he woke thinking of Dewey. A man should be watching TV and eating cereal with his son. He tried to go back to sleep but thought of Betty, too. A man should be in bed with his wife. Where is Chicago? East of L.A., east of west, easily forgotten. He doesn't know exactly how many miles. He doesn't know what they're doing there. He doesn't know if they're thinking of him. All he knows now is that he needs to head into the artery of La Cienega Boulevard and cop some flake. He's dreaming of a white Christmas, which comes earlier every year.

He stops in a doorway to scratch his arm and check his watch again. It's a nice watch but not too nice. He doesn't want it taken off his arm. Up Adams, near Crenshaw, there's a woman walking across the street. She has a fine ass—so round, so firm, so fully packed. Sad to see, then, that she handles it all uncertain, like she's a renter and not an owner. Foxx thinks the problem is in her heels, which are higher than high. He walks toward her, passes, tips a hat he's not wearing. At the corner is his Santa Claus, a Jamaican dude named Gumball on account of what he's constantly chewing. He's down on his crouch, listening to the radio, Lou Rawls fading down, Brick fading up. Hey, Foxx says to Gumball, bumping fists. My man, says Gumball. Mon, Foxx says. Motherfucker is thin and getting thinner, not more than 130 pounds sopping wet with rocks in his socks. Foxx does the deal, neat and clean, white for green, talks some shit about the fine-ass sister up ahead, and is turning to go when Gumball tells him that Sonny Boy has been looking for him. "I don't think so," says Foxx. "Because I been looking for him."

"If you see him tell him I told you," Gumball says. "Don't like it when that one's mad at me." He pops another piece of gum into his mouth. The radio's playing the Spinners now, and Foxx makes like a rubber-band man himself, bounces.

He slides on down the street to Rollo's pool hall. Rollo is as fat as Gumball is thin, and he's sitting at the bar, straining the seams of a leather coat that is far too heavy for the light weather. "Float On" is floating on the jukebox. There seems to be music pouring out of every hole now, like leaks or wounds.

"Hey," Foxx says. "Ace."

"Joker."

Foxx jerks a finger toward the jukebox. "You got anything good in there? Five Keys? Penguins? Orioles?"

"What is that? Some of the shit that was popular when you were. I don't listen to that dinosaur music."

"Your mother and I used to lay around in bed and listen to it all the time."

"You fucked my mother? Shit, man. That would make you my daddy. But that can't be, because I don't even think of you as someone with a name." Rollo grins coldly.

"You seen Sonny Boy?" Foxx says, sitting down.

"Sure enough."

"You want to tell me where?"

"Right in here. That fool comes in here talking some nonsense about how he's been busy at the gym, but he's still the same scrawny piece of shit. The only thing he's lifting is my eyebrows."

"Well, I heard he's looking for me."

"He's looking for anything he can use. You're probably just about right for him."

An older man enters the bar and approaches Rollo, wiry dude with something vicious fucking up the skin on his face, leaving him looking like a basketball left in the weather to crack and peel. "How much you give me for this pack of cigarettes?"

Rollo turns the pack in his hand. "These aren't cigarettes. What are they, clarinet reeds?"

"I guess." The man shifts from foot to foot, blows on his hands. When he blows, flecks of skin drop off his cheeks. "They're from José."

"He's out of jail?"

"Since last week. He wants to sell them."

"What? One box?"

"How much you give?"

"A dollar? No. Forget it. What do I need with these? Get out of here."

"He wants to sell them," the man repeats, and leaves.

"You got clarinet reeds?" Foxx says to Rollo. "I'll pay you top dollar."

"Like you got top dollar."

"I got what I got, and that's a hell of a lot," Foxx says. "Been a bigger bank but I'm not out of bank yet."

"Oh, yeah?" Rollo says. "Sonny Boy will be happy to hear that. He might be thinking that his golden goose has no eggs left."

"You think Sonny Boy's coming back around here later?"

"He said he had to go see someone out in Century City. But anything's possible."

"You see him, you tell him I was in here, looking."

"I'm not your fucking message service."

"Don't talk that way to your father," Foxx says. He puts his shoulder into the door on the way out, show of force, walks until he finds his car, goes home through Boyle Heights. Shouts of *vato, vato* ping against his windows.

The house that Foxx is renting is a Spanish-style up in Benedict Canyon. Some mornings Foxx stands outside in nothing but a robe, waving at his famous neighbors. Man of the people, man of the world. Then he goes back inside to the blond-wood kitchen and the plush red living room and the bathrooms, four of them, one by the front door, one off the living room, and two upstairs, one in white marble, the other in black. He showers in the black one, but he won't use the toilet in there. He can't see what has just come out of him. And if he can't see where the shit begins, he can't see where it ends.

It isn't sweet, exactly. It isn't sour, either. But there is definitely a smell in the room.

The living room is mostly red, from the leather couch to the pile carpet to the chairs that line the wall. The ashtray is red, except for the gold drawing of an eye on the bottom. On the small table next to the couch there is a glass of wine, and even that is red. Ash floats in the wine like a clot. The table, designed by a famous furniture designer, is round with teeth, buzzsaw-shaped, and from where Foxx sits it looks as if it is about to cut into the head of Anita, who's down on the floor. She isn't wearing red. She isn't wearing anything. She drags a finger through her pubic hair as she watches Dinah Shore, sound down too low to hear.

"Is there any more fruit up there? This one is mealy." Anita holds up an apple. One bite is missing, and the white meat has already begun to brown.

"I saw an orange, I think."

"Really?"

"I think so." He doesn't remember where.

"I know there are apples in the kitchen. I'll go get them in a minute. So, you finally caught up with him?"

"I did. After I left Rollo I gave him a call. He was doing a deal in Century City but we talked."

"What did he say?"

"You know Sonny Boy. He's not sure what he can get, or when he can get it. But he'll get it."

"I think he makes you overpay." Anita is doing her daily exercises. When she interlaces her fingers behind her head and does a sit-up, the muscles in her stomach stand out like the cords of a bridge. "How much you giving him for a key, anyway?"

Foxx reaches for the ashtray and stubs out his cigarette in the center of the eye. "Hey," he says. "That's business. You know I hate to mix that shit with pleasure. And anyway, I got no choice. I can't go to Gumball or some shit like that. This is a big score."

"Ooh," says Anita. "Shaft."

"No, no," Foxx says. "It's a party, baby. I got to impress people. It's not for personal use. Think of him as a caterer."

"Well, I'm just saying you have to be careful with your money."

"Careful's for someone else," he says. But she's right. The last time he had a party at the house, some skinny sister came up to him and told him she needed some cash or else her boyfriend was going to beat her. Foxx peeled off four hundreds and just handed them to her. His neighbor, Lance Marker, was watching. "Very magnanimous," Marker said when the woman had gone.

"Fuck," Foxx said. "I don't know what those big words mean. Next time just say *munificent.*"

Marker laughed. It was his last laugh of the night. On his way back down the Canyon road he got busted for driving while flying. One of the deputy chiefs, a dude with long hair who probably lit up himself now and again, talked about it on the radio. "There are many people in the film and music business," he said, "known to have drug problems. We will not tolerate that in them simply because they are famous." Why not, Foxx thought. Wasn't that the point of getting to the top?

"Okay," says Anita. "Just know that if you get picked up, I'm not coming in to bail you out." She flops over on her stomach, then pulls herself to her feet and goes to the kitchen.

Foxx picks up the camera from the coffee table. "I've said it once and I'll say it a thousand times," he says. "Baby, you should be an ass model."

Anita turns and scowls. Foxx takes the picture anyway. He loves his camera, an Electric Zip with a red body.

"I wish you could see it," Foxx says. "And now, thanks to the miracle of modern technology, you can." He shakes the picture to develop it. It's not bad, either—the ass like a black heart upside-down in the center of the frame, the blue square of the TV a cool fire in the middle of the red room.

"Hey," Anita says, returning with the apple in her hand. "Will you put some lotion on my feet? They're starting to get dry again." She pulls up one of the dining-room chairs and puts her feet up on his lap. He squeezes lotion into his hands and begins to work it into the grooves between her toes. When he's done with her toes, he does her calves, then the outsides of her thighs. He knows where he's going. "This apple is the best yet," she says, reaching up to wipe the juice off her chin. He parts her legs and slides his middle finger into her. She is wet. She always is. She holds the apple out so that he can take a bite. Then she says, "Let's listen to some music. Maybe something old, like Stevie Wonder." He can smell the apple on his upper lip. Underneath it, he can still smell that other smell, not quite sweet and not quite sour.

"Stevie Wonder's not old," he says.

"You know what I mean," she says. "*Talking Book*. What is that, four years already? And don't get on me anyway. I was talking to some of the girls down at the studio and one of them didn't know who Smokey Robinson was."

"Which one you talking about?"

"She's the one who looks Japanese but she has a monster Afro."

He can see into the hallway from where he sits. There is something that looks like a spot of dirt on the wall, but it is moving.

"Keiko. She's one of Reggie Lee's girls."

"Well, she never heard of Smokey." Anita absently plays with one of her nipples.

Foxx laughs with scorn. He hasn't listened to the radio much lately, and when he has he hears lots of old singers dressed up new: Johnnie Taylor, O'Jays, even that overripe brother Lou Rawls. And Lucas Sanders, of course. But not the Lucas he knew: Lucas Sanders, bassist for the Foxxes, was a distant memory, as distant as Lucas Sanders, cousin. Now he's Lucas Sanders, solo star. After "We," Foxx thought L would hang it up: point proved, blood. But "We" was only the first spark. Then came the fire: "You Make Me New," "Take a Chance on My Love," "If Ever Was Right Now." Four years after setting down the funkiest bass in the world, Lucas is a stone soul man with two great big eyes and one great big voice. He has the girls swooning in Seattle, down on their knees in Miami Beach. They cry out for him but they're also crying because he is a good man, always photographed with his new wife, always standing up at charity events to show how upstanding he is. Just the other day, Foxx had seen him on Gerald Atkins, bass-booming his latest and biggest hit, "The Valley." It pushed the gospel plow but with a lover's hand, and it was already number three.

I've lived my whole life in the valley
Watching the mountain above
Wondering what was up in the sky
Dreaming of a perfect love
I've lived my whole life in the valley
I've been here for days, and nights too,
The valley is low, but what's lower
Is how low I feel without you

Foxx listened for something that would sell him on the performance, a note of real sorrow in the words, a whiff of loneliness in the spaces between them. Instead he heard his cousin, greasy with sincerity. Foxx spit out the bit then and now he spits it out again.

Anita is still talking about Keiko. "I'm just saying that she doesn't have good taste."

"Girl don't have to have good taste, looking like that. Remind me to invite her to the party."

"You still haven't told me what this party's all about."

"Business, baby. Business."

"Will Leon be there?"

"Probably. Why? You not getting along with Leon?" Leon has moved up through Turn, and now he's in charge of most of the soul and funk acts, which the label is still calling R&B. Ripped off and beaten down, Leon likes to say, but still the toast of the motherfucking town.

"We're cool," says Anita. "It's just that I haven't seen him around in a little while."

"Yeah," says Foxx. That's true: Leon has been angry with him because he hasn't been working on his new record. Company tightens its belt and it's bad to be out of the loop, Leon said on the phone, half joking, half serious. With Leon you never could tell. Man, said Foxx, Brother Man, did I not deliver unto you the solo record *Coming Back for More*, certified gold, certified bold? You did, said Leon. Back For More in '74. And since then, all you've given me is smoke and mirrors. Foxx clucked his tongue: You know better, he said. Songs come when songs come. I hear you talking, said Leon, but I don't know what you're saying. Do you have the songs or do the songs have you?

Foxx doesn't know the answer to this question. There is something wrong with it at the root. There aren't songs, exactly. There's just a song. One. It's the new song he's working on, has been working on for months, and he has written enough of them to know that the new one is the only one. It is a song and a dance and a sweet romance, an alpha and an omega, a pork chop and a pie. But he is keeping it in the hip pocket of his head, not letting it go just yet, mainly because he doesn't have the band to make it work. The studio cats he hired to dig around in the litter box of *Coming Back for More* couldn't scratch the surface of his new song. In fact, he won't let anyone touch the new song; whenever Leon has suggested that he give it away to a band who can take it top ten, he just slaps the idea down like he's knocking back a particularly stupid dog. It's his song to keep, and for now that means keeping it secret. He doesn't even dare to think of the title most days, unless it slips out. "Please Step Back." That's it, slipping out.

Who can make sense of inspiration? Not him. He is a bullhorn through which a higher power sometimes speaks, and this time it's telling him that he is the once and future king, hold for throne. The song came to him—came out of him—as he shaved one morning, the opening lines at least:

> *The world is*
> *Pushing up on me*
> *Yes it's pushing up on me*
> *I wish the pull*
> *Would have its full*
> *Effect*
> *Lord save my neck*

It was the first time in years that a verse had been so strong in him. He left the foam on his face, went into the bedroom for a pencil and paper, and started scribbling right there. The piece of paper's still there on his desk. He hasn't sung the song for anyone, hasn't dared to. Making it real will make it unreal. That much he knows.

The spot on the wall is still moving. Now it's on the switch plate for the hall lamp. He gets up to take a look, but by the time he makes it across the room, it's gone. On the way back, he ducks into his bedroom for a joint. There is a bright-blue stain on the white chair next to the window. There were plenty of stains in the world that weren't big mysteries. Brown could be dried blood or shit. Red could be new blood or makeup. But what the fuck is blue? He pulls out his shirttail and tries to rub it off, but it only smudges slightly.

"Hey," Anita calls. "You coming back to finish up?"

When he comes back out, she has her panties on.

"Why you dressed?" he says. "I thought you wanted to finish."

"My feet."

"In that case, I'm finished."

"You gonna let me sing some more backup soon?"

"I told you," Foxx says. "Not on this record." Girl can't carry a tune; everything she sings has to be wiped off, and it's stretching out the tape. "For the next one, I'm writing you your very own song."

Anita holds the apple at arm's length, inspects it. She sets it on the table, next to the first apple. Then she motions for Foxx to pass her the joint. "What's it called?" she says on the intake.

"I ain't got no title for it yet. Just a melody.'"

"But you promise me there's a song."

"There's a song," he says. "Listen, do you smell something funny?"

"How am I gonna smell by listening?" she says. "Anyway, all I smell is this reefer." She puts the joint back into his mouth. Her fingers are soft when they brush his lips. Then she goes into the bedroom and comes out wearing a bra and carrying a needle, a small bottle, and a book. She sets the book on the table next to the two apples. She sits on the chair opposite him and spreads her legs, the bottle between them. Then she fills the syringe and finds a spot on her thigh and stabs herself. She picks the apple back up and takes a big bite. This time she makes no attempt to wipe the juice away, and it runs down her chin and drips onto the floor.

"Don't let that shit get on the floor. We'll get bugs."

She walks over and climbs up on the couch, straddling him. Her breasts are against his face and he presses his ear flat to them and listens for her heart.

"There anything left in the bottle?" he says. "We have company coming over later."

"This bottle's empty," she says.

"Just make sure that you don't use up the whole stash. And throw that apple away."

She carries one of the apples into the kitchen. When she comes back, she doesn't return to the couch. She stays at the dining room, in one of the other chairs.

"Why didn't you take the other apple?" he says.

"I thought you might want it."

"You told me it was bad. Why the fuck would I want a bad apple?"

"Hey, baby," Anita says. Her voice is soft. "Don't yell."

"And why did you bring this book out if you weren't going to read it?" he says. She stops in the doorway, her face crinkled, and he is suddenly happy that he can do this, that he can *run* her.

"That's the book you told me to read," she says. He doesn't remember telling her to read anything. It is *King Lear*. "I started it, but you didn't tell me it was poetry."

"It's not," he says. "It's a play."

"Oh, good," she says. "When I took acting classes, the teacher said I had potential."

"Here," he says, throwing the book. "Read me some." He even has a scene in mind: the one where the king is out alone, when he talks about the storm going under the skin. He always thinks of needles when he reads that, of the deceptive calm in the dropper's neck, and the weather it unleashes in his mind. He wants to hear Nita read that part, maybe while he fucks her. But the book thuds against the chair and falls to the ground. Foxx bends down to get it and the first thing he sees is an apple core under the couch. It's dried-up and brown, and there aren't any bugs on it anymore. But that's the smell. He's sure of it.

Sonny Boy's shoes are sharp as shit, polished new black motherfuckers the same color as his car and jacket. He even has a matching box for his works, black with a gold eagle on it. Foxx can barely see him in the room with the shades drawn the way they are. The only light comes from the TV.

"Yo, Foxx. Where was that show where you didn't come out?" Sonny Boy asks as he unpacks his needle and his spoon. When Foxx tells him, Sonny Boy sings, "They're fighting up in the streets of Dee-troit." Then he spins around the room, touching things while his girl heats the tip of the needle with a lighter. Foxx calls her Sonny Girl. He doesn't remember her real name.

Sonny Boy touches a stapler. "How they get these things to stay together?" he says. "I mean when you buy them from the store, they're all jammed in a long line. How does something like that happen? And don't it seem like a little bit of magic?"

"I don't know," says Foxx. "Ask the Shell Answer Man."

"This you and Mick Jagger?" says Sonny Boy. "That's superstar."

"Yeah," he says. "Keith gave me a bottle of scotch. I think I still have it."

"I'll get it," says Boris. He jumps up, happy to have something to do. When he's not busy, he gets like dogs get, a little helpless, ears drooping down.

"Wait," says Sonny Girl. Her voice is like a little child's voice. "There's a bottle over here."

"But that's not the good stuff," Foxx says. "That's what we make the nigger maids drink. Oh, I'm sorry. Is anyone in the room Afro-American?"

"Thanks anyway, baby," says Sonny Boy. "Good to have a girl who's looking out for you. How is Anita, anyway? I thought she'd be here."

"She's dancing tonight. Still bugging me to sing on the record."

"Woman's got to have it."

"She says it's not fair if she's not famous. Not fair to me, I mean, because I'm famous, and I should be with a chick who is famous."

"That is some unimpeachable logic, my man."

"Sure is."

"You should get married onstage," Sonny Boy says.

"Yeah," Boris says. "That's a good idea."

"I wouldn't invite none of you," Foxx says. "Don't want you, don't need you."

Sonny Boy pretends to cry, says, "Man, you're hurting my feelings." He rubs the spoon on his shirttail to dry it off. Then he uses the fingernail of a pen cap like a shovel and scoops some of the powder into the spoon. "You know what I'd get you for a present. That which cures." With the syringe, he drizzles a little bit of water over the powder. "Speaking of inviting, man, let's talk about this party that you mentioned on the telephone." Sonny Boy lights the candle.

"What?"

"Telephone, man. Ring, ring? Ring a bell?"

"Oh, yeah. I was just seeing what episode this is." Foxx turns from the TV. "Anyway, it's like I said. Leon is bringing around some of his friends next week, and he wants to throw a real party. I'm letting him use my place so he can be the man."

"But you're the man. You're the superstar. What you want? Blow? Junk? Gash for the bash?"

"All of the above," Foxx says.

Sonny Boy runs the numbers out loud: twenty thou for the powder, ten for the girls.

"That's some major motherfucking coin," says Foxx.

"Here's something on the house," Sonny Boy says, throwing Foxx a taste bag. "Anyway, think of it as an investment." He's the second person today to say that. Floyd Hughes had called early in the morning, his voice with too much energy in it to be straight. "Is this the pizza parlor?" Hughes said. "I'll have a large."

"You already large," said Foxx. He had been deep in a dream of a threesome, Nita and one of those Japanese girls from the studio, and the phone had shattered everything. "Larger than large. You fat. You got bitch tits."

"Shit, man, that hurts. Well, I may be a giant, but you two dwarfs," said Hughes.

"What?"

"Sleepy and grumpy."

Foxx laughed. "What you want?"

"Just calling to tell you we're going to be doing some wreckin' in your neck of the woods. Next Friday at the Forum."

"Cool."

"And I want you to come down and see us."

"All right." Floyd, who was up on him almost every week around the time of *Revolution,* rarely called him now. "What's the occasion?"

"Nothing special," he said. "Well, that's not true. Something special." Hughes shifted into white voice: "I am pleased to announce that I have just reached an agreement with the Western Recording Corporation to distribute music under my own label, to be known as Formula Records."

Foxx sat up in bed. "No," he said.

"Yes," said Hughes. "Now will you marry me?" Then he loosed that rumble-chuckle of his and replaced the receiver.

The next call, about an hour later, was Leon. "Blood," he said. "You hear about Floyd?"

"Yeah," said Foxx. "He called me himself."

"So you know my thinking?"

"No," said Foxx.

"It's a masterstroke," he said. "I want you to switch over to his stable, and I'll go with you. I haven't talked to Floyd about this, but I can't imagine that he'll have any problem with it. I mean, shit, man, you're his Christ and Buddha both."

"Wait up," said Foxx. "Why would I want to do that?"

Leon sighed. "We've been through this," he said. "Because you haven't had a hit record in more than two years or a great record in twice that time. Because Anchor is the hottest thing going. Because you need some fuel and some strip so you can take off. You can record that song you've been talking about." He waits for Foxx to fill in the title, but Foxx won't do it.

"So you want to put me next to the hottest thing going and hope I catch fire?"

"Something like that."

"I'm starting to think that you're just a cracker with a burnt-cork-job."

"You can blow all the air in the world at me," said Leon. "But I'm gonna get you back where you belong."

Foxx sighed. "What do you want me to do?"

"Just go along with me. I want you to make nice to him, have this party. It's an investment, a way of ensuring returns. That's all."

Now Foxx replays that conversation in his head. He looks around at the house, remembers calling his accountant to make sure the rent checks are clearing. He knows how many of his cars he owns and how many he leases. He knows that his bank accounts are shorter than a midget on his knees. He knows that Leon knows.

"But listen, man," says Sonny Boy. "I need to know what kinds of pussy you want. I gots your black. I gots your blonde. I gots your cherry red."

"I'm not a racist. I'll try anything once," says Foxx. "Only no dirty bitches. Get me nice clean ones. Ones you would have for your own." He bats his eyelashes at Sonny Girl, who lets out a delicate, musical laugh.

Sonny Boy laughs, too, and holds the spoon over the candle. Soon the C&H is boiling, white foam chattering at the edges. "Soup's on," Foxx says. Sonny Boy ducks under it to look at the bottom, which is as dirty as the bottom of a foot. He takes a piece of cotton and sops up the hot mix.

"I ever tell you about the time I heard your shit in jail? It was right after I got sent down. I was freakin', because I couldn't get any scag in the joint. I used to wake up in the middle of the night scratching up my own fucking legs. There was this fat piece of shit a few cells down who was also going cold turkey. He was always singing to keep himself busy. Mostly it was gospel: Jesus be a fence around me, God put your hand in my pocket, that kind of shit. One day I started yelling at him to sing something else. And you know what he started singing? 'Wednesday Ain't So Bad.' Half the cell joined in with him. It was like a movie."

"And was he any good?"

"He was like Wednesday," Sonny Boy says, laughing. He takes up the syringe and stabs it into the wet cotton. Then he pulls back on the dropper. When it has sucked up all the liquid, he turns the syringe needle-up and leans on the dropper to clear the air. Then he calls to Sonny Girl. "Yo, baby. Why don't you do this for Foxx? Go on over there and help him out."

"No need, man. No need. Last time I got help it was one of Boris's girls, and the bitch tied me off up around my wrist like it was a bracelet."

"She was a nice girl," Boris says.

"She was," says Foxx. "But nice girls here are like white dudes in hoop. You don't need them for anything but kind words and comedy."

Sonny Girl uncurls herself from the chair next to Sonny Boy. She is taller than Foxx thought, and she doesn't walk across the room so much as she glides. "I'll hold this," she says, extending the syringe. Foxx ties himself off, looping a length of rubber tubing twice around his left arm, just below the elbow.

"Shake my hand," Foxx says, and the girl shakes it. "Really great to meet you," he says in a white voice. "It's more than swell. It's swelling." When the vein thickens enough so that he can see it, he takes the syringe from Sonny Girl and sticks it in. Blood races up the needle and fills the trunk of the plunger. "You want to do the honors?" he says, and Sonny Girl nods. "Careful," Foxx says, but he knows this is worthless advice. She is intensely careful, and she pats his back with her free hand as if she is burping him.

"There you go," she says. He slips the needle out. He can feel the shit already moving up his arm. It turns the corner of his elbow, races toward his shoulder, then skids into his heart. Sonny Girl's hand on his shoulder is light, then heavy. He reaches for it. Then he leans back into her stomach, feels the bottoms of her breasts on the top of his head.

"Hey, there," Sonny Boy says. "Don't be rubbing up on the nurse."

Foxx's mouth is as dry as a desert. A picture rises into his mind, a picture of a desert. There is a figure in the center of the yellow sand. Foxx squints but can't recognize him. He half turns and buries his face in Sonny Girl's stomach.

"Aw, what the hell," Sonny Boy says. "Rub up on the nurse."

Sonny Girl smells like soap. Foxx isn't sure how he knows this, because he can't breathe. Air is precious. He feels nothing in his shoulders or his chest. He feels like there are fingers on his neck, cold fingers, and that there are hot fingers on his lips. Maybe that's the girl. But when he looks, her hands are where they had been since the shot, one on his shoulder, the other on her own hip. With a start, he wonders where his cock is, and he flops a hand into his lap to test for it. He pinches the tip, and though he doesn't feel much, it's enough to reassure him.

"You the king," Sonny Boy says. "The little king of everything."

Foxx opens his mouth to tell him that lately he's had too much of kings, everyone crowning him and it's drowning him, but nothing comes out except a sound like a door creaking open. He opens his eyes and tries to see Sonny Boy and Sonny Girl, but they are only shapes now, shapes melting into other shapes, which he assumes are chairs, lamps, pictures hanging on the wall. He tries to guess which pictures are pictures of him. "Ain't no harm to take a little nip," he rasps. "But don't you fall down and bust your lip."

"Hey," says Sonny Girl, and reaches down and draws a finger gently across his mouth. Foxx leans forward into the finger, melts. "I don't know where Boris is," she says. Foxx realizes he must have called for him. "I think he went out for a few minutes."

Sonny Boy comes and stands next to them. "Blood, I'm gonna step into the next room and dip. Come on, baby." Foxx hears Sonny Boy and Sonny Girl in the next room, legs bumping furniture, mumbles, whispers. The dope is beating in his blood, and the noises sound closer than they are, louder. The veins pulsing in his temples are like eggs just about to hatch chicks. They quiver. His vision is still blurry.

Across the room there is a blue chair, and a small table next to it that holds a scatter of records. On top of the records is a gun. "Forty-fives," he says, eyeing the scene. That number hangs there, too, next to the word. In the other room, Sonny Girl sounds like she is crying, but Foxx knows better. He hears Sonny Boy grunting, and every once in a while, both of them breathe heavily.

Careful not to let the nausea overcome him, he tiptoes to the table, hoists the gun into his hand and sticks the tip of his little finger into the hole in the barrel. "Boom boom," he says. The first gun he bought was in late '74, when Sonny Boy first started coming around. It was something he liked to look at but didn't really believe in, an artifact from someone else's religion. The second gun came four months later, as a gift from Boris, who told him that he wasn't always going to be around to protect Foxx so he might as well get used to the weight of the thing in his hand. Then there was a third, for the Rolls, and a fourth, for the Jag, and a fifth for the bed stand, and a sixth for the little closet in the hall, and before he knew it he had guns in every corner of the house. They are well hidden, though, and most aren't even loaded. He tells Nita it's because Dewey might visit. But that's not it. It's the house: It doesn't trust Foxx and Foxx doesn't trust it.

It hadn't always been that way. The first month he had loved it. It brought him friends at all hours, pyramids of coke, new mistresses on old mattresses. But over time there was a turn. One day he was standing over a red guitar and he noticed that the neck was pointed at his neck. A chill sprinted up his spine. If that guitar wanted to kill him it could. Maybe it was already plotting. He had no studio to keep the guitars busy and so he was sure that they were up to no good. He mothballed the guitars and he put the guns out instead. He knew they could hurt him, but at least they were clear about it.

In the next room over, Sonny Girl is moaning but not moaning, singing a kind of song, working a rhythm, tossing in the occasional lyric. When she's done she says Sonny Boy's name in a whisper that propels Foxx backward through time. Nita is a high rocket in bed, no doubt about that. She can fuck all night and hold down the sun in the morning. But Foxx wants to hear his own name spoken softly. He wants to feel a woman's tenderness, fluttering like a butterfly in the hollow of her neck.

He lays back down on the couch, closes his eyes, rides the end of the high, tries to dream. He isn't trying to dream just anything. He's trying to dream a day back in October, a fall day so bright that he had to draw the curtains in the living room. He is almost there, and then he's there, in October, on this same couch but sitting upright again, smoking a joint instead of nodding, and the telephone is ringing. "Go," he says, picking it up.

"Robert?" It's Betty. He hasn't heard her voice for more than a month, and he hasn't heard it like this for more than a year.

He softens his voice to match it. "Everything good? Dewey okay?"

"He's fine," she says. "He's taking a nap."

"He been getting my packages?" Foxx has been sending Dewey letters every few weeks, sometimes straightforward reports, sometimes little songs.

"He has," she says. "I read him the letters and let him look at the pictures." Foxx always includes photographs of himself with famous people. "But I'm calling with bad news. My mother passed."

"I'm so sorry to hear that," he says. There's nothing in his tone but what he means, and this surprises him.

"The funeral is Saturday," she says.

"I'll be there. Can I talk to the boy?"

"A nap," she says. "Remember?" The voice is back to what he's accustomed to. "Anyway, I have lots of calls to make."

Foxx calls Leon. "I need a ticket, quick," he says. He flies mostly straight, just pills, and in the car on the way to the cemetery he keeps checking himself in the mirror.

Betty is already there, with a little boy at her side. His little boy, holding a stuffed animal that is either a dog or a bear. Foxx parks the car a few hundred yards away so he can approach on foot. When he's close enough to identify the animal—a bear— he notices a man coming toward Betty, a slick young guy with a Teddy Pendergrass beard. Foxx and the man arrive the same time. "Miss Cobham," Foxx says.

Betty gives him a quick kiss on the cheek. "Robert," she says. "This is Jeffrey, a friend." Foxx shakes the man's hand, watches as he puts his other hand at the bottom of Betty's back.

Dewey hasn't spoken yet, so Foxx gets down on one knee. "You there," he says, smiling. "Do I need to introduce myself?"

"Hi, Daddy," Dewey says. His face breaks into a shy smile. How can a boy be shy with his own father?

"What's the bear's name?" Foxx says.

"Wendell," Dewey says.

"Hi, Wendell. You taking care of Dewey, or is Dewey taking care of you?"

Dewey laughs and, after a few seconds of delay that are eternities for Foxx, comes forward with a hug. There's nothing more to say, so Foxx doesn't say anything. Above them, Betty and Jeffrey are silent, too. The dream fades out on Foxx, like it always does, right at this moment. Real history had more in it: Foxx straightened back up;

228 | Ben Greenman

tried to meet Betty's eye; failed, took a measure of Jeffrey; found him lacking in some regards but not in others; sat as the preacher delivered Betty's mama into the arms of the Lord; wondered what the old woman was seeing now in the hereafter, whether she would stay blind or suddenly get her vision back to gaze upon the angels she believed would greet her; drove back to the house where he shook hands with Lonnie; hugged Charlotte; kissed Dewey, sat with him on his lap for a minute that he can't remember, can't recover, and that he, as a result, questions the existence of; shared a painful embrace with Betty at the door; told her he had to go to the airport.

He didn't. He spent the night in a hotel and drove back out to Betty's mama's house, which was Betty's house now, which was Dewey's house. He waited down the street until he saw Betty and Dewey come out, crept after them in the car. They went to a playground. He sat there and watched. A ghost can see without being seen. He imagined that he was protecting Dewey from freaks and demons. Then he saw a police car across the way and it hit him. He was the freak. He was the demon. He drove back to the airport short of breath and needed two drinks on the flight just to settle down. When he touched down in Los Angeles he felt his blood warming up again: He had all the smack and blow and pussy he needed, plus a plan to get the rest back.

He surfaces from the dream, there on the couch. He can't hear Sonny Girl anymore. The radio is playing "Reaching for the Moon." He considers it, goes back to sleep instead.

Two young dudes in suits are closing up shop in the lot of the dealership when Foxx drives in. He does this every few weeks, so they know him. The taller one wanders off when he sees who it is. The shorter one smiles and starts the routine. "Looking to buy?" he says.

"Looking to look," Foxx says. The front row of cars are all Stingrays, and Foxx runs his finger over the hood of a red one. "Don't like the steering wheel," he says. "Feels cheap."

"The four-spoke? Yeah. They brought it over from the Vega. But the horses are back up over two hundred. Seems about right for a man like you." Foxx isn't sure that the guy knows who he is, but he likes the idea that even as a normal man, he rates two hundred horses.

"What'll it run me?" Foxx has shifted into a white voice now.

"I think we could get you out of here for ten."

Foxx strokes his chin in mock thought. "Ten, you say? One of the guys down at the company, Dennis, just bought himself a Camaro and I don't like hearing about it every day. He's ruining my coffee breaks."

"You won't hear me say it," the salesman says, "but the Camaro can't compare to this car. The horsepower isn't even one sixty."

"I'm going to be sure to tell Dennis that," he says, still white. "It's like apples and slower apples." He shifts back to his normal voice. "When are the new models coming in?"

"A few months. You seriously thinking about getting one?"

"I need the muscle, Russell."

"Well, you know where to find me."

Foxx walks back to his car. "That I do."

"Where you off to now? Another dealership? Going to try to get a better price?"

Foxx laughs. "You know I wouldn't do you like that. Got errands to run. Planning for a big party."

"And I'm not invited?"

Foxx goes to the liquor store. He stops at a pay phone and calls Sonny Boy to make sure he's set with the dope and the girls. He calls Leon to make sure he's set with Anchor. Then he calls Anita, whom he hasn't seen in two days. No answer. He doesn't have a watch on, so he asks a passing man what time it is. Eight: That'll mean that Anita's probably working a hostess shift at the social club on Banker Street. That's how he met her, as a customer, eating a French dip and watching the fine black girl in the front. He left his number folded under his plate, and she called him the next day, pretended that he had left a hat at the club.

Foxx gets back in the car, smokes another joint, cruises around for an hour, and then parks the car across the street from the club. He waits. There's another car waiting, too, a Camaro. "It's Dennis from the office," Foxx says, funning with himself. He lifts his hand in a wave. "Hey there, Dennis," he says. "It was great seeing you at the company picnic the other day. You have a lovely wife. Too bad your car's such a beater. You ain't got but one sixty in that bucket." The radio plays the theme from *S.W.A.T.*, then the Sylvers, then "Mixing Board." Foxx turns it down until he hears Yvette's voice, turns it off. Foxx taps out some of Sonny Boy's coke onto a pocket mirror and takes a snort. After a few minutes the side door of the club opens and a girl emerges, followed by another. Neither of them is Nita.

He considers tapping out some more powder. He's so busy with the bag that he almost misses Nita, who comes out of the door with her purse clutched tight to her side. Foxx waves to her but she doesn't see him. Instead she heads straight for the Camaro, comes up alongside the driver's side, leans in so that her ass is perfect in the air, and kisses the dude in the front seat. Foxx blinks, blinks again, like the scene is a blurred-up windshield he's trying to clear. Then he slouches down to get a better look at the motherfucker. It's a young dude, no more than twenty-five, with one of those caterpillar mustaches crawling across his lip. Nita drifts back and then forward again, like a curtain in the breeze, and then the two of them are kissing again, this time a deep kiss that lasts. Finally, she walks around and gets into the passenger side, and the two of them drive away.

Foxx sits in the car, numb from what he has just seen. He knows that Nita some-times goes with other men—when wine's so fine, there's a battle for the bottle—but the thought of losing her seems wrong, just when he's at the brink of getting it all back. He pounds the glove box with the heel of his hand, and the bag of coke falls to the floor. Or rather, it flutters, like a bird coming down. He shoves it back into the box and lights up a joint. The car purrs. He is part cured. He stubs out the joint. He drives home.

Now Foxx is going like a ghost through the Forum, where he has come to see Anchor throw down. Like a ghost because it's been so long since he was here, since he was in any arena. He's a little late and the ends of rows have fallen off and flowed toward the exit doors. The diehards are staying put, stomping their feet, waving their arms. Marionettes, Hughes calls them. In fact, that's what he's calling them now. "Marionettes," he screams, "how good does it gets?" The crowd roars in reply: "It gets so good it's bad."

Foxx stops near one of the exits with a good view of the stage, watches Hughes hold court. The papers say that Anchor has picked up where the Foxxes left off, but each time Foxx sees them he's struck by how different the two bands are. When he led, Foxx demanded tightness. He turned the songs over, checked for leaks. Hughes just stands in the middle of the stage and lets it dangle. And while the Foxx shows were short and sweet—give the people what they want but not so much that it steals their appetite—Anchor's shows are marathons. Tonight's show started at eight. It's now past eleven thirty, and "Claim on Your Brain" is winding down with its odd end harmonies—they sound like the shit that hangs off a jellyfish, beautiful and stinging. But Foxx knows that Floyd isn't done, and so does the girl next to Foxx, and so does everyone who is left in the Forum, eyes fixed on the stage through the haze of smoke and sweat. In the dark, the basic stitch of the cymbal comes creeping, one beat, then three, then two, then three again. The crowd roars at the signature. Then the bass, Potter Lee's fatback temblor, rumbles through the arena, and suddenly all the people making for the exits are back in their seats.

"Hey-ohh," says Hughes, and ten thousand voices answer back. "Ohhh-hey." "Hey-ohh," he says, and gets it back reversed again. "L.A., how's it shakin'? You get big with the pig, you'll be big with the bacon." Then Gene Pine's drums drop like a bomb, the lights come up with a loud flash, and the place erupts again into a bumping, thumping, roast-your-rumping carnival.

The encore lasts for forty-five minutes. Every other song, Hughes disappears into a hole in the floor and pops back out dressed in some new costume. He plays in overalls. He plays wrapped in an American flag made up like a jungle toga, stars and stripes for the Tarzan types. For the next-to-last song, "Get Your Feet on the Floor," Hughes jumps from stage right disguised as a giant foot, the five foam toes splayed over his head like a crown. "Sole music," he calls out. After that, it's all choreography: the band introductions, which take ten minutes for the whole troupe, not just Shank and Ring and Fluke but Jack "Mynah" Bird, Anthony "the Tiger" Ward, Donald "Ill-Gotten" Gaines, each name announced by Floyd from the wings and echoed by a trio of backup singers. Finally, Floyd emerges. Now he's dressed in a sharkskin suit, superslick, superbad. "Stop the dizzy games, you dizzy dames!" he screams, and the band winds up and delivers "Anchor What?" The girl next to Foxx mouths the chorus:

Anchor what?
What you saying?
Shake your butt
When we playing
Free your mind
Never fear

In a bind?
Anchor's near.

Foxx nods his head, feels his hips give in to Porter Lee. Motherfucker can certainly deliver the bottom. But he's wearing a monkey suit just like the rest of the band—his is a Negro League baseball uniform. Hughes, who has been called "the new face of funk," is just the old face with a clown's mask.

As antidote, Foxx starts to hum "Please Step Back." He knows exactly how it will sound, the way he'll tell the drummer to lay out at times and gallop forward other times, the staccato he needs from the horns, the weave of the bass and the lead guitar. Is there a band anywhere that can do it justice? The Foxxes could have, but they're in the past, or in the ground. Even the two living ones are gone: Kevin's working for Jerry in management and Tony's in A&R. Foxx hasn't spoken to either of them in months, and the last time it was an accident—Foxx was in for a meeting at Polyphone records, rounded a corner, and there was Tony, clean-shaven and suited up. He was going on about a new act he had just signed, a rock band that processed all its guitars through a little black box. "I know it sounds busted, but it's the future," he said. "Programming."

"I'll take the past," Foxx said.

"You had it," Tony said. A secretary appeared at his side. "Yeah," he said. "I have a meeting in a few. But you should come around again."

"I may be in business with you soon," Foxx said. "Here to talk with some of your people about a deal." But he didn't, and he wasn't.

Foxx wonders if he'll have to record "Please Step Back" all by himself, and then sets the thought aside with a quick motion. He doesn't want to rush it. He'll get there when he gets there, and he'll be at the top of the mountain. Plus, he has other songs that will help Leon get him real paid. There's "Time to See Things Through," which puts a new spin on the Spinners; "Survive," which Holy Toledeos the Ohio Players; even "Let's Wake Up Tomorrow," a slow killer that would bury Barry White. They're all right, or they're all wrong. He can't tell. He needs to get to "Please Step Back," but how can he do it? Get straight, Alexander the Great.

The guts of the Forum are arranged along a central hallway. Rooms branch off to the left and right. At the dead end of that hallway, there's a big room with a big-screen television and a circular couch. When Foxx started down the hallway, the TV was on, showing a basketball game. Now, though, the TV is dark, and the room is dark, too. Foxx steps in. "Hey-ohh," says Hughes's voice. Foxx squints but can't see him. Then his eyes adjust. Hughes is sitting on top of the table in the middle of the room with a naked girl on his lap. "You want me to switch on a light, man?" says Hughes. "I thought I was giving off enough glow fo' sho'." He cackles and pats the girl on the head. "Ain't this the life, man? And just think. Some poor folks just get old and die." He reaches a hand over the girl's shoulder, points down at her crotch. "You can reach me at my new address," he says. The girl giggles and Hughes dives in.

Foxx goes into the small room, flops down on the couch. Finally the giggling stops, and Hughes comes through the door in a robe. "I'm going to have some T-shirts made up that say 'Bicentennial Dick' and 'Bicentennial Pussy,'" he says. "State of the union. Place your order now." He falls into a chair. "So how you been blowing, captain?" He doesn't wait for an answer. "Tonight we smoked that joint, don't you think? I mean, it started a little sluggish, but we shook the ice out of our beards and got the fire fired up. Do you know that when we played down in San Diego the other night someone said that they saw Tricky Dick in the audience? If I'm lying, I'm dying, and I ain't dead yet. Hey, you want?" Foxx opens his eyes, which he hadn't realized were closed, to see Hughes holding out a coke spoon. Foxx shakes his head. "Suit yourself," Hughes says.

Foxx is suddenly exhausted. "Listen," he says. "I'm gonna jet in a second. I just came by to see the show and make sure you're in for the party tomorrow night at my house."

"Yeah," says Hughes. "Leon mentioned it. We'll be there." He snorts the spoon clean. "Did you see any of the other guys from the band? I wanted Fluke to play you this new track we're working on. It's a motherfucker, eight minutes of lava. We're also thinking of recording an album of Sinatra songs. You know that one that goes, 'Every kiss, every hug acts just like a drug...'" Hughes's Sinatra is surprisingly good.

"Yeah," says Foxx. " 'You're Getting to Be a Habit with Me.'"

"You got it," says Hughes. "Frankie baby." He reaches into a backpack on the ground and brings out a bag of powder. "Want?" he says. Foxx shakes his head. "Maybe you can sing on it," Hughes says. "Would you do that? You can be a link between the past and the future."

Out in the parking lot, after he has gone past the two naked girls in the anteroom, past the less lucky groupies clustered in the hall, past the kids still milling in the arena, Foxx stops and leans on the nearest car. No sound comes out but he is screaming. He's sure of that. Past and the future? Who died and made Hughes king? And then he remembers: He did.

"When the saint comes marching in," Hughes says to Foxx, who is paused in the middle of the doorway of the bathroom, fresh from doing a line with Keiko. In the middle of the room, on the table where Foxx had set the apple just a few days before, there is an incense burner, and it's letting off a smell that he doesn't recognize. Two seconds later he knows what it is. Someone's burning weed in the incense burner, which means that anyone who draws more than two breaths in the room is high.

"All night long, we did the bump, bump, bump." That's what the stereo is saying. There's a clock on the wall but he doesn't bother looking. He has a clock inside him. Six hours since the last fix, one hour to go. Time takes time, and then it takes everything else.

Sonny Boy has brought girls, as promised. All shapes, all flavors, most of them wearing sky heels and skirts so short that they might as well just put a picture of a pussy on the outside. In fact, Sonny Boy has brought so many girls that he has forgotten his own girl, who is curled up in the corner with a drink and a magazine. Perfect, Foxx thinks. Her with no man and Foxx with no girl, on account of Nita not answering her motherfucking telephone all day. "Hey," Foxx says to her. "Where'd you come from?"

"From your best dream," Sonny Girl says. Foxx talks to her for a little while about the headlines, her sister's high school graduation, her plans to go home to Houston for the Fourth. "So that's me," she says. "What about you?"

"Just hosting with the mosting," he says. He has been trying to get to Hughes since the beginning of the party, but each time he approaches him, another girl swoops in from the side and Hughes disappears in a tangle.

"I heard Leon and Floyd talking. It sounds like they're cooking something up."

"Oh yeah?"

"Out by the pool," she says. Foxx dips a hip, slips around a fine blonde girl and a finer redhead, glides onto the patio. The party is starting to broil. Hughes, who is down to his boxer shorts, is snorting a mountain of coke off the patio table. Leon has a snifter of brandy and an Asian girl with a tattoo of an open book on her hip. Sonny Boy is smoking some ditch weed. Behind him, a short white chick is thrusting out her ass toward the bulge in some cat's pants. There doesn't seem to be any space between the two of them. After a few minutes of grinding and groaning, the girl climbs down the chrome ladder into the pool. The cat with the hard-on walks over to Hughes and whispers something to him; Hughes responds with a hoot and belly flops into the pool.

"Floyd," Foxx calls. Hughes looks up from the pool, smiling the widest smile Foxx has seen all night. It's a shit-eating grin, but all the shit has been polished away. It gleams. "You got the party going," Foxx says.

"We're Anchor, not Anchorites," says Hughes. He hugs the Asian girl, whom he introduces as Sweet and Sour Chicken, and motions for Foxx to come to the edge of the pool. He pulls the girl's tit out of her bra. "Be my guest," he says. When Foxx touches the nipple Hughes bags up. "Such a gentleman," he says. "I thought you'd use your mouth."

"Listen," says Foxx. "Leon tells me that you want to talk about something."

"Pleasure before business," Hughes says. "Rules are rules. But we'll talk in a little while, man."

Foxx wanders back inside. Now someone has dropped the needle on Stevie Wonder's new record. As usual, Stevie has some melodies that are like birds, and others that are like bullets. They're killer bee, all of them. But the lyrics—man, what does that bat-eyed motherfucker think he's doing? Still, the shit makes Foxx move, especially "All Day Sucker," which has that nasty synth line strung tight across the chorus and that other sound that's like a telephone ringing. Or is that the telephone ringing?

He jogs to the nearest phone, picks it up. Dial tone. He finds Boris in the living room. "You answer that call?" he says. He tries to keep the beg out of his voice.

"Yeah," says Boris. "It was no one."

"Oh."

"You still haven't heard from Nita?"

"Fuck her."

"I can call her up for you."

. "No, no. I mean, fuck her. You go fuck her." A girl nearby laughs, and Foxx turns to take credit for the joke. But she's not laughing at him. She's laughing at Hughes, who is coming down the hall jaybird-naked except for a narrow band of bright fabric that turns out to be a pair of red panties. Probably took them off the Asian girl.

Hughes stops in the middle of the room, bows like a gentleman, then moves the panties to expose his cock. A girl appears like magic, and Hughes lifts her skirt over her head. "I asked her friends about her but all their lips were tight," says Hughes. Foxx starts laughing. Motherfucker has the mind to quote Little Richard while he's fucking. Then Stock Miller, who is nearby, starts laughing, too.

"Big beat keeps her rocking in her seat," says Hughes. Everyone is laughing even harder now, even the girl. Hughes pushes her away. "Show some respect," he says. "What would your daddy say?"

Foxx wanders off. Someone hands him a drink. Someone else passes him a stick. Across the room he spots Anita. He raises his chin at her, a backwards nod. "Hi," she says, walking toward him.

"Where the fuck you been?"

This stops her. She scowls. "What do you mean? I'm here now."

"How's Tijuana Joe?" he says.

"I don't know who you mean."

"Fuck you don't. I saw you outside of Captain Bonner's."

"Oh," she says. "You mean Anthony. He's just a friend. He has good shit."

He stares at her coldly. "Go make yourself useful."

Foxx's head is buzzing so low that he can't hear it but loud enough that he can't hear anything else either. He ducks into one of the side dens and does a quick line of coke. He's not ready to go back out, so he sits in the dark, singing bits of his old songs to calm himself down. "I need you more than ever now," he sings. "I need your hand upon my brow." And, "How can you find your way back home? With a child's eyes, a child's eyes." And, "Take the left track, take the right track, turn the horns up, play it all back." He gets on a roll, and he's midway through "A Place in the Sun" when the door opens a crack. It's the girl who was in the pool earlier with Hughes. Her eyes are bright but shallow. "Hey," he says.

"Hi," she says.

"What's your name? Your real name."

"Need-to-know basis," she says. "And you don't need to know." She sits down next to him. "I'm going to spark up," she says. "Want?" He shakes his head. She wanders over to the table next to the boxes, where there's a stack of records and a portable player. "You got 'Car Wash'?"

"No," he says. "I don't got fucking 'Car Wash.' Got EWF if you want it."

She puts a record on, unbuttons her shirt, unzips his pants, and puts his cock between her breasts. Then she takes him in her mouth. He looks at the mirror across the way and tries to fashion an expression of indifference. More: He tries to get rid of the things around him, not just the noise, but the eighty-watt nuisance from the bulb above, the sweet rot of weed rolling through the house, the click of her bracelets against one another. He becomes liquid and then he comes. Foxx flips her like a coin, heads to tails, and slides his tongue between her legs. He sticks her with the point of it, licks the ridges and the rims, then starts to think slick thoughts. "Hey," he says, surfacing. "How close are you to Floyd?"

"Right now," she pants, "not so close."

"Naw," he says. "That's not what I mean. What I mean is this: You have his ear?"

"What?"

"We're going to do business, and I want to make sure he sees things in the right light."

"You want me to do work for you?"

"You could say that."

"Okay," she says. "If you stay down there."

When he's done, he taps her on the ass and she comes to sit next to him on the couch. "Sing a Song" is on, and she's singing along, but it's like someone put a cat in a bag and the bag in the river. "Beautiful," he says. "You ever think of becoming a professional?"

"I am," she says, laughing. "The oldest professional."

He's loose, happy. He fires up another joint and tells her about "Please Step Back," even singing a verse. "I may just be a girl who doesn't know when to stop," she says, "but that's beautiful." When she kisses him and puts her tongue into his mouth, he can smell something musky and medicinal, probably pills. He has a flash of anger. Why isn't she sharing?

He leaves the girl in the room and is halfway down the hall when he hears a woman's voice. "I don't know," she is saying, soft in volume but not in meaning. He backs up to the door and hears it again. "I just don't know." It is Anita.

The next voice he hears is Hughes. "I'm afraid I'm not familiar with that answer," he says.

"I should go."

"I should come," Hughes says.

Foxx hears another voice. "Maybe this will convince you." He goes back into the hall closet, takes the pistol from the shoebox, tucks it into his waistband, and comes back to the doorway. He doesn't hear Anita's voice anymore. He puts his shoulder into the door and knocks it open. Anita is on all fours, with Hughes taking her from behind and Sonny Boy in front of her. One of his hands is on the side of her face. It looks gentle until he sees the knife that's in the other hand. It's a switchblade, closed, but it's still a knife.

"Man," he says, "what the fuck?"

"Nothing here to see," Hughes says.

"Stop it."

"Go away, man. Circulate. Isn't that what a party's for?"

Foxx yanks the gun out of his waistband. It feels like he's taking out his cock, and he waves it that way, proud. Anita screams, like people scream in movies.

Hughes snorts. "Number one with a bullet," he says. "Is that peashooter even loaded?"

Foxx notices that Sonny Boy has stepped back, away from Anita, and that he's holding the knife, which is now open, at chin height.

Hughes chuckles at Foxx. "Man, you so dumb you brought a gun to a knife fight."

Leon has appeared in the doorway. "Hey," he says. "Let's all cool it."

Foxx's hand is shaking so bad he cannot possibly aim accurately. But it is shaking so bad he knows he might squeeze off a shot accidentally. Hughes is losing his nerve and he knows that Foxx can tell, his limp dick out of Anita and in his hand now. Leon can tell, too. He takes a step into the room with his palm up, like he's about to ask a question, and then he makes his move, taking hold of Hughes by the shoulder as Foxx goes for Sonny Boy, slapping the knife out of his hand and then whipping him across the face with the pistol. Then he resets the barrel on Hughes. "It's loaded. Now get up and get out."

"Let's up and atom," Hughes says. "I'm the bomb." But he doesn't move.

Sonny Boy runs his tongue over the place where his lip is split. "You're going to be sorry," he says.

"Don't tell me what I'm going to be," Foxx says.

"I'm telling you how it's going to be. I'm putting the word out not to sell to you. And if my boys don't sell, you're going to need to go out on the street."

"So I'll go out onto the street. You think I'll get lost?"

"I think you will," he says. "But not how you think. You buy from me, you get good shit. Controlled. But do you know what's out there? It's purer than you know, or less pure. How much you gonna put in your blood? You don't have any idea, do you? But here's the catch: Guess wrong and you won't just lose your high. You'll lose your life. You know how many motherfuckers go into the ground their first few months on the street?" He takes a careful look at his knife on the ground and nudges it with the toe of his shoe. "I don't need that. I got the longest blade there is."

Hughes has pulled up his pants and shrugged on his shirt. "Come on, man," he says to Sonny Boy. "I think the time has come."

"Come and gone," Foxx says. "You go on back to Annapolis and learn your manners."

"Talk big all you want," Hughes says. His face hardens. "You're on my had list, bitch."

Foxx goes out into the hallway. Anita is there with Boris. She's not crying anymore; rather, she's staring at Foxx like she's waiting for an answer. He covers the distance between them and slaps her once across the face. She staggers back, but her eyes don't show any shock. It's as if she's been waiting for this one for a while.

Boris pushes him away. "Take a walk," he says.

"Fuck off," Foxx says. "This one cost me more than she's worth." He goes to the bathroom, where he finds the bag he has stashed under the sink, fumbles the zipper, finally gets it going, draws the dope into the dropper, puts it in his arm. He has spent the last year trying to invent a time machine to take him back to '74, back to '66. Now he will settle for a more modest trip, back not years but minutes. He shuts his eyes as tight as he knows how, and then squeezes them tighter. But when he opens them, he hasn't managed to reverse time, or even slow it down. He wanders back out, goes by Anita, whose head is still on Boris's shoulder.

"God damn you," says Anita.

"He's trying his best," Foxx says, in melodrama. But when he makes it to the end of the hall, the remark is still with him, and he begins to sob.

The radio is playing "Oh, What a Night." Foxx remembers December 1963, and there wasn't no motherfucking *doo dit doo dit dit doo dit doo dit dit.* There was a dead president, a shooter who got shot, and a country tipping over. He snaps the dial sharply to the left, and the radio clicks off. He is healthier at once; what is sicker than music that won't tell the truth?

Boris is driving. If he was mad before, he's not mad now, and that's why Foxx keeps him on: The best dogs never bite the hand that hit them. Los Angeles comes into the car, loud noises, loud light. They go by a short, stacked girl standing on the corner. Foxx can't see her face, only her dress, which is the same color red as the carpet in his red room. "Hey, hey," Foxx says to Boris. "Pull over. See if I can get that bitch to pitch me a few." The car slides to the curb. Foxx gets out, introduces himself as John with a laugh. "And a tear," he says. Then he gets into the backseat with her and tells Boris to go. "Put the radio back on, will you?" he says. "But one of those stations where people are talking. We need the company back here or else how are we going to become a corporation?" He lights up a joint and passes it to the girl. "The brakes are burning. Smell them?" She nods, though it's not possible she has any idea what he's talking about. "What's your name?"

"Vernessa."

"No shit."

"No shit," she says. "And you know it's real, because who would change it to that?"

"Sounds like someone poor. But you're about to be rich." He pulls out a roll, peels off a bill, and lets it flutter to the seat. "There's oh so much more where that came from."

"You want me to go looking in your pocket?"

"Smart girl."

She goes looking. "Drive around," he says to Boris, and they take Avalon to Century and head West. He looks out the window as they drive and tries to fashion an expression of indifference. More: He tries to get rid of the things he is hearing, seeing, or feeling. First, the chatter on the radio disappears. Then he shutters the rest, the bright sunlight, the smoke rolling around in the car, the slurp of this Vernessa in his lap, the black wave of her hair. He decides to feel absolutely nothing when he comes, and that's exactly what he feels. "Baby, you like an aspirin," he says. "I had a headache this big and now where has it gone?" He taps her on the head and she sits up, lips glistening. "You want to come on over to my house?"

"Sure," she says. "You think I don't who you are?"

"That's right," he says. "I think you don't know." At the house he takes her right into the studio, shows her the gold-record wall, the pictures of him with Diana Ross and Stevie Wonder. There's a picture of Anchor that makes him flinch.

The two of them sit on the black love seat. Vernessa cuts some coke. Foxx declines showily. "I have a story for you," he says.

"Tell me," she says. Her dress is off now, bloodred on the floor. She takes his hand and puts it on her snatch.

"I'll tell," he says. "Just don't shoot." She giggles. "Once upon a time in Boston," he says, "there were two boys." He closes his eyes. The room is big but it seems small because he's in it. A radio in the corner that he doesn't remember turning on is playing "Al Di La," not Jerry Vale but the Ray Charles Singers, and this is the beginning of, or part of, his story. He slides his pointer into Vernessa. "Itchy trigger," he says. While he's fucking her with his finger he drifts into another memory, a present that Betty bought him once when she went to Chicago to visit her mama. It was a figurine of a man standing on a mountaintop. Foxx had made a joke about it. "What?" he said. "Is this because I like to get high?" But the truth was that the gift had stuck with him. What was it about that little man that made Betty think of him when she was in a faraway place? He tries to remember the expression on the figurine's face: It was somewhere between thoughtful and peaceful, which used to seem like close cousins but now seem like enemies. He can't quite get it, though. And he's distracted, mainly because there's a smell coming up from between him and Vernessa. Is it him or her? He smells his hand. It's her. But a little odor can't kill his motor, and he's like dinner in a diner: He comes in a minute.

Afterwards Foxx sends Vernessa to take a shower, and while she's in there he wanders downstairs and starts to go through the closet. He isn't looking for anything in particular. Or rather, he's looking for anything that can lift him on out of the present, which still smells like shit even though the stink is gone. The boxes in the closet are like a museum, or a tomb, stuffed with old tapes, tickets, backstage passes, photographs, and one blue envelope labeled "Important." What the fuck is in there? His soul? It's flat enough. But when he opens the envelope, all he finds are some folded-up sheets of legal paper. "Fuck," he says. These are his handwritten lyrics from *Wreckered*, *Pitch*, and *Revolution*. This is the Bible that Betty wanted, probably still wants. How did they survive the fire? Why hasn't Boris put this in the safe-deposit box? Foxx shouts for Boris, but no one comes. He knows that in twenty minutes he'll be back upstairs pumping another three hundred dollars into Vernessa's pussy. But for now he is alone with the words that he once wrote. He spreads the pages out on the floor and touches them softly with his fingertips. These are a man's thoughts, but what happens when he stops thinking them? These are a man's hopes, but who is the man? He grabs for memories, anything within reach. He remembers when he was a boy and his cousin Andre died, how he sat in his mother's kitchen, in a straight-backed wooden chair whose crossbars were painted red, and how he tried so hard to make sense of what death was. His mother tried to explain it to him. She used love and poetry and still couldn't bring him an inch closer to understanding it. She held his head and told him stories about his father, and how a good man makes for a good boy. Foxx brushes his fingers over the pages. The decade drains away. Blind men see what other men can't. Brave men see what other men won't. There's space at the bottom of the last page, and he writes down the lyrics to "Please Step Back" in neat block letters. It's the first time he has seen them all together like this. He has to get into the studio to record it. That'll get him on track. That'll clear his head. He lies down next to the pages, careful not to roll on top of them, and closes his eyes until he can't hear the noise from the shower. He can't hear any noise at all. He tries his best to wake up but then he realizes he's not asleep.

The next day Vernessa has Foxx drop her at a downtown hotel, and he sits in the lobby for a while, thinking about taking home another girl. Instead he heads down into Westlake, circles the park a few times to see where the sleepwalkers are going, follows them in. The kid's named Leonardo. "Like the painter," he says. "How much you need?"

"I don't want a bad bag, you understand?" Foxx says. "No lemonade, no flea powder."

"I got what's good, man. Treat you right." Leonardo points at Foxx. "Tell you what. Take the bag, take a taste, then give me the money. What's fairer than that?"

Foxx takes the bag back to his car, takes a pinch, and snorts it. Then he gets out of the car and starts walking toward downtown. It's a nice day, not too hot, and he figures he'll walk as long as he wants. He's starting to feel the distance in his legs a little bit when he runs into a fat man outside of a taco stand. The fat man has just eaten, and his greasy lips shine like ripe cherries. "Robert?" the man says, crinkling his brow. "Robert Franklin?"

Foxx is about to tell the motherfucker that he has the wrong idea, if he has any idea at all. "It *is* you," the fat man says. "It's Carl Chandler."

"My God," Foxx says, and means it.

"How long has it been?"

"Forever and a day," Foxx says. He is still staring at this soft middle-aged specimen, trying to understand the joke. This is Carl Chandler, the sharpest shark in Boston? Foxx thinks for a little while and then gives a tentative smile.

"Man, I think about you all the time," Carl says. "But I never thought I'd run into you like this. I mean, I've only been in the city since yesterday."

"You live here now?"

"No. I'm here on business."

"With a band?"

Carl laughs. "No band. I'm a salesman now. Plumbing supplies. Doesn't sound too exciting, I know, but I'm making a good living. And I have to. I'm married now, with three kids." He reaches into his pocket for a wallet. "This is Louise, my wife. Henry and Willie are the twins, and Lucy's the baby."

Foxx takes the wallet, stares at it for a moment blankly, hands it back.

"I can't say I miss the music much," Carl says. "It was a hard life. Most everyone ended up sorely disappointed in themselves. Very few got to be stars. Like I have to tell you. I have all your records, though. I always tell people that I was the first one who knew how great you were going to be and tried to keep you down because of it."

"That you did, my man."

Carl shakes his head, disapproving of his own past. "Well, we were hotheads. Young men are supposed to be."

Foxx needs something in his hands. He fumbles in his pocket, past the bag of dope, for his own wallet. He's trying to remember if there's a picture of Dewey in there. There is: a snapshot from his third birthday party, which Betty said was a big success. "This is my son," he says to Carl.

"Wonderful," Carl says. "Another rock star, you think?"

"Maybe I'll put him on the next record."

"He was on one already, remember? When he was a baby." Carl laughs. "I told you I have everything you've made. When's the next one?"

"Soon," Foxx says. "That's what I was doing just this morning, meeting with a label. They call every record a comeback, like I've ever been away. I got a hot new single that should be out real soon."

"What's it called?" Carl's eyes narrow and for a minute he's the man Foxx remembers, the cat with the scratch.

"'Please Step Back,'" Foxx says. "I mean, you don't have to go nowhere. That's the name of the song."

"Well, that's great," Carl says, soft again. Was that what happened over time? Your real self got buried in layers of padding until you couldn't even prove that it was in there anymore? "I'm so happy to hear there's another record."

"I'll send you a copy."

"No, no. I'll buy it. It's my pleasure." Carl looks at his watch. "I have to go take a phone call in my hotel in a few minutes. But this was something, seeing you like this. Louise will never believe me." He holds out his hand for Foxx to shake. Foxx complies, and Carl bows deeply like he's praying. "This really was something."

SIDE FOUR: GOING SOLO

Betty
Los Angeles 1980

"It's hot, Mama."

At eleven thirty they picked up their rental car and drove out of the airport.

"The weather's the same here as at home," Betty said.

The highway was dry and clear and patches of it shimmered in the distance. "See where it looks like water?" Dewey said. "It's a mirage. You know how it works?"

"No," she said. "But I'll bet you're about to tell me."

"It's like a mirror," he said. "It shows you something that's not there. You're seeing a piece of the sky reflected on the ground but you think it's a puddle." He leaned further over the backseat. In his hand he had a bag of candy he bought at the airport. "With my own money," he said when Betty protested.

"Sit back and put on your seat belt, Professor," Betty said. "Notice those other cars all around us? They're real, and solid, and I need you where you're safe."

"I want to see when we get close to the mirage. It'll disappear. What's cool is that if you take a picture of it, it shows up on the picture. It's a real illusion." He settled back into his seat and pointed at a limousine. "Look," he said. "That car is so long. I'll bet there's a TV in it."

"It's not like we went to the moon," Betty said. "I used to live here. In fact, you know, you used to live here."

"How old was I then?" he said.

"Just a baby."

"Not true," he said. "I was never that age." He was a Chicago boy, bluff and dreamy at the same time. When he was six years old, his first-grade teacher had them look at a few drops of Lake Michigan under a microscope. "There's a whole world in there that I can never go to," he said. But he went, in a way: He had his books about sea animals and about the history of airplanes and about electricity. He was suspended between at least two existences: He was an only child surrounded by four cousins, the youngest but also somehow the oldest. "I feel sort of like James," he said, rotating one hand in front of him to buy time. "It's just that when he talks about things that are for older kids I'm more interested. I think I'm going to like being that age." Belief that he would find a comfortable stretch in life: That was one of the things that made him young.

They were past the mirage now, off the highway, onto surface streets. Betty pulled into the parking lot of the hotel. It had seen its better days; in fact, she had seen them, been present for more parties than she could count. They were distant memories, but she could close her eyes and see every curve of the lobby mirror, every corner on every piece of furniture. Kevin had been making a girl in the stairwell next to the elevator. Kevin? Was that a character in a movie she had watched?

Betty had not seen Robert since her mother died. He had come to Chicago for the funeral, made an impression by hardly making an impression, left to go back West. "He was quieter than I expected," Jeffrey had said. Jeffrey? Was that another character from another movie? He had been a kind man, and Betty had wondered if she might love him, and she made love to him as if she did. But then one day she got a letter from Robert. It wasn't even for her, but rather for Dewey, a handful of words scribbled on hotel stationery and a picture of Robert standing near Rod Stewart. Betty tried to give it to Dewey without reading it, but she caught a glimpse of what Robert had written—"Baby bird," the note said, "tell me what you've heard. Tell me a thing. Signed, the Big

Wing"—and she was gone to him again. The next week she broke it off with Jeffrey. She didn't mention Robert, but she could see in Jeffrey's face that he blamed him. How could you not blame a man like that?

"Let me carry something, Mama. Who's the man here, anyway?"

Dewey went on ahead, the bag bumping behind him. Betty had written Robert letters over the years, and once or twice even mailed them, but she didn't deceive herself that they were still in touch. When Dewey was seven, he had made a birthday card for Robert. He wrote his own song, which rhymed *child* with *smiled*, and drew a picture of the two of them on a crooked staircase, Robert on a top step, Dewey down below. Betty lied and said that she had mailed it, because it was easier than trying to explain why she couldn't. The card went into a shoebox where she kept other mementos from that period: photographs of Robert holding Dewey at three months, postcards from the road, and of course the packages that Robert had sent her whenever he had finished a record.

Before coming to Los Angeles, she dug around in the box and found the papers Robert had sent her. They were handwritten on legal paper, and they had the lyrics to *Wreckered* and *Pitch* and *Revolution*. There was another song on the back of the last page; she hesitated to call it a new song, but it was a song he had written and never recorded. She put the pages in an envelope. It was the perfect present, and she resolved to give it to him. "I want him to have it," she told Charlotte. Charlotte just stared at Betty and patted her hand. What was she thinking? That Betty was pitiful, harboring a distant hope of reunion with a man who had moved on? Betty didn't know what was distant and what was close, and she didn't know how to find out for sure. Mirrors lied. Lenses lied. Even the highway lied. But she did know that when Charlotte heard the record, she heard the guitar and the horns and the vocals. When Betty heard it, she saw Robert sitting cross-legged in a chair, tapping his right heel in time to the song, unaware that he was even doing it. She heard through the record to the man, remembered the things he had promised, the things he had delivered. She remembered the trip to Italy that they never had a chance to take.

"Dewey, come out of there." He was in the bathroom, fiddling with every switch and knob. "Stop messing around."

He came out, ducked back in, grabbed the bag of candy from the counter. "How can you be thin as a rail with all the junk you eat?" Betty said.

"It's metabolism," he said confidently. "People sometimes get it from their parents."

Betty ran a hand over her stomach and smiled. "You were in there, you know."

Dewey frowned a little and went back into the bathroom. "Do you think the light goes off immediately when you turn the switch, or does a little bit of time pass?"

"Doesn't the signal have to travel along the wires?" she said.

"No," he said. "All you're doing is breaking a circuit. Remember that electronics kit you got me? It's like that." He dropped his bag of candy next to the TV and went to stare out the window. "Mama, can we see where Daddy is from here?"

"Not exactly," she said. "I think if we were on the other side of the hotel, we'd have a better view. But we'll drive over there later."

"What time?"

"We'll leave in an hour or so."

"Oh," he said. "I forgot to change my watch. How many hours earlier is it in California?"

"Two."

"But what about the time it takes to change the watch? You have to add that in, too." Betty must have looked confused, because Dewey laughed.

They two of them sat and watched a movie on TV, a comedy about an exiled princess who snuck back into her kingdom disguised as a commoner. It struck Betty as too documentary, and she changed the channel, settled briefly on a national news report on Mount Saint Helens, came to rest on a baseball game. The green comforted her. A player struck out. Another one walked. The inning ended. The broadcast went to a commercial, which showed an old woman counting pennies from a jar. Then there was a commercial that used "Highway Car" in the background. Betty remembered Robert making the record, then she remembered that he had made it before he ever met her. It was all mythology, wasn't it? The song played out while an attractive young woman drove a sedan down a sunny road. The melody was beautiful. "Talent's just another close friend," Robert had said once on TV. "You can count on it to let you down." Gerald Atkins had laughed. The actress sitting down the couch from him had laughed. They heard it as cynical comedy but maybe he wasn't doing anything but telling the truth.

"Game's boring," Dewey said. He got up to get more candy and switch the channel back to the special about Mount Saint Helens. On that channel, there was a commercial with a man singing about detergent in the middle of a crowded city street. "Sounds like Uncle Lucas," Dewey said. He was right. Moreover, the man looked like Lucas: tall brother, thick mustache, deep voice, expression on his face pitched somewhere between judgment and self-satisfaction. She had seen Lucas on television a few weeks before, on a new talk show that was running opposite Gerald Atkins. Lucas lived with his second wife now in Dallas, in a big house where he held Bible sessions and played with his three children, including a new baby. The baby gave him the illusion of youth, though he was starting to show signs of wear. On TV, he chatted with the host and then pretended to consider a request to play a song. "I hadn't planned on it," he said, "but I suppose I could." The staginess of the moment offended Betty, in large part because Lucas managed it so well. She had seen Tony, too, not on television but in person, in Chicago, where he was scouting rock groups for his label. She had him over for dinner. "You look just like your father," Tony told Dewey.

"But younger," Dewey said.

After Dewey went to bed, Tony repeated Dewey's comment. "The funniest part about it is that he's almost wrong. When I met Robert, he wasn't much older than that." He crushed out the cigarette he hadn't yet lit. "It's possible that in the end he was simply smaller than the things around him."

"I never thought it was about size. It was about shape. He didn't fit."

"I'm no expert anymore," Tony said. "If I ever was one. No one could figure that man out, which was part of what made him what he was. Whatever that was." He felt along the edge of his mustache. "You know what's funny? I keep waiting for him to call me. Isn't that stupid?"

"What makes you think he won't?"

Tony laughed softly. "I just think it's unlikely."

The volcano show was over. "Turn it off," Betty told Dewey. "The weather's nice. Let's not sit in here all day."

"We're going to see him?"

Betty wasn't ready yet. She couldn't call ahead, couldn't even think about it. "Soon," she said. "On the way I can show you the street we lived on when you were a baby."

Betty had told Dewey a thousand times about the fire, but he was still disappointed to learn that the house they were looking at was not part of his past. He frowned at it like it was interrupting him. He said he didn't like the windows or the way the lawn was cut.

"There's a little boy waving from the window right now," Dewey said, but there wasn't.

There was a record store in a strip mall near the house, and as they went past it, Betty thought she saw Robert. She brought the car around. It wasn't him. It was Jimi Hendrix, but a terrible likeness, flanked by Stevie Wonder on one side and Mick Jagger on the other. She laughed: What kind of woman couldn't even recognize the man she married?

Betty checked her watch. "About an hour more, and we'll head over there," she said.

"Ow," Dewey said. "My stomach hurts."

"I wonder if that could be from the candy you've been eating since you landed." She tried to sound disapproving. "Just relax," she said. "We have time. Let's go to the drugstore."

"Okay," he said. "But don't drive so fast or else I might throw up."

"I'm not driving too fast."

"Well, you're not driving too good."

"And you're not speaking too good," Betty said. "It's too *well*, you know."

"I know," Dewey said. "I was just kidding."

"Sure you were, Professor," she said. The drugstore was on a familiar street, at the end of a long stretch of memory: past a restaurant where she and Robert used to eat and a park where she and Robert used to sit. Her mind drifted backwards through time. She was in the house with Robert after the separation, and then she was in the apartment in San Francisco. The two of them were sitting at the kitchen table reading the newspaper and drinking coffee. Dewey was tiny, or maybe just a notion. Robert was smiling at her. Though the memories comforted her, they were false. Robert didn't drink coffee. He did coke. And the mornings at the kitchen table had been few and far between, rare exceptions scattered among the mornings hiding in bed or dragging him to the bathtub. If she could do it all over again, could she have stopped him? She always meant to ask him that, but she could never find the right time. She wondered if she was strong enough now, or if her fear was weak enough. Maybe she could pack the whole question into his name. "Robert," she'd say when she saw him. Meaning: Could I have stopped you? Would you have let me? Where does love go when it doesn't go away but it isn't there any more? Are you proud of your son? Do you see yourself in him? Do you regret what you've lost? "Robert," she'd say, meaning everything.

One day, Dewey had come home from the third grade with a question. "We need to write about someone famous. Can you help me do a report on Daddy?" What she did shocked her for its cowardice. She went to the bookshelf and tipped down a thick encyclopedia of rock and roll that someone had sent one year as a Christmas present. "The Foxxes were a popular Bay Area rock and soul band led by the Rock Foxx (born Robert Franklin). The group made its name in the late sixties with a pair of ebullient anthems, 'Make It Better' and 'We All Need a Place in the Sun.'" That was how the paragraph began; it ended soon enough, after an account of Yvette's death and the band's dissolution. She counted the total number of words: four hundred and seventy four. Dewey's report was longer. The paragraph didn't weigh what it should have, not with nine hundred for James Brown, seven hundred for Aretha. Robert had more ink than Mandrill, but not as much as Anchor. Even Lucas had more. The encyclopedia went back on the shelf. Cowardice again.

"Sit here while I go into the drugstore," she told Dewey, but he insisted on coming in with her, and explaining to her how the generic medicines were the same as the brand names. Back in the car, Betty made him take a pill with a can of ginger ale and teased him about the teenage cashier and the way she had smiled at him. "That girl was in love with you," she said.

"No she wasn't."

"And I think you were a little in love with her."

"Was not," he said. But the denial had no force. Denials of love never did.

When Betty had turned thirty, she had not been in love. Dewey was nine then, in fourth grade, too small for the clothes she bought him for that school year and too big for the books she read to him before he went to sleep at night. "Tell me a story about you and Daddy instead," he said, but Betty needed to sleep too, and she couldn't think of a story that didn't end in a nightmare. That was the year that Thomas—who was the man after George, who was the man after Jeffrey—was sent packing, and she and Dewey were alone together again. On nights when she was lonely and a drunk would have turned to drink, she played Robert's records and pretended she was just like anyone else hearing them for the hundredth time. "They make me want to get up and dance," she told Dewey, but she stayed in her chair.

She was dating again. This time his name was Kenneth. He was a teacher and coach at the middle school down the road. He had a flat stomach and soft eyes and a scar on his right hand. He had taken her to the islands for a weekend. They made love as the wind bellied out the curtains in the hotel room. "You're beautiful," he told Betty. "Like a mermaid."

"You're just saying that because we're near the water," Betty said. But at the mirror she saw what he meant. She was fuller of figure than at twenty-five, with amplitudes.

He laughed and put his arms around her. He was the first man she had dated who didn't know about Robert, or at least the first man she hadn't told. When Kenneth asked her about Dewey's father, she looked off into the middle distance like she couldn't quite reach the answer he was seeking. "Someone I knew in Los Angeles," she said. "I was very young."

"And now you're so old," Kenneth said, and led her to the bed, and tried to make her young again.

"That medicine worked perfectly, Mama," Dewey said. "Do you know that it's made from the same chemicals as an eggshell? I read about it in a book. Guess how long it takes a chicken to create an eggshell?"

"I'm guessing longer than it takes a person to break it," she said.

Dewey laughed although the idea struck Betty as tragic.

She turned left on Santa Monica, went past Western and past Wilton. She parked the car. Her heart quickened. Would she be strong enough to see Robert without feeling afraid? It wasn't that he got in her head; it was that he had never gotten out. She took Dewey by the hand and went down the middle of the lawn toward Robert. She fumbled in her purse for the papers. She laid them on the tombstone, turned the last page over, and began to sing.

Please Step Back

The world is
Pushing up too hard
Yes it's pushing up too hard
I wish the pull
Would have its full
Effect
Lord save my neck

The world is
Giving too much lift
Yes it's giving too much lift
I wish the ounce
Would stop its bounce
So high
Lord tell me why

Please step
Please step back
The pill on the hill
Is still killing Jack
It broke his crown
It put him down
It beat his white eye black
Oh, please step back

Well, what good is my money?
What good is my fame?
Every solution begins with a single flame

The world is
Spinning much too fast
Yes it's spinning much too fast
I wish the poles
Would play their roles
And freeze
Lord help me, please

Please step
Please step back
A peach out of reach
Never fails to attract
There goes a bird
Without a word
His song is so abstract
Oh, please step back